D1454932

## THIS IS THE WAY
## THE WORLD ENDS

"Joe," Mary said, "I hired a lawyer yesterday."

"What do you mean, you hired a lawyer?" he asked and lay back with his hand over his eyes, not wanting to accept what was happening.

"Joe, we've been separated for nearly a year. It's time!"

"It is *not* time!" he bellowed. "I know you, Mary, you . . . you're going through something right now. But I can wait, goddam it. Even if it takes years, I can wait. No, we don't need a lawyer!"

"That's why we do need one, Joe," she said. "Because you *are* waiting . . . "

# THE BROWNSTONE CAVALRY

## HOWARD CROOK

BERKLEY BOOKS, NEW YORK

With special thanks to my agent, Freya Manston, for her unwavering belief; Jim Silberman, the wisest and gentlest of editors, and not least to my living mentors of many years, Norman and Hedda Rosten.

This novel is a work of fiction. Names, characters, places and incidents are either the product of the author's imagination or are used fictitiously, and any resemblance to actual persons, living or dead, events or locales is entirely coincidental.

This Berkley book contains the complete
text of the original hardcover edition.
It has been completely reset in a typeface
designed for easy reading, and was printed
from new film.

THE BROWNSTONE CAVALRY

A Berkley Book / published by arrangement with
Summit Books

PRINTING HISTORY
Summit Books edition / May 1981
Berkley edition / May 1983

All rights reserved.
Copyright © 1981 by Howard Crook.
This book may not be reproduced in whole or in part,
by mimeograph or any other means, without permission.
For information address: Summit Books,
1230 Avenue of the Americas, New York, New York 10020.

ISBN: 0-425-05935-9

A BERKLEY BOOK ® TM 757,375
Berkley Books are published by Berkley Publishing Corporation,
200 Madison Avenue, New York, New York 10016.
The name "BERKLEY" and the stylized "B" with design are
trademarks belonging to Berkley Publishing Corporation.
PRINTED IN THE UNITED STATES OF AMERICA

*For my mother and father, with love*

# PART
# ONE

# CHAPTER
# ONE

Joe Tiernan struggled to keep his balance in the swaying subway car as the IRT number 3 train sped in a noisy screel under the East River toward Brooklyn. It was nearly six o'clock on Christmas Eve and the train was crowded with last-minute shoppers on their way home to their families. His own daughter's present, an expensive doll he'd purchased with the major part of his unemployment check, dangled in a red plastic bag from his free hand.

His other hand was clenched tightly onto the overhead grip as he tried to keep himself from being thrown against a young blond woman who happened to be sharing the same grip. It was taking nearly every muscle in his tall lean body to resist the lurching of the train and at the same time maintain the little smile of nonchalance he was affecting for her benefit.

Each time he was bumped against her he modified this expression to one of mild discomfort by briefly shutting his eyes and exhaling through his thin Irish nose, then to one of amused resignation by raising an eyebrow, then back to nonchalant half-smile. And each time, the young woman's expression changed not at all—not a twitch.

Among the other passengers, puffed in their heavy winter coats and struggling with their packages, there was a rare mood

3

of cheerfulness. It had started back at Fourteenth Street when four black youths in leather jackets had squeezed into the car and called out for everyone's attention.

"Hey, all you people! Listen here, peoples! Christmas present from the Mandingos!"

Then one of the youths had switched on his portable hi-fi and filled the subway car with the mellow baritoning of Bing Crosby on a taped Christmas album. The usual cold stares and repressed anger evoked by such youths with their radios had flickered for a moment but then gave way to smiles and shrugs of approval. By Wall Street, where the young blonde had got on, many of the passengers were talking to each other. A derelict had offered a sip of his wine to the woman sitting next to him. And some of the riders had even relaxed their grips on their packages.

And all the while, Joe Tiernan's mind and eyes had been on the young woman jammed in so close to him. She was so beautiful with her green eyes and smooth, deeply tanned skin. He could smell the newness of her fur-collared brown suede coat. Probably just back from a Caribbean vacation, he surmised and mentally stripped her down to a string bikini. Her freshly glazed lips looked so sweet and moist that he literally hungered for them. Her eyes were crystalline and warm like the waters off a tropical beach. He was swimming in her pale green eyes. Eyes, unfortunately, that continued to stare unswervingly, almost somnambulantly, at a point on his dimpled chin.

He was practically holding his breath to keep from panting directly into her face. Behind his precarious nonchalance he was again struggling with his shyness and fear of rejection. He had almost forgotten about it during the ten years he'd been safely married to Mary. But now, with their separation, he felt like a nervous adolescent again. It was maddening.

There were moments as the train rumbled through the tunnel when he felt his courage mounting to the point where he thought he might break the ice—force a few words up through his fear. Just a few words. One even. The singing of Bing Crosby had created a congenial mood. Surely he could say something about Bing Crosby. But each time he phrased an opening line in his mind he shrank back, thinking she would see through him, see his tongue hanging out. Oh, god, he thought, let her say something. *Please!* If she would only just raise her eyes a fraction and look into mine. God, they're so beautiful. Come on, baby, you do it. Say anything. Even cough, for Christ sake.

She sniffed. How delightful, he thought. He responded by clearing his throat toward the window. When he returned his gaze, she turned away. The periodic flashes of light in the dark tunnel passed through her reflection in the glass. She looked at herself and moistened her lower lip. Their eyes finally met in the reflection on the rushing window.

At first she seemed to be looking at him with no more interest than if he were one of the "Learn to Be a Secretary" advertisements over the car's windows. But then there occurred an almost invisible little softening of expression in the corners of her eyes, that ancient, almost melancholy sign of a woman's first opening to a man. And in that instant in which the blood perceives more quickly than the mind, he felt a warmth move down through his body, tingling his skin, swelling his penis. She continued to look long and softly into his eyes. The pulses of tunnel light running across their images seemed to be marking the beats in his chest. He responded by smiling genuinely, and then almost without thinking he formed the word "hi" silently on his lips.

She smiled back but then pursed her lips and made a little guilty frown, an expression that seemed to indicate that something was tugging at her conscience. His lips asked, "Married?" She nodded and then shrugged wistfully. Then her eyes inquired the same of him. He shaped the word "separated." She nodded sympathetically.

They were still looking thoughtfully into each other's eyes in the glass as the train approached the Clark Street station in Brooklyn. The increasing light in the tunnel began to erase their reflections. By the time the train squealed into the brightly lighted station their reflections were gone. She turned without looking up at him and began squeezing past him to get out, brushing her soft bosom against his chest.

"Bye," she said quietly without looking up.

"Bye," he said sadly.

He watched her disappear into the crush of standing passengers as she made her way toward the door. Down, Tiernan, he thought, she's married. But, oh, god, she did look at me so sweetly. A woman like that . . . For a woman like that I could put it all back together again. So what if she is

married! What the hell does that mean? He pictured her
husband as a stump-shaped little Mediterranean type with wiry
black hair and a perpetual scowl on his face. Married doesn't
mean shit these days, he thought. So he's rich, takes her to the
Caribbean every winter, has her living in a fancy brownstone.
But that look in her eyes, the way she looked at me.

Then he heard the subway doors hiss and he knew it was too
late to try to follow her. Goddam it! he thought and gritted his
teeth. He leaned forward and peered out the window at the
people walking along the platform toward the elevators. Clark
Street, he thought. That meant she lives in Brooklyn Heights.
His friend Richie Gemetz worked in his father's appliance store
in the Heights. Richie's probably seen her around, he thought.
Maybe he and Richie could prowl around the neighborhood
some weekend and try to find her. He'd mention it to Richie
tonight when they got together with Len Talbot for the
Christmas Eve party at Larsky's bar.

Tiernan was still thinking about the blonde when he emerged
from the subway station in Park Slope, a little brownstone
neighborhood bordering Prospect Park. It was nearly dark and
he could see the floodlights illuminating the Grand Army Arch
near the entrance to the park. Instead of walking toward the
Arch and continuing along Prospect Park West to his apartment, he turned off toward Lincoln Place, where Mary and
Lynn lived—where he used to live.

Yes, he would talk to Richie about the blonde tonight, but
first he had to stop off at Mary's to leave Lynn's doll under the
tree. They were expecting him, so there'd be no danger of
Mary's little Italian boyfriend from upstairs being there. It was
impossible that Mary could be sleeping with someone else,
particularly that little effeminate creep, he thought. All those
years together and now he felt he had never known her. He felt
his anger rising again and tried to quell it.

This time it would be different. He'd made a fool of himself
when he'd gone over to have dinner with them on Thanksgiving. He'd cried and begged her to let him come back. God, he
still shuddered when he remembered the dead expression on
her face as she had sat there listening to his desperate pleading.
Something had indeed died in her. And the weeks of total
drunkenness and depression he'd gone through afterward. No
more of that, he thought, turning down Lincoln Place. Besides,

Richie and Len had sworn they'd kick his ass if he went back begging again.

No, this time he'd spend a little time with Lynn and then: Good night, Mary, I'm off, he thought. He'd look at Mary and think of the blonde—that would be his shield. He'd warned her . . . he'd told her that he wouldn't wait forever, that someone else would come along. It's happened, Mary, he thought, and she's younger than you, Mary. Prettier, too. I'll find her again and, by god, I'll never think of you again, Mary. Never! he thought and felt a lump growing in his throat as he imagined Mary pining away for him.

She did like me, too, he thought, remembering the way the blonde had looked at him in the window. Hey, I'm no slouch, he thought, jutting his chin a bit over his navy wool scarf and squaring his shoulders inside his trench coat. Not bad for thirty-four—still got those all-American looks. Right? Then he thought again of Mary's swarthy little Italian and closed his eyes in rage.

Len Talbot growled at the stitchy pain in his side and stepped up his pace as he jogged across the deserted south meadow of Prospect Park. Darkness was filling the park, and he still had another two miles of running before him. The large grove of tall winter-bare trees ahead was suffused in deep shadow, increasing his sense of isolation. He panted tiny jets of frost into the cold evening air and listened to the steady soft striking of his white jogging shoes into the crisp grass.

He felt a mixture of foreboding and primal joy as he moved wolflike through the dimness toward the trees. In the past year his running had become his only escape from the disintegration that was his life in the brownstone world just outside the park. In moments like this, alone and pushing his body to the edge of its limits, each stride of his long muscular legs seemed to bring him closer to something he had always wanted but could never identify. Something he had felt close to as a boy hunting deer under the live oaks in East Texas. The feeling intensified as he drew closer to the grove.

As he neared the edge of the meadow the pathway lamps came on, setting a line of somber islands of light against the murky undulations of the park. Entering the light of one of the lamps, he was tempted to follow the path out to the park's side entrance, which was only a few hundred yards from the rooming house where he lived.

But then in his mind he saw again his son's kindergarten-scrawled Christmas card lying on the gray military blanket that covered his sagging bed, and his mood darkened to equal the shadows that lay ahead in the grove.

She had mailed it from her parents' home in New London, without enclosing any greetings of her own, let alone a few words of apology for suddenly taking the boy out of town for the holidays before he could hold him close to him and wish him merry Christmas from Daddy. Well, there were ways of dealing with ex-wives, he told himself.

The grove stretched through a two-mile area of the park, and within its looming shadows it concealed a steep gorge. At the bottom of the gorge there ran an ice-covered brook and parallel to the brook a cinder-path trail for the riding stable at the north end of the park.

He felt a sudden excitement as he slipped into the trees, digging his steps roughly through the leafy mulch and sending animal grunts into the silence before him.

In a few minutes he was at the edge of the gorge. But instead of slowing down he slashed through a hedge on the rim and plunged down its side, struggling to keep his feet and dodging trees as he descended. Halfway down he stepped into a drift of dry leaves that upset his balance and cast him into a staggering slide toward the brook, which he landed in on his hands and knees, breaking through its thin sheath of ice and soaking his arms and legs in cold water.

Rising to a kneeling position, he shook his thick mane of black hair and began to laugh. He picked up a large pane of ice and bit pieces out of it, spitting them out with more great blusters of laughter.

"Oh, yeah!" he cried. "Oh, hey, a merry fucking Christmas, folks." He heard his voice reverberate through the gorge. "Christmas!" he yelled again, his dark eyes looking for the small remnant of light above the trees.

For a few seconds more he continued yelling and whooping and cracking out more of the ice with his fists, flailing the water all about him.

Finally he sprang up and was off and running again, zig-zagging on the bridle path and prancing like a show horse. As he cavorted down the path he began chanting in rhythm to his step. "We wish you a merry Christmas, we wish you a merry Christmas . . . Oh, we wish you a merry Christmas, and a happy New Year."

The pain in his side had left him and in his exhilaration he felt he could run another twenty miles. He clapped the icy drops of water off his hands and boxed the air Ali-fashion. His gray sweat pants were dripping with water and his shoes squished each time they hit the ground.

About a half a mile farther down the trail he was still singing and chanting when he saw the first tiny flickering of a fire up ahead. Coming around a curve, he could see that someone had a little campfire going under the ornate bridge that crossed the riding trail. He stopped singing and slowed his pace.

As he drew closer he could see two men huddled near the fire, and he was tempted to turn off and skirt the bridge altogether. But something made him go on, a growing heat inside of him, a tightening of his fists, an eagerness for an encounter with danger.

"Oh, we wish you a merry Christmas . . ." he began again and continued to lope toward the bridge. As he got within the glow of the fire under the stone arch of the bridge, he could see that the two figures were elderly derelicts, sitting with a single dirty blanket draped over their shoulders and also sharing a gallon bottle of white wine.

"Merry Christmas, gentlemen!" he said, saluting them as he trotted past.

"And the same to you, sir!" one of them returned.

"Hey, sir!" the other shouted with a raspy voice.

He circled around and faced them across the fire, still jogging in place "Yeah?"

"Hey, sir, come have a Christmas drink with us," the man said, rising from under his blanket and holding out the glistening bottle on his dirty finger.

"Warm you up for the run," the other said. "Come on."

He started to decline, but the novelty of everything that was happening appealed to him and he turned back to join them.

"Here, let me wipe it off," said the man with the bottle, rubbing the mouth of it with the edge of his blanket. "It's Gallo, very nice for a cold night like this."

After handing him the jug, the man smiled and pulled the blanket close around his shoulders. In the glow of the fire Talbot could see that he was not as old as he had thought, perhaps not yet even fifty. But he had derelict aging, a haggardness of missing teeth and skin creased from too much weathering, so that he looked near seventy. The other had very white hair and a long stringy beard and was indeed probably seventy.

Seeing the water running off the bottom of his legs and out of his shoes, the older derelict began to laugh. "Boy, you fall into the creek?"

"Yes, one of the joys of jogging down here," he said, raising the bottle to his lips. The wine tasted sweet and warmed him as it went down. He brought it down and started to hand it back.

"Naw, go on and take some more," the younger one said. "Looks like you could use it."

"Well, merry Christmas, fellas," he said, taking a long drink this time.

"Merry Christmas to you, too," the older one said. "Guess you got young ones to go home to tonight, hey?"

"Yeah, I . . ." he said and stopped as the anger started to rise. "Well, not this year. My ex took him outa town. Guess I'm not much better off than you guys."

"Give him another drink, Jimmy," the older one said.

"No, I'm going to wind up with all your Christmas cheer if you don't take it back," he said, laughing.

"Hell, man, we got plenty," the one called Jimmy said. "It's Christmas, ain't it? Drink up all you want. Hell, you want to stay down here with us tonight, you're welcome."

"Hey, what's that song you was singing as you came up?"

"Oh, that," he said, raising the bottle again.

"I know this one," the older man said. "Silent night, holy night, all is calm, all is bright . . . ," he sang in breaking voice and then stopped. "You know it?" he asked.

"Maybe he don't wanna sing, Haskel."

"Yeah, sure, I know it. Let's try it," Talbot said.

They began singing the song, all together at first, and then the two older men dropped their voices back to let Talbot's clear deep bass carry in the echoey space under the bridge. At the end of the song they remained silent for a moment, letting the glow of fire connect with the glow they were all feeling inside. The younger derelict's eyes were brimming and he turned away for a second.

"Well, I better get back before I freeze to death in these clothes, fellas."

"That's right," said the older one. "Merry Christmas to you."

"Yes, this has made it a good Christmas for me. I want you to know that," he said, handing back the bottle.

"Go ahead and take one more for the road," Jimmy said, snuffing his nose.

After bringing the bottle down for the last time, he said, "I gotta meet some buddies of mine later tonight; we'll drink to you."

"All the best to you," the older one said.

"Merry Christmas," he said a last time and began trotting out on the other side of the bridge. Before the bridle path went around another curve Talbot took one last look at the campfire scene and saw the younger derelict still standing there and waving to him. "Good men there, Lord," he said to himself. "Take care of them."

Night had taken dominion over the park now and he could see stars up through the skeletal branches of the trees. His toes were becoming numb in the wet shoes and he ran harder to warm them. The wine had made him feel loose and energetic, with the warmth in his stomach spreading throughout his body as he ran. After another half-mile he climbed the small hill at the edge of the grove and prepared to cross the last meadow near the main entrance of the park.

The meadow sloped gradually downward in a series of gentle undulations, and moving onto it he felt a great desire to fly. Slowly his speed built up until he was aware of the cold wind in his tearing eyes. The sky was clear and bright with stars and there was a gray penumbral glow over the meadow. His blood was coursing and he was running now with all of his speed. He watched the grass flowing under him and felt a rising joy in making it flow faster. Everything that had ever tethered him was breaking loose and falling away behind him. In a moment he felt he would be flying.

Finally he became so light-headed that he grew dizzy and had to slow down. He was at the edge of the north meadow near the main entrance. His breathing was coming in great sighs. The stars now seemed to be spinning overhead. After staggering a few more steps he fell to his knees and shook his head.

In a few minutes he got up and wiped his brow and started walking a little shakily out of the park. He was shivering and his head still felt a little light. Beyond the entrance the traffic swirled in a great river of headlights around the illuminated Grand Army Arch. He waited for the intersection light to change and then crossed Prospect Park West.

Walking the eight blocks up Prospect Park West to his rooming house, he was haunted by the brightly lighted windows of the elegant nineteenth-century brownstones along the way. The world of the living was going on behind those soft-sculptured facades. A world of festively lighted Christmas trees, wreaths of holly in the windows, candles glowing to demark civilization from the night.

Moving past this tableau, he ached for what had been taken from him. In one window a young couple toasting punch glasses of eggnog to each other. In another a child's glowing face. At one door four guests arriving for a party, bursts of affectionate greeting, the door closing behind them.

At Garfield Street he glanced down the gaslighted sidewalk to see if there were any familiar faces outside. He and Susan had put most of their eight years of marriage into fixing up the brownstone apartment a few blocks down on Garfield. She had kept the apartment. And the friends.

It had been his idea to take the apartment after they had come up from Austin so he could take the teaching job at Brooklyn College. She had thought the place was too big. Six big rooms. That first winter all they had had was a mattress on the floor and the cord of wood the previous tenant had left for the two fireplaces. Those had been the best months of their marriage, he had always felt.

But slowly the house had filled. The big piano for Susan, the bookshelves for his study, each new piece of furniture carefully selected as they created their fantasy of nineteenth-century elegance. Even when Teddy was born they had spent two weeks deciding on the right blue wallpaper for his nursery.

On Christmas Eve there would be a few friends over for late-night oysters and champagne. He remembered the single yellow rose in the long thin glass vase on the piano while Susan played Beethoven and the guests drank from the silver goblets sent as a late wedding present by his grandmother. How beautifully Susan had played and how secure and mellow he had felt sitting on the Persian rug smoking his pipe and listening.

"Bitch!" he growled. "Bitch!"

Richie Gemetz quietly let himself into his apartment and began tiptoeing toward the candle glow coming from the room at the end of the long dark hallway. Halfway there he paused and awkwardly shifted the large brown bag of take-out Chinese food in his arms because the bottom of it was burning his hands.

"Helloooooooo?" Verna warbled from the candlelighted studio room. "Is that the burglar?"

"Naw," Gemetz replied in a gruff voice. "He couldn't make it tonight. I'm his cousin—the rapist."

"Oh, thank god!" she exclaimed. "Your cousin has such filthy breath."

As he neared the end of the hallway he stepped on something soft that let out a screech and darted scratchily across the floor.

"Dammit!" he yelled.

"What happened?"

"I just stepped on Brombly."

"Oh, poor old Brombly. Is he hurt?"

"I don't know. Now I probably got a gimpy rabbit."

Entering the big high-ceilinged room, he could see Verna's shapely legs dangling over the edge of the loft-bed where she was lying on her back and idly tracing a long fingernail along the ceiling.

He barely noticed the dried pellets of rabbit shit crunching under his shoes.

"That's really amazing," he said.

"What?" she asked, turning over on her stomach and swinging around to see him. In his old navy peacoat and close-cropped brown beard, he always looked to her like he'd just come in from the sea. Her Jewish Viking, she called him. Well, half a Viking, anyway, she would amend, allowing for his five-foot-nine height.

"Why did I get so furious, when *he* was the one who got stepped on?"

"You're probably upset because he startled you. Jesus, Richie, I wish the hell you'd get the lights turned on."

"No way!"

He walked around the cluttered Formica bar that separated

the kitchen from the rest of the room and put the bag on the drainboard of the sink, which was full of encrusted dishes. In a corner nearby were four bags overflowing with garbage. As he took the white cartons of Chinese food from the sack, the warm spicy odors for the moment overwhelmed the stale effluvium coming from the garbage.

"Yeah, I know, you don't really live here. For fourteen months now this has been your unaddress. At least get the gas turned on! What do you do when your kids come over for the night?"

"They love it. We play campfire in the fireplace."

"But think of how nice it would be to cook for them."

"They hate my cooking."

"When did *you* ever cook?"

"At the hotel, right after Linda and I split. I told you about that. I had this little two-burner stove and I cooked up some pretty good stuff—pork chops, corn on the cob, spaghetti—all kosher."

"So?"

"So they hated it. It was always 'Mommy cooks this or that better, Daddy.' The only time I ever beat Mommy was about a month ago—we had a weenie roast in the fireplace. They both owned up that it was better than Mommy's hot dogs. I almost broke down and cried. A very important moment for me."

After setting out all the cartons, he began removing his clothes and piling them on top of the dirty dishes in the sink.

"See, there's progress," she said. "Today hot dogs, tomorrow eggs Benedict."

"Hey, I'm getting used to living primitive," he said. "There's a pristine wilderness evolving here. Think I want to desecrate it with Con Edison and Brooklyn Gas?"

"Desecrated? Hmmm, yeah, that's the word I was looking for for this place. The motif is definitely Early Desecrated."

"Wash ouw," he mumbled, walking naked across the room with the chopsticks in his mouth and both hands loaded with the white cartons.

"Just look at this," she said, "you've even got candle wax on the sheets. Candle wax and roaches and rabbit shit—and probably bubonic plague growing in that bathtub. Yugh! Every time I take a shower in there I get the feeling those shower curtains are sneaking up on me."

"Grah dese," he said, inching his thin hairy body up the

ladder and holding out the cartons to her. She took them and sat up, her blond head nearly touching the ceiling, her large pendulous breasts white against the tan that remained from summer.

"Ooooo, I'm starving," she said. "What'd you get?"

"Oo goo ay han," he said through the chopsticks as he slid into the bed and pushed her over on her back away from the food. Falling on top of her, he kissed her with the chopsticks still in his mouth.

"Oo oo ay an?" she asked under his lips.

"Uh-ha, an oo oo ork," he answered while parting her warm silky thighs with his hand.

"Oo oo ork?" she asked, searching for his penis with her hand.

"Ung," he affirmed.

"An aht el?"

"An oah uck," he said, moving up between her thighs.

"Um um, oast uck," she said, starting to laugh and guiding him into her. She was still wet from their lovemaking before he had gone out for the Chinese food.

"Ung, ung, uck, uck," he said as he began plunging with increasing passion. Then his foot struck something and there was a loud *splat* below on the floor.

"Oh, shit!" he said, taking the chopsticks out of his mouth.

"Damn, I bet it was the roast duck," she said.

He started to withdraw from her to go down and get it.

"No!" she pleaded and locked her legs around him. "Don't go. Fuck the old roast duck!"

"Fuck the duck?"

"Oh, Richie, just fuck . . ."

First he glanced back over his buttocks to make sure his legs were not in danger of knocking any more of the food off the bed, and then he slowly began to move inside her, knowing the variations in rhythm that would quickly bring her to climax. One of the things he liked about Verna was that she reached orgasm so easily. With his wife it had always been work, never in the moment of his own passion, which certainly wasn't premature, but afterward when it had made him feel like a machine pushing her toward her destination, an uphill grind.

"Oh, god, Richie!" Verna exclaimed, thrusting wildly against him with her pelvis. He rose on his arms, locking his elbows and driving into her forcefully, the expression of abandon on her flushed face igniting his own orgasm. As he felt it coming he threw his head back in ecstasy, striking it painfully against the ceiling.

"Yaagh!" he yelled as the pain shot through his scalp and momentarily short-circuited his orgasm. At the same time he wanted to laugh at the ludicrousness of the moment. He crossed his eyes and wobbled his head and then sank slowly down against her soft breasts.

"Poor baby," she said.

"God, that smarts! Gimme another 'poor baby.' "

"Poor baby."

As the pain in his scalp lessened a bit, the urgency in his loins grew warm again. He felt himself filling her. She pulled him closer and bit him sharply on the shoulder. He was tingling with pain and fire. Grabbing her hair with both hands, he pulled her head back against the pillow and kissed her forcefully on the mouth, at the same time driving deeply with his penis, his passion mixed with anger.

"Oh, good, Richie, come, come, come . . ." she moaned as he rose on his arms again and drove harder and harder.

It was one of the strangest and most satisfying orgasms he'd ever had; and afterward, lying next to her, listening to her sighing exhaustion, he felt great tenderness for her, not exactly love, perhaps, but gratitude that she had taken his anger into her flesh and held him there until it was gone. He traced the tips of his fingers over the edge of her perspiring upper lip, then kissed her eyes and smoothed back her damp hair.

"Oh, woman," he moaned into her ear. "Woman, woman."

She smiled at him and there was a great calm in her brown eyes. Then he lay back on his pillow and felt the faintly pulsing echoes of his orgasm radiating warmly over his body. In a moment he drifted into a light sleep.

About fifteen minutes later he awoke from a dream in which his father and a rabbi in a surgical mask were attempting to circumcise him. The father had been complaining that they had left some of the foreskin when he was an infant. He opened his eyes but still felt something happening to his penis. Then he slowly looked down and saw that Verna was having him with chopsticks.

"Thought that would wake you up," she said. "Let's eat!"

"Looks like you've started without me. Jesus, that feels strange," he said, pushing the sticks away from his penis.

"It wasn't the duck," she said, handing him the carton with the duck in it.

"Oh?"

"You got moo goo guy pan all over the floor," she said. "I just hope the rabbit shit doesn't mind."

"What time is it?" he asked, digging hungrily into the duck.

"Ah, zee time ees eight ah fivteen, monsieur."

"Still want to go over to Larsky's with Joe and Len?"

"We could stay here and fuck."

"Larsky's it is," he said. "One more today and I'm going to need a transfusion. Besides, I'm supposed to go over and fuck my shiksa wife for Christmas tomorrow."

"You're kidding, right?" she asked, her face deadly serious.

"Right," he said.

"Richie?" she asked again.

He took another bite.

# CHAPTER
# TWO

Overhead, there was a current of cigarette smoke eddying around the gently swaying Tiffany lamps. Below, the persistent pulsing of rock music from the jukebox could be heard in the lulls of the clamorous waves of shouting and singing from the crowd. And behind the long mahogany bar the three fat Larsky brothers looked like sailors bailing out a rapidly sinking boat as they tried to serve up the Christmas Eve free-beer hour.

Tiernan was sitting at the far end of the bar gloomily staring into the amber depths of his mug of beer when Gemetz and Verna pushed in through the swinging front doors. Despite the huge crowd and the party uproar, they spotted him almost immediately, his bowed blond head illuminated under one of the Tiffany lamps.

"Jesus, just look at that face on him," Verna said, shaking her head.

"We'll perk him up. Come on," Gemetz said, gently pushing her ahead of him through the crowd. "Hey, Joe!"

Tiernan's face came up blinking as he recognized his friend's voice. After a while he saw them squeezing toward him.

"Hi, Joey!" Verna yelled. "Smile goddam it!"

He gave her a quick fierce smile and then waved at Danny, the nearest of the Larsky brothers.

Danny nodded tiredly at Tiernan and went on filling five mugs of beer at the tap, unmindful of the sweat beading off his brow into the beer. In a moment he grabbed up the overflowing mugs in his two big hands and swept them down the bar to a group of young women who now had their backs to him and were talking to some young men in three-piece suits, styled hair and gold neck chains. Danny figured them for electricians.

"I'll get it," one of the electricians said, slapping a twenty on the bar.

"It's on da house, pal," Danny said in his hoarse Brooklyn voice.

"It's my round," the young man said, feeling awkward about losing his big-spender play.

"Whatta you, nuts, Tony?" one of the girls asked.

Danny jerked the twenty off the bar, turned and banged the register with his big wet fist. The change was dug out of the drawer and slapped onto the bar and then Danny was wading toward the beer taps again. An ex-Marine, he was one of those muscular fat men who move with the slow inherent violence of bears.

"Beeahs?" he called over to Tiernan.

"Two!" Tiernan answered as he got up to let Verna have his stool.

"Seen Len?" Gemetz asked, nearly having to shout over the noise.

"Hasn't come in yet."

"So, how would *you* have known?" Verna asked. "You with your long face down in your beer. What a sight! The whole place is jumping and there's Joey sitting by himself looking like he was composing suicide notes. Anything wrong, Joey?"

Danny brought the beers over and winked at Verna. His red "Larsky's" T-shirt was soaked through. What little hair he had was hanging down in wet strings.

"Hey, Danny, you just get out of the shower?" Gemetz asked.

"Yeah, Richie. Screw you, Richie. How ya doin', Verna? I hope ya didn't have ta come in wit dis joik."

"Great Christmas Eve party, Danny," she said.

"Yeah, it's breaking my goddam back, dis great party," he grumbled as he lumbered back to the taps.

"Sweet guy," Gemetz said. "Had a brilliant career as a brain surgeon before he lost his nerve."

"I, uh, had a lousy evening," Tiernan said distantly, finally responding to Verna's question.

"Huh?" she asked.

"A total bummer," he sighed. "Mary dumped all over me, and then on the way out a dog bit me. God, I used to like Christmas," he said.

"You went over there after all," Gemetz said, giving him a frown.

"Jesus, I hate her now," Tiernan said, almost under his breath. "For the first time I really *hate!*"

"Wait a minute, wait a minute!" Verna said. "What are you talking about? Whatta ya mean, a dog bit you?"

"Hate!" Tiernan shouted and slammed the bar with his fist.

"What's he talking about?" she asked Gemetz.

"What's he talking about?" Gemetz answered with exasperation growing in his voice. "Remember how he was last Thanksgiving? No, he was never going to do that again, right, Joey? Same shit, right, Joey? Goddam it!" he muttered, and slammed his hand on the bar.

"I know, I know," Tiernan said.

"Shit!" Gemetz hissed. "She's a killer; you know she's a killer. What'd you expect? I bet you even went through the begging shit again. Right?" Gemetz was really fuming. For a minute Verna thought he was going to punch Tiernan, who was now staring rigidly ahead, his jaw muscles grinding, his face nearly as red as his sweater.

"Richie, go take a piss or something," Verna said, pushing him away. "I want to talk to Joey."

Gemetz finished most of his beer in one long drink and looked at Tiernan again and shook his head in disgust. "Jesus, where's Talbot?" he asked. "He got crapped on this week, too. Susan took Teddy up to Connecticut without telling him."

"Hey, can we get off of ex-wives tonight," Verna protested.

"He's probably sitting in the dark slugging bourbon, if I know him," Tiernan said. "Maybe we should go over and dig him out."

"Richie, why don't you go? I'll stay here and talk to Joe," Verna said. "Did you say a dog bit you?" she asked Tiernan.

"Yeah, that was the final frosting," Tiernan said, raising his

leg and showing them a two-inch flap hanging off the thigh of
his tweed slacks.

"Jesus, he broke the skin, man," Gemetz said, leaning over
to inspect the hole in Tiernan's pants. "You put anything on
it?"

"Did Mary get a dog?" Verna asked.

"No," Tiernan said glumly. "It was down in the lobby after
Mary dumped on me. Christ, what a night! There's this crazy
woman who lives on the first floor of Mary's building. You
walk past her door and you'd swear she was keeping a dead
body in there. Anyway, she's coming into the building with this
black mongrel of hers. The dog is as crazy as she is—teeth like
this," he said, turning his fingers into fangs and clamping his
hands together. "Almost got the part for *Jaws.*"

"Yeah . . . So? So?" Gemetz asked impatiently.

"So, being mentally retarded, I hold the door open for her to
come in. And in she comes with Jaws and he rears up on his
leash and chomps my leg."

"What'd *you* do?" Verna asked.

"I, uh, admonished him sternly."

"Good!" Gemetz said with a nod and took a sip of beer.
"Hey, Danny!" he then yelled to the bartender. "You got
anything to put on a dog bite?"

"Ony a shot of whiskey," he answered, coming over. "Who
got da bite?" he asked, looking over the bar at Tiernan's torn
pants. "Joey? If it was Joey, it's da dog should get da
whiskey."

"Arrrroooooooo!" Gemetz howled. "Give him the shot!"
Then Gemetz finished his beer and started to put on his
peacoat. "I better go get Talbot."

"No, I'll go," Tiernan said, holding his arm. "I need some
air anyway." He shook his head as Verna tried to hold him
back. In a nearby corner he took his trench coat off a rack,
slipped it on and started through the crowd toward the
entrance. Gemetz watched him for a minute and then turned
back to the bar, where Danny was setting down the brimming
shot glass of whiskey and looking off toward Tiernan with
confusion on his face.

"I'll take it," Gemetz said, throwing a five-dollar bill on the
bar and picking up the shot glass. Downing the whiskey in one
gulp, he winced, then gasped, then coughed, then stood there

for a moment looking into Danny's impassive face. Then he started barking.

As Tiernan neared the front door buttoning his coat, he saw Juliet down by the jukebox at the farther end of the bar. She was illuminated in the red and blue lights of the jukebox and dancing to the Eagles tune he'd played so often when he wanted to torment himself over Mary. "You get the best of my love . . ." The refrain seemed to say everything he felt.

Juliet saw him about to leave and waved as she continued to dance sensuously and slowly with Rico, a muscularly built little Puerto Rican who seemed to be all arms and shoulders. Tiernan paused for a moment and watched her, liking the way her long dark hair swept softly around as she danced. She was wearing a thin white peasant blouse and cutoff jeans.

Ah, Juliet, he thought. The first girl he'd met at Larsky's after Mary had turned him out. She'd seemed a little interested at first, but his constant blubbering about Mary had put her off. Friendly conversation at the bar, but she would not go out. Richie had had a little more luck after that. At least she'd gone out with him a couple of times. Then Richie struck out, too— called her a "professional virgin." Still, she was the most beautiful girl in the place and lately Talbot had been talking about taking a run at her. Yeah, Juliet might be just the thing to get Talbot to come out of his cave tonight, he thought. He'd tell him she was there looking fantastic.

Walking from the bar up Fourth Street to get to Talbot's rooming house, he thought of all the women the three of them had gone through at Larsky's. Mostly one-night stands, mostly too young or too homely or too crazy—so many depressed women with depressing stories. He thought of the blonde on the subway and reminded himself to ask Richie about her. But already he sensed she was slipping from his mind.

God, he'd really felt something there for a moment. Then a few minutes with Mary and he was back to square one again. He didn't know what his feelings meant anymore. So many women who came to nothing. So many changes since the long drowsy years of marriage.

"Fuck her," he muttered under his breath as he came to the rooming house, a tall crumbling brownstone with a flight of stone steps up to the front door.

At the top of the steps he took a coin from his pocket and, leaning over the stone balustrade, he struck it against the curved glass of Talbot's bay window. There was a dim light on behind the peeling green shutters inside the window. After a minute, the shutters opened and Talbot's glum face appeared, nodded at him once and disappeared.

The buzzer sounded and Tiernan pushed the high oaken door inward and stepped into the gloomy churchlike foyer. There was the smell of fresh linoleum mixed with the clinging staleness of old men's clothes. The house was occupied primarily by elderly men, grey-stubbled pensioners who seemed expansive and friendly sitting out on the front steps on warm days, but inside reminded him of hermit crabs with their furtive scuttling in and out of their rooms. For some strange reason it seemed natural to him that Talbot had chosen to live there after his marriage had broken up.

"I didn't feel like going," Talbot said by way of greeting at the door. He was wearing a white T-shirt and faded Levi's and was in his bare feet. And he seemed unwilling to open the door all the way.

"You will when you see Juliet. Come on, get your . . . ," Tiernan said, straining to see past Talbot's shoulder into the room. "Oh . . . Got a little chickie in there?"

"Nope."

"So what's with the door?"

"What's the password?" Talbot asked with a mischievous look growing on his face. Before Tiernan could reply, he slowly drew a gleaming cavalry sword from behind him.

"What the hell is that?" Tiernan exclaimed.

"Present," Talbot said, turning and walking into the room.

As Tiernan followed and shut the door behind him, Talbot went over and sat on the bed. There he picked up a gray palm-sized whetstone, spit on it and began stroking it along the sharp edge of the sword. For a minute, as Tiernan watched in silence, there was only the muted rhythmical singing of stone against steel as Talbot calmly sharpened the sword.

Except for the mantel over the tiny fireplace on which Talbot had half a dozen crayon drawings made by his son, there was a barracks Spartanness to the room. The wood floors still had the smell of fresh mopping. Near the bay windows was a round oak table and chair. On the table was Talbot's old upright Underwood typewriter and a clutter of books, file cards and manuscript pages for a history paper he was preparing for publication. Nearby there was a glass-enclosed bookcase and behind that a whole wall of shelves stacked with books. On the other side of the room was a sink, gleaming clean, a small stove and refrigerator. And in the middle of the room an old four-poster brass bed, tightly made with a gray military blanket. The only other furniture was a small wooden stool near Talbot's knee on which stood a half-filled bottle of bourbon.

After a while, Talbot placed the whetstone on the stool and picked up the bottle and took a long drink. Then, blinking as the fire in his throat made his eyes water, he held it out to Tiernan. He took it and walked over to the sink and picked up one of the three glasses that were washed and sitting in a row on the drainboard.

"Ah'll be taking a little branch water with mine," he said, turning on the tap, which rumbled and hiccoughed before it began to flow evenly.

"It came in the mail today," Talbot said, sighting down the sharp edge of the sword. "It's been in my family for more than . . . well, since the Civil War."

Tiernan returned with his drink and placed the bottle back on the stool. Talbot turned the sword around and handed it to him. "That, my friend, is a real cavalry fighting sword, not ceremonial," he said.

"Goddam," Tiernan said, hefting it and swishing it about in the air a few times. "You mean this little muthah done tasted blood?"

"Yankee blood!" Talbot said evilly.

"Lovely Christmas presents you rebels give each other," Tiernan said, walking over to the mantel. Touching the sharpness of the blade, he inspected it closely and imagined the little black pit marks were blood from old battles. It made him slightly dizzy holding something that might have ended men's lives.

"Curious feeling, eh?" Talbot asked.

"Yeah," Tiernan said, coming over and tossing the sword on the bed. Then he walked over to the table near the window and sat down with his drink.

"You know you got a hole in your pants?" Talbot asked, picking up the sword and sharpening it again.

"Dog," Tiernan said and took a drink.

"Oh, dog, huh?" Talbot said, sensing Tiernan was in some kind of mood.

"Black," Tiernan said, looking into his drink.

"Black dog," Talbot said and nodded.

"Yeah."

Talbot continued sharpening while he waited until Tiernan was ready to tell him what his problem was. Tiernan pushed some of the papers aside on the table and draped his leg over its edge and then took a drink from his glass.

"What's this?" he asked, zipping the manuscript page from the typewriter.

"Careful of that. It's my ticket to making associate professor this spring," Talbot said. "I hope."

"Who's Lorenzo?" Tiernan asked, looking at the page.

"Ah, yes, Lorenzo de' Medici," Talbot said, stopping his stroking with the whetstone for a minute and looking off into the distance. "He did for the Italian Renaissance what McDonald did for the hamburger."

"I don't wanna talk about Italians," Tiernan said, tossing the page on the table. "Mary's going with this little squirt Italian."

"So how's the scene at Larsky's?" Talbot asked as he picked up the sword and started sharpening it again.

"Half of Park Slope's down there," Tiernan said without enthusiasm and tossed down half his bourbon and water. "Richie and Verna sent me to get you."

"Good party, huh?"

"Yeah, sure," Tiernan said and slumped down in the chair and rested his leg over the edge of the table.

Talbot stopped stroking the sword for a moment and looked at Tiernan's morose face and then started stroking again. "So what's the matter?" he asked.

"Nothing, nothing. . . . I, uh . . . Ah, you know. Mary."

Talbot lowered his head and closed his eyes. After all he and Richie had been through with him on Thanksgiving he couldn't believe the big sap had gone back there again. He could feel his anger and impatience with his friend growing, but as he looked up and saw the deep pain in Tiernan's face he checked it. Goddam poor fucking boob, he thought. No, he didn't need anybody jumping on him now.

"You went over?" he asked.

"Yeah." Tiernan sighed. "You know, just to drop off Lynn's present."

"Got sucked in again, huh?"

"Yep . . . bad," Tiernan said without opening his eyes.

"Well, at least you got to see your kid," Talbot sympathized. "See all those presents under the bed? Teddy's. I won't get to give them to him till after New Year's. Fucking Susan split for New London with him without even telling me."

"I'm sorry," Tiernan said, looking at the presents. "I just got Lynn a doll—all I could afford this year."

"So what happened?"

"Jesus," Tiernan took another long swallow and put the glass on the table.

"As bad as Thanksgiving?"

"Worse. I really blew it. It all really got to me, you know— the tree, the Christmas decorations, Lynn saying good night with her arms around me . . . I want . . . wanted to be there. You know?" he said, his eyes beginning to brim with tears.

"Yeah," Talbot said softly.

"Mary was sitting on the couch and I, uh . . . You know, I just came in from putting Lynn to bed. And, well, we had a couple of drinks. You know, listened to some Christmas music. Then, I didn't wanna leave. I, ah—"

"Ah, forget it, Joe," Talbot said, putting the sword aside and going over with the bottle to pour some more into Tiernan's glass. "Belt this shit down fast. Cures everything."

"You know what she said, man?" Tiernan said and gritted his teeth. "I was on my knees, man, holding on to her and . . . Oh, god, Len, I was . . . I was begging, man."

"Come on, drink this down," Talbot said, handing him the glass of nearly straight bourbon.

Tiernan took a long drink and gasped. "And she, ah [gasp] . . . Christ, that's strong," he said, grimacing as the bourbon continued to burn in his chest. "She . . . she said I was defective." He laughed and bit his lip.

"What?" Talbot asked incredulously.

"Yeah, that was it," Tiernan said, nodding his head. "She said she didn't wanna live with me again because I was defective."

"What the fuck does that mean?"

"Who knows? Something. . . . She said my moods

changed too quick or something for her—made her crazy. Said she never knew what I was going to do.''

"Defective, that's a new one." Talbot laughed. "Maybe she wants you to be like one of those computers she works with.''

"That's right—she's been programming computers so long she's become one. Oh, god help me, Len, I hate . . . I wanted to just grab her and . . .''

"What'd you do?"

"Nothing. I couldn't even talk after that. I had this creepy feeling I was in the room with a robot or something. I don't know her anymore, Len. . . . She's all wheels and wires inside." He looked up at his friend and shook his head. "Defective? Defective? Jesus, man, how'd you like to be written off as defective?"

"Yeah, well, it's your own fault, you know. I warned you about using that low-grade oil. And when's the last time you had your plugs cleaned? And you've been pinging for months now. Even Richie noticed it. Just the other day he said, 'Joe's gotta get something done with his pings—before he becomes defective.' ''

Tiernan laughed and started making motor noises interspersed with coughs and belches.

"See?" Talbot said with a knowing nod and headed back toward the bed. "Defective. I can understand why Mary would say that."

"Yeah, I know—my own fault," Tiernan said, feeling warmed by Talbot's effort to cheer him up.

"Gotta stay oiled," Talbot said, raising the bottle and taking a long swig.

"So let's get our defective asses down to Larsky's before they run out of free beer."

"Nah, I hate Larsky's," Talbot sighed and flopped down on the bed, spilling some of the bourbon from the bottle on his T-shirt.

"Come on, man. Richie and Verna are waiting. And wait'll you see Juliet tonight."

"I really feel like staying in tonight," Talbot said, putting the bottle back on the stool and starting to sharpen the sword again.

"So this is the way to spend Christmas Eve?" Tiernan said, coming over and taking the sword from him. "Sitting here all night slugging booze and sharpening a fucking sword? Forget her, man. When she comes back you can lay down the law about Teddy. Sic your lawyer on her."

"We must keep our weapons sharp," Talbot said.

"This is going to come as a shock to you, old man," Tiernan said, hefting the sword and looking down the blade, "but old Cracker Land done lost de woah, Colonel Talbot, suh. In fact, I may have to confiscate this weapon."

Tiernan clicked his heels together and began flourishing the sword around the room, nearly knocking Teddy's drawings off the mantel over the tiny fireplace.

"Hey, careful!" Talbot yelled and ducked as Tiernan swept the blade near his head. "Okay, okay, I'll go," he said as Tiernan came at him with the point of the sword, his face grinning maniacally.

". . . and that, and that, and that!" Tiernan exclaimed, turning and slashing the sword at some other imaginary enemy.

"I say, old boy," Talbot said, getting up. "That's not really proper form, you know." He held out his hand for the sword.

"Oh, blahst, I'm in disgrace," Tiernan cried, throwing his arm over his face. "Mummy and Daddy had so wanted me to kill *properly*."

"Nothing to it, old man," Talbot said, taking the sword and assuming a modified fencing stance. "Done with this sweeping motion, don't you see," he said, slicing the air with the blade. "Wrist and arm, wrist and arm, ever so in harmony. Takes the head off ever so brightly."

"Jesus, Mary and Joseph, now where'd ye larn a thing like that?" Tiernan asked in an Irish brogue. "Military school, was it?"

"No, my father was a tank cavalry officer in the army—went out a lieutenant colonel. But he loved the old horse cavalry stories and rode with a number of 'ceremonial' cavalry units on weekend parade drills. This was his grandfather's sword."

"So he sends it to you for Christmas?"

"Yeah, with a note. I mean, what a note!"

"Yeah?"

Talbot took the blade in both hands and went back and sat on the bed. "He said, 'When a man loses his woman, he can find solace sleeping with his sword.'"

"Providing he doesn't cut his pecker off," Tiernan laughed.

"I think it's something from way back," Talbot said, taking up the whetstone and stroking it along the blade again. "When men joined the army to forget a rotten situation. Like the Foreign Legion. But I mean, what a thing to say, huh? In our times. I've been thinking about it all night—and about Susan.''

"And sharpening the sword.''

"Yeah, it's very pleasant to sharpen a sword and drink bourbon whiskey when you're angry. My god, it brings a deep, deep calm.''

Tiernan looked at him for a long moment and then went over and leaned on the mantel. He thought of his anger at Mary and wished that he, too, had the solace of a sword this night. Then Talbot got up with the sword and began pacing back and forth between the bed and the kitchen, his brows knitted in thought. Tiernan remained silent and watched him, sensing something building in his friend.

Talbot continued to move silently, catlike in his bare feet, pacing back and forth, his face tightening, and then his arm sweeping out with the sword, taking cuts across the air. Finally he walked over to the refrigerator and took out a large grapefruit.

"You okay?" Tiernan asked.

Talbot did not answer but placed the grapefruit on one of the bedposts, balancing it carefully until it remained by itself.

"Like this," he said calmly, "arm and wrist so." Then he swung the blade cleanly and powerfully and halved the grapefruit. Tiernan watched the two halves roll across the floor and felt a shiver go through him as speckles of its juice stuck to his face like blood.

Talbot dried the sword off on the bed and sat down, still deep into his dark mood, and began stroking the blade again with the whetstone. For a moment Tiernan watched and then went back over to the table and sat down. Taking a long swallow of bourbon, he closed his eyes and listened to the rhythmical striking of stone along the blade and imagined himself sitting around a fire after a hard day of riding with the cavalry.

"Okay!" Talbot declared suddenly and got up, startling Tiernan out of his reverie. "Off to Larsky's.''

"Right," Tiernan said and watched as Talbot picked up the grapefruit halves and tossed them in the sink. Then he put on his boots and white turtleneck sweater and left the room to go to the community bathroom on the floor above.

When he was gone, Tiernan went over to the bed and picked up the sword, sighting down its sharp edge and taking a few cuts at the air with it. Then he walked over to the refrigerator, opened it and took out another grapefruit. After a moment he had it balanced on the bedpost.

Gripping the hilt with both hands, he drew the sword around his shoulder.

"Defective!" he grunted, and with murderous energy he slashed through the grapefruit so cleanly that for an instant the halves remained together before it toppled to the floor and fell apart.

"How easy," he whispered. "How sweet and easy."

When Tiernan and Talbot got back to Larsky's, the bar was considerably less boisterous than when Tiernan had left it. That was because the Christmas Eve free-beer hour was over and because Millie and Buffalo were singing on the tiny raised platform behind the jukebox. Millie, looking thin and exotic in her black leotard top and tight-fitting jeans, waved to Tiernan and for a few moments directed her deep haunting voice solely toward him.

"Great. Millie's singing 'Vincent,'" Tiernan said, smiling at her and rubbing his cold hands. He and Talbot had jogged the four blocks from the rooming house.

"Let's hope they can get through it without fighting for a change," Talbot said, referring to the many times the young couple, who lived together in the neighborhood, had interrupted their performance with bickering because Buffalo had objected to Millie's impromptu styling.

Tiernan called them the beauty and the beast—Millie sensually graceful with dark soulful eyes and long black silky hair, and Buffalo an elongated gangle of bones with a face that was a whorl of brown beard and erupted skin.

Near the end of their song Millie motioned for Tiernan to come down to that end of the bar. She liked Tiernan and usually joined him for drinks after her singing. In recent weeks she had suggested a little "exploratory" affair. Her living arrangement with Buffalo had an "exploratory" clause, she had said, and her open propositions to Tiernan had never drawn any more reaction from her dour partner than a *tsk* through his wide-spaced teeth. Still, with Buffalo you never knew what would trigger his sudden fits of temper.

The anger that Tiernan had felt over Mary's rejection earlier in the evening had now turned to predatory heat, and he was blazing a look into Millie's eyes. Tonight, Millie, he thought. As she finished her song she pointed to a table near the jukebox where Tiernan could see Gemetz and Verna sitting with their backs to him.

"Come on, there's Richie," he said, giving Talbot's arm a little shove in that direction.

"Millie looks a little eager," Talbot said.

"Ah, yes, think I'll have a jolly go at Mildred tonight. Don't you think?"

"Oh, rawther," Talbot said. "And I'm sure dear old Buffalo will play accompaniment on the guitar."

"Yeah, you're right," Tiernan said, cooling to the idea as he usually did whenever Buffalo was around. "I don't trust that arrangement of theirs. All I need to deal with right now is a berserk Buffalo."

As he and Talbot got to the table Millie and Buffalo were putting away their guitars and shutting down their amplifiers. Buffalo plugged the jukebox cord back in and Larsky's was again filled with pulsating rock music and a rising volume of chatter and laughter from the patrons. Talbot unzipped his red ski jacket and scanned the room for Juliet. He saw her sitting at the bar talking to Rico and a few of his friends. After a moment Rico and the other young men put on their jackets and started out.

"Hey, where the hell you been?" Gemetz exclaimed as Tiernan sat down and took his mug of beer.

"Slicing grapefruit," Tiernan said and took a long swallow.

"Why don't you have some beer?" Gemetz groused and grabbed his beer back.

"I'll get some," Talbot offered and headed toward Juliet at the bar.

"Feeling better?" Verna asked Joe.

"Yeah, fine," he sighed and looked up over his shoulder at Millie, who was just climbing down from the band platform. "Jesus, is the kitchen still open? I'm starved."

"Yeah, me, too," Gemetz said, making a pained expression and rubbing his stomach. "Gotta get something on my ulcer before it eats a hole in me."

"It's nearly twelve o'clock," Verna said. "I think Frieda has closed the kitchen, Richie."

"Well, I nominate Joe to go over and find out," Gemetz said.

"C'mere, tiger," Millie murmured suggestively and plopped herself in Tiernan's lap and gave him a big hug.

"I've got an idea," Gemetz said, watching Millie fondling Tiernan's face. "Why don't *I* go see about the food?" Then, shaking his head at Buffalo, who was standing just behind Tiernan and Millie *tsk*ing his teeth, Gemetz got up and walked toward the little fry-kitchen window at the end of the bar.

Frieda Loaman was bending over the sink splashing soapy water over her hot face when Gemetz poked his head in through the window and startled her with his loud greeting.

"Mein gott!" he yelled. "Ist das ist meina Frieda all shtigging oudt der?"

"Richie, you deffil!" she exclaimed, angry at being caught in such an awkward pose, even though she was quite used to his mimicry of her German accent. With the sudsy water draining from her handsome face, she groped for the stringy towel hanging over the sink.

"Feed me, Frieda, my love, or I'll bite you on the bum."

"Bum ist not on the menu," she said, drying her face and smoothing her blond hair back with the towel. "Anyway, the kitchen is closed, Richie."

"Frieda, no!" he protested, leaning farther in. "Zis couldt loose zee war. You couldt be seriously shot!"

"Twelff o'clock, Richie," she said, smiling at his contortions and brushing a few drops of water off the sleeves of her black wool sweater.

"Frieda baby," he whined.

"No, go to Eddie's Pizza!"

"Eddie's?" he yelled and pounded the serving counter. "You know what Eddie's does to my ulcer."

She liked Gemetz but she was tired and she wanted to get drunk and forget it was Christmas. For a forty-nine-year-old woman, Frieda still had her smooth-skinned good looks and a firm shapely figure. As she untied the apron from around her deep-green velvet slacks she did a little lackadaisical striptease for him.

"I have *nothing* to giff you," she said, looking back over her shoulder at him like a weary hooker.

This time he did not say anything to her but looked into her gray-blue eyes appraisingly. He liked her mature sensuality, and for an instant he imagined her in creamy nakedness lolling

voluptuously on pale green silk sheets. That's all I need, he
told himself, me and the Kraut.

They all had fantasies about Frieda, this older somewhat
mysterious woman who worked as a cook at Larsky's on
weekends and holidays to help pay her bar tab. The rest of the
evenings she was usually at her "place" at the end of the bar.
Frieda was always there in the evenings to talk to, to listen to
their tales, to laugh and flirt with, the one they wound up with
when they had struck out with the younger women—though
she, too, always managed to unhook herself from their drunken
propositions before she left for her tiny apartment each night.

"Come on, Frieda," Gemetz pleaded again.

She walked over and leaned wearily on the window counter,
pouting her lower lip and looking into his eyes as a mother into
a child's. He pushed farther in until his face was close to hers,
his eyes all innocence and need. But his expression changed
slowly to sadness as he continued to look deep into her eyes
and was strangely reminded of the December blue sky over the
cemetery slope in Queens last year when his mother was
buried.

"You are hopeless, Richie," Frieda said, pulling gently on
his beard. "Perhaps I have a little ham yet. Where are you
sitting?"

"I luff you," he said, kissing her sweetly on the cheek. "Mit
moostard, undt piggles, undt rye bredt, I luff you."

"Idiot," she said, smiling, and pushed him back from the
window and looked out. "Ach," she sighed as she saw Talbot
and Juliet arriving at the table with two trays of filled beer
mugs. "How many are there—two, three, six!"

"And make one for yourself and come join us," Gemetz
said, rubbing his stomach as his ulcer began stabbing out a
hollow pain again below his solar plexus.

"You will buy Frieda a little drink, Richie, *ja?*"

"Ja, ja, meina Liebling," he said, starting to lean back into
the window for another kiss.

"Out!" she said and pushed him away. Then she turned and
went over to the refrigerator to begin making the sandwiches.
Gemetz started back to the table, frowning at the pain in his
stomach.

"You don't look too good," Verna said as he came over and
slumped down in his chair beside her.

"Gut," he said, narrowing his eyes.

Gemetz looked up and saw Millie still sitting on Tiernan's lap and whispering something in his ear. Tiernan gave Gemetz a sickly smile and then glanced apprehensively over at Buffalo, who was chewing on a hangnail and looking otherwise unconcerned.

"Frieda's making some sandwiches," Gemetz said.

"Great," Talbot said, "I'm starving." Then he raised his glass to Juliet and took a long swallow. Juliet smiled back and then, feeling a little self-conscious about the attention he'd been giving her, she looked at Gemetz and shrugged. She had recently discouraged Gemetz from pursuing her, but she still felt a little awkward being friendly with his best friend.

"What happened to Rico and his merry crew?" Gemetz asked her.

"Stealing Christmas trees," Talbot said with a laugh.

"Yeah, I told them they were nuts," Juliet said.

"They wanted us to go with them," Talbot said. "You know that lot next to the Food Fair market? They're going to try to pinch a tree while the guy is sleeping in his truck."

"Rico said they always steal their Christmas trees," Juliet said.

"Well, that makes it a Christmas tradition then," Gemetz said. "Kind of sweet when you think about it. The young men going off to bring back a tree."

Meanwhile, Tiernan was becoming more and more uncomfortable with Millie's attentions. Not only because she seemed to have made his lap her permanent seat for the evening but Buffalo was now staring steadily into his eyes and *tsk*ing at a faster rate.

"Let me up, Mil," Tiernan said, pushing her gently from his lap. "Gotta go see Mother Nature."

"Hurry back," she said, patting him on the behind as he walked away toward the men's room.

"Whyn't you go and hold it for 'im," Buffalo said sarcastically and *tsk*ed again.

"What I hold or don't hold is none of your business, fuzzy face," she said, sneering at him.

"Christ," Tiernan whispered to himself and shook his head as he continued to the door of the men's room. He had to find some way of turning Millie off or he was sure there was going to be an explosion from Buffalo.

When he entered the men's room Alan Curtis was leaning

over the sink splashing water on his pale chubby face. The forty-year-old lawyer and his wife, Fredricka, had been in their circle of friends when he and Mary were still together. The friendship had cooled shortly before the breakup when the Curtises, who lived in their building, had suggested a little strip poker one night after a party at their place. They had declined, but then Tiernan had started avoiding Alan altogether a few weeks later after Fredricka confided to Mary that Alan was bisexual and found Tiernan very attractive.

"Joe!" Curtis exclaimed cheerfully as he noticed Tiernan behind him in the mirror. "We were just talking about you."

"Hello, Alan," Tiernan said without enthusiasm and walked over to the urinal.

"So this is where you've been hanging out."

"Yeah," Tiernan replied glumly and turned away slightly as Curtis stood by the sink looking down at his penis.

"You still job hunting?" Curtis asked, moving around to Tiernan's other side for a better view.

"I may have something after the first of the year," Tiernan said, flopping his penis up and down to taunt Curtis.

"No kidding," Curtis said and then coughed in embarrassment as he looked up and found Tiernan glaring at him angrily. "Hey, there's a young woman with us tonight I want you to meet. She saw you and Len come in and asked about you."

"Oh, yeah," Tiernan said, zipping up and going over to the sink.

"Ellen Williams—a very classy lady, Joe. Just your type. I'm handling her divorce. She was married to a gynecologist, of all things."

"She's here tonight?" Tiernan asked, thinking it might be a good way to avoid going back to the table and dealing with Millie again.

"Yeah, her first night out. Know what I mean? Joe, you'll love her: great looks, owns her own brownstone, graduated from Bennington. Just one thing—watch what you say to her. She's really hyped up on women's lib."

"Forget it. I've been out with that type before," Tiernan said and was about to head out the door.

"Wait a minute, will you?" Curtis said, grabbing his arm. "I'm telling you she's ripe, man. Fredricka says she's so horny she's got smoke coming out of her."

"Yeah, well . . ." Tiernan said, rubbing his chin and

reconsidering. Then he thought of Millie and Buffalo waiting at the table and nodded. "Sounds like my kinda girl. Let's go have a look."

As he and Curtis walked past Gemetz's table on their way to the other end of the bar, Tiernan waved and said he'd be back in a little while.

"Joe!" Millie called with a puzzled look on her face.

"Merry Christmas!" he said and blew her a kiss.

About midway down the bar Tiernan stopped and had to step aside as Rico burst in through the front doors followed by three of his friends. They all looked out of breath and frightened.

"Hey, where's the tree?" Tiernan called after them as the four young men headed down toward the jukebox end of the bar.

"He came at us with an ax!" Rico replied over his shoulder and kept going.

"What's that all about?" Curtis asked.

"Tree specialists," Tiernan laughed.

"There she is," Curtis whispered as they neared the end of the bar and saw Fredricka talking to an elegantly dressed young woman who was sitting with her back to the bar and sipping a martini. Not bad, Tiernan thought as he drew nearer, liking her close-cropped blond hair and slightly blushed face.

Slipping up behind Fredricka, Tiernan grasped her around the waist and pulled her against him, breathing passionately into her ear. "I need some help, lady," he moaned. "I'm just a little lonely."

"Gak!" Fredricka exclaimed and tried to pull away until she saw who it was.

"Ellen, this is Joe Tiernan," Curtis said, laughing.

"Hi," Tiernan said, taking one of his hands from Fredricka's waist and extending it to the young woman, who was blushing even more and switching her drink to shake hands with him.

"Yes, our local neighborhood sex maniac," Fredricka said, turning and tweaking Tiernan's cheek.

"Hello," Ellen said, her big wide-spaced blue eyes twinkling. "You're the college professor?"

"No, that's Len Talbot, the guy I came in with," he said, continuing to hold her hand. "I'm a professional horny bachelor, as Fredricka claims."

"Me, too," Ellen said, giving his hand a large affirmative

shake and spilling some of her martini on her white angora sweater.

"Ellen, you just blew your air of mystery!" Fredricka exclaimed.

Just then there was a commotion down at the other end of the bar and Tiernan could hear Rico and Juliet arguing. Stepping up on the bar rail, he looked over the crowd and saw Rico gesturing wildly and complaining about something to her, with the other three young men adding in their comments. Gemetz and Talbot were sitting at the table looking disgusted.

"Let's go see about the sandwiches," Gemetz said to Talbot, and both of them got up and went over to the end of the bar near the kitchen window. "Jesus, what a night," he sighed.

"Why does Juliet bother with them?" Talbot asked him.

"They've been friends since grade school," Gemetz said. "She feels responsible for him."

"If they go back there, that guy's likely to chop them up this time."

"Idiots," Gemetz said and leaned over the bar and looked into the kitchen. "Frieda? How's it going?"

"I'm coming," she said, turning out the light and sliding a large tray of sandwiches onto the serving-window counter. "Please take them, Richie," she said and then put her overcoat on her arm and slid her long fox fur around her neck. When he took the tray, she opened the door and stepped into the area behind the bar.

"Give her a hand, Len," Gemetz said, taking the tray and turning back toward the table. There was only one way from behind the bar and that was over it. Talbot stepped onto the rail and held his hands out to Frieda.

"Up we go," he said, grunting as he picked her up under her arms and lifted her over the bar and down to the floor on the other side.

"Oh, so strong," Frieda said, blushing a little as she straightened her sweater and glanced up at him.

"Light as a feather," Talbot said, touching the bottom of her chin lightly with his fingers. "Come on," he said, leading her over to the table, where Rico and his friends had stopped arguing with Juliet and were parading out of the bar again.

"Frieda, you're an angel!" Verna greeted her. "We're all starving to death. Richie and I had Chinese food earlier, but you know what they say about that. Come sit next to me."

"Where's the merry crew off to now?" Talbot asked.

"Dopes!" Juliet exclaimed and sat down with a scowl on her face.

"The lads are going off to avenge their honor," Gemetz said, reaching for one of the sandwiches.

"I'm gonna split, too," Buffalo said, getting up and putting on his sheepskin coat. "You coming, Millie?"

"I wanna stick around," she said, trying to spot Tiernan at the other end of the bar. "You go on."

"Yeah, right," Buffalo said, picking up his guitar and giving her an angry *tsk* of his teeth. Then without looking at the others, he started out.

"Good sandwiches, Frieda," Talbot said after taking a bite and washing it down with a long swallow of beer.

Frieda sat back and smiled at him, her eyes telling him he was welcome—but something else, too, something that made him feel warm and uneasy at the same time. She had put on some makeup, and for the first time Talbot was caught by the almost aristocratic beauty of her face—a classic line of nose and chin that in some women brings the face to its finest sculpting in middle age. A touch of decadence, too, he thought, looking at the battered fox fur draped around her neck with the heads lying on her breasts.

A different Frieda tonight, it seemed as he looked back into her eyes. A light flickering somewhere within where he'd only seen pain before. She'd always been a little closer to him than to the others, opening up to him a little more on those evenings when she drank too much. She had told him the story of the girl—her eight-year-old daughter—who had drowned. Poor wounded Frieda, he'd always thought—until tonight. She had told him of walking out on her husband in New Jersey two years ago. He was a retired army captain whose discovery of Jesus at fifty-eight had ruined the only thing they had had in common in recent years—drinking. They had met in Berlin during the occupation after the war. Now he sent her a little money each month along with religious tracts and sad little reminiscences about their daughter, Maria, drowned in the officers' club pool at Fort Riley, Kansas, where they had been stationed in the sixties. Yes, that was how it had come up. Talbot had been telling her of how he had gone swimming in that pool as a child when his father, the colonel, had been stationed there.

"Frieda, you look lovely tonight," Talbot said, putting down his mug of beer and smiling at her.

"Oh, *ja,* sure—like a cooked herring," she said, feeling embarrassed by his compliment. "So hot back there . . . Um, do you have a cigarette maybe?"

He picked up Verna's pack of Salems from the table and offered it to her. She took one and put it in her mouth and then dug into her coat pocket for a match. Picking up Verna's butane lighter, he flicked it and held the flame out to her. The sexy way the cigarette dangled from her lips made his hand shake slightly as he held the lighter.

Frieda glanced up at him and touched his hand with her fingers to steady it. *"Danke,"* she said, leaning back and exhaling wearily.

*"Bitte,"* he replied and then smiled quietly as she found him looking hungrily at her. She smiled back and shook her head in amusement.

"Well!" he exclaimed and raised his glass. " 'God bless us, every one.' "

An hour later Tiernan was leaving Larsky's with Ellen Williams, ostensibly to walk her home, but she had given him enough hints in their conversation at the bar that he'd be invited in. Thank god they had been able to slip out of the bar without Millie seeing them, he thought as he buttoned up his coat. Gemetz had seen them leaving and had given him a conspiratorial wave.

As they walked under the corner streetlight, Ellen pulled up the collar of her mink coat and smiled at him. He smiled back and slipped his arm around her waist.

"We could go to my place for a nightcap," he said. "Just around the corner."

"I have to let the sitter go," she said. She had told him about her six-year-old twin girls during their conversation, and they had discussed her bringing them to the park playground some afternoon to meet his Lynn.

"Just a wee nightcap?" he persisted.

"We'll have one at my place," she said. "Come on before we freeze to death on this corner."

"Right," he said eagerly and guided her across Fourth Street and headed down Seventh Avenue.

The rows of small stores along Seventh were darkened except for strings of colored lights in windows here and there.

The sound of their footsteps echoed with a twanging hollowness along the sidewalk. He held her close and listened to the alternation of his heavier step with her clicking high heels. Above the amber glow of the streetlamps he could see a few stars shining feebly and sighed his frosty breath up toward them.

Mary would be asleep by now, he thought, picturing her peaceful face lying on her pillow. It seemed like an eternity since he had last lain beside her. So many nights had his steps echoed through this deserted night world she knew nothing about. Just then Ellen let out a little groan and fell against him as she turned her ankle on the uneven sidewalk. He grasped her close to him to support her and then as she looked up at him he kissed her warmly on the lips.

"I liked that," she murmured and kissed him back once more.

Three blocks farther down they were passing in front of the little lot adjacent to the Food Fair store where Rico and his friends had tried to steal a Christmas tree. The trees were leaning in a great pile against the side of the store and the place was dark and deserted. A large mud-spattered truck was parked at the curb, and Tiernan thought he could see someone slumped down inside.

"Mmmmmm, I love the smell of Christmas trees," Ellen said. "Did you get a big one this year, Joe?"

"No, I, uh . . ." Then the thought occurred to him that this was the first year he had not bought a tree. He should get one for his apartment for when he brought Lynn over, he thought. "Hmmmm, I wonder if the old geezer in that truck would sell me a small one."

"Well, let's go ask him," she said, walking away from him to the truck.

"Wait, Ellen!" He had just remembered what Rico had said about the guy having an ax and a bad temper.

"Hey!" she shouted and knocked on the window of the truck.

He walked over to Ellen's side and together they peered into the cab of the truck. Inside they saw a large man in a checkered jacket resting across the seat with his head against the opposite window. As his vision grew accustomed to the darkness inside the cab, Tiernan could see that the man was looking at him, his hawkish face glowering, two close-set eyes sending back a message that made Tiernan shiver for an instant.

"Hello," Ellen said.

"How much for a little tree?" Tiernan asked.

He was about to knock on the window when the man raised his dirty farm boot and positioned it directly in front of his face against the window.

"Well, if that's the way he's going to be," Ellen said and backed away.

"Yeah," Tiernan said, giving the man a finger and walking away. "I know where I can get one tomorrow. Thanks for the idea. God, what a creep." They put their arms around each other again and continued down Seventh toward Berkeley Place, where she lived.

Her street was very much like Lincoln, where he and Mary had lived for so many years, rows of grand old brownstones with gaslight lanterns out in front.

"A few more doors up," she said. "The one with the steps."

"Uhuh," he said, nodding. "Maybe we should really go to my place. What if your kids wake up?"

At the steps she stopped and looked through her purse for her keys.

"Sure it's okay?" he asked.

"God, will you stop it," she said. "I'm the one who's new at this."

"I'm sorry," he said, smiling, and took her arm as they walked up the steps. In a few minutes he would have this wonderful woman's warm and naked body in his arms. Quit fighting your own good luck, he told himself.

After she opened the outer door, he followed her into the little foyer in front of her apartment door, which was also locked. In a moment she had it opened and was moving ahead of him into her darkened apartment. Then, just as he was about to follow her, her apartment door flew back at him with such force that it knocked him staggering into the foyer. Then her door slammed shut and its locks were clicked into place. As he recovered himself, he heard the anguished voice of a man.

"He's not coming into my home! I'll kill him first!" The voice was full of pain and anger.

"It's *not* your home anymore, you bastard!" he heard Ellen

cry out. "How dare you come here and do this! How dare you!" she wailed in rage.

The husband was now pleading: "It's Christmas, Ellen . . . I had to come home. I want to be home, Ellen."

For a few minutes there was just the sound of a man crying and then pleas for forgiveness. Then silence.

"Joe, you still there?" Ellen asked.

"I'll kill him if you let him in, Ellen. I . . . I don't know how, but I'll murder the sonofabitch!"

"Joe?"

"Yeah," Tiernan said, rubbing his sore arm where the door had hit him. "You gonna be okay?"

"It's okay," she said after a moment. "I'm very sorry this . . . You hear what's going on? It's my husband. . . . I . . ."

"It's okay," Tiernan said. "I understand, really. Tell him I'm sorry. I'll go."

"I'll call you," she said.

"Yeah," he said. "Take it easy."

"Joe?"

"Yeah?"

"Never mind. Good night."

He walked down the steps to the sidewalk haunted by the pain he'd heard in her husband's voice, remembering his own desperate pleading to Mary earlier in the evening. Tears filled his eyes as he understood the longing to be home on Christmas—to be in from the dark. They didn't understand about the dark, the Marys and Ellens who stayed home and kept the same hearth going, kissed the children good night, slipped under their familiar fresh sheets—while he walked the streets at night, taking his bearings from the lights outside the bars along Seventh Avenue. In a moment he was running toward Larsky's.

As he made his way past the Christmas tree lot, he saw the door of the flatbed truck hanging open and the hulking farmer who ran the lot standing a little ways up the sidewalk with an ax in his hands. He was looking across the street, where Rico and his cohorts were crouched down behind some cars.

"It's too crazy, it's too crazy," Tiernan kept murmuring to himself as he continued running toward Larsky's. It was Mary's fault that he was out wandering in this madness on Christmas Eve.

Frieda was just coming out of Larsky's when he got to the door. "Merry Christmas, Joe," she said.

"Not a damn thing merry about it," he said, going inside with his head down.

Only Talbot and Juliet and Millie were still at the table. His head felt like it was in a vise and he wanted to drink himself into oblivion. Too much for one night, he thought as he went directly to the bar and ordered a straight Scotch.

"Hey, that was quick," Talbot said as Tiernan came over to the table and slumped wearily into a chair. "Christ, what happened to you? You look like you've seen a ghost."

"Where have you been?" Millie said, pouting her lips and then smiling and sliding her chair over next to him.

"I had to walk someone home—to her husband," Tiernan said, glancing ruefully over at Talbot. Then he downed his drink and got up for a refill just as Millie was reaching for his arm.

"What's with him?" Millie asked Talbot.

"He's got a lot on his mind lately," Talbot assured her.

When Danny brought another Scotch on the rocks, he downed it in straight gulps. Then he took off his coat and ordered another. And then another, which he brought back to the table. He was finally beginning to feel a little numb.

"Where's Richie?" he asked Talbot.

"He was feeling lousy—his ulcer. Verna took him home."

"Poor bastard," he sighed and took another drink.

"Joe?" Millie asked hesitantly.

"Millie!" he said expansively and threw his arms around her. "Where have you been all my life, Millie?"

"Waiting, goddam it," she said and punched him in the shoulder.

"What you been waiting for, Millie?" he asked, smiling softly at her and lifting her black hair back from her face with his fingers.

"For my Christmas present," she said, pouting and then smiling as he drew her face to his and kissed her long and gently on the lips.

"And tonight you're going to get it," he murmured.

"Um," she sighed and looked deep into his slightly bleary eyes.

"Well . . . ah, er . . . Ah, where were we?" Juliet

asked Talbot, feeling a bit embarrassed by the intimacy going on between Tiernan and Millie.

"You were about to quit your secretarial job and become a full-time student at Brooklyn College."

"I was not," she protested. "I just said I'd like to take one of your courses."

"Okay, so I'll take you on as a private student," he said, putting his arm around her. "Evenings at my place. I'll open your mind to all the wonders of ancient and modern history. You'll—"

"Not so fast, Professor," she said, taking his arm from around her shoulder. "I've got an idea of what kind of wonders you're planning."

Just then the sound of sirens and clattering fire trucks filled the street outside. Talbot stood up and looked out the half-curtained window and saw a glow coming from farther down on Seventh Avenue. Fire trucks were converging on the area from several directions.

"Hey, it's just down the street," he said and grabbed his coat.

"Oh, boy!" Juliet said, getting up and going over to the bar to get her coat. "Come on, you guys, a fire," she called to Millie and Tiernan, who were smooching at the table, oblivious to all the commotion outside. Some of the patrons had already gone outside and big Danny was heaving his bulk over the top of the bar.

"Good, I hope they burn Brooklyn down to its sewer lines," Tiernan shouted and then reached for Millie, who had just gotten up, and pulled her into his lap. "We got a better fire going right here, right?" he asked her. She nodded and kissed him again.

Going out the door with Juliet, Talbot took one last look back at Tiernan and laughed. At least Joe's gonna score tonight, he thought. Juliet had been nimbly skipping out of his own snares all evening. No one-night stand, this girl, he thought, walking beside her down Seventh Avenue toward the fire.

"Oh, god!" she exclaimed. "It's the Christmas trees! Oh, I don't believe they'd do that!"

"Rico?" he asked.

"Oh, if he gets sent to jail once more his poor mother's

gonna just die. Damn you, Rico!" she cried and stamped her feet.

"Maybe he didn't do it," Talbot said as they got to the scene.

Not only the trees, but the entire side of the food store was in flames. Seventh Avenue was jammed with fire trucks, and firemen were just starting to turn their hoses onto the blaze. More trucks were sirening into the area and large numbers of people were gathering.

In the glow of the flames he saw many of the patrons from Larsky's. Danny the bartender was standing with his heavy arms folded around his chest trying to keep himself warm. There were now half a dozen arcing currents of water being played into the flames, but they seemed to have no effect. Inside the store he could hear cans of food exploding.

"Juliet!" A husky young woman with a whiney voice rushed up to Juliet and pulled her away from where Talbot was standing. It was Juliet's roommate, Annie, who had stayed home this evening. "I gotta talk to you," she said. "Rico's over at our place. He said to come get ya."

"Oh, that idiot. Do you see what him and his dopey friends did?" Juliet said angrily.

"He says they didn't do it," Annie said. "But he's scared as hell and wants you to come."

"Okay, let's hurry," Juliet said and started hurrying across the street.

"Juliet!" Talbot called.

"Good night, Lennie!" she called back. "I gotta go."

"Want me to come?" he asked, hurrying after her. "Maybe I can help."

"No, please. Good night, Lennie. And . . . ah . . . merry Christmas."

"Yeah," he said and gave her a little wave.

For a few minutes more he watched the firemen battle the blaze and then was about to head back to his rooming house when he saw Frieda leaning out of her window over a storefront opposite the fire. Her fox furs were hanging down around her neck, the glass-bead eyes glittering in the light.

"Frieda!" he called, but she didn't hear him for all the noise of the trucks. He walked down the sidewalk stepping over fire hoses and hopping over icy puddles until he was directly under her window.

"Frieda!" he called up to her again.

"Lennie, isn't this terrible?" she said and smoothed back her hair.

"How did it start?" he asked.

"I don't know. I had just come in and poof! I see a big light. How is Joe feeling?"

"Don't ask."

"Poor Joey. You want to come up?"

"Yeah, ring me in."

She gathered in her dangling fox heads and withdrew from the window. In a moment he heard the buzzer and pushed the door open. There was a chemical smell from the new carpeting on the creaky stairs as he walked up to Frieda's floor.

She opened the door and stepped back to let him pass. There were no lights on in the small room but he could see clearly in the glow from the fire outside the window. She had closed it, but he could still hear the squawking noises on the fire radios and the shouts of firemen battling the blaze.

"Just like the war," she said.

Sliding the fox fur from around her neck, she threw it on the bed and sat down in the small stuffed chair exhaustedly.

"I could use a drink," he said.

"Help yourself, Len, dear, I am too tired to move." She rubbed the back of her neck and turned her head to ease the muscles there. "Beer in the frig, Scotch in the drawer near the bed."

"Can I get you one?"

"Ah, *ja*. Scotch. Straight, please."

In the night-table drawer he found the half-filled pint of Scotch. There were also various bottles of pills for sleeping and nerves. Also a small gold-framed picture of a young girl looking up with Frieda's eyes. He started to ask and then closed the drawer.

"Straight up," he said, handing her about two inches of Scotch in a glass he found on the sink.

"*Danke.*" She took a long sip and rested her head back, looking at the flames. She kicked off her shoes and stretched out her legs. His beer popped behind her and she heard him throw the tab in the sink.

"Take off your coat and relax awhile," she said, feeling the warming effect of the Scotch moving down through her.

"These shadows are eerie," he said. "Strange watching a

building burn down so close." He looked at her from the window. With her head resting back she looked very beautiful in the glow.

"I have seen many burn."

The beer tasted good but he suddenly felt very weary. "God, what a night," he sighed, flopping down on her bed and watching the shadows play along the ceiling.

"You look tired," she said.

"Long night and I jogged ten miles earlier this evening."

"Yes, we are both runners, I think. Only I found I get more miles from this," she said, sliding the amber liquid around in her glass and then draining it down in one gulp.

"Why were you looking at me tonight?" he asked her.

"You would laugh."

"I won't laugh."

She sighed and got up and poured another drink, this one completely filling the glass. She drank down about half of it and sat down again smiling.

"So?" he said, rolling over on his side on the bed to look at her.

"Well, I was looking at the corners of your mouth."

"What?"

She turned and looked over at him very tenderly. "Frieda is crazy, *ja?*"

"*Ja!*" he said, lying back.

She bit her lip and for a brief instant something painful crossed her face. Then she began speaking in a soft and distant voice. "There was a boy during the war. His lips were like yours. He had much different eyes but his mouth was like yours. And he was a soldier and he tried to seem very brave. And in the corners of his mouth . . . a child trying very hard not to cry."

"What happened?"

"He died."

"Did he ever cry?"

She got up and walked over to the window. The flames were almost out now, leaving little flickerings in her tearing eyes as she watched. "I always hoped . . . that he cried."

She finished the drink in another swallow and walked over to the bed and looked down at him. He smiled and reached out to stroke her thigh.

She intercepted his hand with hers and as she squeezed it he pulled her down on top of him. When he tried to kiss her she put her finger to his lips and drew back, looking into his eyes, calming him with the calm in hers.

Then slowly she leaned over and softly kissed each corner of his mouth and drew back again. Leaning slightly over him, she stripped her sweater over her head and let it fall to the floor. Then she bent slowly to him again and kissed him lightly again on the lips, drawing back again as he was about to respond.

As he lay there in a lake of utter calm she undid her bra strap in the back and let her full white breasts fall free and lovely. When he reached for them she gently pushed his hands back down and leaned over until her nipples were barely touching the edges of his lips. He wet each one with his tongue and then as the hunger grew in him she leaned further into him and let him suck.

Again she drew back from him and got up and moved over near the light in the window and slowly slid her pants to just below her pubic mound and stopped. As he watched she walked pantherlike around the room stopping at the bureau to light a cigarette and brush her long blond hair.

Still tasting her breasts on his lips, he rose from the bed in a fury of desire. She seemed to be laughing at him as he tore off his sweater and began pulling off his pants. She was still nonchalantly brushing her hair when he whipped the cigarette from her mouth and swept her up in his arms.

"Ho, ho, ho!" she laughed, pushing her nails through his thick dark hair as he carried her to the bed. At the bed she took his face in her hands and kissed him long and hungrily, moaning like an animal. They fell together like this onto the bed and his hands tore at her slacks until he had stripped them from her writhing legs. Then he slapped her thighs apart and forced his throbbing penis into her.

"Oooooooh," she screamed and suddenly relaxed as he churned powerfully within her. Then she slowly began to move with him until she was matching him stride for powerful stride, riding in ecstatic muscular harmony.

No, no, no, he told himself as he felt the explosion coming. He wanted it to last. He began to falter, to slow down, to delay.

"No, don't stop," she said, pulling his neck down with her arm. "It is beautiful. Good, good!"

When he could hold it back no longer, he finally let himself fly into her, hearing his own crying moans of relief distant in her ears. Frieda held him and rocked him rhythmically, making a cradle of her womb.

"God, I'd hate to see you when you aren't tired," he sighed.

"There is always something left. How do you feel?" she asked, kissing his eyes.

"Good. You didn't come. I'm sorry."

"Shhhhh. I enjoy." She felt very old thinking of the last time she had had an orgasm. In another life, a brief unreal life separated from her now by fire and ashes.

"Anyway, it's your fault for exciting me so much. The European touch," he sighed.

"Now, I *am* very tired," she said, slipping under the sheet. "Ooooh, sooo tired. Tonight no pills for Frieda. *Danke.*"

For a while he lay there looking at the streetlight glow in the window, listening to the clatter-roar of the fire engines starting up as some of them prepared to move away.

"You think it was Juliet's friends—that, uh, Rico—who set off the Christmas trees?"

"No."

"Well, they had a beef with the guy who runs the lot. A weird old galoot. I think he sleeps in his truck on these cold nights." Then it struck him that he had not seen the truck when he'd gotten to the fire.

"The truck," he said, slipping out of bed and going over to the window.

The walls of the store stood in charred ruins under the glare of the fire-truck spotlights. Ice was beginning to glaze the sidewalk down to the curb, where water was running in a glistening stream. But there was now a space where the black truck had been parked for the last two weeks.

"They are just boys," she said, rolling over and closing her weary eyes. In a while he heard her gentle snoring.

# CHAPTER THREE

Tiernan awoke at noon with his daughter tying Christmas wrapping ribbons in his hair. Her tiny fingers were cool and light against his throbbing forehead as she pulled gently at his locks and whispered motherly admonitions.

". . . an' never don't lose your ribbons. 'Chwanna look pretty? 'Chwanna look pretty?"

He kept his eyes closed and tried not to wince when she occasionally pulled his hair too hard. He felt as if he were awakening from brain surgery, each pulse at his temples hitting with a wicked snap. The familiar jabbing of a spring against his ribs told him he was lying on Mary's old couch. But how had he wound up at Mary's? It was impossible, he thought. If he were stark raving insane he would not have come back here.

He could vaguely remember being at Larsky's. Verna encouraging him to drink and siding with him against Mary. Then feeling good and playing with Millie's legs under the table. So drunk. Couldn't remember leaving. Images floating through his memory. Millie pulling his shoes off. He was lying in bed someplace. Where? Millie naked and lying beside him . . . small tits, large black pubic bush. Must've gone home with Millie. And now waking up on Mary's couch? It was frightening.

He hated this couch particularly. There had been months of
exile on it after Mary refused to sleep with him. So many
nights of sailing into oblivion on this goddam couch, he
thought, nights of inhaling its cloyed sweaty smells, murmuring his drunken sorrows into its cushions, punishing it with his
lonely masturbatory writhings. So many despairing nights—
until his despair had turned to fury and finally given him the
courage to quit the marriage.

The phone rang in the kitchen at the far end of the apartment
and he could hear Mary answering it. "Well, merry Christmas
to you, too," he heard her say. A girlish tone he had not heard
in her voice in years.

He remembered again the clinician's voice telling him he
was defective. He felt the void opening around him again,
again sliding into darkness on his asteroid couch. He opened
his eyes in panic.

"Mommy!" Lynn exclaimed.

Lynn's face seemed to float over him for a moment, her little
mouth smeared with candy cane, her fine yellow hair tied out at
the sides with red ribbons. Then she was gone.

"Mommy, Mommy, Mommy! Daddy opened his eyes!"

Sunlight was streaming in through the windows and through
the tinseled branches of the tree. The floor was littered with
Lynn's gifts and Christmas wrappings. He looked for the doll
he had bought her and finally saw it lying on its face near the
coffee table.

"I'll call you back," he heard Mary say.

He scraped his carpeted tongue with his teeth and spit dryly.
Gotta get outa here, he thought, get out before he would have
to confront her. But his strength seemed as scattered as the
papers on the floor.

"Well, I'd sure hate to have *your* head this morning," Mary
said, coming into the living room. "How about a couple of
aspirin?"

"Naw, I, uh . . . ," he half moaned, throwing his arm
over his eyes to shield them from her. It made him furious to be
so helpless under her eyes. How in hell's name could he have
ever come back?

"Little hair of the dog maybe?"

"Don't, uh, don't," he croaked, trying to shut her out. He
needed to be away from her.

"I made a pitcher of Bloody Marys," she said, sitting on the coffee table in the middle of the room. She could still feel the tenderness for him that had begun shortly after 4 A.M. when she had finally gone down to the sidewalk and claimed him from the police.

His loud lamentations below her third-floor bedroom window had roused the neighbors, as well as making Michael, her lover who lived upstairs, more than a little nervous. Lying next to him in the dark, she had felt the tension building in his small wiry body.

"Shit, Mary!" he had finally blurted out and sat up after Tiernan had bellowed her name for the thirtieth time. "Get rid of him, goddam it," he had said, reaching for a cigarette on the night table. In the glow of the cigarette lighter his long black hair and delicate Italian features had given him an almost girlish beauty. She was aware that she cared for him in the way that she had been fond of certain dolls when she was a child.

"I hurt him tonight," she had said, reaching over and tracing her nail down Michael's narrow back. He had flicked the cigarette lighter on again and turned to look at her for a moment, reading the deep sadness in her eyes.

"Okay," he had said, nodding in resignation. "I'll get back upstairs to my place." Darkness in the room again. "You can make it up to him. It's okay." She had felt him rise from the bed.

"I can't," she had said.

"Can't what?"

"Make it up."

"Do you want to?" he asked and walked over and parted the drapes to peer down at Tiernan. "Dumb bastard, look at him. He doesn't know about me, does he?"

She had heard the jingle of coins in his pocket as he took his pants from the chair near the window.

"No. It would surprise him. He thinks you're a fag."

He had not replied and she knew that she had hurt him. Hurt him, too. God, she was so tired of being careful with men. For the first time in her life she was becoming honest and men were staggering away from her bleeding from her honesty.

"I'll see you."

"You don't have to leave, Michael."

"I'll see you," he said curtly.

After Michael had left she had lain in the darkness with the feeling of him still within her and Joe's plaintive calls echoing off the brownstone walls outside. She had known that he would come back. He had never been able to heal his own wounds, always coming back for her to remove the pain she had given him. But now she needed to wound, needed to allow the suffering. The why of that she did not know.

"Hey, down there! Beat it or I'm callin' the cops!" She had heard a gruff male voice from one of the windows across the street.

"Eat dog shit!" Joe had hollered back.

"Mr. Tiernan, please go home," Miss White had called from above her window.

"Home?" he had called back. "Home? You tell me where that is!"

When she had heard the police car she got up and put on her housecoat. She had known what would happen if the police tried to get tough with him. Joe was basically easygoing and had a great Irish playfulness about him, but an authoritarian challenge could trigger some deep reserve of snarling anger in him. Throwing open the window, she had called to officers walking toward him to wait, she'd be right down to bring him in.

When she got downstairs in her bathrobe the two young officers were trying to humor Joe, telling him they knew it was Christmas but urging him to go inside and try to sleep it off. He just gave them a look of disgust and waved them away and kept calling Mary's name. Then when he saw her come out he just stood there smiling at her like a guilty child.

"Come on up, Joe," she had said, taking his hand and leading him toward the door.

"See?" Joe had said to the officers, who nodded their approval.

Riding up in the elevator with her, he had not looked at her but leaned heavily on her shoulder murmuring, "Not fair, Mary, not fair."

After she had brought him up to the apartment, he went in and looked at Lynn and then returned to the living room, slumping heavily onto the couch. His eyes were red and weary and he seemed not to have the energy to speak. Watching him with his head back and staring at the ceiling, she had decided she would try to draw him out, help him to get it off his chest.

"How'd you tear your good pants?" she had asked.

"Old Lady Petri's dog bit me—when I was leaving."

"Damn, did you put something on it?"

"It's all right."

"You want to talk?"

"Yeah."

He had looked at her for a long while with those tired eyes, and then he had said again she had been unfair. It had not been fair to make him hate her. It hurt him more to hate her than to lose her, he had said.

"I think I can accept it, you know, going away from you. But I don't want to hate you, Mary. That takes everything away from me. You're in my . . . you're . . . I can't *forget* things. I cursed you tonight. First-class bitch, right? Then, I'm lying in bed with this girl and . . . Jesus, I'm thinking of how you looked—your face when you . . . the way you looked, you know, so tired . . . that morning in the hospital when you had Lynn. I, uh, just . . . just can't . . . hate you." Tears were spilling from his eyes and he could not go on.

She had started to cry, too, and had got up and walked into the kitchen to make him some coffee. Waiting for the water to boil, watching the tiny bubbles gathering in the bottom of the chrome pan, she tried desperately to fight back her emotions. Yes, there were times that she missed him terribly, missed his open loving nature, missed his humor and wit, all his crazy schemes and dreams.

That part of her would always love him, but there was another part—a greater part—that needed quiet and solitude. Joe was like a roller-coaster ride, wild and often exhilarating, but she never knew when he was going to be up and when down, always changing his plans. She had always felt she had to go along, never having the courage to tell him she didn't want to. You went along or you got left behind—the way her father had left her and her mother behind when she was only nine years old. Yes, it was better to have no man than to live in fear that he would leave.

Her mother had told her there was a wonderful peace in living alone. And now she understood it. And she wasn't entirely alone for she had Lynn—as her mother had had her. How much like her mother she'd become, she thought. She had her daughter, her work, her plants, her music—even a casual non-demanding affair with Michael upstairs.

Poor Joe, she thought as she took down the jar of instant

coffee, spooned out some into the cup on the stove counter. It's not your fault. I'm sorry I called you defective. If anyone's defective it's me. . . . Can't live with my fears. She smiled sadly as she thought of him again in those early days, so full of ambition and joy. How he had believed in everything he did, building public appreciation for his accounts, selling his enthusiasm and belief like so much merchandise. This belief of men had always puzzled her; and men, like her father, with passion behind their beliefs threatened her. She felt hollow and alien around such men. This believing—it was a trick they had, something they had learned to perform long ago and one that women were only beginning to learn. But it was a trick, she felt. The truth was that you tried to make things work, tried to keep it together, tried to get through each day without destroying something.

When she had returned to the living room, Joe was lying stretched out on the couch sound asleep. She had taken his shoes off and cried softly again looking at three of his toes sticking out of his torn sock.

All morning she had kept coming into the living room to see if he had awakened. Now as he rose wobblingly from the couch, his eyes looking ravaged, she moved to his side, reaching for his waist to steady him.

"No!" he yelled with a rage that surprised her. She moved away from him. He stood there pushing his fists into each other and trembling to contain his fury.

"Lynn, go wait in your room for a few minutes," she said to the girl sitting at the end of the couch with her feet tucked up inside her cottony red nightgown.

"What's wrong with Daddy?" she whined.

"Nothing. He's just not feeling too good. I'll come in in a minute. Go on now." The child looked at them both for a minute and then went to her room and closed the door.

"Where the hell are my shoes?" he said, kicking some of the wrappings aside on the floor.

"Joe, what's wrong?"

"I just woke up inside a goddam nightmare, that's what's wrong! How'd I get here? They bring me here?"

"You don't remember?"

Finding his shoes sticking out from under the couch, he flopped down and began putting them on, cringing with shame as he noticed his toes sticking out of the sock.

"No, I have to assume I was dragged here. Goddam, you must be eating this up. Well, to hell with you, see. Blackouts don't count!"

"Joe, it's a bad sign when you start having blackouts."

"Yeah, it's *defective*, right?"

Suddenly she started laughing. The sight of him full of outrage, furiously trying to put his shoes on and his hair full of ribbons was too much. He stopped tying his shoes and looked at her. She pointed to his head and was laughing so hard she had to sit down on the coffee table.

"Joe, you're not defective," she said, trying to control her laughter. "You . . . you're . . ." And then she broke down again almost shrieking with laughter.

"Are you drunk, goddam it?" he shouted.

What the hell was with her anyway? he wondered. At the same time he was moved by her beauty when she laughed. The long gold-streaked hair falling around her lovely flushed face reminded him for an instant of how she looked astride him in sexual ecstasy. In the months they had been separated she had become slim and buoyant again; and even now, hating what she had done to his life, he loved the curve of her hips in the faded blue jeans she was wearing.

"Oh, Joe, please forgive me. Look in the mirror." She couldn't stop laughing and hoped that his old sense of humor was still there. She watched as he slowly reached up and touched one of the ribbons Lynn had tied in his hair. And then as his hand found that nearly the entire top of his head had been tufted and tied with ribbons his face began to relax and a smile started at the corners of his mouth.

He stood up and turned to look in the mirror on the wall over the couch and then burst into laughter. "Jesus, I can't believe this!" he exclaimed.

"I tried not to laugh," she said, still erupting. "You were so angry. And those ribbons!"

"Well, I *was* angry. I mean I *am* angry," he said, touching the ribbons lightly and preening girlishly in front of the mirror. "Oh, god," he said, feeling suddenly weak again and flopping down onto the couch. "Jesus, the fates have me . . . they've got me typed for comedy. I want a serious part, goddam it!" he yelled at the ceiling.

She looked at him warmly and shook her head.

"It's damned frustrating," he said with a sigh. "Last night I knew . . . I mean I really *knew*, right?"

"What?"

"That I was never, but *never*, going to see your rotten face again for the rest of my life. I mean, I was going to let you go to hell, right?"

"Right!" she said, raising her glass in toast.

"So what happens? I fall asleep for a minute. I mean I fall asleep with your replacement—well, your latest replacement. Right?"

"Right."

"And I wake up back on your goddam couch—and dressed up like the Queen of the May. It just ain't fucking fair, goddam it!"

"Poor Joey. So, who's my replacement, huh?"

"Never mind, she'll probably never speak to me again. I think I will have that Bloody Mary."

"Good, I'll join you," she said, rising to go to the kitchen.

Watching her move lightly in her white tennis shoes, he felt a pang of desire and began pulling out the ribbons and smoothing down his hair. He had enjoyed laughing with her again after so long. But something at the back of his mind sent a little warning. He could see Richie's look of disgust. No, there would be no letting down this time. A friendly Christmas drink and he would take Lynn out for a brief walk in the park.

"Lynn! Wanna go to the park?" he shouted.

"Do I have to?" she answered glumly.

He got up and went to her room, where she was lying on her bed and reading one of her books.

"Whatta ya mean, 'Do I have to?'" he said, going over and tickling her and sweeping her up in his arms. She started to giggle.

"Do I have to?" she repeated, teasing him and laughing harder as he tucked her against his chest and walked from the room.

"I haven't had my breakfast yet. Think I'll eat you up," he said, softly biting her arm through the cotton nightgown.

Mary came into the room smiling and handed him one of two tall drinks while Lynn hugged his neck and squealed joyfully.

"Yum-yum," he said in his giant's voice. "Okay if I have this juicy little girl for my breakfast, Mommy?" he asked, sitting down on the couch with Lynn snuggled against his chest. He angled his head around the girl to take a long swallow from the glass. The peppery tomato taste was good and he nodded his approval to Mary, who was licking her lips.

It moved Mary to see Lynn so happily nestled against his red sweater. Their child had his fair coloring and his nose. She liked the way he looked at the moment, at peace and his hair pushed down on his brow Roman style. There was an attractive ruggedness that came through when he wasn't all combed and dressed for the world outside.

"What's the latest on the Alma Reed job?" she asked, remembering that he had told her on Friday that he thought he would be hired by the small public relations firm that mainly promoted restaurants in Manhattan, as well as a few business and industrial accounts in the Bronx and New Jersey.

"God, that's good," he sighed after taking another long drink. "I'm supposed to phone Alma after the holidays, but it looks like I got the job. Going to be strange working for a woman."

"You've never had any trouble impressing women," she said.

"Jesus, what a woman," he said, shaking his head. "You should have been at my interview. I mean she has me standing in the middle of her office, you know, firing nonstop questions at me, and all the time she's walking around sizing me up. All the time talking about how I'd need the right touch for her big society clients—only she comes on like Vince Lombardi buying backfield meat. Come to think of it, she looks a little like Vince Lombardi, too—only bigger. She must be six feet tall, and shoulders like this," he said, extending his arms.

"Well, it'll do you good to have a little money for a change," she said.

"Yeah, and maybe kick in a little support money," he said, glancing sideways at her.

"I wouldn't complain about that," she said with a laugh. "Want another drink?"

"Naw, I want to take Lynn over to the park for a little while and then go home and crap out. Come along."

"I've got a hundred and one things to do around here this afternoon, including cleaning up these papers," she said, scooping up a handful of the Christmas wrappings.

"Hey, boober, what'd Santa bring you?" he asked Lynn as he put her on the floor and got up. "Boy, all this loot yours?"

"Daddy, Santy Claus forgot to bring my puppy," Lynn said and pouted her lower lip.

"That's about all he forgot. Look at all this stuff!" Seeing the expense Mary had gone to for Lynn's presents made him feel guilty. The doll he'd bought looked pretty small now amidst all the other gleaming toys—a tricycle, dollhouse, games, a huge pink and white stuffed dog and dozens of other odds and ends. He picked up the doll he'd purchased and straightened its dress. "This is nice," he said and looked over at Mary and raised his eyes.

"David got a puppy, Daddy," Lynn said, ignoring the doll he was holding.

"The boy downstairs," Mary said, walking toward Lynn. "He's already been up this morning. Come on, young lady, let's go get dressed for the park. You didn't tell Daddy how much you liked the doll."

"It's okay," he said with a little smile as Lynn walked slowly into her room with a glum look on her face.

"A dog? I didn't—" he said.

"I didn't tell you," Mary said. "I was hoping she'd forget about it. I sure don't need a dog around here." She looked at him holding the unwanted doll and gave him a sad smile. "She likes it, Joe. It's the best doll she's ever had."

Tiernan shrugged and went over and sat wearily in the bentwood rocker with the doll in his lap. "A dog—Christ," he sighed, looking down at the doll.

"She'll get over it in a few days. You know Lynn," Mary said and then went into the bedroom to start getting Lynn into her snowsuit.

The sunlight flooding into the living room through the front windows forced him to close his eyes. Yeah, Lynn would get over the dog thing in a few days, he thought. But, God, he wished he could have bought her some other nice things. The doll was a stupid choice. She has tons of dolls, he thought. It was the first time he'd ever bought anything for her without Mary along.

He thought of the previous Christmas when he and Mary had walked up Fifth Avenue together stopping in at the various stores buying presents for all their friends and relatives. She was so good at that, knowing just the right things, having him along just to show them to, knowing he'd smile and nod an approval. He had always liked that.

He'd missed her so much yesterday, passing the same stores like a fugitive, envying all the happy young couples so bright with purpose. He'd felt like a shadow moving through the lively throng on Fifth Avenue. And in the toy store near Central Park he'd almost cried out with bewilderment as he walked along the aisles seeing things Lynn might like. If he'd only had more money, if Mary had only been there, if only his head hadn't been throbbing with migraine. He'd seen the doll and grabbed it off the shelf and hurried to the cashier with it, half mad with his need to hide.

Afterward he had almost run to the entrance to the park, where he could get away from the crowds. But even there he was oppressed by the living, whole armies of young families, young mothers and fathers out with their beaming children. He'd continued through the little zoo area and kept walking until he found an empty park bench under some trees. And there he had sat for more than an hour with his face buried in his hands.

The park had often been his refuge in the months he'd spent halfheartedly job hunting in Manhattan. After the breakup, he'd gone on a two-month drinking binge and lost his public relations position with the bank. He might still be bingeing if Talbot and Gemetz had not come along and encouraged him to straighten up and quit feeling sorry for himself. They were going through the same thing in their lives: about his age, fathers, married about the same number of years before their breakups. But they couldn't be with him all the time, and in those lonely hours out on the street or at night trying to sleep he'd start to come apart at the seams again.

If he could only understand what had made her change. Yes, she had said that they were too different, that she had tried to remake herself to suit him. She needed peace and quiet, she'd said. She had grown up in a fatherless home where problems and emotions were kept to a minimum. He was too flamboyant, she had said, too full of change for her, up one day, down the next, this plan one day, another the next, too . . . defective. But she had seemed so happy in those early years, he thought. What had changed her? Things had started to grow cold right after Lynn was born. Five years of good times, he remembered. And then Lynn and five years of steadily cooling feelings.

He heard Lynn protesting about her clothes in the next room and opened his eyes. The sunlight in the window in front of him was nearly blinding. He let out a moan and closed his eyes again as he remembered sitting in this same rocker with the sun in his eyes ten months ago. The day he had left home. He had been rocking gently and looking at Mary, who was standing in the glare at the window, her back to him and her arms folded. If only she'd turned around and asked him to stay. They were down to their last minutes. All the weeks of sleeping on the couch, his howling protests, the destructive drinking, crying, glasses being thrown against the wall, ultimatums . . . over.

He had sat there waiting and finally—not believing it could be happening—he was rising from the chair, his eyes brimming, his insides feeling like they were being torn from him.

"You just have to call, Mary," he had said through his choking sorrow.

But she had remained with her back to him and in that last moment he could not even see her anymore for his tears and the brightness at the window.

"Call," he had gasped and then turned and walked out with his suitcases.

And that was ten months ago and an eternity of pain ago. He looked down at the doll in his lap and turned it over to face him. Wide blue eyes and cherubic smile. Yes, the doll would always smile—and Mary would never call.

Driving along the shoreline road in New London, Talbot could smell the snow in the air. The little Connecticut city lay quiet and waiting under a pillowy overcast. Off to his left were thickets of white sailing masts around the marinas where the private boats had been dry-docked for the winter. Farther out over Long Island Sound the horizon was darkening as the storm lowered in.

In a few minutes he would be turning off Pequot Avenue to the wealthy neighborhood where Susan's parents had their rambling green Victorian home. He looked at his watch— nearly 3 P.M. The family would be gathered now in the living room or in the den around the great fireplace for their annual Christmas Day party.

He smiled grimly as he heard Teddy's gift-wrapped presents

bouncing around on the back seat of his old red Volkswagen. Susan should not have taken his son away from him on Christmas. And now like a malevolent Santa Claus he was descending upon her unsuspecting family gathering to find the child she had denied him in Brooklyn.

That morning, lying awake in the first light in Frieda's apartment, he had listened to her soft breathing and thought of the great trials she had passed through over the years. There had been the war and the young soldier she had loved. A war so long ago and a face ever young in her memory. And there had been her daughter who had drowned. A child she had created from her flesh, had nursed with her milk, had held and bathed and tickled. He thought of Teddy and heard his laughter. Does a child's voice ever die?

I am lucky, Frieda, he thought, moving his fingers over the pillow close to her slightly parted lips. Teddy is alive and probably opening his presents right now. Not my presents, goddam it. Poor Frieda. How you would fly, my German friend, if your daughter were alive in New London. Only a three-hour drive, he thought. Then he had rolled over on his back and knit his brows as the thought hit him. Quietly he had slipped out of bed and got dressed.

Stepping into the cold morning air outside Frieda's building, he had been stunned by the grotesque beauty of the ruined store across the street. Charred walls draped in icicles—like the memory of his marriage.

Snow was now falling lightly outside his car window, bringing him out of his reverie. He glanced over the New London harbor area again and stretched his fingers out and then closed them tightly on the steering wheel. The reception Susan's two brothers were likely to give him at the door would be anything but friendly. Charles and Edwin Cope were big good-looking twins who were attending college on football scholarships. Susan had told him that the brothers had wanted to drive down to Brooklyn and thrash him the previous year for the beating he'd given her after finding her in bed with Garnand.

She had gone home to Connecticut with her bruises the next day but not, he knew, with the full story of how she got them. Her father had urged her to divorce him, reminding her that he had warned her about the inbred violence of Southern men.

Cecil Cope had spent most of his life trying to forget the

violence in his own lower-class upbringing. After the war he
had married into a small ceramics factory and apprenticed
himself to his wife's class. The family worked at being
straitlaced and acceptable except for Susan, whose four years
of analysis had loosened some of the Cope corset strings. They
would not want any unpleasantness, Talbot told himself, and
perhaps they would let him complete his mission.

"I have only come to see my son on Christmas," he said
aloud, rehearsing the declaration he intended to make at the
door.

Turning the wheezing little car up Atlantic Avenue toward
the Cope home, he could feel the fear knotting around his
heart. The large homes along the street sat far back on wide
sloping lawns. No gaudy display of Christmas sentiment save
the proper wreaths hanging on the heavy wooden doors. He
looked in vain for a child playing along the street. There was
an eerie stillness over the area and he cringed at the noisiness
of his broken exhaust muffler.

"I only wish to see my son," he rehearsed again.

As he approached the big Cope house, he saw the long
driveway filled with large glittering cars—Cadillacs, Chrys-
lers, a Mercedes. Biting his lip, he kept the Volkswagen
moving past the house. He would go around the block and
regroup, he told himself.

So, the Copes were throwing the party early this year, he
thought. Eggnog from the big silver punch bowl, Susan at the
piano. He felt a pang of loss at not being part of these quaint
Cope Christmases anymore.

"I don't wish to intrude . . . ," he experimented. For an
instant an image of Edwin and Charles standing at the door
flashed into his mind. "Fuck!" he shouted in frustration and
banged the steering wheel with the heel of his fist.

He turned the corner and pulled the car over beneath a
leafless mulberry tree at the curb. He waited a minute, listening
to the engine idle unevenly, and then took a thin pewter flask of
bourbon from his red nylon ski jacket.

"I say, have a spot, old man?" he asked himself.

"Um, quite," he answered, downing the entire contents of
the flask and then slumping down into the seat with a gasp.

"Pip, pip!" he said. He wiped his lips with the back of his
hand and returned the flask to his pocket.

"Yes, pip, pip—and rot!"

"Rot?"

"Rot!"

"Not rot, surely?"

"Rot, absolutely!"

"Rot, then."

He swung around and looked at the half-dozen presents in the back seat. His son's presents. Teddy's rightful presents! Not let his son have his presents? *Who* were the bloody bastards who'd keep Teddy's presents away? Edwin and Charles? Ha! He'd cut them to the ground with his fists first!

"Yeeeeeehaaaaagh!" he yelled from the bottom of his Southern soul and leaped the car forward.

In the living room Susan had just filled Mrs. Moran's little silver cup with eggnog when she heard the familiar sputter-backfire-sputter out front. The Volkswagen had always done that after the ignition was turned off and the motor was too hot—continuing to fire explosively long after they had walked away from the car. "Fuel farting," Len had always called it.

"My god, it's Len!" she exclaimed, running to the window.

It had started to snow and through the soft tumbling flakes she saw Talbot down at the end of the lawn leaning into the back door of the little red car trying to get something out. The car was still blasting and lurching and looked like any moment it might run off and leave him standing alone at the curb.

"Goddam you!" she cried, stamping her thin high heel on the floor. She was wearing a long burgundy velvet house dress, but with her luxuriant long blond hair and the anger radiating on her high-boned face she looked like a lion ready to pounce.

"Susan!" exclaimed her mother, who had just come into the room and heard her.

"Oh, he's really gotta be kidding!" Susan said as she watched him turn with the gifts piled in his arms and close the car door with his heel. He looked up at the house and then, ducking his face against the thick falling snow, he started up the long sloping lawn.

"Oh, my, what's *he* doing here?" her mother said, coming alongside her at the window. Virginia Cope was taller than Susan but had the same small nose and deep-set blue eyes. Without turning, she whispered, "Better stop him before he gets to the front door, child."

"Just who in the hell does he think he is?" Susan hissed.

"Did you hear what I said?" her mother said under her breath. "Do you want your father to sic the boys on him?"

"It would serve him right!" Susan whispered back as her mother turned and then moved quickly away to intercept Charles, who had just come in from the den for more eggnog.

"Charles, there you are! I need your help in the kitchen, dear," his mother said, making an effort to control her anxiousness.

"Right," he replied in a husky voice as he tried with difficulty to place his little silver cup on the table with fingers that were taped together as the result of a recent football scrimmage. "Long as I don't have to join Dad's little festival of song in the den again. Hey, Susan, they need a piano player in there real bad!"

"Well, well, who is the good-looking young man out there in the snow?" Mrs. Moran asked as she joined Susan at the window.

"Where?" Charles asked.

"Never mind. Come with me now, Charles. Please," his mother said, tweaking the sleeve of his brown sweater and trying to tug him toward the kitchen.

*"That* is my former rat-fink husband, Mrs. Moran, and if you'll excuse me a minute I'm going to send him on his way," Susan said, heading toward the door.

"It's Len?" Charles asked, pulling from his mother's grasp and going to the window. "What's he doing with all those presents? You invite him, Susan?"

"No, I certainly did not!" she said, brushing past him on her way out.

"Let Susan handle it, Charles," Mrs. Cope said, placing herself in front of her strapping big son.

"What if he hits her again?" Charles asked. "I better get Eddie quick!" he said, hurrying toward the den.

"I don't think he looks angry, Virginia," Mrs. Moran said, peering out at Talbot still coming up through the snow with his presents.

"Oh, dear!" Mrs. Cope said as she saw Susan come into view, her jaw jutted defiantly and the snow swirling around her long dark dress.

As Charles strode into the den, most of the guests were gathered around the massive stone fireplace where Cecil Cope was leading them in song. The elder Cope's pudgy-cheeked face was red from his vocal exertions as well as from the heat being generated on the broad seat of his pants by the four blazing logs in the fireplace.

Farther down the room, near the tall richly decorated Christmas tree, Edwin was plinking awkwardly on the piano, seemingly two or three songs behind the fireplace singers, who were at the moment winding up the "sixth day of Christmas" and heading unevenly for the "seventh."

". . . and a partridge in a pear tree!" Edwin bellowed, those being the only words he knew of each chorus.

"Eddie, come on. Len is here. I think he and Susan are gonna tangle on the front lawn," Charles whispered into his twin brother's ear.

"You got it!" Edwin said, getting up quickly and heading out of the den with Charles.

Cecil Cope watched his two sons leaving and wondered if something was amiss in another part of the house. Whatever it was, however, there were still four and a half days of Christmas to get through with his eager singers.

Meanwhile, Susan was standing in front of Talbot on the whitening front lawn. Her hands were on her hips and she was forced to shift awkwardly as her high heels sank into the snow.

"What the hell is this, another one of your dramatic gestures?" she asked, brushing angrily at the white feathers of snow that touched her face.

"Nothing more dramatic than a father wanting to see his son on Christmas," he said, feeling his anger rising at the sight of her severe expression. "I've brought his gifts and I'd like a few minutes with him."

"Teddy's asleep, and Father won't have you in the house!"

"Well, just tell *Father* that I'm not leaving until I see my son!" he shouted, spitting out the flakes of snow that collected on his lips.

As they stood arguing in the swirling snow, Charles and Edwin appeared at the open front door of the house. Their mother held them in place by the backs of their sweaters. "Just wait!" she said. "Susan will probably be able to handle it."

"Listen, goddam it!" Susan yelled at him. "I'm trying to keep you from getting your brains knocked out. Charles and Edwin are dying to get at you. You can leave the presents with me and I'll give them to Teddy when he wakes up."

"You had no right to take him away without consulting

me . . . goddam willful bitch! No one else exists in the world! Now take me to Teddy or by god I'll kick my way into that house if I have to!"

"This is *my* home!" she shrieked, the old anger bursting out. He was bullying his way into her life again, stepping on what she had staked out as hers. Draw a line and defend it, Dr. Fischer had told her.

"Not one step further!" she snarled at him.

When he started to take an exaggerated step past her she lunged at him and scattered the presents from his arms.

"*My* home!" she screamed and came at him with her nails as he continued to move past her.

"And I want *my* son!" he said, flinging her aside into the snow. "Teddy!" he called out and started picking up the presents.

"Go and help your sister!" Virginia Cope cried and let go of her two sons.

They came hurtling from the house like two bulls into an arena. Susan looked up from where she was sitting in the snow and saw them heading for Talbot, who, unawares, had his back to them as he went about picking up presents.

"Len!" she cried out instinctively.

Hearing her warning, Talbot stood up just in time to have Charles plow into his back with a bone-jarring tackle that sent them both sliding across the thin coating of snow on the grass.

"Hold on to him!" Edwin yelled, coming on so fast that he skidded past them and fell. Charles had Talbot pinned down with a viselike grip around his legs.

"Hurry up, Eddie! Stomp his head!" Charles yelled.

Talbot struggled to a sitting position and popped Charles on the top of the head with his fist and felt like he'd broken his hand. He was shaking it in pain when Edwin kicked him in the face.

"Stop it! Please stop it!" Susan screamed and grabbed Edwin by the tail of his green sweater and then, slipping down in the snow again, pulled him on top of her.

With his vision slightly blurred by Edwin's kick, Talbot again tried to pry loose from Charles's bearlike hug. Grabbing a fist full of Charles's blond hair, he raised the young man's grimacing face and kept belting him powerfully until Charles finally relaxed his grip and rolled over unconscious.

Meanwhile, Edwin had got free of Susan and kicked him in the face again.

"Bastard, I'll kill you!" Edwin yelled as Talbot rolled away from him. Just as Edwin delivered another murderous kick, Talbot ducked and rose up under him, catching him in the groin and throwing him down.

Now Talbot was the only one standing. "Get up!" he bellowed as he watched Edwin struggling to his feet. The pain in his hand was almost unbearable but he felt he had enough left in it to mess up Edwin's face.

But Edwin managed to duck his punch and caught him with a solid right on the chin that made him suddenly feel numb all over. For an instant they both stood there looking at each other appraising the blow. Then Talbot discovered that he couldn't move. At which point, Edwin opened up on him with a barrage of heavy punches to the head and ribs that staggered him and sent him reeling. He found himself leaning over and dripping blood onto the snow and wondering where he was and why his nose was bleeding profusely.

"And this is for Susan!" Edwin said, smashing his knee up into Talbot's face, sending him to the ground.

"Stop it, Edwin! Something's wrong with Charles!" Susan screamed, crawling over to where the other twin was lying face down in the inch of snow that had already accumulated on the grass.

By now Cecil Cope and several of the male guests were hurrying from the house toward the little war on the front lawn. It was snowing even more heavily now and Susan and the three combatants were covered with it.

"My god! My dear god!" Mr. Cope exclaimed, seeing the bloody-faced Talbot lying stretched out and Susan and Edwin trying to raise Charles to a sitting position.

"Hi," Charles said, opening his eyes as Edwin rubbed snow on his face. "Oh, man, the first snow! I told you it would snow, Eddie."

"Charles!" the elder Cope exclaimed, rushing to his side. "Son, are you all right?"

"Yeah, he's okay, Dad," Edwin said. "He was just out for a minute. You okay, Charles?"

"I knew it would snow on Christmas—oww!" Charles said, suddenly discovering that his jaw was throbbing.

"Did you boys do that, son?" Mr. Cope asked Edwin, pointing over to Talbot, who was beginning to stir.

"Yeah, Pop, I—"

"I'm proud of you, son. You boys stopped that Southern scum. I'm *proud* of you!"

"Thanks, Pop," Edwin said, beaming.

"Take him inside," the father said, trying to get an arm under Charles. "Ralph! Andrew!" He motioned to two middle-aged guests who had come out with him. "Give Edwin a hand with Charles. It's all over now. My boys took care of this hoodlum."

To Talbot, who was trying to clear his head and sit up, it all had a surreal quality—voices, people milling around, snow getting into his staring eyes.

"Let's go in, everybody!" Mr. Cope directed. "He won't be bothering *this* household again."

"Daddy, I want to see about Len," Susan said, beginning to shiver from the cold.

"I said go inside. Now!"

She looked for a moment at Talbot sitting with his legs out in front of him and his nose bleeding onto his snow-smeared red ski jacket and she began to cry, her nerves finally disintegrating.

"Now!"

"Yes, Daddy."

While the others struggled to the front door, Cecil Cope stood alone over the dazed Talbot. Snow was collecting on Cope's bald head and on the paunch bulging his yellow sweater.

"You know where you are, Len?" he asked when Talbot finally looked up into his narrowed eyes.

Talbot spit some blood onto the snow and ignored him.

"You are on my property!" the head of the Cope household declared.

"I'm not leaving till I see my son," Talbot said, drawing his legs up under him Indian fashion.

"No, I don't think so," the old man said, starting to walk back and forth in front of Talbot. "You've upset enough people for one day. No, young man, you will—"

"Aw, piss off, fat ass!" Talbot yelled at him, making him jump back nervously.

"Yes, I see," Mr. Cope said, recovering himself. "Then I

invite you to wait and enjoy the snow. Teddy should be coming out tomorrow to try out his new sled. Yes, by all means, wait!"

"Pompous ass," Talbot muttered, turning to spit out more blood.

"Now, if you will excuse me, I have guests waiting. And, Lennie, I wouldn't try coming in. Not if you don't want more of the same." With this the old man turned and waddled back through the deepening snow to the door, where several of the guests were watching.

For a few moments more Talbot stared back at them breathing heavily and squinting to keep the snow out of his eyes. Then he heard a laugh and the door closed with a thud. Many faces were now looking out of the lower-floor windows of the house but they did not seem real to him.

The snow was collecting on him more thickly and it felt good on the back of his throbbing right hand. After the storm of kicks and punches and Susan's fiery anger he felt strangely at peace in the quietly falling snow.

She had tried to warn him just before Charles had crashed into his back. That was nice. He even felt a certain fondness remembering how fiercely she had tried to defend her ground. That flinty New England spirit he had admired when he had met her at the University of Texas. Yes, it was her independence that had attracted him then. She had rebelled against her father by going to a Southern university and then she had rebelled against just about everything when she got there. In fact, they had met at an anti-war demonstration.

Looking at the broad two-story home, he saw light in several of the upstairs windows and wondered where she was right now. Probably with Teddy. He thought of his sleeping child and felt at peace in the peacefully falling snow.

"Charles seems to be all right now," Susan's mother said, coming into her daughter's room upstairs. The bedroom was dim and Susan was sitting in the window wearing a white terrycloth bathrobe with her hair wound up in a yellow towel.

"He's still just sitting down there, Mamma," she said with sadness and exasperation in her voice.

"I know," her mother said softly, coming over and sitting in the little cushioned window seat next to her. "Men live in a different world," she sighed.

"To hell with men," Susan replied. "And Daddy's no better. He's talking down there like he stopped the whole Confederate

army on his front lawn. Why can't we let him come in? He just
wants . . . All he wants to do is see Teddy," she said,
looking over at the sleeping child lying on her big bed.

"Don't press it, sugar. Your father said he would call the
police if Len takes another step toward the house. God, I hope
he *does* get up soon. He's nearly all covered with snow."

"He's stubborn enough to sit there until he freezes to death,
dammit!" Susan said, getting up and pulling the cover up
closer to Teddy's chin.

"You are both very stubborn," her mother said. "I used to
think it was a male trait, but you've become . . . Oh, I don't
know what's the word for it."

"I've learned a lot in recent years, Mamma," she said,
looking down at the boy and seeing the father's brooding
seriousness already evident in his little face.

"Ah, yes, from your Dr. Fischer."

"I've learned you have to fight to stay alive."

"You were always a fighter, Susan."

"Well, I lost it for a while. Slowly, after we were married I
just got more and more— I felt like I was playing a part. Not
*my* part, either. It was really *Len's* life and I was given a role in
it."

"Marriage is—"

"Do you know what men remind me of sometimes?"

"No, what?" her mother asked.

"A bunch of taxidermists!"

"Well, I never heard *that* one before!"

"Really, Mamma, they look at you and like you and then
they want you. But what they really want to do is scoop you
out and stuff you. And then they'll have you—pretty and
mounted in their trophy case just the way they want you. Total,
but I mean *total*, ownership!"

"There's a difference between being owned and being a part
of something," the mother said, smiling philosophically.
"Like being part of a family."

"Not for a woman. You should know that," Susan said,
returning to the window seat.

"Do you think your father owns me? Do you think I've been
stuffed and mounted, as you say?"

"No, I suppose not," Susan lied. "Look at him sitting there!
The way it's snowing he'll be buried. Damned stubborn males!
They'll turn into ice before they'll concede a point. And at the

same time they'll expect you to concede every goddam point there is."

"Honey, you used to be very much in love with Len. There was a time when—"

"Len is the worst taxidermist of them all! My god, I felt like I almost had to strike a perpetual pose for him. Noble heroic wife staring at noble heroic husband. How's this for going through life?" she asked, striking a heroic adoring pose.

"Or this?" she continued, slipping down off the window seat and kneeling with her eyes raised and her hands clutching her breast.

"I never understood why Len suddenly became so violent with you," her mother said, looking out at him sitting Indian fashion in the snow. "He always seemed to be so gentle before."

"Maybe I got tired of being heroic," Susan answered, knowing that her mother suspected there had been another man involved. It was their way of telling oblique truths.

"Don't tell me you'll never think of marrying again," her mother said, moving on. "No one in your life right now?"

"There you go again!" Susan said, getting up and straightening the towel wound around her head. "The one desperate thought of all women—marriage, marriage, marriage. Mother," she said soothingly, "we don't insist on our lives. We don't fight for our lives. Hell, we don't even know we have lives!"

"Well, we'd all get pretty lonely just keeping up with our own lives," her mother said, getting up to leave.

"*Men* seem to do it pretty handily and you don't hear them complaining about being lonely."

"Everybody gets lonely, child," her mother said gently, closing the door as she left the room.

Susan rested her head back against the window casement and watched Talbot through the falling snow. It had completely covered his long dark hair and collected on his eyebrows so that he looked like an old man sitting there staring up at the house. The gifts that he had brought for Teddy were now just white shapes scattered around him in the deepening snow.

"Go home, Len, please go home," she whispered.

Talbot by now had slipped into a comfortable drowsy state, almost hypnotized by the soft veils of snow descending around him. His nose and lips had stopped bleeding and though he felt the cold it did not seem to bother him.

In a while he knew he would have to get up or freeze to death. Little she cared, he thought. Back in the bosom of her murderous family. No, he knew better. She was not like them. But she was stubborn. She would stick to a point—perhaps until it was too late. Then she'd be sorry. He smiled. Let her explain to Teddy someday that she let his father freeze to death out of stubbornness.

No, he would have to get up and go home. Fuck the Copes! Fuck her stubbornness! But not right now. The cold was not too bad. It felt good not to move. A little longer and maybe he would win after all. He would sit there impervious to all, strong and stoic like the Indians he had seen as a boy.

He watched the snow covering the scuffle marks on the lawn and began to think of the morning it had snowed when he was eight and they had lived for a year near the mountain in El Paso. He could still hear the bomber circling around in the low clouds trying to come down.

His father was away fighting in the Korean war and his mother had been walking with him out to the highway to wait for the school bus. They had lived in a trailer camp for Fort Bliss families just north of El Paso and he remembered it as a happy time when he and his mother had been very close. She seemed a freer spirit then, and he remembered her laughing and telling him many things—things about her childhood in Oklahoma.

And on that morning, walking and stumbling through the foot of new snow, he had hit her playfully with a snowball and she had let out a *whoop!* and had chased him with a handful of snow.

"Come back here, you little coyote!" she had cried out happily as she had galloped after him and finally caught him and rolled him in the snow.

Then he had jumped up and showered her with wild flurries of snow and then they had thrown snow over each other until they were both so tired of laughing and throwing that they had fallen into the soft snow together out of breath.

"Oh, I haven't had so much fun in years." She had sighed, brushing the snow from his face and kissing him sweetly on the lips.

He remembered the glow on her cheeks and nose and how beautiful her brown eyes looked. It was that image of her smiling and nuzzling him in the fine crystals of falling snow that he would always remember.

"Mom, you're pretty," he had told her.

It was then that they had heard the somber engines of the bomber droning in the heavy clouds overhead. The thick gray clouds had been so low that they had covered half the red granite mountain that towered from the desert floor about a mile away.

"My, he's very low," she said, getting up and brushing the snow from her long cloth coat. "Probably going to land at Biggs Field, I imagine."

"Boy, that sounds like one of them big ones with all the engines. A B-36, Mom!"

As the sound of the engines passed over them they had started walking toward the highway again. They could see the mountain hazily through the falling snow farther on.

"I bet none of the other kids are going to school today, Mom. I bet they get to stay home and play in the snow. It hardly *ever* snows, Mom."

"And what do you think your father would say to that?" she had said, continuing on slightly ahead of him.

"You wouldn't have to tell him," he had said, feeling slightly uneasy about suggesting a conspiracy against his father.

"Oh, yes I would, young man. And if I didn't your poor marks would tell him."

"But what if he gets killed in Korea?" he had asked, blurting the question out before he had time to try to call it back. It had sounded wicked but he had not meant it to be wicked.

"Leonard Talbot, never say anything like that again in your life! Do you hear me?" she had said, whirling on him with more fright than anger in her face. "Do you hear me?"

"Yes'm," he had said. After that they had walked in silence the final few yards to the highway.

When they had got to the highway she had turned to him, but instead of chastising him further she had seen the sad look on his face and had knelt down and pulled him toward her. A truck had roared past nearly knocking them over with its wind, but he had felt warm and secure again pressed against her.

"I know you love your daddy, Len," she had said. "And you're Mommy's bright angel. Will you remember that?"

"Yes'm," he had said.

Just then they had heard the big plane lumbering overhead again, this time much lower. They could feel the shuddering vibration of its motors as it moved through the clouds toward the mountain.

"Oh, my Jesus!" his mother had exclaimed as it passed over them. "It's going to ram the mountain."

As she stood up and pulled him to her side he had seen a bright glow just above the cloud level on the mountain and an instant later there was a massive boom that sent the wind against his face and clothes.

Then he had seen particles of fire raining down through the clouds and off to his right a pair of enormous wheels bouncing down the slope of the mountain.

"Oh, God have mercy on their poor souls," his mother had said as they had clung to each other.

Several cars had pulled over on the side of the highway and he had seen men running toward the mountain.

"Mom, let's go see!" he had said.

"No, they are all dead," she had said, trying to turn him back toward the trailer camp and holding on to his jacket collar with a tight grip.

Looking back at the mountain as she pulled him away, it suddenly struck him that men were lying dead just behind the clouds. It was the first time that he had ever been close to dead people. They were men who were alive just a moment before, flying in the clouds in their giant airplane, he had thought. He'd had a picture of them in his mind, sitting in their seats, wearing their uniforms like his father. And then a second later they were all dead and mangled on the mountain. He had begun to tremble and cry.

"Mom, I want Daddy!" he had cried as she stopped and held him in the snow. "I don't want my daddy to die."

"Daddy? Daddy!"

It was Teddy's voice. Talbot looked up from under his encrusted brows and saw his son standing a few feet away in the thickly falling snow. For a moment he thought he was dreaming.

"Daddy?"

"You? Is that you, Teddy?" he asked, breaking a frozen strand of blood at the corner of his mouth.

Looking past the boy, he saw Susan standing about fifteen

feet away, her arms folded and wearing a terrycloth bathrobe and a towel wound around her head. Her look told him she was making a painful concession. He held his arms out to Teddy, who then ran to him and nearly bowled him over backwards with a hug.

"Daddy, you made yourself into a snowman!" the boy exclaimed as Talbot hugged him desperately and cried silently.

"Yeah, Daddy's a snowman," he sobbed. "And guess what the snowman brought you?"

"What, presents?"

"Yep, let's find them," he said, crawling around in the snow with the boy and uncovering the scattered gifts.

"Mommy, look what Daddy brought me!" the boy yelled, running to Susan with a large red box.

"That's wonderful, darling. Hurry up, now. Mommy's freezing to death," she said, taking the gift.

Teddy then ran back to his father, who was uncovering the rest. In a moment he and the boy carried them over to her and placed them in her arms.

"It was dumb of you to come up here," she said. "You look terrible."

"I'm okay—now. I have what I came for."

"You've got to go home now. Dad is threatening to call the police."

"In a minute," he said, leaning down and sweeping the boy up onto his shoulders. "Okay, ready for a little horsie ride in the snow?"

"You can't be a horsie!" Tedddy yelled happily. "You're a snowman!"

"Right! But don't you know that snowmen are magic? They can turn themselves into anything. Even daddies," he said, looking over at Susan.

While Talbot trotted back and forth on the snow-covered front lawn, Cecil Cope watched disapprovingly from the front window surrounded by his sons and several of the guests. Virginia Cope watched from a window upstairs.

Seeing her son and his father romping so happily, Susan knew she would never be entirely free of Talbot. He would always be near as a necessary part of Teddy's life.

Finally he brought the boy over to her and put him down at her side. They looked into each other's eyes for a moment—understanding enemies.

He nodded his gratitude. "When are you bringing him back?" he asked.

"On Friday."

"May I have him for the weekend?"

"I suppose."

With that, he squatted down and gave Teddy another hug and a kiss. "See you Saturday, cowboy.

"About noon," he said to her.

"Bye, Daddy," the boy said, hugging him one last time.

Talbot turned and started walking down the long snow-laden lawn toward his car. It was still snowing and the afternoon had darkened into dusk. He had been bloodied, but he felt better than he had for a long time.

"Merry Christmas, Daddy!" the boy called after him.


Gemetz was chopping the ice from the sidewalk in front of his father's store when he saw Linda coming toward him with a look as inviting as the old coal shovel he was using. Pulling his woollen seaman's cap down around his ears, he turned his back on her and continued chopping.

He had not heard from her in the three days since Christmas, when he had walked out in the middle of the elaborate dinner she had prepared for him and the boys and a couple they had known before the breakup. Good, sweet, treacherous Linda, he thought, remembering how she had served him the best slices from the turkey—and then tried to leave a carving knife in his conscience.

I don't know you, lady, he thought, as he speeded up his chopping. The shovel bit through the crust of ice and spanged against the concrete. The morning was cold and gray under new snow clouds and there were still a few Manhattan-bound office workers gingerly making their way over the ice to the subway station at the top of Montague Street. But it was unusual for Linda to be out at nine-thirty—early for her. A chorus soprano with the Metropolitan Opera, she rarely went to bed before 2 A.M.

He sensed her standing directly behind him waiting for him to turn around, to "face reality," as she called it. He preferred the reality of chopping out the ice. How easily it cracked away under his thrusts, a matter of knotting his shoulders and driving down the steel. The trail he was making through the sheath of ice was nearly complete.

"Richard!" she exclaimed finally.

A voice for disciplining schoolchildren, he thought. Perhaps he'd swing the shovel around and smack teacher in the face with it. With a grunt he bashed out a large piece of ice.

"Richard, we have to talk, goddam it!"

Just a little more, he thought, puffing from the exertion. The old man was afraid someone would fall down in front of the store and sue him. So, he thought, looking at the solid glaze all the way up the sidewalk to the corner, let them sail safely past Gemetz Appliance and then fall on their asses in front of the boutique next door. While they're lying there they can admire the bathing suit display.

"I'm not going to talk to your back, Richard!"

He shoveled the last shards of ice off into the pile of snow along the curb and then turned and walked toward the store. Linda scurried after him and caught the door just as he was closing it behind him.

The elder Gemetz was standing behind the counter near the window eating a hard-boiled egg when they came in. The store had not yet warmed up and the old man was still wearing his long black coat with its handsome fur collar. But with his stringy neck and emaciated head he looked like a wispy-haired buzzard looking out the window.

"You are a total creep, Richard!" Linda yelled as she rushed past the old man trying to keep up with Gemetz. "Excuse me, Papa," she called over her shoulder.

"Mazel tov," Martin Gemetz replied, watching them disappear into the big storage room in the back, and then he gloomily went back to eating his egg and looking out the window.

Midway through the rows of washing machines, refrigerators and other appliances in the cavernous storage room, Gemetz yanked his hat off and suddenly turned to face his ex-wife, who had nearly been treading on his heels. Bumping into him slightly, she backed up and glared in silence, waiting for him to apologize. He found his hands tightening around the handle of the shovel that stood between them. The breath of her determination oppressed him.

He brought the shovel up and clanked the blade of it down against the cement floor near her toes as a warning for her to back up.

For a moment they stood facing each other in silent

territorial combat. She measured her breathing and shifted her high-heeled boots to a slightly wider stance. They were about the same height, but he kept his glance down on the buckle of her brown leather trench coat as he waited for her to move.

Slowly he raised the shovel and then brought it down hard near her foot causing her to jump back a few inches. Still not enough, still standing in my life, he thought. He looked at her coldly. The nostrils of her slightly aquiline nose were flared, her large hazel eyes beginning to tear with defiance.

His own anger was collecting around the handle of the shovel again. He could feel her Mexican-Irish pride mounting to the flash point, but he was determined to drive her back. He started to bring the shovel up again. This time she slapped him stingingly across the face. He smiled and brought the shovel down with a loud clank, again forcing her to jump back.

"I'm not moving again, jerk," she said calmly and he knew that she meant it.

"So, talk," he said, leaning the shovel against a washing machine and unbuttoning his peacoat. He knew that he had frightened her, turned her from attack to defense. She was much better at defense. He grudgingly admired her courage in that position and it was not the first time he had tested it.

She took the silk scarf from her head and shook out her long chestnut hair. Her olive skin was still ruddy from the cold outside. He wished she would take off her black kidskin gloves: her long sharply taloned fingers had a dangerous quality that had always excited him. But she kept the gloves on, drumming her sheathed fingers on the top of a dishwasher as she collected her thoughts.

"First I want to know what all this shit with the shovel is all about," she said.

"You know exactly what it's all about. Now what do you want? I'm busy."

"Somebody better tell you you're acting sick in the head. You're getting so fucking weird I don't even know you anymore. Even Amy and Bob said—"

"What do you *want*, Linda? Money, right?"

"Look at you right now! I—"

"Money, right?" He cut her off again, shouting with impatience.

"Hey, don't yell at me, see," she said, turning back to

the dishwasher and slamming her gloved fist down. "You little prick you. No, *you* don't ever yell at me. See?"

He looked at her for a moment in silence and smiled. "Money, right?" he whispered in mocking compliance.

She turned and looked at him, shaking her head slowly. Her long-suffering superior look, he thought. Her "You're a bug" look.

"Okay, you wanna be El Creepo, you got it. What time is it?" she said, pulling off her gloves.

"Almost ten," he said, looking at his watch.

"Right, and the kids haven't had breakfast yet. And at noon they aren't going to have lunch. And at six they aren't going to have supper. Get the picture?"

"Aw, gee, don't tell me you're all out of food stamps?"

"Look, I've got two kids, a baby sitter and two goddam cats to feed and nothing on the shelf but a can of tomato paste!"

He looked down on the floor and waited for her to continue. A can of tomato paste. Not bad, he thought, that little touch. Kids waiting around starving. Mommy out in the snow begging a few pennies from Daddy. And that can of tomato paste sitting on the shelf.

"Excuse me," he said, stifling a smile, "I'm trying not to laugh. I, uh, did give you a hundred and fifty three days ago, right? Pretty expensive tomato paste."

"It all went for rent. We're still half a month behind."

"Uh-huh."

"Uh-huh. And the hundred-fifty the week before went for Christmas presents. None of which you bought."

"Your idea to raise them Christians."

"At least I'm raising them, Jew boy! This is *shit,* Richard. Give me some goddam money or your kids aren't going to eat today—or the rest of the week. If you'd give me the money you're supposed to, I wouldn't have to come here and go through this total crap."

"Another cheap shot," he said, reaching for his wallet. "Just like that food-stamp bullshit you pulled in front of Amy and Bob during dinner the other night."

"I told them later I only borrowed them from Helen."

He was still kicking himself for being suckered into going to her damned dinner. All too cozy. He had known in his bones it was a trap. And sure enough, right in the middle of the meal she had tried to shame him by announcing that all of the food had been purchased with welfare stamps. What a bitch! He had simply lowered his fork, dabbed his lips with the napkin, smiled and got up quietly and left.

"You bet your ass you did! Thirty-one thousand a year hardly qualifies you for food stamps."

"I'm paying *everything* out of that—including Mark's shrink bills."

"And *your* shrink bills."

"Look, I don't even have to argue with you. The court says you have to pay me two hundred and twenty-five a week."

"And *your* tennis club bills," he continued.

"I could just have Papa send it to me out of your checks, you know. Want me to go out there and tell him his grandsons are starving to death?"

"Right, go out there and give him another ulcer. One more operation ought to just about do it for him." As he said it he was counting out eighty dollars in twenties from his wallet.

"When are you going to start giving me what you owe each week?" she asked, smiling slightly at the money.

"I can't right now. I'm trying to get a car. Anyway, you're living on nearly twice my income now."

"When?" she asked again.

"I don't know. Maybe in the spring when I get my tax money back. You want this?" he asked, waving the crisp bills in front of her face and then jerking them back as she grabbed for them.

"Richard?" she said, smiling as he gave her a look she recognized. Game time again, she thought. She looked around the vast dimly lighted room and felt her excitement growing.

"What'd you expect from Simon Legree?" he asked, taking off his coat.

"Don't start, Richard," she said, backing up but feeling that old weakness as she looked at the bulge in his Levi's.

"You say your children are starving, dearie?" he asked, twisting the ends of his mustache and moving toward her. He shoved the money down into his front pocket and stroked slowly over the bulge.

"Damn it, Richard, it's cold in here," she said but did not try to move away as he moved up against her and started unbuckling her coat belt.

"You have no choice, Linda," he said evilly and slid his hands inside the coat caressing down over her sleek hips. "The children are waiting—hungry children." He breathed the words into her ear and pulled her awakening body against his erection.

"Children . . . ," she sighed, slackening her thighs as he pressed between them. "No, stop, we can't—Oh, god, ummm . . . No, Richard. What if Papa comes back here?" She tried feebly to push him away but loved it when he held her more forcefully, loved the boldness of his hands already pulling up the light jersey dress. Loved the game.

He knew he had her. He could always have her if he made it sinful enough, dangerous enough. All those convent school years under the nuns had given her an exquisite sense of sin. She had lived her life inhaling and exhaling guilt, had ruined their marriage with it, but could abandon herself to sex with the passion of those who would give their souls for it. He had often thought that they had ruined their relationship by legitimizing it with marriage.

"You have to, Linda," he said.

"Ooooh!" she exclaimed as he slid down her panty hose and pushed her warm bare buttocks back against the cold metal surface of the dishwasher. But then his fingers were moving into her wet vagina and the mixed sensations delighted her, made her dizzy.

"Richie!" It was the old man calling from the front of the store.

"Oh, god!" she exclaimed. There were other voices out there, too. Customers. They were coming toward the back.

As she tried to push him away and pull up her panty hose, his hands gripped the top of her shoulders and slowly forced her down to the floor.

"No, Richard, we can't," she whispered forcefully. "I think they're coming back—"

"Shut up," he said, pushing her over on all fours and kneeling behind her. In a moment he was inside of her, moving with long sensuous strokes.

"Jesus!" she cried half in fear, half in ecstasy.

"Hey, Richie!" the old man called as he stepped into the storage area with two young housewives just behind him. "Show these ladies the new Kelvinator! Richie?" he called, squinting his eyes in the dimness.

"Is there a trade-in allowance, Mr. Gemetz?" one of the women asked as she walked behind him.

"No. No trade-ins. We deal in new. Richie? My son, he'll show you. A beautiful piece of equipment."

Gemetz laughed and held Linda's soft white buttocks. "Yes, beeeautiful," he said.

"Goddam it, hurry up!" she whispered. "Oh, god, this is insane."

"You love it," he said, moving his hips faster.

"It's dark back here," the other woman said as they made their way slowly down an aisle two rows over from where Gemetz and Linda were down on the floor.

"I'm coming!" Gemetz yelled suddenly.

"What was that?" one of the women asked, stopping and putting her hand on the other's arm.

"You bastard!" Linda hissed.

"Oh, god, it's coming!" he yelled again, raising his satyr's head up over the top of the washing machines.

"Richie?" the old man asked, squinting his eyes.

"Aaaah, aaaaah, ooooooooooh!" he exclaimed as he felt himself pulsing into her.

"I can't believe you're doing this, Richard!" Linda said, but still moving back against him and enjoying his final thrusting.

"There's my son now," the old man said, still not noticing Gemetz's ecstatic head sticking up but pointing in the direction of his voice. "He'll be able—Ladies?"

When the old man turned the two women were scurrying out of the storage room and heading for the front door.

"Ladies!" the old man called as he pursued them. "My son"—the front door of the shop slammed shut on his words—"will show you." He stood there for a moment under the white neon lights of the display floor and scratched his head. "Every Christmas it gets crazy."

Back in the storage room Gemetz and Linda were straightening their clothes and laughing. She could be wonderful at times, he was thinking as he watched her buckling her long coat. She had a smudge of dirt on her chin and he wet his finger with his tongue and wiped it off. Then, holding her face gently in his hands, he looked into her eyes and kissed her softly. In the old way. But as he did so he felt her long fingers slipping down into his pocket and taking out the eighty dollars.

"Was I worth it?" she asked, kissing the bills and putting them into her coat pocket.

"Every cent," he replied, resenting the distance she was beginning to insert between them again.

"What about Papa? Think he knows what we were up to?"

"I doubt it. But those two women won't be back soon."

"At least they didn't see me. I think I recognized one of their voices. Cynthia Heller. Her Jason comes over to play with Jonathan sometimes."

"Guess you'd better go feed the boys," he said, moving quickly to shut off the little crack of feeling she had opened in him. You had to be on top of it every day. He had no intention of becoming a basket case like Tiernan.

As they walked through the display room, the old man was standing behind the counter looking out the window again.

"He doesn't look good," Linda said. "How's he been feeling?"

"I don't know. I think he's still depressed about her. It's like they buried a part of him out there with her."

"Hi, Papa," she said cheerfully. "We missed you on Christmas."

"What'd you want, Papa?" he asked.

The old man turned and looked at them for a moment as though they had materialized out of thin air.

"Oh, Linda!" the old man said, smiling. "How are those two grandsons of mine?"

"They miss their grandfather, Papa. You don't come over much anymore."

"It's the business. Soon, soon. And look at this one," he said, pointing to Gemetz. "Late again. I get no help."

"What did those women want, Papa?" he asked.

"What women?"

Gemetz looked at Linda sadly and nudged her toward the door. He was glad there was still a bond between her and the old man. His father often forgot they were divorced and he was not interested in adding to the old man's sorrow.

"Linda has to go feed the boys, Papa," he said.

"Yes," she said, moving toward the door. "Promise me you will come over soon. We are only a few blocks. Come for lunch."

"Soon," the old man said, nodding and slipping back into himself.

When the door closed behind her Gemetz walked over

behind the counter and stood beside the old man. For a while they both looked out the window in silence. Linda smiled and waved to them, trudging carefully across the pocked ice, avoiding the path Gemetz had chopped.

# CHAPTER
# FOUR

The three young children in bright nylon snowsuits were kneeling on the subway-car seat looking out the sooty window as block after block of empty and decaying South Bronx tenement buildings swept past. The fourth child, Gemetz's seven-year-old son, Mark, sat beside them glumly turning over a toy racing car in his mittened hands.

Sitting opposite him across the slush-streaked aisle, Gemetz frowned and tried to figure out what was troubling the boy. Mark had surprised him by not wanting to go to the zoo when he had shown up at Linda's with Tiernan and Talbot and their two children. Even Jonathan, his five-year-old, had been a little reluctant until Talbot's Teddy had started talking about the polar bears. Mark had agreed to come only after Linda had scolded him and said that it was too late to arrange a baby sitter and that she was leaving immediately for her opera matinee.

Gemetz wondered if it was because Mark was still upset about not getting the bicycle he had wanted for Christmas. It was something that he and Linda had agreed to withhold from the boy in order to surprise him with it on his birthday in February.

"Get that for Christmas?" Gemetz asked, leaning forward

and pointing to the blue and white racing car Mark was holding.

"Mark?" he had to ask again when the boy remained silent and did not look up.

"Traded Josh Segal for it," Mark finally mumbled, still not looking up.

"Traded what?"

"Nothin', just old stuff," the boy replied, a little impatiently.

"Oh," Gemetz said, leaning back in his seat and jamming his hands into his peacoat. The hell with it, he thought.

Tiernan, who was sitting in between Gemetz and Talbot, listened to the short exchange and understood Gemetz's frustration. His policy with Lynn when she was being silently angry at him—and the Gemetz boy definitely seemed to be down on his father—was to wait until she was ready to bring it out. Gemetz was right not to push it, he thought.

Then Tiernan went back to watching the young Puerto Rican woman who was sitting a few feet farther down from Lynn. The heaters under the long plastic seats had warmed the car up almost uncomfortably and the young woman had just taken off her yellow wool bandana and was shaking out her lush black hair.

She had noticed him looking at her from time to time and twice she had returned his look, exciting him with her beautiful dark eyes. Probably about twenty-five or twenty-six, he thought. Not married—didn't have the look. But she did look like she was very much aware of him. He imagined her thinking of him, wishing he would make a move to enter her life. Of course she would fall in love with him. The Latin women really knew how to take care of their men, he thought. How fiercely loyal and devoted she would be.

Then he thought again of the blonde in the fur collar he had talked to silently in the subway window coming back Christmas Eve. He had fallen in love with her, too. He seemed to be falling in love a couple of times a day lately—women passing him on the sidewalk, sitting across from him in restaurants, waiting in line at the unemployment office, once even with a woman he'd seen sitting in her car waiting for a light to change. God, she didn't even have her window down, he chided himself.

What the hell was happening to him? he wondered. He

would have sworn that even Verna was coming on to him last night at Larsky's when they had been talking about taking their kids to the zoo. She and Richie did seem to be cooling down, he thought. No, it was more of his craziness. But she *had* kept her knee against his thigh most of the evening. Maybe that was because Richie seemed to be looking down the bar at Juliet all night.

Shit, it was all Mary's fault, he told himself. She had slammed the door on his life, and now he was running around like a lunatic, attaching his heart to anything with a nice-looking face—or ass. Yes, he certainly did love Verna's ass. He wondered if the young Puerto Rican woman had a nice ass. Couldn't tell anything with these big winter coats. Nice calf and ankles, though. Shit, I'm going nuts, he thought.

Talbot was sitting sideways on the seat with his arm resting on the window, looking out at the urban wreckage rolling past. The elevated tracks were turning up ahead and he could see the rubble-strewn streets and the storefronts that looked like they had been bombed out. There was snow on the flat littered rooftops of the tenements, and the fire-scorched windows reminded him of pictures he'd seen of war-torn cities in Europe. This whole section of the Bronx looked like it was undergoing a slow-motion blitz.

More signs of people giving up, he thought, more signs of the collapse of individual will in the twentieth century. Well, he would not sink into the shit with the rest of them, would not lie down and call it man's natural position. He was a rider and he had already ridden against the odds, tilted with the Cope windmill, and he had taken his victory. He snuffed through his still-swollen nose and was proud of his wounds.

"God, it's depressing," Tiernan said, looking out at the decay.

"It looks like World War Two out there," Talbot said.

"Yeah, you're right," Tiernan said, nodding. "I saw this documentary about the battle of Stalingrad last Sunday on TV and it reminded me of the Bronx."

"I saw that, too, *The World at War.* I watch it every Sunday. Damned good. Jesus, those Russians really held out, didn't they? All those months in bitter cold, fighting from cellar to cellar. I wonder if the American people would fight like that?"

Gemetz, who had been quietly listening, turned and asked,

"Wasn't that the battle where they cut off about a quarter of a million Germans?"

"Yeah, they wanted to hightail it back to Germany but Hitler told them to stay put," Tiernan said.

"And then the Russians finally broke out and turned the whole bunch of them into hamburger," Talbot said.

As the train pulled away from the next stop, Tiernan noticed that the Puerto Rican woman had gotten off. She was tying her bandana on as she stepped through the snow on the platform. Still can't tell about her ass, Tiernan thought.

Four stops later they came to the Bronx Zoo station and hurriedly moved to get their respective children out the door.

"Okay!" Tiernan shouted. "Let's go challenge the elephants to a snowball fight!"

"Yea!" Lynn cried.

"I bet the elephants could make a big snowball, Daddy," Teddy said as they stepped through the slush on the platform to the long flight of steps down to the sidewalk.

Walking the three blocks to the zoo entrance, the children pelted them with snowballs and the three fathers lumbered along with their arms hanging down and made sounds like bewildered elephants.

It was a bright, clear Saturday afternoon and as they entered the zoo grounds they could see the sunlight flashing off the windows of the slowly moving Skyfari cable cars crossing over the treetops toward the far side of the zoo.

"Daddy, I wanna ride on the cable cars!" Jonathan said.

"How about it, you guys want to? Then we could catch the animal exhibits walking back," Gemetz said.

They all agreed and, after paying their admission at the Skyfari station, decided to split up into two groups because the little enclosed cars were too small for them all. Tiernan and Talbot and their two children went in the first car and Gemetz and his two sons in the next.

From the cable cars they could see over most of the vast snowcovered animal preserves in the park. Here and there herds of antelope and various types of horned African animals could be seen in corners of the open compounds. But most of the beasts seemed to be snugged inside the snow-topped buildings at various points along the winding trails below. In the distance they could still see the tombstone skyline of the Bronx.

About midway they were passing over the lion preserve, in the middle of which three of the big yellow cats were cavorting in the snow, jumping long distances and breathing little clouds of vapor into the frosty air.

"Daddy, that big lion looked at me!" Lynn exclaimed excitedly as she pressed her head against the glass of the gently swaying cable car.

"Oh, he's a magnificent one," Tiernan said, leaning over to her side and looking down at the big male standing near the two females that were still leaping about.

"I'll say he is," Talbot agreed. "Look how he stands guard over those two females."

"Don't forget about Liberation," Tiernan said. "You mean, he *thinks* he's standing guard."

"Ha!" Talbot laughed and sat back as Teddy climbed over his lap to see the lions.

"Do the lions like the snow?" Teddy asked.

"It sure looks like it," Talbot answered.

"Daddy, can the lions catch us when we come down?" Lynn asked.

"No, baby, they can't jump over the moat," Tiernan said.

"What's the moat?" she asked.

"It's a big trench that's all around the place where the lions live. And it's so wide they can't jump over it."

"What if the big *big* lion, though, jumped over the moat and ate you up?" she asked.

"Then I'd tickle his belly until he laughed me up," Tiernan said.

"Then he'd eat you up again."

"Then I'd tickle him again."

"Then he'd eat you up *again*."

"Tickle him again," he said, tickling her through her pink snowsuit.

Talbot smiled and looked back over his shoulder and wondered how Gemetz and his two boys were doing in the car just behind him. It was a swell idea of Gemetz's to get together for an outing with the children. It was important for children to know that fathers had a place in their world, that they just weren't *visitors* in their lives.

The cable cars were nearing the farther end of the park and Gemetz was trying to steady Jonathan, who had just lurched

across the car to his window to watch a deer that was running
through the snow just below.

"Easy, Jon, you're making me seasick," Gemetz said as he
tried to pin the boy between his knees.

"You mean *air*sick," Mark corrected without taking his
gaze from the treetops and the animal enclosures passing
beneath them. Mark was also wearing a nylon snowsuit, but
the string-tied hood only partly concealed the irritation on his
face.

"I don't care what kind of sick," Gemetz said, trying to hold
on to the squirming Jonathan. "You guys cool the jumping
around or Daddy's gonna lose his lunch."

"Jon, I can see the bears!" Mark exclaimed, pointing off in
the distance.

"Where's the bears?" Jonathan cried as he scrambled over
to Mark's side and caused the car to sway again.

Gemetz shook his head at Mark's sabotage and regretted the
amount of beer he had put away the previous night at Larsky's.
He was also feeling a little bushed from the lovemaking that
morning with Verna. Lovemaking that had turned a little sour
because of an argument they had had. He had told her he
thought she was becoming a little too possessive and he
thought maybe they should drop it for a while.

He had also told her he did not want her to come along to the
zoo. One of the reasons was that he wanted to be free of her—
for a while anyway. And the other reason, the one he told her,
was his policy of not involving his children with the women he
was dating unless he was sure it was going to be a long-lasting
relationship. So far they had not met any of the women he had
known since the breakup.

Once, after he had dated Juliet a few times, he had planned
an afternoon with all of them together at the boat pond in
Central Park. It had never come off, because she had broken
the date and never accepted his invitations after that. Getting
too homey for her, he guessed.

Watching his sons looking out the window, Gemetz was
amazed at how these two beautiful children could have come
from two such antagonistic spirits as his and Linda's.

But he wished he knew why Mark seemed to be drawing
away from him lately, not wanting to hold his hand anymore on
walks and even initiating little attacks on his patience to
frustrate him.

"Daddy, we're going down," Jonathan said.

"Dad, can we ride on the camel?" Mark asked, finally turning away from the window.

"I doubt they're gonna have the camel out riding in this snow," Gemetz said, relieved that Mark was now talking to him.

"Can we at least go see, Dad?" Mark persisted.

"I get to ride the camel, too, Daddy!" Jonathan said.

"Okay, we'll go see," Gemetz said. "But I still can't see them having—"

"Never mind," Mark said, turning back to his window.

"Hey, Mark, what's this 'never mind' business?" Gemetz asked, leaning over toward his son.

"Just . . . never mind," the boy replied.

"No, don't look out the window and say, 'Never mind.' I told you we'd go see. Now what's eating you? I said, look at me!"

"It probably costs too much money is all," Mark said, turning and looking him coldly in the eyes.

"No, money's not the problem," Gemetz said, trying to speak softly to the boy. "I just don't think the camel is going to be out in this snow. You see all that snow down there, don't you? But we'll still go see. Okay? Ya gonna quit being a big grouch?"

"We probably better save the money for food," Mark said, turning back to the window.

"Food, huh?" Gemetz said, sitting back and eyeing his son. "Where did you get that?"

"Daddy, we didn't have no food in the house," Jonathan said, sitting next to Mark. "And . . . and Mommy told Steve you liked us to get hungry. And then Steve—"

"Who is Steve?" Gemetz asked in astonishment.

"And Steve bought us a whole big bunch of—"

"Be quiet!" Mark warned his brother.

"—food!" Jonathan continued.

"Well, Mommy told a big lie," Gemetz said, still flabbergasted. "And who the hell is this Steve?"

"Steve is gonna be our new daddy," Jonathan said.

"Oh, Mommy said that, huh?" Gemetz said, feeling dizzy with outrage.

"That's not true, Jon!" Mark exclaimed. "She just said he wanted to be our new daddy."

"Oh, well, that's different," Gemetz said. "Well, look, I hate to disappoint you guys, but I haven't resigned as daddy yet. And now will somebody tell me who the heck Steve is?"

"Daddy, Steve is stronger than you," Jon said.

"He is not, Daddy is stronger!" Mark said. "Steve is just taller."

"He is too stronger!" Jonathan protested. "He picks me up stronger than Daddy!"

"I think I'm actually going to kill her." Gemetz sighed in bewilderment, leaning his head back against the window.

There was complete silence for a minute as Gemetz looked out over the park grounds. Then Jonathan suddenly began wailing, startling him out of his angry reverie.

"Now what's the matter?" Gemetz asked.

"I don't want you to kill Mommy," the boy said, his face red and wet with tears.

"What? Who said I was going to kill Mommy?"

"You did!" Mark said, pouting his lower lip and starting to blubber, too.

"I didn't mean it," Gemetz said, trying to pull Jonathan over to his seat. "I've never hurt Mommy, have I? And I never will. I was just saying angry words. Dumb, dopey words, but I was angry because she told you things that were not true. I'm sorry. Okay?"

But both boys kept up their crying, holding on to each other and playing it just a bit to punish him.

"Jesus, I can't believe this is happening!" Gemetz said.

When Gemetz's cable car finally rocked to a halt, Tiernan and Talbot were standing on the Skyfari platform waiting. The attendant opened its door and two red-faced sobbing children hopped out and ran toward Lynn and Teddy, who were standing farther back near the exit. After that Gemetz stepped down from the car with an expression of seething fury on his face.

"Hey, what happened?" Tiernan asked in amazement.

"You guys better go on," Gemetz said, swinging his arms angrily across his chest. "I'm taking them home—and then I'm going to kick the shit out of their mother. That *bitch!*"

"Richie, for god's sake, cool down a minute," Tiernan said. "What happened?"

"Oh, well, not much, man. She just told the kids I was trying to starve them. And then she tells 'em this jerk named Steve, whoever the fuck that is, is going to be their new daddy.

Too much, man. Now I'm—Owwww! Damn ulcer is killing me," he said, stooping over.

"Richie, come on," Talbot said, putting his hand on Gemetz's shoulder. "Let's walk around a bit and talk. It isn't worth getting like this."

"No, I'm going back right now and kick her ass! Right now!" Gemetz said, straightening up.

"Look, she ain't gonna be home anyway," Talbot said. "Hasn't she got two opera performances today?"

"Jesus, what a dumb thing to tell her kids," Tiernan sympathized. "I mean, kids get jerked around enough as it is when a marriage breaks up."

"And that's why you gotta stay cool, Richie," Talbot said.

"Cool? I'm gonna break her—"

"No, man," Talbot interrupted. "With a mother like that it's especially important for you to have your act together. Right? Man, they need you more than ever. You gotta be there like a rock, strong and steady. You gotta be a rock of love for them. That's what a father is, right?"

"A rock of love, huh?" Gemetz said, beginning to laugh in spite of himself at this kind of sentiment coming out of Talbot.

"Yeah, a rock," Talbot said, laughing, too, and cuffing him on the shoulder. "Come on, Rocky, let's see your stuff!" he continued, sparring around Gemetz like a boxer.

"Wanna see it, huh?" Gemetz said, starting to punch back at him despite the sharp aching in his stomach. "Wanna see the old Gemeter, huh?"

"Yeah, whatta ya got?" Talbot said, ducking and feinting.

"You pussy, I'll tear your head off!" Gemetz huffed, driving Talbot back with light punches to his chest and arms. "Left, left, feint, left—and right, pow!"

"All right!" Talbot approved. *"That's* the old Gemetzer!"

"Hey!" Tiernan exclaimed. "Where the hell are the kids?"

"Oh, Christ!" Gemetz said looking around and seeing the Skyfari platform nearly empty.

The three fathers took off on the run, jumping up and looking into the departing cable cars, peering through the maze of station supports. Then Talbot looked over the iron fence near the exit ramp and saw the four children running along the park trail below toward the big new primate house.

"Come on, I see them!" he yelled.

The black asphalt trail was wet from melting snow, and the

three men splashed through its slushy puddles as they ran after their children. The path kept winding and along its sides the sunlight was glittering on the filigrees of ice covering the tree limbs. Far ahead they could faintly hear the children's excited voices.

"Mark, slow 'em down!" Gemetz yelled.

Rounding a final turn onto a straight stretch of trail, they could see the four children some twenty yards ahead about to go into the modern buff brick primate house.

"Okay, they're going in," Gemetz said, breathing hard. "Let's walk the rest of the way."

"How you doing, Richie?" Tiernan asked.

"Okay . . . just out of breath. . . . Don't worry. Len . . . you were right. Thanks."

"Yeah, I just hope *I'll* be able to remember it next time Susan pulls some shit," Talbot said, clapping him on the shoulder.

"Goddam it, this is really bullshit!" Tiernan said, slapping some of the ice from a nearby branch. "I mean, what's it been now—nearly a year? And we're still having marriage hangovers."

"*Now* you're getting the picture," Talbot said, smiling.

"The three basketeers!" Gemetz yelled and raised his fist in the air. "Basket cases, unite!"

"No, that's over, goddam it!" Talbot said, turning and holding them back with his hands planted on their chests. "Look, it's going to be a new year in a few days, and I say we make a pledge right here and now that it's going to be a *real* new year for all three of us. We leave *all* this bullshit behind. A new ballgame, right? Whatta ya say?"

"Right on!" Gemetz said, smiling.

"Right, Joey?" Talbot asked.

"Oh, sure. On the stroke of midnight all the frogs are going to turn into princes," Tiernan said in disgust.

For a moment Talbot just looked at him, his bruised face tightening in anger.

"Yes, goddam it, right on the stroke!" Talbot said.

"Fat chance," Tiernan said and started to push past him, ready to knock his hand aside if he did not move it.

"Joey, goddam it, you've got *shit* for a backbone!" Talbot cried out, grabbing a fistful of Tiernan's coat and shoving him back.

"Leggo, Len, or I'll break your face some more," Tiernan said, feeling that dead calm that came over him before he went into a fight. At the same time he was feeling pity for Talbot, who seemed to have gotten more than just physically hurt in New London. Something had been building up in him for several days now.

"Len! Cool it for Christ sake!" Gemetz yelled, moving quickly to get between them.

"Wait," Talbot said, letting go of Tiernan's coat. "I . . . I'm really sorry, Joe. Jesus, I'm getting crazy," he said, smoothing the coat down. "Wait, Joe, hear me out. We gotta put this year together. They've turned us into a bunch of wimps!"

"Just once, I wish we could get together without rapping about our wives," Gemetz said, walking with his head down and his hands jammed into his coat.

"It's Christmas; it's tearing us all to pieces," Tiernan said.

"Man, it isn't just Christmas," Talbot said, slamming his fist into his palm. "I feel like I've been walking around in a swamp for a year."

"Look, maybe you're right," Tiernan said, putting his arm around Talbot as they continued down the trail. "Maybe we *can* turn it around this year. I mean, like you said, really work at it. But, Len, it ain't as easy as just making a lot of goddam New Year's resolutions. You don't just talk something like this out of your system with a few brave words. Hey, Len, I'm still in love with her. I can't . . . There ain't no way I'm gonna wake up on New Year's Day and look in the mirror and tell myself I no longer give a shit. Right?"

"That's not the point, man," Talbot said. "Sure, and I guess I'm still in love with Susan. And way down deep Richie is still in love with Linda."

"In a pig's ass," Gemetz said.

"So what's the point then?" Tiernan asked.

"Okay, want me to boil it down to one simple truth?" Talbot said, turning on them again, putting his hands up to halt them.

"Wait a minute. I don't think I can take any more of these truths," Tiernan said, smiling and putting his hands up pretending to defend himself.

"The hard simple truth is . . . they don't *want* us anymore," Talbot said quietly and slowly. "We've got to forget everything else we know about them but keep that."

"Yeah, I guess that boils it down all right," Tiernan said, feeling a sudden hollowness growing in him.

"Joe, the truth is also what you just said about waking up on New Year's and looking in the mirror—seeing that love, thinking about that love. That's the swamp, man! And all I'm saying is we gotta get on our horses and ride like hell for open country."

"How, goddam it?" Tiernan asked.

"The same way they did back in the old cavalry days. How do you suppose those men left home for years at a time? You think they took it all into battle with them? No, they kissed 'em good-bye and tucked that part of their lives into a shirt pocket like an old love letter. And that, by god, is what we are going to do—put it away into a small corner and get on with the bigger part of our lives. Joe, we are men! And our wives and our lost marriages are only a small part of our world. *Our* world is still out there. The world between destinations—that's the world man owns."

"The world that—what?" Gemetz asked, looking at Tiernan.

"All right, let me tell you my theory," Talbot said, pausing at the entrance to the primate house. "I asked myself, What is the real fundamental difference between men and women? I mean the bedrock essential difference planted there by nature. And I threw out everything I ever thought I knew or heard or read or whatever. And I tried to come to it by associations. You know, the images that naturally collected around each one when I thought of man and woman."

"Hey, ain't this the guy who was knocking Freud the other night at Larsky's?" Gemetz asked.

"You want to hear this or not?" Talbot asked.

"I'm fascinated, but let's finish it inside," Gemetz said, pushing him toward the front door of the primate house. "I wanna make sure the kids haven't crawled in the cages with the gorillas by now."

Inside the great circular room of the primate house there were about thirty or so people, mostly parents with children, milling past the illuminated cages along the sides. The high ceiling was domed and in front of the bars of each cage there was thick glass to further protect the apes. The air inside the house was warm and humid and in addition to the mingled smells of disinfectant and excrement there was the almost overpowering funkiness given off by apes in captivity.

"Whew!" Gemetz said. "Smells like King Kong's armpit in here."

"There they are," Talbot said, pointing to the four children who were clustered at the far end of the room looking at a family of gorillas, including two young ones jumping about the cage.

The children were so engrossed that they did not notice their fathers coming up behind them. Talbot put his finger to his lips for Gemetz and Tiernan to be quiet and then he crept up behind the children and dangled his arms over them, snorting and making apelike grunts.

"It's Daddy!" Teddy exclaimed.

"No, it's King Kong!" Talbot said, putting his arms around Teddy and Jonathan and pulling them up against his chest. "And I'm going to carry you off to my tree for running away."

Then Talbot let out a huge growl and loped halfway across the great room with the squealing children tucked under each arm. Just as he got to the center of the room, a real ape in another part of the primate house let out a large noise that sounded like *kreeeeeeeega!*

Talbot stopped in surprise and looked all around, making grunting noises and then he let out his own startlingly loud *kreeeeeeeega!*

"Did he say, 'Kreeeegah'?" Gemetz asked, affecting an English accent.

"Yes, of course," Tiernan said, eyeing Lynn. "And in gorilla talk it means 'Let's catch some little children!'" he said, sweeping the open-mouthed girl up in his arms and loping toward Talbot in the center of the room.

"Kreeeeeeeega! Kreeeeeeeega!" Tiernan shouted.

"Kreeeeeeeega!" Talbot answered.

While the two fathers aped around in the middle of the room, drawing laughter from the other visitors, Gemetz stood alone with Mark at the railing of the gorilla cage. The boy looked at him anxiously for a moment and then turned and watched the young gorillas playing in the cage.

"Mark, listen, I just wanna say something to you for a minute and then we'll forget it for the rest of the day, okay?" he said, squatting down next to the boy and reaching over and turning Mark's face to his.

"Okay," Mark murmured.

"I, uh, I'm really sorry about what happened in the cable car. It's really just something that's between Mommy and me and I'm sorry I upset you and Jon. Mommy and me will talk about it in a nice way. Mark, I know this whole thing has confused both you and Jon, but there's one thing you never have to be confused about: I love you very much. Okay?"

"Yeah," the boy said, looking a little embarrassed.

"Now, you know what?"

"What?"

"We're going to go find that camel and see if he'll give us a ride. Okay?"

"Yeah, but, Dad . . ."

"Yeah?" Gemetz asked, beginning to cringe because he was certain Mark was going to start it again about the food thing.

"Could you be a gorilla?"

"Could I be a gorilla?" Gemetz asked. Then he smiled and began snorting and walking around the boy at a squat. Then as Mark let out a cry of frightened joy, Gemetz swept his son onto his shoulder and ran toward the center of the room.

"Kreeeeeeeega!" he yelled in true primate happiness.

Later, as they were all standing in front of the orangutan cage—with the children making faces at the big-bellied male sitting in a suspended tire swing—the fathers resumed their discussion.

"So, what's the difference between men and women?" Gemetz asked, nudging Talbot.

*"Vive la différence!"* Tiernan exclaimed.

"Well, it's a theory I got from that association thing, right? I mean it's just one way of looking at it for our purposes."

"For *my* purposes, I know the difference," Gemetz said.

"Come on, let him talk, Richie," Tiernan said.

"Okay, all the associations that come to mind for women—and I ain't going into all of them—had to do with home or, ah, call it destination. But for men they seemed to have to do with traveling or moving. Like, man is a traveler, woman is a destination. Sperm and egg—man is equipped to journey, woman to stay and build."

"You're forgetting one thing," Tiernan said.

"What's that?"

"We aren't out journeying, we were *kicked* out."

"That is exactly what's wrong with modern man—he's been

hanging around the house for so long he's *had* to be kicked out. I think one of the reasons women are so much up in arms these days is not because they want to get into man's world, it's because underneath it all they're resenting man taking over their turf."

"Okay, answer my question," Gemetz said. "If woman is destination or home, whose destination are we talking about? Man's, right? Which means man really just wants to go home."

"You know, they had this really good program on the other night about the sexes," Tiernan said. "And it showed that at one point in embryonic development all fetuses have a kind of opening like a vagina. Like at one time we were all females. Then as sex gets determined nature plants a penis on top of the vagina and you got a man."

"You guys are hopeless," Talbot said, getting a little impatient. "Look, I don't give a crap how nature did it. All I'm saying is that nature made man to travel. And she gave him the equipment to make it to a new destination if we just use it, dig?"

"Pack up your penis in your old kit bag, and smile, smile, smile!" Gemetz sang and started doing a vaudeville shuffle toward the next gorilla cage.

As they moved slowly around the succession of cages, Talbot's mood grew gloomier and gloomier. For a few minutes as the others moved ahead toward the exit, he stood exchanging stares with a big male gorilla that was sitting near the front of his cage.

The massively armed gray beast seemed to be sunk into such boredom and demoralization that Talbot felt like taking a sledgehammer and breaking him out. This is what was happening to modern man, he thought. Gradually being closed in until one day he, too, would be trapped in a single neon-lighted room staring out in stupefication and breathing his own stink.

He waved a commiseration at the staring brute and moved on, passing a female gorilla playing around her cage with two young ones. Of course, he thought.

When he stepped outside into the refreshing cold air and sunlight, he saw Tiernan and Gemetz talking down at the bottom of the steps. Meanwhile, the four children were slipping away down the trail unnoticed by the two fathers.

"Don't look now, but the elves are disappearing again!" he shouted.

"Oh, no!" Tiernan exclaimed and started running after them.

Since they had not gotten very far, Gemetz let Tiernan do the running while he waited for Talbot. In a few minutes Tiernan caught up with the children and continued running with them, waving the other two on toward lion country.

"To hell with it," Talbot said. "I ain't running this time. We'll catch up with them. Joe can have all the fun."

"Hey, Joe just had a great idea while we were waiting for you," Gemetz said as they walked briskly after the others.

"Yeah, what's that?"

"Fits in with what you were saying—a way of doing something different this year. Something positive instead of shitting about our wives for a change."

"What, for Christ sake?"

"A party. You know, for New Year's Eve."

Talbot stopped and looked at him for a moment. His depression seemed to have been suddenly snatched off of him. A New Year's Eve party. It was brilliant! Goddam Joe hadn't had an inkling of the idea he was propounding, and a few minutes later he puts it into reality. An image of the big gray gorilla climbing out of his cage flashed into Talbot's mind.

"No, we can't have a party," he said, starting to walk on again.

"Well, it was just an idea," Gemetz said.

"We're gonna have a goddam orgy!" Talbot shouted and pounded Gemetz on the head and started running toward Tiernan and the kids.

For the next hour as they walked along the trail, stopping at the various exhibits, Talbot talked of nothing else, drawing the others into it, making detailed plans. Tiernan was a little skeptical about it being an actual orgy but he was relieved at the light-hearted change that had come over Talbot. They had agreed that it should be at Gemetz's because, although he only had a studio, the room was immense and just right for a party gathering.

"God, you know what would really be decadent?" Talbot asked. "I heard about these European parties where all the women come in paper dresses and the men squirted them off with seltzer bottles."

"Great, I'll bring the seltzer bottles!" Tiernan said. "Mary has two of them I could borrow."

"Oh, wait, you won't believe this," Gemetz said, rubbing his hands. "Verna was telling me about this wild party these nurses had last year somewhere in Queens and a bunch of them came in paper surgical gowns so they could be ripped off. Only, *we* could squirt them off."

"Shit, that's great!" Talbot said. "Only, do you think Verna would come?"

"Will *Verna* come? Hell, I'll get her to bring all the nurses, too. Jesus, we really actually might have an orgy. Joe, there's this one named Carol you gotta meet," Gemetz said, holding his hands out on huge imaginary breasts.

Tiernan smiled but he was really thinking about what Verna would look like cavorting around in an orgy. Then he felt a pang of fear when he imagined *himself* at such a party.

Riding back on the subway later that afternoon, Talbot subsided into himself and was looking out the window as the train swept past the rows of crumbling buildings. God, the whole world seems to be in ruins out there, he thought. Chaos had invaded the American civilization like some medieval plague—destroying the cities, marriages, families, individuals—returning it to barbarism.

He thought again of his paper on Lorenzo de' Medici that was to appear in the *American History Journal* shortly after Easter. It was a mistake, he now thought—too conservative. Tiernan had read it and called him a closet fascist. The board of faculty at Brooklyn College would read it and probably deny him his associate professorship.

Why had he submitted it? "Lorenzo, a Tyrant for Our Time," he had entitled it. He had compared Lorenzo's rule of fifteenth-century Florence to a kind of highbrow Mayor Daley. His thesis had been that there could be no real revival of America's crumbling cities until they drew into themselves and submitted to a benign but autocratic rule by men of wealth and culture—men like Lorenzo of the Renaissance.

But he now saw his publication of the paper as almost suicidal, considering the liberal cast at Brooklyn College. Perhaps he *was* seeking self-destruction—showing up many times for his classes unprepared and badly hung over. His life since the breakup had been like some kind of kamikaze dive.

Fuck it, he thought. Everything was falling around him anyway, better to go down in defiance.

"Christ, every time I look out at the Bronx I think of that Stalingrad movie," Tiernan said, interrupting Talbot's thought.

"Hey, you just named the party!" Talbot said, snapping his fingers. "We'll call it the Stalingrad Breakout Party! Just like the Russians, man. We're coming out of our cellars and god help the Nazis!"

"Can I go to Stalingard's party, Daddy?" Teddy asked.

# CHAPTER
# FIVE

Tiernan and Gemetz were sitting on the floor of Gemetz's bare studio apartment sipping cans of Budweiser, having spent most of the afternoon cleaning the place for the Stalingrad Breakout Party that night. Talbot had been in earlier helping move most of Gemetz's dilapidated furniture temporarily into Marion and Phyllis's apartment next door. Then he had left with the two young black models to pick up the caviar, vodka and other supplies before the stores closed.

The shutters on the two bay windows at the front of the big studio were open for a change and the pale light coming in was glowing softly on the newly waxed floor. Slumped against the cheap Formica bar, Gemetz let out a long stream of cigarette smoke and looked tiredly around at the unfamiliar cleanliness of the place.

"Ain't such a bad dump," he said.

"It'd be a good dump if you took care of it," Tiernan said, sitting against a wall and looking up at the elegant molding bordering the fifteen-foot-high ceiling.

"I forgot how big it was without the furniture," Gemetz said.

"Furniture?" Tiernan said, shaking his head. "Where'd you get all that old shit?"

"Used place on Fourth Avenue."

"I've been to those stores. Most of the stuff looks like it was thrown out of windows in Bed-Stuy."

"Hey, I wouldn't talk, man," Gemetz said, remembering Tiernan's living-room furnishings, which consisted of a new couch and a card table.

Tiernan smiled and took another drink of beer. It was peaceful sitting there in the fading light of day letting his muscles relax after the sweaty cleaning effort. For some reason the anxiousness he had been feeling about the party had disappeared and for a moment he was just enjoying the transformation they had wrought in Gemetz's apartment.

"Richie, when're you going to finish scraping that mirror?" he asked, gesturing with his can of beer toward the large baroque framed mirror over the fireplace.

The previous tenants had covered over the huge mirror when they had painted everything in the apartment in off-white. Gemetz had made a halfhearted effort to scrape the mirror when he had moved in, but after making a dozen or so inch-wide slashes through the paint he had given up, telling himself he would finish it when he was less depressed. That had been months ago and now the same reedlike slashes were reflecting the meager light in the room.

"Wanna see if we can finish it before the party?" Tiernan asked.

Gemetz seemed to be off in another world, just sitting there looking at the mirror and thoughtfully sipping his beer.

"No," he said finally. "I may paint it again."

"Well, that would be better than just seeing pieces of yourself in it. But, man, that's a great mirror. It would create a whole new space in here."

"Maybe I don't want to see *me* in that space," Gemetz said and downed the rest of his beer.

"It's getting dark in here," Tiernan said, turning to the windows. "I hope they get back with the candles soon."

"What, are *you* gonna start about the electricity hookup now?" Gemetz asked, rising and going around the bar to the tiny kitchen area to get another beer.

"Hey, Richie, I know where you're at," Tiernan said sympathetically. "Okay?"

"Want one?" Gemetz asked, holding up a can of beer.

"Yeah, this is one time I want to be polluted *before* the party."

"Floor's dry now. I think I'll let Brombly out of the bathroom," Gemetz said, walking over and handing Tiernan a can of beer.

"Ha! Old Brombly—"

"Can't have an orgy without a bunny, right?" Gemetz said as he walked toward the long hallway.

"Hey, Richie?"

"Yeah," Gemetz asked, turning.

Tiernan was staring at his can of beer, his face clenched in consternation, his thumbs pressing dents into the sides of the cold can. "You think it's going to get . . . ? I mean uh, you know . . . pretty wild?"

"Who knows?" Gemetz said, continuing down the hall. "I'll be surprised if we really bring off an orgy. I figure we'll just get drunk and have a good time."

Tiernan sat for a moment in the dimming light and tried to imagine the room full of naked people cavorting around and doing whatever the hell people did at orgies. It just didn't seem logistically possible. Aside from the high loft-bed in one corner of the stripped room everything had a starkness to it. He heard Gemetz scolding Brombly for shitting in the bathroom.

"Richie?"

"Wait a minute, I'm up to my knees in rabbit pellets!"

"I don't think I can fuck with a lot of—"

"What?" Gemetz called from the bathroom.

"—people around."

"What?"

"Nothing."

When Talbot returned to Gemetz's place shortly after 7 P.M., he found his two friends sitting in the dark slightly bombed on beer. Marion and Phyllis came in a few minutes later after putting their things away. It had been a funny afternoon driving around in the car with them picking up supplies for the party. Both had been smoking marijuana, giggling and sharing their joints with him. At one point they had staggered into an army surplus store in lower Manhattan where the two women had bought themselves some well-worn and oversized combat boots to wear to what they kept calling the Stalingrad Breakout Prom.

For the next half hour they lighted the big holiday candles around Gemetz's apartment and put away the caviar and drinks and other party snacks. Then Talbot and Tiernan left to get cleaned up for the *grande débauche* ahead.

"Hey, bring your sword!" Gemetz called down the stairs after Talbot. "I wanna show it to Verna."

"Yeah, bring your sword, Lennie," Marion hooted and tickled Phyllis in the ribs.

Standing under the shower in the communal bathroom of his rooming house, Talbot wished he had brought along one of the candles from Gemetz's place, because the light bulb in the dank little room had blown out. There was just the flickering glow on the peeling walls from his Ronson lighter, which he had left burning on the toilet seat. There was also the lingering stench of a bowel movement left recently by one of the elderly tenants.

He envied the better living conditions Tiernan and Gemetz had with their apartments, but felt good about spending less than half what they did for rent. His life was Spartan, but that was his style now. Everything lean and strong, he thought, taking pride in the sinewy strength in his arms and chest as he lathered the soap on. He was toughening his body and his bank account was growing and he was moving spiritually toward the open country again. The country he had known before Susan.

The party was an important occasion for him, he thought. And for Tiernan and Gemetz as well. It was an assertion, a first skirmish against the miasma of defeat and loneliness their wives had cast them into. He would lead them and they would take their women like cavalry, lustily and without sentiment, and then they would ride on. Yes, the sword was a good idea, he thought. He would bring it and it would be a symbol of their independence.

On his way to the party that night, Talbot made a detour and walked down Garfield Street, drawn for some reason he could not explain to parade with his sword past Susan's apartment. She would probably be tucking Teddy into bed now and she would feel his ghost passing into a year that would hide him from her.

Walking up the narrow path shoveled through the sidewalk snow, he moved carefully to avoid the great drifts that nearly covered the cars along the curb. The streetlights gave everything a yellow hue, and light crystals of snow blown off the brownstones were swirling around in the air. And as he passed he saluted her lighted front window with his sword, tasting the cold steel as he kissed the blade.

An hour later Talbot was laughing at Gemetz, who had found an enormous overcoat, which he was wearing backwards with the sword belt tied around it. With a thick Russian accent he had been brandishing Talbot's sword and demanding to see everyone's papers. Then he had run off to find Marion's big fur hat in the next apartment.

Even Tiernan seemed to be relaxing at last, and Talbot had to chuckle to himself as he watched him being cornered by Fredricka over in front of the fireplace. He'd invited the Curtises over Tiernan's objections, because Alan had cornered him at Larsky's one night and asked about the party.

"So how does that sound to you?" Fredricka asked, her tiny coal-chip eyes glittering in the candlelight.

"I'm thinking about Alan," Tiernan said, leaning against Gemetz's mantelpiece and giving a little wave to one of the nurses who padded past them in her bare feet and wore a yellow paper surgical gown.

"I'm not asking you to go to bed with Alan," the tall bony woman said, trying to be heard over the disco music. "Although I'm sure he wouldn't mind."

"Huh, what?" he said, pretending to be surprised.

"Everybody knows about Alan," she said. "Why do you think I bop around with other men?"

"Why do you stay with him?"

"Oh, I'm very comfortable with dear old Alan. Besides, I've always needed plenty of variety, so it makes it sort of ideal."

"Ah, finally an ideal marriage," Tiernan said and began searching through flickering candlelight again for Verna. They had had a very friendly moment together an hour before when she had arrived with the three other nurses and had asked him to Scotchtape a tear on the rear of her surgical gown.

"Well?" Fredricka asked, kicking his shoe lightly with hers.

"You mean just sort of come over some afternoon?"

"Or evening. Or morning," she said. "Why, you like afternoons?"

"No, uh, I mean . . ." he stammered, backing up and

feeling a slight anger percolating up through his mild drunkenness.

"When?" she asked, moving after him. "Joe, I told you I've been celibate for six goddam weeks. Joe, I'll be *fantastic!*"

"I'll call you . . . ah, pretty soon," he said.

"Call me when, Joe?" she said, moving into him, stroking her long bony hand over his red sweater front.

"Hey, uh, I . . ." he said, shaking his head to clear the gathering hostility at being cornered. "Just, uh, back up. *Back up!*" he finally shouted, causing her to flinch and nearly spill her drink.

"I'm sorry. I've gotta find somebody," he said, moving away toward the Formica bar.

"Joe, wait!" she said, and then shrugged as he turned away.

Phyllis and Marion were standing at the bar wearing long white thermal underwear and combat boots. Phyllis was swinging her hips to the loud Bee Gees recording on the portable record player and eating spoonfuls of caviar from the tin on the bar.

"Hi, sugar. Try some of this," she said, feeding Tiernan a spoonful of the glistening black delicacy.

"Ugh!" Marion said, making a face as he licked some of the tiny eggs from his lips.

"Russian soul food," he said, reaching for one of the half-dozen vodka bottles sitting atop the bar.

"Remind me to stay out of Russia," she said.

"My darlink, tonight ve only breaking oudt of Stalingradt!" he said, raising his glass and then drinking down about a third of it.

The party was nearly two hours old and most of the thirty or so people who had come were sitting around on pillows and sofa cushions near the walls or standing in little groups near the windows and under the high loft-bed supports. Talbot was standing near the window talking to Frieda and Verna.

"Where's Richie?" Tiernan asked.

"You mean the mad Russian?" Phyllis asked. "Last time I saw that nut he was rooting around in our little garden looking for dry leaves."

Tiernan laughed, remembering the famous garden in the

nextdoor apartment. The girls had a big walk-in closet that they had filled a foot deep with dirt and planted with marijuana, keeping it going with plant lights.

"Okay, white boy, let's see what kinda ass you got," Phyllis said, pulling him out to the middle of the floor as a new tune started on the Bee Gees album.

"All right!" he shouted, shaking his hips in an exaggerated hustle.

"That ain't no kinda boodie, man," she said, moving her body suggestively at him. "You call that boodie a boodie?"

"I ain't got no boodie," Tiernan sang and tried harder to shake his ass.

Just then Gemetz came into the room with the overcoat on backwards and the sword hanging so low over his hips it was dragging the floor. He was merrily puffing on a big marijuana joint and he had Marion's big silver-tipped fur hat on his head.

"Tovarich!" he exclaimed, taking Tiernan's drink from his hand and drinking it all down in one gulp. Then he threw the glass across the room into the fireplace.

"Comrades, enough of this corrupt capitalist danzing!" he continued. "Is hustling is being shot! Ve danzing old-time Russian style!"

With his blazing marijuana cigar clenched in his teeth, he latched onto Tiernan's and Phyllis's shoulders and started kicking his legs straight out in a wild kazatsky. But after a few kicks he managed to pull Phyllis down on top of him and had to finish his dance lying flat on his back and aiming his kicks at the ceiling. Phyllis, lying beside him, kept right in step until one of her combat boots flew off.

"Unfortunately, comrades, that's the *old* old style," Tiernan said, standing over them, "and your next dance vill be for de firing sqvadt!"

"Hey, Richie!" Talbot called. "Try not to bend the goddam sword."

"Who are all these people?" Frieda asked Talbot as more young couples got up from the floor and began dancing around Gemetz and Phyllis, who were now writhing around on their backs doing a sort of horizontal hustle. Two of the young men drew some applause when they began doing the Russian kazatsky in time to the hustle music.

"Oh, god, don't ask," Verna said, smiling at Tiernan as he joined them at the window.

"I have never seen most of them," Frieda said.

"Well, we figure that about half are our friends," Talbot said. "And the rest are Russian laundromat refugees."

"Russian what?" she asked, looking incredulous.

"Yeah, see, good old Richie posted a notice at this laundromat where he does his clothes. What did it say? Oh, yeah. 'Free New Year's Eve Orgy for the sons and daughters of mother Russia. Relive the freeing of Stalingrad!'"

"You are kidding?" Frieda asked.

"No! I thought Joe was going to have a fit," Verna said.

"Well, good old Richie didn't tell us anything about his little joke until all these strange people began showing up in Russian peasant blouses," Tiernan said. "See that little group of guys under the loft-bed? I haven't heard 'em speak English since they came in. Probably off a freighter or something."

"Well, I'm not orgying with any of *them*," Verna said, creeping up close to Tiernan.

"Ha, that is just a joke about the orgy. Yes, Lennie?" Frieda asked.

He looked at Frieda and smiled. She looked very attractive in her long-sleeved white silk blouse. Her hair was brushed back smoothly along the temples and there was a soft glow to her skin. They had not slept together again since the night of the fire, nor had she mentioned it or acted in any way proprietary toward him at Larsky's since then.

"What's the matter, Frieda, afraid of catching a cold?" he chided her. He knew that she would not stay around when—and if—the party started getting orgiastic.

"Lennie, why do you need sex to bring in your New Year?" she asked.

"It's going to be an important New Year, a liberating year," he said, the humor going out of his voice for the first time that evening.

"So why do you want to degrade it with cheap—with sex that has no meaning? You will begin the year by insulting your sensitivity? How will you *feel*? Verna, you can't be serious."

"This is the year we put the sword to *feelings*," he said, looking out at the park through the window. He squeezed powerfully on his cocktail glass daring it to shatter.

"I'll try anything once," Verna said, smiling sheepishly at Tiernan.

Frieda looked around the room. Everyone seemed to be having a warm good-natured time. There was a calm friendly atmosphere—at least among those sitting quietly talking on the cushions around the floor. No, it was impossible that these lovely civilized human beings would suddenly throw off their clothes and leap into a sexual bonfire, she thought.

"At least don't have your orgy until after midnight," she said, smiling at Talbot. "I want to be around to wish you a happy New Year."

"It's a deal, my fearful fräulein," he said, bending down and kissing her cheek.

"I remember when I was a little girl," she said, "Papa would let us wait up until after our big hall clock struck the New Year. And then we—there were six of us children—we would place our wishes on the windowsill."

"On the windowsill?" Tiernan asked.

*"Ja,* it was a little family tradition that my grandmother had invented. We would each come to the window one at a time and kneel down and make a little prayer for what we wanted in the coming year. And then Papa would leave the window open just an inch at the bottom so God could come and slip them out during the night."

"Oh, that's beautiful, Frieda," Verna said.

*"Ja,* and the next morning we would know if our wish was going to come true."

"The next morning?" Tiernan asked.

"Oh, *ja,* there would be a sign. In the morning we would all gather around and then Papa would pull the big curtain back and the first thing we each saw outside would be a symbol of what God had to say about our wishes."

"What if it was snowing?" Talbot asked.

"That was not always bad. You see, Papa was the one who interpreted what each of us saw. And Papa was a generous soul."

Just then Talbot heard a commotion in the hall as new guests came into the party. First there was Rico and then Juliet's roommate, Annie, and then Juliet, who was lugging a child's sled under her arm.

"Happy New Year's everybody!" Juliet called out, taking off her stocking cap.

"Juliet! Where's Juliet?" Gemetz yelled, rising up from behind the bar, where he had been sitting on the floor drinking from a vodka bottle and smooching playfully with Marion and Phyllis. His fur hat was cocked sideways on his head and he was waving his vodka bottle.

"Hi, ya, Richie!" Juliet said, resting the sled against her side as she took off her shawl. "We just dropped by for a minute to wish you guys a happy New Year's."

"A sled?" Gemetz exclaimed, tottering toward her. "I invite you to an orgy and you come with a goddam sled? Now I've seen everything."

"Yeah, well, I don't see no orgy goin' on," she replied and then started laughing as she noticed his sword clanking along after him.

"What? You don't call this an orgy?" he said, pointing to the dozen or so couples dancing now.

"It looks like Polish night. Oy, it's hot in here," she said, taking off her coat. Under it she was wearing a black turtleneck sweater and a tight-fitting pair of jeans.

"You're right—this ain't no orgy," he said, nodding. "But we were waiting for you. Here, gimme your coat. And your sweater, and your—"

"Give me a break," she said, waving to Talbot, who was coming toward them through the dancers.

"Better than that, have a drink," he said, handing her the bottle of vodka and taking her coat.

"Hey, I'm not drinking out of a bottle, Richie!" she called after him as he clanked off with his sword toward the closet down the hall.

"Here, let me," Talbot said, taking the bottle from her and guiding her gently behind the bar.

Rico had taken his coat off and was digging a can of beer out of the ice in the sink. He resented the way Talbot had moved in on Juliet but he respected the muscles that were rippling under Talbot's light wool sweater too much to make anything of it. The bruises that were still on Talbot's face gave him an even more forbidding appearance.

"Hey, let's dance, Jule," Rico said, moving to her side. "Then we'll split for the park."

"No, Rico, you're with Annie tonight," she said. "Now how about gettin' off my case!"

"Rico, how's it going?" Talbot asked, scooping a handful of

ice from the sink for Juliet's drink. "The cops still bugging you guys about the store fire?"

"Na, that weirdo who was selling the trees admitted that he accidentally did it trying to keep warm."

"Oh?" Talbot asked, handing Juliet her drink.

"Except it wasn't no accident," Rico said. "How come he didn't have no fires going all the other nights, right? It was an insurance job."

Talbot nodded.

"Hey, come on, Jule, one dance," Rico said, grabbing Juliet's arm.

"I said no, Rico, and I mean it," she said, pulling away.

"Well, I'm splitting," he said, moving away.

"Go find Annie," she said.

"She ain't my type."

"Well, I ain't either."

"Hey, Rico, stick around," Talbot said, smiling. "We got a bunch of nurses you might like, and they're all wearing paper dresses."

"No shit? Made outa paper?"

"Yep, and after midnight we're going to squirt them off with these seltzer bottles," he said, indicating two seltzer bottles near the end of the bar.

"Oh, yeah?" Juliet said, looking at two of the nurses dancing wildly with two of the laundromat refugees. "Well, that's when I squirt right outa here."

"Hey, no shit?" Rico said, picking up one of the bottles. "Man, this is gonna be a *class* party!"

"Ha! Caught you," Gemetz said, slipping in beside Juliet and putting his arm around her. "Soon as my back is turned I catch you fooling around with Lennie."

"Richie, stop it, I'm spilling my drink," she said, pulling his arm away. "Hey, you look great—a cossack or something, right? Is that a real sword?"

"Oho! Let me show you this sword, my little darlink!" he said, pulling the long sharp blade from its scabbard.

Just then a window was flung up and a cold blast of air swept across the steamy room, causing a chorus of complaints from the dancers.

"Len! Richie!" Frieda cried out as she pushed her way through the dancers toward them. "Please come! Joey is going to be hurt. Please stop him."

"Where?" Gemetz exclaimed, placing the sword on the bar. Talbot was already pushing toward the windows with Frieda following close behind him.

"He got mad because one of those Russian fellows made a pass at Verna," Frieda said. "Then Joey challenged him to a Russian drinking duel."

"Drinking duel?" Talbot asked. "What's Joey know about a Russian drinking duel?"

"I don't know. Even the Russian didn't know. Joey said he read it in *War and Peace*. He's going to stand outside on the window ledge without holding on and finish a whole glass of vodka. Len, he's going to fall down and break his neck!"

When they got to the window, Tiernan was already outside and yelling at Verna to let go of his leg. There was a small crowd around her, including the three supposed "freighter" Russians, who were singing something in Russian and clapping.

"Stop him!" Verna pleaded as she saw Talbot and Gemetz rush up.

"Goddam it, let go, Verna!" Tiernan yelled from outside as he swayed in the freezing air and looked down at the row of covered garbage cans two floors below.

"Joe, if Verna lets go, will you come in?" Talbot asked, leaning his head out the window.

"No, this is a question of *honor!*" Joe declared drunkenly, flourishing his drink and nearly falling off. "When I finish my drink I will come in. Len, my goddam honor is at stake! The honor of the whole Russian nobility is at stake!"

"The Russian nobility?" Joey, what the hell are you doing out there?"

"Shhhh," Tiernan said, leaning down and giggling. "I can outdrink any Russian sonofabitch. Len, he's gonna fall on his ass. The C.I.A. will probably give me a medal."

"Are you kidding?" Talbot exclaimed. "*These* guys probably are C.I.A."

"That's even better!" Tiernan shouted and stood up laughing his head off.

"Better let him do it," Talbot said, coming back in. "If he stays out there too long I know he's going to fall off."

"Len, it's two stories down," Verna said.

"He'll be okay," Talbot said, pulling her back and praying he was right.

"Staleeeeeeengraaaaaaad!" Tiernan howled and then put his head back and drained off the entire glass of vodka. Then he flipped his glass over his shoulder and lowered himself back into the room.

As he came in flushed with victory, everyone went wild and cheered and clapped him on the back. Then Tiernan's opponent in the duel stepped forward and shook his hand. And after a gallant bow to Verna the young man climbed out onto the window ledge. His two comrades held his legs as he rose to a standing position and called for a drink. Tiernan took a nearly full glass of vodka from one of the nurses and handed it out to him.

"Staaaleeeeen—" the young Russian shouted but was interrupted when Verna stepped closer and indignantly declared that it was not a fair duel because his comrades were still holding his legs.

Whereupon they let go. Whereupon the young Russian fell off the window ledge because he had not been prepared for their sudden release. He never uttered a sound but they heard him crash onto the garbage-can lids below.

"Jesus Christ!" Gemetz exclaimed.

"Misha?" one of the comrades called down, looking out the window.

Then they all rushed to the window and saw the young Russian lying in the soft snow where he had landed after bouncing off the covered garbage cans. He was still clutching the unbroken vodka glass in his hand. Then, just as they were about to rush downstairs, they saw him sit up and shake his head. After a moment he looked at the glass in his hand, and then he looked up at the window.

"Staleeeeengraaaaadt!" he shouted and got to his feet.

He was answered by a cheer from the window.

"Tovarich!" Tiernan yelled down to him.

"Tovarich!" the young Russian yelled back and saluted with the glass. Then he started walking with a slight limp toward the front door.

"Buzz him back in," Tiernan said.

When the young Russian came back there was more celebrating and the party got louder and drunker.

At about eleven-thirty, when the party seemed to be catching its breath, Frieda put on some mellower music and asked Talbot to dance with her. Most of the couples were sprawled

about on the pillows. Fredricka and Misha were heading down
the hall toward the bathroom. Alan was ensconced like a pasha
on some pillows under the loft-bed supports with Phyllis lying
with her head in his lap. Marion had become sick and gone
back to her apartment. Rico and one of the nurses had been
dancing steadily, with and without music, for nearly an hour.

"Having a good time?" Talbot asked.

"*Ja*, a good time," she sighed.

"Still going to leave after midnight?"

"If it gets too wild," she said. "I'm too old for your
orgies."

"Don't believe it," he said, enjoying the softness of her
body against him. "You dance really nice."

"I just follow the music. It requires no effort."

"Oho, look at Joey and Verna," Talbot whispered.

Verna had both her arms around Tiernan's neck and their
bodies seemed to be welded together as they danced slow
and sensuously to the music.

"Richie will be jealous," she said.

"Not tonight. He's only got eyes for Juliet tonight."

"Ah, then you will be jealous," she said.

"What, me and Juliet?" he asked, looking at her.

"I have seen you look at her."

"Maybe you are the one who's getting jealous," he said,
squeezing her side playfully.

"Maybe—just a little," she said, resting her head softly
against his chest.

Tiernan was becoming very aroused as Verna held her
thigh against his erection. She was sighing her breath
against his neck. He loved the soft curve of her narrow
waist and had his arm all the way around her so that his
hand was caressing down inside her hip toward her pubic
mound. She moved her body slowly around so that he
would touch it and bit him lightly on the neck.

"Verna, Verna," he moaned quietly.

"Ummmm," she sighed and then pulled away from him.
"We better cool down or we'll never make it to orgy time.
How about a drink?" They walked over to the bar arm in
arm.

Juliet was sitting on top of the bar where Gemetz had
hoisted her. He had finally taken his fur hat off and was

leaning on the bar looking at her, his sweaty blond hair matted against his head.

"Hey, I haven't seen Brombly all night," she said, shifting her hips a little to get farther from the point of the sword lying across the bar.

"He's hiding out. I saw him a while ago in the closet."

"I don't blame him," she said, frowning a bit as she watched Talbot dancing with Frieda. "This definitely isn't any place for a nice rabbit like Brombly."

"You still going over to the park tonight?" he asked.

"I may have to go alone. I think Rico has finally found true love over there. And Annie is trying to teach English to those Russian guys."

"It isn't such a bad party," Gemetz said softly. "Why don't you stay?"

"We'll see," she said, reaching over and pushing some of the matted hair off his brow.

"Let's dance," he said, waving to Tiernan and Verna as they came over. Gemetz was relieved to have Verna moving out of his life and into Tiernan's.

"Hey, why won't you go out with me anymore?" he asked as Juliet hopped down from the bar to dance with him. "I thought we had a lot of fun."

"I didn't say I wouldn't go out with you," she said, slipping into his arms on the dance floor.

"Look, I got the picture. How many times does a guy have to get turned down?"

"You were just coming on a little strong, you know. I'm really not into getting heavy with nobody right now."

"Juliet, I like you. Is that okay? I mean that doesn't have to mean heavy, right?"

"No . . . and I kinda like you, too, Richie. I don't know anybody nuttier."

"So?"

"So, give me a call next week and maybe we'll talk about it."

"Next week," he agreed, smiling, and pulled her closer as they danced.

"Richie, what did you do, lose the sword already?" Talbot said, passing them on his way to get another drink.

"It's on the bar," Gemetz said.

"Here it is," Tiernan said, picking up the sword from the bar.

"Ah, yes, the famous sword," Tiernan said, slipping into a W. C. Fields voice. "Many a man has lost his head over this lovely blade," he said, swinging it about.

"So, how'd you guys come by the sword?" Verna asked.

"Len's father sent it as a bed warmer."

"A what?" she asked, ducking back as Tiernan continued to swish it around in the air.

"His father's a general, and this, my dear, is an actual cavalry sword. Goes back to the Civil War days. Right, Len?"

"A lieutenant colonel—and it's been in campaigns from the Civil War, the Indian wars and even the First World War," Talbot said.

"This innocent-looking piece of metal has taken actual lives," Tiernan said, looking at it for a moment and holding it up to her.

"Ugh!" she said, pushing it away.

"Here, let me have it," Talbot said. "I'll show her how it's handled."

"No, thanks," she said, walking away as the music on the record player ended and Gemetz came back with Juliet. "You guys have fun with your toy."

"Ah, yes, women and children always have been frightened by the instruments of war," Talbot said, striking a fencing stance and pointing it at Juliet. She had been avoiding his eyes since she came in.

"Point that someplace else," she said, pushing it aside as she passed him.

"Hey, Len, show us the grapefruit trick!" Tiernan said. "Wait a minute. . . . Richie, you got any grapefruit?"

"What's the grapefruit trick?" Gemetz asked, going over to his refrigerator.

Juliet, meanwhile, had gone out to the middle of the room and was dancing by herself to a Bee Gees tune. Talbot leaned back against the bar and aimed the tip of the sword at her. Seeing him leaning smugly back and pointing the sword toward her made her angry. At the same time, she felt a growing excitement as he kept it trained on her. It was as though they were dueling. His sword against her hips. She felt a power in her dancing and hurled it against him.

"I've only got one," Gemetz said, handing a grapefruit to Tiernan.

"Okay, everybody. Custer here is going to show us how to properly lop off a head!" Tiernan announced.

"You do it, Joe," Talbot said, starting to hand him the sword. "You did it perfectly the other day."

"No, I'm too drunk. I'd probably miss the damn thing."

About a dozen of the guests began to come over to see what was going on. Talbot shrugged and walked over and took the grapefruit from Tiernan. He grew a little angry as he noticed Juliet still dancing and ignoring it all.

"The wrist and arm—show 'em, Len!" Tiernan said, motioning people to come over.

"Of course, this sort of thing was done during a cavalry charge while the man was on horseback," Talbot said. "So I'll have it relatively easy." He looked over and saw that Juliet was still dancing and looking very unimpressed.

"You have to try to imagine an Apache coming down on you pell-mell on horseback and you are racing at him on your horse," Talbot said, placing the grapefruit on a corner edge of the bar.

"Wrist and arm, wrist and arm," Tiernan chanted.

"And just at the precise moment," Talbot said, bringing the sword up, "when he is bearing into you, when he thinks your life is his . . ."

He let the sword finish his sentence, slashing it through the grapefruit and sending the top half of it flying over Juliet's head.

"And another Apache warrior bites the dust," Talbot said, bowing as the group that had been watching him applauded.

"Yeah, they were just marvelous at Wounded Knee!" Juliet shouted angrily from the center of the room. "Tell 'em about how they used to stick women and babies with those swords!"

The people standing around Talbot stepped back and he saw her standing alone in the middle of the room, her face a masterpiece of contempt. For a minute he just looked broodingly into her eyes. Then she started dancing again, taunting him.

Talbot smiled and pointed the tip of the sword toward her again.

She danced slowly over to where the half of the grapefruit was lying near the fireplace and kicked it over to him.

"Which one is easier, baby Indians or grapefruits?" she asked, and continued her provocative dancing.

She watched Talbot smile evilly and lower the sword with the pommel against his crotch and the tip pointing toward her. Then he began walking toward her, slowly, deliberately.

She paused for an instant as a wave of panic crossed through her but it was brief and there followed a feeling of great sexual excitement and power. He was coming toward her and the look in his eyes was one of surrender, not conquest—blind eyes, not seeing the abyss she had placed before him. She pushed her long beautiful dark hair high over her head, beckoned him further with her hips. She pulled the pulsing music into her body and cast it over him like nets.

When he got to her he did not stop until he had passed the sword between her legs, gripping the hilt with his powerful hands, the blade glistening in the candlelight out behind her.

Then as everyone watched entranced, she let her hair fall down over her face and danced slowly and sensually, touching her breasts against him, making his head swim with the beauty of her abandonment.

"Oh, Juliet," he sighed, his head beginning to sway.

She pushed her hair back and looked deeply into his dreaming eyes. She smiled and moved sexually against him.

"Too bad you don't have a real one," she said contemptuously.

His stomach suddenly felt as if she had turned the sword into him. His mouth gaped and his eyes stared out of his pain. For an instant he saw Susan's face and he could feel the anger rising in him. His hands trembled on the sword and he had to fling it down to keep from giving in to his hurtling rage.

"Ha!" she laughed and, snapping her fingers around his ears, she danced slowly away, winking at those who were watching with held breath.

Talbot watched her for a moment and then looked at the sword gleaming on the floor. Then he walked over to the mantel and leaned against it, trying to calm himself, breathing deeply. He looked up and saw slices of his angry face in the scraped portions of the mirror. And behind him Juliet still held the floor alone.

He turned and looked at her. She had her back to him and she was taunting him with her ass. Slowly he reached down and drew his sweater over his naked chest.

"Huh-oh," Tiernan said. "It's orgy time."

When Juliet finally turned around, Talbot was standing in front of the fireplace totally naked, candlelight glimmering over his powerful torso. She finally stopped dancing.

He walked over and stood before her for a moment looking calmly into her eyes. Her gaze began to falter before his, and she started to look down. He reached forward and in one quick movement swept her sweater off over her head, causing her hair to fly out over her face and down over her beautiful small white breasts.

"Let the year begin!" Talbot shouted and grabbed Juliet's hand and started toward the loft-bed.

"Not with me you don't, Tarzan," Juliet said, pulling away from him and running to pick up her sweater. In a minute she had it on and was running to get her coat from the hall closet. Talbot laughed and climbed up the steps to the loft-bed.

"Better go home, little girl!" Talbot called to Juliet as he sat with his legs dangling over the bed. "Don't forget your sled, little girl! Somebody get the little girl her sled."

But all they heard was the front door slamming.

Gemetz stared at Talbot for a moment and gave him an angry look. Then he put on his fur cap and let the sword scabbard fall from his waist to the floor. Picking up the sled, he ran down the hall to find Juliet.

He managed to catch her just as she was heading for the big front door downstairs. "Juliet, wait!" he said, holding her back.

"No, I gotta get outa this place, Richie," she said, crying with outrage and pulling away from him. "I can't believe myself tonight," she said, finally relaxing and crying against his chest. "Oh, Richie, it really was my fault, wasn't it?"

"Well, yeah, I guess you provoked him a little," he said, holding her close.

"I just couldn't help it. I just lost my head with all that sword crap. And, Richie, they really did kill women and babies. How can Lennie be like that?"

"He's dealing with a lot of anger," he said. "Mostly about his wife. I kind of understand it because I know how Linda gets me sometimes. But lately he's been like a coiled spring. He isn't really a bad guy."

"Look, I wanna go now, okay?" she said, pulling away.

"This has all been too freaky for one night. Gimme my sled. Richie?"

"Tell you what, it's almost the New Year and I bet they're still having a great time over in the park."

"Lemme just go home, Richie. Really."

"Just sitting there all alone when the New Year comes?"

"I'll watch it on TV."

"Come on, Juliet, we'll be Jack and Jill and slide down the hill," he said, opening the door. "A couple of nice slides and I'll take you home."

"No funny business?"

"So, who could get funny in twelve inches of snow in Prospect Park—on a sled yet?"

"Oh, god, Richie, what got into me up there?" she said, putting on her shawl and following him down the steps.

"People do strange things at orgies."

From where he was lying stretched out on the loft-bed, Talbot could see out the window and he saw Juliet and Gemetz crossing the street toward the park. Gemetz still had the big coat on backwards and the fur hat on his head. He was carrying the sled under one arm and Juliet was holding on to the other. They passed under a streetlight on the far sidewalk and stopped when they came to the low wall bordering the park. Below him in the room Talbot heard the guests begin counting down the last seconds before the New Year and he sat up.

"Ten . . . nine . . . eight . . . seven . . ."

Tiernan, too, was watching out the window as Gemetz climbed over the wall and reached back to help Juliet over. They had just started across the snow into the park when church bells began tolling all over the neighborhood and cars began tooting their horns.

"Happy New Year!" Tiernan heard the guests shouting behind him.

But he was entranced by the scene in the park. He saw Juliet stop, Gemetz going on ahead of her for a few steps until he noticed she was not with him. Then he came back to her. Now they were looking into each other's eyes and now Juliet was reaching her hands gently up to Gemetz's face, drawing him to her, kissing him sweetly. Then Gemetz threw his arms around her and kissed her for a long time.

Talbot was still sitting on the edge of the bed exhorting

everyone to strip. Tiernan shook his head in dismay and looked over his shoulder to see Frieda waving goodbye and turning down the hall to leave. The party was building into an erotic wildness and Tiernan turned from it and looked down once again at Gemetz and Juliet in the park, longing for that kind of idyllic love in his own life. He saw Juliet's hand rising tenderly to Gemetz's face as they ended their kiss and thought of times Mary had reached with love for him.

"All right!" Talbot shouted. "Let's really turn this New Year on!"

He was answered by cheers and a great arc of seltzer spray from behind the bar where Rico was manning one of the cannons. One of the laundromat women leaped up from her cushion and stripped her peasant's blouse over her head and hurled it up at Talbot. Then she danced sensuously out to the center of the room and leaned back slowly shaking her large breasts. Somewhere below him he heard the first paper dress being torn.

"Oh, Christ!" Tiernan exclaimed. "At least let's close the goddam shutters."

"When ya coming down, Lennie?" Carol, one of the nurses, asked, standing just below him, one whole side of her paper dress hanging off.

The first sunrise of the New Year was squeezing light in around the closed shutters of Gemetz's apartment. It created glowing lattice patterns on the littered floor and glittered on the slashes of mirror over the mantel. The big black and white rabbit sniffed through a thin bar of sunlight on the floor and then hopped a few feet farther on to wriggle its nose at an empty vodka bottle lying on its side.

Tiernan sat naked against a wall watching Brombly making his inspections in the dim sun-pierced room. With his legs stretched out before him and his eyes hollowed by exhaustion and a racking hangover, he watched the rabbit hop away from the vodka bottle over to a beer can and then over to a pair of black silk panties. Also strewn over this battlefield were about a dozen bodies, most of them naked, some of them snoring.

He had been awake for nearly an hour and so far no one else had stirred. Looking up at the loft-bed, he saw Talbot sleeping with his arm sticking out over the bed. Curled into his chest was Verna and behind him were another woman's feet. Probably one of the nurses, he thought.

Gemetz had never come back, and sitting against the wall, Tiernan was still haunted by the tender way Juliet had reached up and kissed Gemetz when the bells had started tolling in the New Year.

The beauty of her sweet upturned face under the streetlamp had reminded him so painfully of Mary, her delicate hands reaching lovingly for Gemetz's face, reaching . . . He kept seeing Mary's hands—and then the writhing, grasping hands of the orgy. Seltzer-soaked yellow paper being torn from twisting bodies . . . bodies slithering over him on the wet floor . . . someone pouring vodka over him . . . the hands digging and pulling . . . lips and teeth eating him. And always, even in the midst of that roiling flesh and howling sensuality, Mary's reaching hands passing before his mind. Somewhere in it all, Talbot walking naked toward the loft-bed with the naked Verna clasped around him. Talbot fighting others off the loft-bed. A succession of bodies writhing under him, bony, soft, pushing against him, grinding pubic hair. One, two, three nurses. And Phyllis running. Phyllis down and big-eyed. Surprisingly soft Phyllis, his first black woman, pumping his hot sperm into Phyllis. Hands over him again, dozens of hands. Alan's hands, kicking Alan's face, Alan's bloody face receding. Fredricka feeding on him hungrily. And always Mary's hands reaching—not for him.

He thought of the man he'd been and had a great desire to be away from this room—this hell the fates had cast him into. He wanted to be in his own home, to see Mary's good face again, to forget this holocaust of flesh. He thought of Frieda's sad expression as she had left the party. And of how she had told the story of making wishes on New Year's Eve when she was a child: ". . . and then Papa would pull the big curtain back and the first thing we each saw outside would be a symbol of what God had to say about our wishes."

Tiernan got up and walked over to the shutters of one of the big bay windows. With the light shafting onto one of his shoulders, he stood quietly for a moment and then reached forward and threw the shutters open.

Outside, the morning was clear and bright and the first thing that Tiernan saw were two small dogs fornicating on the sidewalk.

# PART
# TWO

# CHAPTER
## SIX

The last customer for the Valentine's Day sale had left more than twenty minutes before, and Juliet was beginning to wonder if Richie was ever going to show up. She saw the streetlights go on outside the store window and for the hundredth time she touched her fingertips over the fine wool nap on the new black coat lying across her lap. The only sounds in the store now were the faint squeaks of her rocking in the spring-backed chair and the ticking of the little tin clock on Mr. Gemetz's desk.

The old man had said very little to her after she had come in—an awkward greeting and some rambling words about Richie having to rush over to Linda's for a minute. But that was half an hour ago, and now the elder Gemetz seemed to be totally oblivious to her as he sat nodding into a hard-bound ledger and silently tapping the edge of it with the end of his pencil.

Strange old bird, she thought, looking at his starved head and dandelion hair and what looked like a woman's old knitted pink scarf wrapped around his neck. Would she please take the seat next to his desk and wait? As though she had come in to buy a washing machine or something.

Looking around at all the heart-decorated discount signs on

129

the showroom floor, she guessed they must have had a big Valentine's Day sale at good old Gemetz Appliance. Look at him go, she thought, so busy adding up his profits he doesn't even know I'm here anymore.

This was the first time she had met Richie's father in the six weeks since they'd started going together. Things had happened so fast after that night at the Stalingrad party that she still didn't quite believe it. Richie Gemetz, of all people. Something had happened to her after that traumatic moment with Len Talbot at the party. Perhaps it was only against Talbot's savagery that she was able to see the deep tenderness and sensitivity in Richie. God, she had never tumbled so fast in her life. And Richie, too. They'd been seeing each other nearly every night.

Talbot had called her and apologized the next day, and at Richie's persuasion she had agreed to be friendly with him when they met at Larsky's. Something seemed to be going on with Talbot and Frieda now—always talking together at Larsky's and leaving together now and then. A strange man, this friend of Richie's—too strange for her. Goddam it, where is Richie? she wondered looking over at the old man's clock again.

"You don't suppose Richie went home to get dressed or something?" she asked, breaking the long silence.

"Dressed?" he asked, looking up and blinking over his bifocals.

"I mean, I was thinking maybe he hadda go home and put on a suit or something. You know? I mean, Richie said to get dressed up because he was taking me to an opera. And dinner. But dinner before the opera. My first opera. *Macbeth*."

"Oh, most certainly," he said, turning slightly and nodding. "That is, he was dressed for going out for the evening. And very handsome he looked, too. Like a regular, ah, gentleman. Just be a little more patient and he'll soon be back with the tickets."

"Tickets?"

"Oh, of course, Linda always gets us the opera tickets. Even now, ah, that is . . . Well, in fact, she is a member of the Metropolitan Opera Company—a very fine singer in the chorus—so of course she can get free tickets. For family and, er, friends."

The old man coughed his discomfort and smiled awkwardly.

And then he quickly returned to his ledger. Juliet sighed and went back to rocking gently. In a moment the old man was nodding and tapping his pencil again. If Juliet had leaned over a bit, she would have seen that he was looking at two blank pages.

Actually, old Martin Gemetz was counting not figures in his ledger but the rhythmic squeaking coming from Juliet's chair.

Three light squeaks.

One a little louder.

Three light again.

And so on, all of it barely audible to Juliet but followed attentively by the old man. There were moments, too, when she stopped rocking altogether, and he counted the beats in these intervals as well with the tapping of his pencil. An accomplished rocker himself, he was soothed by the regularity of her motion but frowned like an impatient music teacher when occasionally she missed a beat.

It was now five-thirty by the loudly ticking clock on the desk, and Juliet began to wonder if a scene had developed between Gemetz and his ex-wife over the tickets. In the past six weeks, since Juliet and Gemetz had become very close, she had heard him complain about a new and erratic moodiness on Linda's part. Or rather a renewal, he had said, of the sporadic anger she had turned on him back when they were breaking up.

These new periodic storms probably meant the thing with Steve was falling apart, he had said. But it was a goddam pain in the ass, he had said, to have to suffer from her bad weather still.

The children kept him connected to her, but lately he even dreaded phoning to ask how they were. He never knew what kind of reception he would get. There were times she would just yell "Fuck you!" the minute she recognized his voice and then hang up. Then she would call back a few hours later effusively apologetic and friendly. She had also begun calling him at three o'clock in the morning looped on wine and threatening to move with the children to Los Angeles, where her sister lived.

Juliet had no idea what Linda looked like but imagined her as tall and theatrical. Gemetz had told her of Linda's long frustration with being stuck in the chorus at the Met, and she pictured her as always moving tempestuously about her Brooklyn Heights apartment in long flowing robes and railing about the agonies of being an *artiste*. Which was almost accurate except that Linda did most of her railing in jeans and old sweat shirts.

She felt sorry for Gemetz because his ex-wife was giving him hell at a time when he least deserved it. Since the first of the year, he had finally started giving Linda the full amount under their support agreement. This was because his father had nearly doubled what he was paying him to work in the store and was talking about turning the business over to him later in the year.

So where the hell was he? she wondered. They could always go to a movie if Linda didn't come through with the free opera tickets. She felt a little pretentious about going to an opera anyway—all those mucky-mucks in their Fifth Avenue clothes listening to their mucky-muck music. Her own new outfit had cost her a month's wages and the cut was Fulton Street not Fifth Avenue. Damn Richie and his big "freebie" night at the opera!

"Come on." She sighed.

The old man now had his eyes closed and was tapping his pencil in some kind of deep concentration. Probably imagining his washing machines spin-drying dollar bills, she thought. Feeling her leg going to sleep, she suddenly got up and walked over to one of the yellow dishwashing machines nearby. As she left the chair it let out a loud scranging noise that popped the old man's eyes open and caused him to stop tapping.

"He said he'd be right back?" she asked, placing her coat on the machine and stretching.

"Oh, yes," the old man said, leaning back in his chair and gently resting the pencil beside the ledger.

A delicate little thing, he thought, appraising Juliet's trim figure in her new blue silk dress. So young for Richie though. Almost pathetic compared to Linda. Linda had strength and music—and such a mother, Linda. He wondered where Richie would have found such a mere bud as this one. A very pretty face, yes, but no force at all. Still, there was her rocking. He would give her that.

"Maybe we should call," she said.

"I'm sure they are just talking," he said, nodding confidently. "It's only natural. A man and his wife talking."

"I thought they were divorced," she said, turning to him in surprise.

He closed his eyes and waved away the notion.

"They're not?"

"Oh, well, divorced, yes," he said. "But as you know
. . . Ah, forgive me, I have forgotten your name."

"Juliet," she said, feeling her impatience turning into anger.

"Yes, a lovely name," he said, smiling. "Like *Romeo and
Juliet*, right? I read that a long time ago. I always loved
Shakespeare. Oh, we would read all the parts, Sarah and I—
my wife, Sarah was."

"Richie told me. I'm sorry."

"Thank you," he said, clasping his bony hands and shaking
his head. "Such a *strong* woman, Sarah. It is not possible that I
am still here—the wind could blow me away—and she is in the
ground."

"I am sorry," she said, beginning to feel a little tenderness
for this frail old man.

"Ah, well . . . Where was I? Oh, yes, Richie and Linda.
Yes, it is true they got the divorce. Thank god Sarah never
knew it! These days *everybody* has to have a divorce! Look, it
stands to reason. Today we have half as many rabbis and twice
as many lawyers. Now they are advertising divorces on the
television like new cars. Jewish lawyers selling at discount! I
was ashamed. You Jewish?"

"Irish—and some Italian."

"Is that so? So, look, Juliet, don't pay any attention to me.
I'm too old-fashioned, maybe. Yes, they got the divorce, but
when there are children I think that's different. Is a marriage
over when there are children? Always she is the mother. Is that
not so? Could I shut my door to the mother of my grand-
children?"

"Of course not," she said sympathetically. She could hear
Richie's fears about losing his children echoed in the grandfather's lamentation.

"I've met Mark and Jonathan," she said. "They're both so
precious—and handsome like their father."

"Such boys," he said, closing his eyes and smiling. "And,
Juliet—just that you should know—my Richie is a *wonderful*
father. Absolutely devoted."

"Oh, don't I already know it! I mean, it's unbelievable," she
said, coming back and sitting down. "When I see the way
Richie is with his kids it makes me almost jealous."

The old man looked puzzled.

"That I didn't have such a father," she added.

"Yes, it is hard to be a father. At first it seems impossible. A child cries because it is hungry and so the father goes out to earn in order to provide. Yes? And then the child cries because the father goes away. But Sarah, God bless her, she knew the answer. She said, 'Martin, tell him the stories of your life. So that when you are away he will know you will come back to finish the story.' Not too many stories left in me now, I am afraid."

"I see now where Richie gets being so good to the boys," she said. "You really should have seen him at Al's Toyland yesterday. He was trying to pick out a bicycle for Mark's birthday and he had everybody in the shop going *crazy!* 'This doesn't have the right number of speeds! This kickstand doesn't work! Not the right shade of red. I want *deep* red!' What a fuss he made!"

"Mark's birthday?" the old man asked, looking confused.

"Yeah, the party is going—"

"When is Mark's birthday?"

"Next Tuesday!" she said, as though everybody in Brooklyn was aware of the event.

"Why was I not told? How can this be? The boy just had a birthday. I remember, in October it was."

"That was Jonathan's," she said. "He told me about it. He said he had a big party and you gave him a big train set. You have two grandsons who love you very much, Mr. Gemetz."

"Tuesday, you say?" he asked, rubbing his gaunt face.

Just then Richie barged into the store out of breath and red-faced from running in the cold air. For a moment she did not recognize him—so sleek and handsome in his long dark wool overcoat and white silk scarf. His beard and hair were freshly trimmed and there was a crispness about him she had never seen before. She half expected the old man to introduce them, so new did he seem to her.

"Juliet, I'm really sorry," he said, coming over and helping her up from the chair. "Tell me you got here late."

"I can't believe how you look," she said.

"What do you think, the scarf too much?" he asked, still feeling a little uncertain after buying it on an impulse that afternoon.

"No, you look gorgeous!" she said, reaching up and plumping the scarf a bit. "It's just I never saw you so—"

"Peeled? What a friggin' haircut that guy gave me today!"

"I like it, I like it," she said, hugging him.

"Whatta ya think, Pop, isn't she pretty?" he said, hugging her back and beaming at his father.

"She is not pretty, she is beautiful. And you should be ashamed making her wait for so long," the old man said, getting up slowly from his desk.

"Yeah, what the heck kept you?" she asked.

"Oh, god! I'll tell you later. Let me look at *you!* Verrrrry chic!"

"I feel like I'm going to a wedding or something. You should've heard Annie: *'You're* going to the opera?' I'm sure she's gonna spread it around Larsky's tonight. Hey, whatta ya say—want to go to a movie instead? Think of my reputation!"

"Not in that dress we aren't going to a movie," he said, swinging her out and looking at her again. "You look like a princess! Come on, where's your coat?"

As his son helped Juliet on with her coat, Martin Gemetz walked on ahead to hold the door open for them. The old man was caught between enjoying the happiness that seemed to ignite in these two the minute they saw each other and the nagging feeling of being disloyal to Linda.

It was all getting away from him. He would now have to conceal this growing fondness for Juliet the next time Linda dropped in for a chat, something she had been doing more often lately. It had been much easier being a part of Sarah's life, he thought, but now with her gone he was left hurrying after Richie's life like a man trying to catch a train while still putting on his shoes.

"G'night, Pop," Gemetz said, giving his father a light hug around the shoulders as he passed him at the door.

"Night, Mr. Gemetz," Juliet said.

"It's *Macbeth,* did you say?" the old man called after them.

"Yeah," Gemetz called back, "it's all blood and murder and scheming women—the Met's way of saying 'Happy Valentine'!"

Juliet shook her head and waved once more to the old man as Richie hurried her down the sidewalk. The elder Gemetz waved, shivered and closed the door.

Up ahead of them the Brooklyn Savings Bank's digital weather clock was alternately blinking 22° and 6:21. Juliet pulled her blue tam-o'-shanter down over her ears and ducked her face away from the icy wind as Gemetz guided her through the stream of returning office workers coming from the subway station at the top of Montague Street.

"Um, you feel good," he said, holding her tightly around the waist.

"So, what's the story, Richie?"

"I don't think we're going to have time to go to La Fleurie before the opera," he said.

"Richie, I'm starving!"

"I know. Linda screwed us. Jesus, I could have slugged her!"

"What happened?"

"She couldn't find the tickets. I mean, she wouldn't find the tickets. What do you say we just grab a quick snack at O'Neal's and eat at La Fleurie after the opera?"

"Okay with me. Where's O'Neal's?"

"Just across from Lincoln Center. You've never been to O'Neal's?"

"I've never been to Lincoln Center."

"What say we take a cab?" he asked as they came to the subway steps at the corner of Montague and Court.

"Ho, ho, Richie Rockefeller!"

"No, wait," he said, holding her back as she started down the steps. "Let's make tonight really special."

"Richie, it will cost a fortune!" she protested, pulling on his hand.

"I'll make a deal. If we don't get a cab in five—no, ten—minutes, I'll take the subway. Okay? Hey, it's Valentine's Day! Did I tell you happy Valentine's Day?" He pulled her close and kissed her lightly on the lips. Meanwhile he kept his eyes open for any cabs heading toward the Brooklyn Bridge.

Being alone with Juliet in the crisp air had lightened his spirits after the maddening half-hour with Linda. For nearly the whole time he had followed her around the apartment cursing under his breath while she sipped a glass of white wine, giggled and tried to remember where she had misplaced the opera tickets. At the same time, she kept flashing him glimpses of her nudity under the thigh-length Japanese robe she was wearing.

Knowing that he was practically blazing with impatience, she kept making exaggerated apologies and then running off to a new crevice in the apartment to look for the tickets, all the while giggling to herself. Back and forth she had gone, up and down from the sofa, her home base for each new foray, until he had started cursing out loud and threatening to leave. The two boys were in their room watching television after supper. Finally, Gemetz had yelled "The hell with it!" and stormed out. He was halfway down the hallway to the stairs when she rushed from the apartment waving the little white envelope with the tickets.

"Richie, wait, I found them! They were under the Monet book."

"Great," he said in tight-lipped fury. "All the good they'll do now. She's probably gone home already."

"Who, your little bar baby? Don't worry, she'll be there. Say, how'd you ever talk her into an opera, anyway? A teenybopper rock concert, maybe, but—"

"Linda?"

"What is it, Richie baby, honey, sweetie, teenybopper's sugar-daddy dream man?" she teased, cuddling close and stroking his beard.

"Shove it, okay?" he said, tapping her on the end of her nose with the ticket envelope. He headed down the thickly carpeted stairs.

"Nice thanks I get!" she called down the stairs as he disappeared around the landing.

"Richie? Richie?" she yelled louder.

"What, goddam it?"

"Hey, if she's not there— Ha, fat chance! Look, if it turns out she ditched you, come backstage after the performance and I'll give you a ride home."

"Fat chance!" he called, continuing down the stairs.

"I might even let you play grabbies while I drive!"

"Kiss my ass, Linda!"

"Whatever turns you on, sweetie!"

As he was heading for the front door he heard the wine glass shatter just behind him where Linda had tried to sight-bomb him while hanging over the stairwell three floors up.

He could still hear her laughing as he waited near the subway entrance with Juliet. When a cab finally did come by the driver failed to notice his frantic waving. Gemetz shook his head in disgust and was about to concede and head down into the subway when he noticed the bridge lights glowing over the top of Cadman Park. The bridge!

"Hey, what a fantastic idea!" he said, smiling devilishly at her. "We've got about an hour and a half to kill, right?"

"So?" she asked, eyeing him suspiciously.

"So, we'll *walk* to Manhattan!"

"Walk, huh? Sure you wouldn't rather go by skateboard?"

"Hey, I'm serious," he said, taking the lapels of her coat and pulling her close to him. The mists of their breathing mingled around their heads.

"Richie?" she said, patting him on the chest and kissing him lightly on the end of his reddened nose.

"Yeah?"

"You a leedle crazy, Richie."

"Oh."

"Come on, I don't mind the subway. It's fast, cheap and dirty. New York's gift to the working girl."

"Wait a minute, Juliet," he said, pulling her back as she started down the stairs again. "I bet you never walked across the Brooklyn Bridge in your life."

"Are you kidding? For nearly a year I walked back over that bridge. When I was going to secretarial school. But not in *February*, Richie!"

"February's the *best* month," he said. "The muggers all freeze to death up there in February. There's a whole statuary of frozen muggers up there. A kind of muggers' museum—quite charming, in fact."

"Richie, it's a swell idea. Really! It's just that, well, see, every time I walk over the Brooklyn Bridge in February I turn navy blue and, see, I got on this blue dress tonight. It's just going to clash terribly. I know it's silly."

"Yeah, I guess you're right." He sniffed. "I keep forgetting about the weaker sex."

"Oho!" she exclaimed, tweaking his beard. "So, you wanna do cold, huh? Don't think I can do cold, huh?"

"That's, uh, really the question," he said, nodding profoundly. "Can you actually do cold?"

"I can do cold."

"Well, cold, yes, but there's cold and there's *cold*. You could maybe do street cold, or park cold even. But bridge cold—that's something else."

"You can do bridge cold?" she asked.

"Certainly."

"*I* can do bridge cold," she asserted and grabbed his hand and pulled him into the intersection toward the bridge.

"I love it!" he exclaimed, catching up with her and wrapping his arm around her waist. "And when we get across, then we'll grab a cab. Should be lots of them around City Hall."

"By then, I think I'd settle for a Saint Bernard." She laughed.

They nuzzled each other passing in front of the massive gray State Supreme Court building and laughed at the ice pompadour on the statue of Henry Ward Beecher standing with his big belly toward Borough Hall. They had to run to dodge the traffic that swept around them on Tillary Street and then kept running under the bare outstretched limbs of the sycamores lining the park.

When they came to the long flight of stone steps leading up to the pedestrian walkway on the bridge, Juliet stopped to get her breath and leaned heavily against his chest, sighing.

For the first time, he began to doubt the sanity of the bridge idea. Where had it come from? What was he trying to do to her? It would be gruesome out on the span exposed to the cold winds. He thought, too, of the pains she'd taken to look wonderful for him at her first opera. And here he was about to subject her to something a Yukon lumberjack might balk at. Did he hate her? Was this another one of his tests?

Linda had complained that he was always testing her love for him, insisting on a synagogue wedding even though she was Catholic and he had not set foot in a synagogue since he was sixteen, nor had he since the wedding; then those first years of living in that urine-smelling building he'd picked out in the East Village, when his parents had offered them a big rent-controlled apartment they were just moving out of in the Heights; and the thing about making her keep her hair long; and bringing his banjo-playing army buddy in to live with them for three months; and on and on, putting one hurdle after another in front of her until she finally kicked them all over and told him to get lost. He heard Linda's laughing again. Linda, who in the end did everything she could to test him—until the war was settled by divorce lawyers.

He didn't want that with Juliet. No more games. He'd had enough games for a lifetime. Lately he had been thinking of asking her to marry him. Certainly he loved her. At this moment, listening to her sighing breaths, he loved her very much indeed. And this frightened him. Yes, the bridge would test her but it would also trap him.

"This is crazy," he said, holding her closely. "We can still turn back. Want to?"

"No," she said without looking up. She, too, sensed something gathering around her life but she was unwilling, at least for the moment, to push it back.

"I just thought . . . there may be ice up there. You know?"

"Yeah," she said weakly.

"Sure?"

"Yeah."

"Ready, then?"

"Uh-huh," she said, smiling at him a little apprehensively and then ducking her head as they started up the steps.

When they got to the top of the steps he was in a turmoil of doubt. Cars were buzzing past on the brad-studded roadways on either side of the pedestrian promenade. The lights running up the two main cables to the top of the first stone tower looked like serial moons against the evening sky. Juliet clung tightly to his arm and pressed against his shoulder to shield herself from the bitter wind that came straight at them from the tower. Each step he took seemed to be a commitment to folly.

"This is terrible," he said through chattering teeth.

She groaned and clung to him more tightly.

The promenade's trajectory rose gradually over the flanking roadways so that the hornet sounds of the cars were less directly in their ears. Ahead the great churchlike arches of the first stone tower were glowing eerily in the silver lights. The webbed support strands from the main cable seemed to flow out from the vaulted passages in the tower like gigantic curtains in the wind.

They had to walk gingerly over the glaze of ice on the wooden walkway as they approached the several steps up to the base of the tower. Just then a tall lean young man clad in clerical black appeared and started down the steps. On the second step he slipped and had to lunge desperately for the railing to keep from falling. Juliet gasped as he recovered himself and then continued toward them.

"Be careful, the ice is treacherous," the young priest warned them as he passed.

"You all right, Father?" Juliet called after him.

"Yes, thank you. Good night."

When they got to the top of the steps, Gemetz took her hand and carefully led her over to the observation railing at one corner of the tower. The wind was now partly blocked by the great tower, but he could feel his frozen beard stiff and prickly as he moved his lips to speak.

"I th-th-think we're gonna die up here," he said.

She nodded and tucked her chin down against the cold.

From where they stood the other tower looked several miles away. Leaning slightly over the rail, he watched the cloudlike ice floes moving slowly in the black waters toward the freighters docked just below Brooklyn Heights.

"We gotta go back," he said, holding her close.

"Can't do c-c-cold, huh?" she teased.

"Look at all this ice. We'd have to crawl all the way to the Manhattan side."

"I can do crawl," she said, leaning down in pretense of getting ready for it.

"God, I can't take you anywhere," he said, pulling her back up.

"Can't do crawl?"

"No," he conceded.

"Can't do cold?"

"No."

"Aw, poor baby."

"We're going to show up at the opera looking like the last survivors of a polar expedition if we don't get off this goddam bridge," he said, shivering so much his shoulders were bouncing.

"Oh, all right," she said, smiling and turning to go.

"I, uh . . . Juliet?" he said, pulling her back.

"Yep?"

"I love you—very much," he said and kissed her softly.

"Me too you," she said, looking down at his white scarf and giving him a confirming hug.

They were both silent as they made their way back with their arms around each other. The wind was at their backs and the promenade descended gradually toward the bridge entrance, and Gemetz felt as though he was being carried away from a moment in which he had profoundly failed himself.

A few minutes later they were huddled against each other in

the back seat of a taxicab, still shaking with the deep flesh-chilling they had taken on the bridge. From where he sat low in the corner of the seat he could see the bridge's cablework flashing by overhead. He held Juliet protectively and tried to stroke away the trembling in her body. On the Manhattan side the cab turned off onto the East River drive and he sat up a bit.

The red lights of a tug drifted by in the darkness that hid the river. He imagined its crew snugged down in the warm cabin playing cards, smoking and perhaps thinking of going home to their families in the morning. Men talking easily among themselves and easily confident about their lives on the icy currents of the harbor. At rest were the hearts of such men who could ignore the chunking of the ice floes against their hull while they sat back with their thick hands full of aces and wild-card straights and warmed their blood with Irish whiskey. Juliet was meant for such men, he thought. Such men did not take their women out on arctic bridges to test their love. How strange she must think him.

"How you doing?" he asked.

"Beginning to warm up," she said, cuddling against him.

"You must think I'm nuts," he said, tucking her chin up so he could look at her eyes.

"Yep."

"I really am, you know. You can ask Linda."

"Linda's the one who sounds a little bonkers to me," she said.

"That whole business with the tickets tonight, I—"

"She's still in love with you, Richie."

"Linda is in love with Linda. Always has been."

"How about you? Would you ever go back to her?"

"Richie's in love with Juliet. She knows that."

"You told her about me?"

"Well, she doesn't know your name."

"Poor Linda, that's cruel, Richie."

"Don't bother feeling sorry for her. She despises you."

"What did you tell her about me?"

"That I was very much in love. That I—"

"What?"

"Never mind," he said, looking out the window.

She looked at him for a moment and bit her lip. Sitting up straight, she reached over and tapped him on the shoulder. "Richie?"

"Um?"

"I think this is nice what's going on between us, you know? I like doing things with you. You're totally nuts but I like that. You don't take me for granted and I like that, too. But lately, you've been getting real, you know, like tense. And I think I know why."

"Why?"

"Marriage, right? And if that's the case you're scaring yourself to death over nothing."

"What, you wouldn't marry me?"

"Especially not you."

"Oh, thanks a lot."

"Well, think about it for a minute. There's a lot of reasons why I shouldn't marry you: Like you're ten years older than me; you're Jewish, which would kill my mother, to say nothing of Uncle Colin, who's a priest; you've got two kids already, who probably resent the hell out of me—and maybe me them. We're very different, you gotta admit that, Richie. I mean, like tonight you're gonna be sitting there really digging that opera, right? And I'm gonna be sitting there wondering what the hell is going on. I know it."

"So?" he asked, not knowing whether he felt hurt or relieved.

"So, all that I just said doesn't even count. That wouldn't stop me from marrying you. If I loved you, which I do happen to, I think I could deal with all these things."

"I'm getting confused," he said. "Are you saying you would marry me or you wouldn't?"

"Wouldn't."

"Why?"

"Linda."

"Linda? You gotta be kidding," he said.

"Look, there was this guy I used to know a couple of years ago, a cop," she said, slumping back down in her seat. "We were going out and he was getting a divorce and I thought he was really good-looking. Anyway, he warned me to stay away from guys just breaking up with their wives."

"What did he say?"

"Mainly that they were bad news."

"Him included?"

"Well, he didn't tell me all this till after I stopped going out with him. I forget why we stopped going out."

"So, why'd he say guys like me were bad news?"

"Oh, I remember. He was a drinker. Every time we went out he'd get loaded. I figured he was on his way to becoming an alcoholic. I think he got married again. Why are they bad news?"

"Yeah, and don't forget I'm in that category."

"Well, he said that guys just out of a broken marriage either wind up going back to their wives or wind up treating you like shit because they're trying to get even with their wives."

"So, where does that leave us?" he asked, looking glumly out the window again.

"Aw, Richie, come on!" she said, reaching over and turning his face toward her. "You really don't wanna get married. Right? The truth. Right?"

"Who says?" His tone annulled his question.

"Can't we just keep it like it is? For a while, anyways? Ain't it kinda nice just that we found out we love each other?"

"Yes," he conceded, smiling. "Hey, look, I don't want to rush you—or me. I guess I just really need to know that you want me. Do you want me?"

"Uh-huh." She sighed and snuggled against him again. "Hey, did I tell you how sexy you looked coming into the store? Oh, I just wanted to take a bite out of you."

"Any particular part?"

"Ummm, my favorite part," she murmured, moving her hand slowly up his inner thigh.

He drew in a deep contented breath and glanced up in time to see the bull-necked Latin driver checking them attentively in the rearview mirror. Caught in the act, the driver gave him a froggy wink and then kept his eyes on the road. They were nearing the 42nd Street exit.

Later, leading her by the arm up the palatial stairs to the Met's grand tier balcony, he could not take his eyes off her. There was still the freshening from the wind on her cheeks, and the lovely sheen in her long dark hair almost drew a whine of happiness from him. She was looking around at everything with the open wonder of a child, and even the great star-burst chandeliers glittering overhead were nothing to the radiance he saw in her blue eyes. Surely she was the most beautiful woman there, he thought.

And still later, sitting in the shadowy darkness awed by the rich spectacle illuminated below them, she turned slightly and glanced at him. Leaning forward with his hand bent under his chin, he was calmly intent on the scene unfolding between Macbeth and Lady Macbeth. Richie, serene and mature in his world—so different from the electric little man he portrayed himself to be at Larsky's. How gallant he had been and how beautiful he had made her feel coming into the Met. And for the first time she began to feel a proprietary love for him. Would this be the man she would look upon all the rest of her life?

Just then she felt something dark pass through her and she shuddered visibly. She saw again the old man's emaciated head shaking as he talked of his son's divorce from Linda. Was old Martin Gemetz right? Was a marriage ever over when there remained the blood linkages of the children, to say nothing of a thousand shared dreams that lived on despite all the certifications of death in the divorce document. Yes, even at the moment that she thought to reach out to take him for her own, there was Linda. About twenty minutes earlier, Richie had pointed his ex-wife out to her as one of the witches in the opening scene. But it had been impossible to judge what she looked like because of the grotesque makeup she was wearing. She would not appear again until late in the opera, Richie had said, and then as a lady of the court. Then she would see what Linda looked like. Or would she? A witch, indeed, capable of so many transformations.

From where she was sitting Juliet could see the light from the stage playing in ghostly reflection on the faces of those sitting in the boxes along the sides of the great opera house. The next balcony edged out just above her like a black cloud. Behind her, at the very back of the grand tier's seating, there was a low-walled standing area; and here, partly hidden by one of the red velvet-covered pillars, a young woman watched them. She was wearing a green dressing gown and her face still glistened in the dimness with the cold cream she had hurriedly used to remove her witch's makeup.

# CHAPTER
# SEVEN

The phone was ringing when Tiernan got to the door of his apartment after jogging with Gemetz and Talbot. He listened to its forlorn pulsing deep in the apartment and cursed as his key failed to turn in the jammed lock. The lock finally slid and he burst into the apartment, but just as he got to the bedroom the ringing stopped. He flopped down on the rumpled bed, grabbed the phone off the floor and dialed Mary.

"You call?" he asked, his voice rasping.

"Yes," she said. "Joe? You sick?"

"No, just a little hoarse from jogging. What's up?"

"Well, Lynn *is* sick," she said. "Fever and throwing up all night. She's better this morning, but I'm keeping her home from school. She wants to speak to you."

"Poor thing. Yeah, put her on," he said, smiling fondly.

"I ought to warn you, she wants that dog again."

"Huh-oh. Well, that's better than a horse, I guess."

"Or a giraffe even," she said. "But, Joe, you ought to think twice about the dog, you're the one who'd have to keep it."

"Thanks a lot," he said.

"Here's Lynn."

"Daddy, I throwed up," the tiny voice said, its frailty bringing an instant smarting to his eyes.

"I'm sorry, sugar," he said sympathetically. "That bad old flu get in your tummy?"

"Yeah," she said. In the silence that followed he could hear her breathing with difficulty.

"What's this about a dog?" he asked finally.

"Do you like a dog, Daddy?"

"Yes, I like dogs," he said. "What kind of dog do you want, sweetheart?"

"A furry one. A little puppy furry one."

"You want a puppy?" he asked sweetly but frowned as he could almost smell the months of dog shit on the floor during the house-breaking phase.

"Yeah," she said.

"Okay, I'll see what I can do. Maybe I can get off early today and see what they have up at the A.S.P.C.A."

He winced as the phone at the other end bounced off the floor. Then he heard Lynn's excited voice farther away. "Mommy, Daddy's going to get me a puppy from the A.P.C.A.!"

In a moment, Mary came back on the line. "Well, I warned you," she said.

"I told her if I found a dog I'd bring it around after supper," he said. "Okay?"

"Sure, as long as you take it home with you. Why don't you stay for supper? I got a big chicken at Key."

"I ever turn down your cooking?" he asked, smiling and lying back on the bed with the phone on his chest.

"How's the job going?" she asked.

"It's getting zooier every day."

"Well, maybe it will be amusing until something better shows up," she said.

"That's what I figure. I've already put some feelers out. Maybe an airline—great travel benefits."

"That *would* be nice. You could finally take your trip to Ireland."

"Yeah," he said, finding it increasingly difficult to speak. She had allowed a little warmth to open up between them and he did not want to risk losing it by giving voice to the longing that was welling up in him.

After a pause, she said, "Well, I guess we'll see you about—What, six o'clock?"

"Yeah. Bye, Mary."

After waiting for her to hang up he replaced the phone on the cradle and lay there thinking of her for a few minutes. He imagined her going into the bathroom to put on her makeup for work. She would be leaning slightly over the sink with her lovely round breasts hanging soft and smooth against her white silk slip. Ah, those mornings in Eden, he thought, remembering the early years when he had but to reach and pluck that sweet globed fruit, carrying her laughing back to the bedroom. Those mornings when his lust licked the back of her neck during eye shadow, pounced during the stretching on of panty hose, took her between the teacups during breakfast.

He rolled over and put the phone back on the floor and then got up and began stripping off the damp jogging clothes. Forget it, pal, he told his tilting penis. Standing under the steaming shower, he began singing at the top of his lungs. ". . . and you can hear the whistle blow five hundred miles!" The shower felt good. He let it blast against his face and then threw his head back and finished the chorus in a gargle.

He was still singing as he emerged from the steam-billowing bathroom, shaved, combed and wearing a towel around his thin muscular waist. Talbot's morning jogging program was really paying off. He was beginning to feel fit again, like the *old* Joe Tiernan. It was also great to be working again, using his mind to do something besides lacerate himself. A great buddy, Talbot, he thought. Fucking Texans know how to fight back. Good old Talbot, he thought, rallying them all out of defeat.

"Yeeeeeehaaak!" he yelled, trying without success to imitate Talbot's rebel yell.

The apartment was a little cold so he put on a fresh white shirt and then headed for the kitchen. He was ravenously hungry. First he filled the little dented tin pot with water for instant coffee, then a look in the refrigerator to see if by some fluke there might be something edible. Not very encouraging: two six-packs of Miller's, a bottle of catsup, a withered hunk of salami and a brown bag containing a four-day-old bagel. He took the bagel out of the bag, inspected it, whacked it a couple of times on the top of the refrigerator and then put it back in the bag. Then he put the bag on the sink counter and hammered it a dozen times with the heel of his fist.

Twenty minutes later—after the breakfast of coffee, salami and pulverized bagel and after five minutes of serious preening

in his new navy pin-striped three-piece suit—he was breezing
down Prospect Park West, his attaché case swinging, his
coattails flaring and his spirits soaring.

By god, I'll have a piece of this day, he thought and took in a
deep breath of the raw morning air. His legs felt wonderfully
charged as he moved between the cars in the crawling morning
traffic on Plaza Street.

Poor Lynn, he thought. By god, I'll get her a pup if I do
nothing else. Aye, lads, sound the drums and the pipes. We're
goin' to bring back a golden pup for the fair young Lynn, and
tonight we'll sup with Lady Mary. He could hear the bagpipes
screeling faintly from somewhere in his ancestral gloom. Now,
my brave boyos, with me into the pit! his mind called as he
leaped down the subway steps and dug deep into his trench-
coat pocket for his token. Out of my way, ye blaggard! he
thought as he hipped roughly through the turnstile and plunged
down another flight of steps to the waiting subway.

As he emerged with the morning horde from the subway
corridor at Grand Central Station he tucked his attaché case
under his arm like a football and headed across the depot's
great passenger hall. Dodging and twisting through the
ricocheting crowds, he made one of his great broken-field
runs of all time. Cheers swelled in the vast domed arena. Then
up the steps two at a time on the other side and out again into
the cold gray morning. They were still cheering as he made his
way down the four blocks to his office building on Madison
and 38th.

In the lobby he strode over to the news counter and ordered a
paper cup of coffee and a *Times* and then sauntered over to the
elevators. The usual crowd of executive types waiting, faces
tilted up watching the numbers lighting over the doors.

He looked down the line of them with a little smile on his
face until he spotted Marna. Shit! he thought. He'd forgotten
about Marna's party. She was the woman he was replacing at
Alma's and they were throwing a going-away party for her at
the office at five o'clock. Marrying some hometown guy and
moving back to Denver. How in the hell would he get away to
pick up Lynn's pup? It would be important for him to show up
at the party, because Marna was a favorite of Alma's old Yalie
husband, Hodding. Besides, Marna had been very kind to him,
getting him acquainted with the accounts he was taking over
from her. Maybe he could duck out at noon and keep the pup in

a box or something under his desk. He moved over behind the reed-thin young woman. "Party still on?" he asked.

"Huh? Oh, hi, Joe," she said, smiling. She had lovely chestnut hair and big green eyes. "I hope so. . . . Maybe I'll get drunk enough to tell Alma off."

"Great, and you'll have all our silent cheers," he said.

As they rode up to the third floor together he bit his lip and tried to figure out how to get free during the day. Maybe he should duck out now and just come in late, before some agency development kept him tied down at noon.

"Joe, Alma's on a real tear this morning," Jean, the secretary, said as he stepped into the office behind Marna. "You're supposed to go right in."

"Me?" he asked, stopping halfway to his desk.

"Right away," she said, making a slicing motion across her throat.

"How bad is it?" he asked.

"About ten points on the Richter Scale," she said and then had to pick up her ringing phone.

He walked over to his desk and put down his things. What the hell was Alma steamed up about? he wondered. Maybe it was finally his turn, he thought. He had seen Alma put her other employees to her verbal lash. Did she think he would submit to it?

Well, it was an interesting situation, something he had thought about often in the past six weeks. Never in his life had he allowed himself to be subjected to the kind of humiliations Alma dealt out. He wouldn't have taken it. Yet, after so many months of being out on the street, he was just beginning to put some sort of order back into his life. The job was an important part of it and he didn't want an upset right now. He wanted very much to show Mary and his daughter that he was not a loser.

He could hear John Harrington coughing his lungs up and slamming the top of his desk with the flat of his hand. All of the desks were arranged in a row on one side of the big room near the windows, while the rest of the room, separated by a low partition, was decorated with sofas and tables and paintings to give the effect of a living room. Harrington, a very thin middle-aged man with an advanced case of emphysema, was grinding out a cigarette and pounding his desk with each racking cough.

Except for Marna, who had gone immediately to the

bathroom, he and Harrington and Jean were the only ones in the office so far. Alma's private office was at the far end of the room and he could hear her talking angrily into her telephone.

"Hey, John, what's with Alma?" he asked, walking over to the florid-faced Harrington, who had slumped back into his chair and was breathing easier.

"My, don't we look dashing this morning," Harrington said, patting himself delicately on the chest with his long fingers.

"Yeah, watch out or I'll beat you out for the best-dressed title," Tiernan said, sitting on the edge of his desk.

"Oh, that wouldn't be difficult. I'm down to rags these days," Harrington said, reaching for his cigarettes and then taking his hand back as another fit of coughing enveloped him.

"Joe," Jean called from her desk, "Alma just buzzed and wants you in there."

Tiernan looked back at Harrington and gave him a questioning look.

"Good lord, Joseph—" Harrington began but was cut off by more coughing. "She got . . . She and Hodding were . . . Oh, dear god, it's too . . ."

"That's okay, just get your breath," Tiernan said. "You really ought to give these things up, John," he added, picking up Harrington's pack of cigarettes and tossing them back on the desk.

"One of *your* clients, Joseph," Harrington began again as he stroked his reddened face and flicked back a lock of dislodged brown-dyed hair. "I think it's absolutely hilarious, Joseph! That little awful Vietnamese general, Van, Van Dong or something."

"Yeah, Henri Van Dong. He owns the French East."

"Well, Joseph, dear boy, your little ding dong general threw . . . [cough! cough! wheeze!] . . . Alma and Hodding out on their derrieres last night. Oh, *god,* I wish I could have been . . ." But he couldn't go on for more coughing and wheezing.

"No shit?" Tiernan whispered as he got to his feet and shook his head incredulously.

Harrington began laughing again. "Oh, dear poor Joseph—" He wheezed and began slamming his desk as another wave of coughing convulsed him. "She . . . they . . . aargh . . ."

"God, take it easy, John," Tiernan said, becoming alarmed

at Harrington's beet-red face. He seemed to be strangling in laughter and coughing.

"Are you okay, Mr. Harrington?" Jean asked, coming over to his desk.

"Try to quiet him," Tiernan said, "while I get some water."

As he was hurrying across the richly carpeted floor toward the water cooler, Alma burst out of her office and yelled, "I wanna see you! Now!"

The force of her anger stopped him in his tracks for a moment. He turned and looked at her with his mouth slightly open in surprise. She was standing with her long legs spread apart in front of her open office door, her hands on her hips and her lower lip jutted up almost to her hawkish nose.

Fuck you, he thought, and looked for a glass. Then he went to the bathroom door and knocked. "Marna, I need a glass," he said. "John's about to choke to death. Marna?"

"Oh, god," he heard her say. "Joe, see if Alma's got one on her desk."

"Right," he said, and nearly knocked Alma over as he turned and headed for her office.

"Did you hear me?" Alma bellowed after him.

He ignored her and trotted into her big sprawling office and snatched a glass off her desk. On the way out he noticed that her sofa had been pulled out into a bed and was piled with rumpled sheets and blankets. Alma had to duck out of his way as he plunged back out and headed for the water cooler.

"Here, sip this," he said, holding the glass to Harrington's lips. As Harrington tried to swallow, Tiernan stroked him gently on the back. Jean, glimpsing Alma steaming toward them across the room, scurried back to her desk.

Seeing Harrington's condition and the cold reserve in Tiernan's eyes, Alma checked what she was about to say and watched for a minute. "What's the matter with him?" she asked finally.

"He was choking," he answered coldly. "What do you want?"

"Come in when you're finished," she said and turned and marched back to her office, closing the door behind her with a room-shuddering slam.

"How you doin', old man?" Tiernan asked.

"Bet— better, thank . . . you, Joseph." Harrington sighed and slumped back into his chair.

"Sure?"

"I'll be all right. Better go see about Alma."

Tiernan shook his head and gave him a last pat on the back. Then he frowned and walked toward Alma's office. He felt sure he was about to end his strange career with the Alma Reed Agency. Goddam it, he thought. He dreaded the prospect of telling Mary he was out of work again. He had even been able to give her some support money in the last month. That had made him feel good even though Mary had never pressed him. But he would not be talked to like that. "I want to see you. Now!" He remembered her authoritative order. She's lucky I didn't backhand her surly puss, he thought.

Alma was sitting behind her desk jotting something onto a white sheet of paper with a gold ball-point pen. He walked over and leaned with two fingers on her glass-top desk. She continued writing without looking up.

"Please close the door, Joe," she said in a calm almost friendly tone.

He walked over and shut the door. On the way back to her desk he saw the pile of blankets moving on Alma's sofa bed. Looking closer, he saw some tufts of gray hair sticking up near the pillow. Christ, it was Hodding, he thought. They must have both stayed over in town after the incident at the restaurant. The little guy didn't make much of a bulge in the blankets, he thought. Hodding Reed at seventy-five was a quarter of a century older than Alma and was her necessary link to New York's old-line upper class. They said he was already senile when he had married the big woman, a former swimming champion at the University of Pennsylvania, ten years before.

"Alma—" Joe began.

"Just a minute, Joe. . . . There! Read this," she said, handing him the paper full of her large scrawl.

"What is it?"

"A letter to the State Department. I want you to polish it up."

"Alma, I, uh . . ." He gestured over to Hodding and lowered his voice so as not to wake him.

"Don't worry about Mr. Reed," she said loudly. "An earthquake wouldn't wake him up before noon."

"Look," he said, tossing the paper back on her desk, "I think you better get somebody else to polish your letter. I'm quitting."

"Quitting?" she said, sitting back and blinking in surprise.

"I don't permit people to shout at me," he said, narrowing his eyes at her.

She put her index fingers together and touched them to her lips. Then she got up and walked around the desk and stood in front of him. Then she turned around and stood with her broad back to him. The back of her tweed dress was unzipped.

"Zip me up, will you?" she said.

He had to use some force to get the zipper up as the dress pushed the muscular flesh below her shoulders together. One last service, he thought.

When it was done, she turned around. "Tell me what you think of me," she said.

"What do you mean?"

"You think I'm a big dumb bitch, right?"

He laughed and rubbed his face.

"Go on, call me a big dumb bitch."

"No, Alma . . . I, uh—"

"Say it!"

"Okay, you're a big dumb bitch. Can I go now?"

"Sit down," she said, and went back and sat in her chair behind the desk.

"This is crazy," he said, looking around and shoving his hands down in his pants pockets.

"We're even, Joe," she said, leaning back again. "I shouted at you, and you just called me a dumb bitch. Right? No, we're more than even. . . . I'm giving you a raise. Fifty bucks a week. So, sit down, goddam it!"

He sat down.

"Now, will you please read the letter? The basic elements are there. Just smooth it out. What do you think?"

"The State Department?" he asked.

"I'm going to have that little gook deported," she said, pounding her desk. "Hodding's cousin is with State and I'm sure we can do it. No little goddam shit-brained—"

"So what happened?" he asked interrupting her fury.

"Joe, it was a national disgrace," she said. "We were humiliated in front of everyone! Hodding, ah, Mr. Reed and I merely complained about the food taking so long. . . . Oh, Joe, you won't believe this! He actually shouted at us, that pint-sized little Napoleon. And when I objected to his tone he actually threw us out. Poor Mr. Reed, Joe, with his bad heart. I was terrified!"

"I know Henri is a little weird, but this is right off the wall," he said, shaking his head and reading the letter.

"He's a monster! And one of his little gook cooks attacked me with a cleaver!"

"What? How'd the cook get into it?"

"Well, when I couldn't get help from the waiters, I went back to the kitchen to see what was holding up our meal. Maybe we can get the whole bunch of them deported."

"Alma, calm down," he said, shaking his head in confusion.

"Oh, Joe, do you know what I said? I'm so proud I thought of it—right in the middle of everybody. I stood my ground, Joe, and I shouted, 'Long live Ho Chi Minh!' Oh, now I understand what all those hippies were talking about, Joe. They were right! We *were* supporting the wrong side in that war. It's true, Joe. I never, never thought I'd hear myself say it."

"Did he know who you were?" he asked, trying to keep a straight face.

"Of course he did. We had reservations. He even asked how you were doing with the publicity."

Tiernan groaned silently. He had a pretty good idea of what had happened, especially if Alma had pulled her Vince Lombardi routine in the kitchen and started spouting things like "Long live Ho Chi Minh!"

Putting Henri and Alma together, he thought, was like Yasir Arafat and Golda Meir sitting down to tea. It was a tough break, because Henri liked him and was on the verge of putting him onto two other former South Vietnamese generals who were about to put *their* C.I.A. payoffs into a chain of Vietnamese restaurants. It would be a big account for the agency.

For the moment he decided to try to stall Alma until she cooled down. Perhaps he could talk to Henri. Jesus, and he had an appointment this morning to see Marvin Green, a major carpet retailer in the Bronx, about his daughter's coming-out ball at the Waldorf, which the Reed agency was handling as a favor to keep his business account.

"So get busy with that letter, young man," she said, getting up. "And phone the State Department and Immigration

. . . maybe the F.B.I., too. These goddam aliens. Who do they think they are, treating Americans like that?"

"I've got a couple of appointments this morning," he said.

"Postpone them, Joe. This is top priority," she said, leading him out.

"'Holocaust'?" he said, reading the letter as he walked.

"Leave that in," she said.

"Alma, you can't describe what happened as a holocaust."

"It was a holocaust."

"Alma, you burn down New York, you kill six million Jews, you blow up Pearl Harbor, and you've got a holocaust. But not when you get thrown out of a restaurant."

"Leave it in," she said, closing the door behind him.

"I've also got to pick up a dog for . . ." he said to the blank door and then shrugged and went back to his desk.

Most of the morning was taken up with rescheduling the Green appointment for later in the afternoon and composing Alma's letter. He also dialed Henri at the restaurant a dozen times trying to find some way to arrange a truce between him and Alma. Calling the State Department was too absurd to even think about. Just before noon he found Henri in, and he agreed to meet Tiernan if he would come right over to the restaurant at 55th and Lexington.

The French East was not a bad restaurant as far as the food went—a spicy French-Asian mixture that had drawn some moderate to good reviews—but making Henri palatable to the public was another matter. There had been that article in the *News* by a former correspondent who remembered him as "firing-squad Henri" and stated that his Hitler approach to command had inspired nearly as many desertions among his troops as casualties, which were considerable.

The restaurant's decor was another problem. It had always struck Tiernan as a cross between a Paris cafe and a rice paddy. The dining room was a vast unpartitioned area with many round tables set in what looked like a grove of pygmy palm trees. Overhead a whole squadron of white ceiling fans stirred up enough breeze most of the time to shimmy the whole grove.

Mel, the maitre d', a tall stooped consumptive-looking Frenchman, met him inside the door.

"Monsieur Tiernan, welcome again. I shall take you to the general," he said, smiling miserably and bowing.

The place was still fairly deserted and in a moment he saw

Henri sitting at a table near a wall on the far side of the room. The tiny fortyish general was wearing a white dinner jacket and smoking furiously as he jotted notes into a thin ledger.

"Please wait here while I inform the general," Mel said when they had come within fifteen feet of Henri's table.

Of course, Tiernan thought, Henri doesn't greet guests. He holds audiences. He watched as Mel stopped in a kind of spavined military attention in front of the general's table and reported his arrival in French. Henri didn't look up but put his pencil down and slammed his little thin ledger shut with the flat of his stubby hand. Then, still without looking over at his guest, he ground out his cigarette and stood to the side of the table, smoothing down his dinner jacket and increasing his height by a few extra millimeters by stretching his neck. Then, just before turning toward Tiernan, he nonchalantly slid one hand down into his jacket pocket. Then he nodded slightly to the maitre d', who bowed and walked back to Tiernan.

"General Van Dong will see you now," he said, bowing and sliding away.

"Hi, Henri," Tiernan said, extending his hand and then withdrawing it as Henri simply looked down at his little gleaming black shoes and slipped his other hand into a pocket.

"I have given orders for your lunch," Henri said, and sat down with his hands still in his pockets.

And the blindfold is a la carte, Tiernan thought as he saw a long afternoon ahead.

"Henri," he said, frowning and drumming the table with his fingers. "This is terrible for you. . . . I mean coming right at this time."

Henri just leaned back and raised an eyebrow.

"I've been trying to cool Alma down all morning, but she insists on dropping the account," Tiernan continued.

"That is quite academic, Joe, because it was *I* who dropped the account. What idiots!"

Henri glanced over and snapped his fingers at a waiter who had paused with a tray containing a bowl of soup. The waiter quickly came forward and placed it in front of Tiernan. Henri waved Tiernan to go ahead and eat and then picked up his little ledger and began slowly turning through some of the pages.

"Ummmm, this is really good, Henri," he said, spooning up the soup. "What is it?"

"Shark's fin, of course," Henri mumbled without looking up.

Tiernan smiled at his little joke and continued spooning. Yes, he was being a bit of a shark, but even if Henri had spotted his fin in the water he knew he was going to get to him.

"Okay, Henri, I won't try to con you," he said, dabbing his lips with his napkin. "I'd like to save the account. I think we can build it into something. I'm right on the verge of really moving this place. But Alma . . . Well, you saw Alma last night. What the hell happened, anyway? What set the big woman off?"

"Your big Alma is a big swine," Henri said, closing the ledger again. "I was led to believe that hers was a prestige agency. Very disappointing, Joe. Very. She came in here and . . . ugh, she was a perfect swine!"

"She's a tough cookie, Henri—but a good business-woman."

"She screamed at my waiters. She upset my customers. She upset my kitchen. She—"

"She said the cook attacked her with a cleaver, Henri. Is that right?"

"Do you know what she called my cook? A dumb gook. My whole kitchen staff threatened to deser— to quit. I had to pull her out. And then she had the stupidity to praise Ho Chi Minh! My cook was— He had four sons killed by the soldiers of Ho Chi Minh. She is lucky to be alive. *I* saved her life."

Tiernan sighed and leaned back from his soup. He nodded to Henri and shrugged his shoulders in feigned defeat. Let him relax and then get him with the Derringer, he thought.

"What can I tell you, Henri? She's impossible. It's a wonder we keep *any* accounts. I'm just sorry Hodding, the old man, saw it. Really screws up my big campaign for French East."

Tiernan did have a promotion campaign of sorts for Henri's restaurant—mainly aimed at getting some of the United Nations lunch crowd and trying to develop the image of the restaurant as an international meeting place. Capitalize on Henri's bad publicity by making it chic to dine amidst an atmosphere of intrigue and clandestine diplomacy presided over by the terrible little general. A hint of evil would be just the thing, he thought. Exactly how he would pull it off he had no idea, but he'd think of something. Maybe have Henri bug the tables and then let the media find out.

"Campaign?" Henri asked.

"Hodding has relatives high up in the State Department," Tiernan whispered and looked around. "A word from him and we could get the German."

"The German?"

"Gemetzschernsteiner," Tiernan whispered and pretended to be spooning soup again from his empty bowl.

"Ge— who?"

"Shhh," Tiernan cautioned. "The German economics guy over at the U.N. Probably the best set of buds in the business."

"Buds?"

"Taste buds. A genius on food. The whole U.N. community watches where he eats. A nod from him and you got Germany, France, Italy and Holland. And, of course, the Russians. They all follow Gemetzschernsteiner."

"Hodding is with the State Department?" Henri asked, leaning forward and lighting up a cigarette.

"No, it's Hodding's cousins. But they are very close to Gemetzschernsteiner. Like this," he said, crossing his fingers; and then had to keep from bursting out laughing as Henri puffed away on his cigarette and wiggled his eyebrows in anticipation.

"And you think we could get Gemetzschernwhatsits?" Henri asked, looking around.

"A call from Hodding," Tiernan mumbled, already seeing Gemetz accepting the role of the influential German—for a few free meals. God, he'd love it. And by the time Henri got to wondering where all of Gemetzschernsteiner's U.N. friends were he'd be able to get his own plan under way. Not bad, Joey boy, he thought to himself, and now all you have to do is stop Alma from trying to deport the entire restaurant.

"I think I can bring Alma around," Tiernan said.

"And what does Hodding say about last night?" Henri asked, remembering the doddering old gentleman trying to shake his hand and thanking him for a wonderful evening even as he and Alma were being ushered to the door.

"Well, he prefers to sleep on it," Tiernan said, sitting back while Henri waved the waiter in with the rest of the food.

The lunch lasted another two hours, with the both of them getting merrily fogged on Scotch and water and Henri lapsing into war stories, crying as usual when he came to the part where he waved goodbye to his troops from the helicopter.

Tiernan could imagine the troops crying, too—with joy. Finally, after getting Henri to agree to write Alma a letter of apology, Tiernan had one last drink with the slightly dissolved general. A few minutes later, they walked arm in arm under the whirling ceiling fans to the door, with Mel smiling and bowing amidst the rump-high palms.

That left three hours to get up to the Bronx by cab and have Marvin Green sign the agency agreement on the Waldorf coming-out ball for his daughter, and then try to get to the A.S.P.C.A. to pick up Lynn's puppy and still make Marna's party.

But this meeting with Green had taken all afternoon and there had been no time to get the dog. By the time he got back to the office it was nearly six o'clock. The office party for Marna was well under way, with most of the people gathered around his desk, which had been appropriated for the bar. Besides Alma's staff of eight, there were half a dozen of her society friends and another ten or twelve people from the two law firms down the hall. He spotted Hodding over by a window hugging Marna and patting her on the behind. The old man's nose and cheeks were already quite pinked with alcohol.

Tiernan's own head felt a little buzzed from all the drinking with Henri and then the two big tumblers of rare Scotch that Marvin Green had pressed on him. "Watch the sociability factor. Ya gotta watch the sociability factor," Green had kept reminding him as they had gone over the list of prominent guests Alma would try to provide for the event. "No bums, ya unnerstand, this is for my kid. The best of the best for my Dawn," he said, pronouncing it Doo-on. "Money's no problem, just get the sociability factor."

Nobody had noticed him come into the party, so he thought he'd touch base quickly with Marna and then try to duck out and get over to Mary's dinner. First he'd better give her a call. He was already running a little late. He hated having to tell Lynn she wouldn't get her pup tonight.

"Joe, there you are, darling," Alma said as he passed her little gathering of society friends. Darling? Where did she get that voice? Oh, her Larchmont voice, he thought, looking at the middle-aged swells around her.

"Where have you been, dear boy?" she said, hooking his arm and pulling him into her circle. Where have you *beeeen,* dear boy? he mimicked her to himself. "Isn't he beautiful,

Margaret?" Alma asked the tall woman with dry green eyes and too much lipstick. "We're finally getting some sex appeal, wouldn't you say, Helen?" Helen, pushing fifty but still toughly attractive, eyed him suggestively and held out her hand.

"Hi," he said and smiled back.

Alma introduced him around to the rest of her circle like a prize horse and then led him by the arm over to the desk with the drinks on it.

"Where in holy blazes have you been?" she asked under her breath. "And what about my letter?"

"Alma, I don't—"

"Never mind," she said, looking over his shoulder. "Oh, Arthur, you haven't met my new man. Joseph Tiernan. Joe, this is Arthur Rankin, our neighbor in Larchmont. Arthur, listen, I don't think Mildred's antique shop will be big enough for that kind of party," she said, turning her back on Tiernan and leading Arthur back to the Larchmont circle. When she had taken the little bald man nearly all the way there she turned and hurried back to Tiernan for a moment.

"We'll talk later, but for god's sake keep your eye on Hodding. He's making a complete idiot of himself! Please, Joe. Oh, god, there he goes again," she said as another woman yelped on the other side of the room with the giggling Hodding standing directly behind her.

Tiernan smiled and nodded as Alma went back to her friends. He was looking through the accumulation of bottles and cups and appetizers on his desk for his phone so he could call Mary when Marna hurried over and pressed into his side.

"Help," she said. "Hodding has me black and blue," she said, rubbing her rear.

"So this is Hodding when he's awake?" Tiernan laughed, watching the little white-haired old man staggering toward them with a gap-toothed smile on his face and his eyes blazing.

"Marna, come to Daddy," he slurred.

Marna leaped to one side, pulling Tiernan after her, as Hodding went crashing into the bottles on the desk. For a minute he just lay there in the mess, an overturned ice bucket draining water down the front of his pants.

"Here, let me help you, Mr. Reed," Tiernan said, lifting the old man to his feet and then having to grab him under his arms as he cried out, "C-c-cold!" and started to collapse.

"My god, get him into my office, Joe!" Alma exclaimed as she rushed over. "Goddam it, look at his pants!" Tiernan thought she was about to slug Hodding, who was still whimpering that he was cold and pouting his lower lip like a child.

After trying without success to get the rubber-legged old man to stand on his own, Tiernan picked him up in his arms and followed the mortified Alma to her office. He stretched Hodding out on the couch and turned to Alma, who was standing with her back to the closed door and breathing through her nose like an enraged bull.

"C-c-cold," Hodding whimpered as he shivered on the couch.

"I hope you croak, you old bastard," she snapped. She rushed over to the sofa, roughly undid Hodding's pants and yanked them off him. Then she whipped off his wet underwear while he cringed and tried to cover himself. "I could kill you!" she cried, reaching behind the sofa and pulling up a blanket and throwing it in his face.

"Mommy," Hodding whimpered and pulled the blanket down over his nakedness and then up over his head.

There was a light knock on the door.

"Alma? Is everything all right?" It was Margaret.

"Oh, yes, darling," Alma said sweetly in her Larchmont voice. "We're just getting poor Hodding tucked away for a little nap. I'll be out in a minute, darling."

There was a brief silence as Tiernan and Alma looked at each other and Hodding peeked out from under the blanket. Alma glared at him and he disappeared under the covers again.

"Stay in here with him, Joe, until he falls asleep," she said. "Usually, when he gets like this he conks out in a few minutes. You see what I have to live with?" she asked, adjusting her hair. "And if he tries to get up, sit on him," she said just before going out and closing the door.

Tiernan cursed under his breath and went over to Alma's phone. Sitting on the edge of her desk, he dialed Mary. The line was busy. He put the phone back down and slumped in exasperation. In a minute he turned and looked over at Hodding, who was still under the covers.

"You can come out now," he said, feeling a little sorry for the poor old guy.

When Hodding didn't move he waited a minute and then

went over to see if he was breathing. The blanket wasn't moving, but he thought he could hear a light snorting under the cover. He pulled it down gently and saw the old man in peaceful slumber.

Tiptoeing out, he rejoined the party, signaling to Alma with his eyes closed that Hodding was asleep. Well, now he'd get the hell out of there and try to make it to Mary's before it was too damned late. Maybe he'd take a cab. He checked his watch: six twenty-five.

He was picking up his coat from the back of his chair and flicking off some of the booze that Hodding had splashed on it when Jean came over and told him that Mary had called.

"What'd you tell her?" he asked, reaching for his phone.

"I told her you were helping out with Hodding and you'd call her back. She said to wait twenty minutes because she had to run out to the drugstore."

"Great!" he said and slammed the phone down. "Well, if she calls again, tell her I'm on my way," he said, heading for the door and pulling on his stained trench coat.

"Joe!" Alma called after him.

"Gotta go!" he yelled back and slammed the door behind him.

Then as Tiernan looked up from buttoning his coat he saw Hodding, naked from the waist down, hop into the elevator just ahead. Damn, he must have gone out Alma's private entrance, he thought, running for the elevator, missing the closing doors by inches.

"Goddam it!" he cried and headed for the stairwell. If Hodding got out on the street Alma would have a stroke. Down and around he plunged, taking the steps two and three at a time and cursing all the way. He got to the lobby just as Hodding was heading bare-assed for the revolving doors.

With a lunge he caught the revolving door and trapped Hodding in its partitions before he could get to the street. The old man danced up and down and thumbed his nose at him through the glass door. The door would not revolve backwards and Tiernan thought of pushing it around so fast it would sweep Hodding back into the building before he could get out onto the sidewalk. There was already a large crowd gathering.

"Call the Alma Reed Agency and tell her to get down here!" he yelled over his shoulder to the uniformed doorman.

Then he gave the door a great push but instead of sweeping

Hodding back into the building, it hurled him out into the arms of the gasping crowd. Tiernan raced out, grabbed him up and pushed back inside through the doors. Then he hustled him behind the news counter and put his trench coat over him. Hodding, meanwhile, was making little growling sounds and throwing feeble punches.

When Alma came down a few minutes later, Hodding suddenly went submissive again and pulled Tiernan's coat closer around his shoulders.

"It's not bad enough you have to humiliate me in front of my friends, my employees," she fumed, "now you want to get me thrown out of the building? Well, this time you are going to that nursing home, Hod! Goddam it, I've had it. Had it!"

"I guess we better get him back upstairs," Tiernan said as more and more of the building's office workers gathered around the newstand.

"Not on your life!" Alma asserted. "Joe, please, you've got to help me. I can't take any more. That horror last night and now this." Alma actually began to cry.

He held her shuddering body to him and patted her on the back. "It's okay, Alma, it's okay. It'll be all right. Come on, stop crying."

"Joe, please. Stay here with him while I go around to the garage and get the car. You've got to drive him back to Larchmont. Joe, I can't . . ." She snuffed back a big sob and burrowed into him again.

"It's okay," he said. "Go get the car, Alma."

Half an hour later Tiernan was out of the city and piloting Alma's big silver-gray Cadillac across the Westchester county line. He was thinking of Mary and Lynn waiting for him and knew that by now Mary would be getting those old feelings again. Those feelings that he was too unpredictable. He thought of all the times he'd had to call her from work and have to change their plans because something had come up. All the times he had chosen his job over the needs of his marriage and home. What a laugh, he thought. Even being out on the street would be preferable to working for Alma. How in god's name had he gotten mixed up with this bunch of crazies? He'd really come down in the world of public relations. This wasn't public relations. He spent more time patching up relations inside the office than outside. Mary was right probably. It was hopeless.

The fates again—playing craps with his life. Hodding was snoring.

There was still a lot of homebound commuter traffic, and he settled back in the plush seat for the long grind out to Larchmont. There was a special darkness about suburbia, he thought, especially after the electric glare of the city at night— a soft folded darkness that made him think of black velvet. Here and there in the distance off to his left the yellow light in a window pierced the gloom.

He turned on the radio and listened to some soft music for a while. Later, when a car stopped suddenly in front of Tiernan, causing him to hit his own brakes, Hodding woke up with a little jump. He snorted through his nose and reached up to scratch his head but stopped and dug his finger into his ear.

"How you feeling?" Tiernan asked.

"Joe, you driving?" the old man asked, sounding surprisingly coherent.

"Yeah, you fell asleep," he said, smiling over at him.

"Where're we going?"

"Home. I'm your chauffeur for the evening," Tiernan said and then suddenly thought that he had no idea where in Larchmont. "You'll have to give me the address."

"Big white house," Hodding said, sitting up straight. "Number Ten Agee Drive. My god, Joe, where are my pants? That party. Oh, my, was I a bad boy?"

"You were okay," Tiernan said, trying to spare him. "You just spilled some water on them. I loaned you my coat."

"That was nice of you, son," Hodding said, covering more of his bare legs with the coat. "How was Alma? I imagine she's fit to be tied."

"Well, I'd lie low for a while if I were you." He laughed.

"You've never been up to our place, have you? You'll like it, Joe. My father built it nearly sixty years ago. You like billiards? I've got a wonderful billiard table."

"Shot a little pool," Tiernan answered.

"You'll have to stay over. Spend the weekend."

"Not tonight. Alma wants the car right back," he said, feeling sorry for the old man, who he knew was trying to set up some kind of defense against Alma's fury when she got home. It was amazing that he could be so lucid at this point, when less than an hour ago he was a babbling idiot.

"Bull! She can come back out with the Rankins. You'll stay

and we'll shoot some pool—and I've got some of the best brandy you've ever tasted."

"I really have to get right back," he said, looking at his watch. Nearly eight o'clock. "It's my kid. She's been a little sick and I told her I'd come over."

"Well, you just be sure you don't spoil them, Joe," the old man said, getting a brooding look on his face and staring straight ahead. "God knows, that's what I did."

"You've got children?"

"All grown, of course," he said. "Two sons and a daughter. Didn't hear from them for years. Now, they're coming around sniffing after my will. Blasted ingrates, the lot of them!"

"What do they do?"

"Both boys became lawyers. Janice, she married a complete idiot. A writer, he calls himself! Never liked him, never liked him."

"I'm sorry," Tiernan said.

"Spoiled them."

"I guess I do, too." Tiernan laughed. "I have a little girl, only five, but she has me around her little finger."

"That's a good age, Joe. Mine were okay until they became teenagers, then I couldn't control 'em. Couldn't whip them anymore. Don't be afraid to use the strap, Joe."

"The strap, huh?" Tiernan said, frowning and wishing Hodding would go back to sleep.

The traffic was still fairly heavy heading out of the city. There were few cars coming back on the other side of the parkway. He recognized Chopin's *Les Sylphides* on the radio— Mary's favorite. He had never been into classical music the way she was. It was the only thing he knew that she had a real passion for. He liked some of it, but the darker, more melancholy stuff. He liked Fauré's *Requiem* because it brought back the Catholicism of his childhood—the haunting beauty of that oppressive world that he had abandoned intellectually. The heater was up nearly all the way in the big car, but he wondered if Hodding was warm enough with his bare legs sticking out from under his trench coat.

"You warm enough?" he asked, turning to the old man. Hodding had drifted off to sleep with a scowl on his face.

Probably thinking of his ingrate children, Tiernan thought.

Hodding was still asleep when he pulled into the drive of the big home on Agee Drive. There was a gaslight on the front steps of the sprawling white stucco mansion, but he continued on the drive around to the rear of the house so that the neighbors would not see Hodding's condition. He could see one of the maids in the lighted kitchen window at the rear.

"Mr. Reed?" he asked and gave Hodding a little shove.

"What is it? What is it?" Hodding exclaimed, startled out of his sleep.

"You're home," he said.

"Oh, Joe, did you drive me home? Where's Alma?"

"She'll be along," he said, and got out and went around and helped the slightly confused old man out.

"So cold out here," the old man complained, not aware that he had no pants on.

By the time Tiernan and the maid had gotten Hodding tucked away in bed, it was after 9 P.M. and Tiernan felt miserable as he searched the big expensively furnished living room for the phone. Finally the maid brought it in to him on a long cord from the hallway. He slumped into one of the deep chairs and dialed Mary.

"Hi," he said.

"Hi," she said. Her voice was tired but not angry. He almost wished she had been angry.

"I'm sorry," he said, pushing his hair back. "I had to drive the old man out to Larchmont."

"I know, the girl told me. I called back when you didn't show up. Where are you now?"

"Larchmont." He sighed wearily.

"Lynn's asleep. Did you get the dog?"

"I didn't have time. It's been a crazy day, Mary."

"Sounds like it. It's just that I told Lynn you got the dog. She's going to be disappointed. I explained to her that your work kept you away tonight."

"How is she?"

"Okay, I think she's over her flu."

"I feel rotten about the dog."

"I'll explain to her when she gets up," Mary said and he could hear the agitation creeping into her voice.

"Do you think she'll be up to going out tomorrow?" he asked.

"Probably, why?"

"I thought I'd take her up to the pound and let her pick out her own dog. What do you think?"

"She'd like that. What time?"

"Noon," he said, feeling a little better.

"Fine, we'll be expecting you."

"Uh, Mary? Any chicken left?" he asked, hoping there was still a chance to see her tonight. He wanted desperately to see her, to touch base with something meaningful in his life after this day of insanity.

"Oh, Joe, it's so late. Can't you grab a bite out there? You must be starved and it will take you more than an hour to get back."

"Yeah, I guess. But, I . . . uh . . . Are you alone?"

"Yes, but I am expecting someone."

"I always seem to step into it, don't I?" he said, trying to keep his voice from showing too much disappointment.

"I'm sorry."

"Hey, don't be sorry. I just missed my place in line, right?"

"Joe, you're tired, and I don't feel like fighting with you."

"I guess you're right—tired and pissed off at Alma. I didn't mean to take it out on you."

"Why don't you have dinner with us tomorrow night?"

"I've got a date tomorrow night," he lied. "I'll come by about noon to take Lynn to the pound for the dog."

"I wish you wouldn't be angry."

"I'm not angry," he said angrily. "Just tired. I . . . I'll see you. Bye," he said, hanging up the phone with a slam. Fuck you, he thought, I *will* get a date tomorrow.

He got up and rubbed his face to clear his head and then walked to the back door. Just as he got outside the maid ran to the door and said that Alma was on the phone.

"Christ," he whined in exasperation and turned back.

Alma started talking nonstop the minute he picked up the phone and said hello. She was speaking in her Larchmont voice, so he knew her friends must be nearby. In the background he could hear people saying goodbye at the party. Alma was ever so grateful about his helping out with Hodding, one of those little embarrassments of old age, everyone had a great time, too bad he couldn't have stayed, but there was one last favor, please, Joe.

"Of course, Alma . . . Anything, Alma," he said sarcastically.

"You're such a dear," she said, ignoring his tone.

Would he mind staying over for the night in Larchmont? She

was going to come out in the Rankins' car, so there was no need for him to bring hers back to the city. She'd just been through too much for one day, she said. She just wanted to get right home. She'd drive him back to the city in the morning. Be a dear, Joseph.

"Alma, I have to go home tonight," he said, desperate to get away from her mad world.

"But I *have* to have my car in the morning," she protested.

"It's okay, Alma," he said. "I'll take the train back. There is a train station here, isn't there?" He was furious.

"Of course, but you—"

"I'll leave the car at the train station, Alma," he said and slammed the phone down again. "Shit!" he shouted and stormed out.

After parking the car in the station's lot, he went in and bought a ticket and sat down to wait. The next train to the city would be along in an hour and five minutes, the ticket agent had said. Sitting there, he noticed the neon lights of a tiny bar across the street and decided to wait over there. He needed some good numbing Scotch to kill the pain that was building into an explosion inside of him. One, two, three drinks down fast and in a little while even the blaring country music on the jukebox started sounding good to him.

Then slow conversational drinks with the bartender about how the best thing a man could have was a good, loving, patient, understanding wife—the bartender had had four of them—and how a man's life wasn't worth a damn without one. At eleven-thirty he looked up at the clock over the bar and realized he'd missed the train. Fuck it, he thought and ordered another Scotch. When the next train was pulling into the station at twelve forty-five, the bartender alerted him and he managed to wobble across the street and jump on before it took off.

As the train slid through the suburban night, he sat slumped in his seat staring at his haggard Irish face in the window. Beginning to look more like my old man every day, he thought, remembering his tough, bad-tempered father. Biggest man on the Worcester police force, he thought. Beat the hell out of his kids, too. Yeah, Hodding, I know all about the strap, he thought. Up ahead the city was glowing over the velvet night.

At 3 A.M. Tiernan was lying in his own room, his bleary face illuminated in the light of the little Sony television set sitting on a bottom corner of the bed. He pulled his tie loose and unbuttoned his vest. Still wearing his new suit. Idiots in new suits, he thought and took a sip from the cold can of Miller's beer in his hand.

"Equipped to travel," he sighed drunkenly and raised his beer to Talbot's theory. Then he patted the five other cans in the six-pack snuggled against his hip. He drained the remaining half of the can's contents in long swallows, belched and laughed and let it drop off the side of the bed.

"Aaaaaah, good cold brine ta slake me pain and drrrown me sorrows." He sighed and popped open another can. "And t'morrow Oy'll lick the whole bloody warld. Meself—just meself. And when did a Tiernan need a bloody woman? Hey?" he shouted.

The television set on the bottom of the bed flickered in his eyes, flashing scenes without sound. A lovely young Indian squaw running through some tall grass after her Indian brave who was being carried away by some cavalry men on horseback. Her face a mask of torment over the loss of her man.

Tiernan closed his eyes and let out a long sigh of despair. "Women, women, women."

# CHAPTER
# EIGHT

There was a light sleeting rain Monday morning and Susan Talbot was hurrying down Garfield toward Seventh trying to keep Teddy from running out from under her umbrella. The sidewalk was full of slushy puddles and Teddy seemed determined to stamp in every one of them, chilling her legs and streaking her nylons with cascades of dirty water.

On Monday mornings she worked for ChildSpace, a parents' cooperative day-care center on Seventh Avenue, and she was hoping to get there early to change out of her good clothes before the other parents began dropping their children off. She was irritated with Teddy's splashing, and she was irritated with herself for not wearing her boots. But most of all she was irritated because Bob Gillet had not come down from New London over the weekend as he had promised. He had not even bothered to call.

"Now, stop it!" she exclaimed, jerking Teddy back from a big puddle he was gleefully aiming his snowboot at.

As she turned up Seventh Avenue she let go of Teddy's hand for a moment to try to button the bottom of her raincoat. She regretted it immediately and cringed as he ran ahead and leaped with both boots into the middle of a small sidewalk lake in front of the Korean vegetable store. Some of the water that

Teddy splashed out of the puddle slapped a crotchety-looking black dog in the face and drew a protest from its master, an elderly little man wearing a black beret.

"I'm terribly sorry," Susan apologized and waited at the edge of the puddle for Teddy, who was wading toward her looking triumphant. "Look what you did to that poor doggie," she admonished as the dog shook itself and tried to snort the ice water out of its nose.

"Come, Pixley!" the old man said disdainfully and walked away pulling the snorting dog along by its leash.

"That's your last puddle, young man," she warned as she snatched Teddy's hand and skirted around the edge of the huge puddle. "Do you understand me?"

Teddy gave her a sly look, a child's echo of the one she had seen so often on Len's face when he, too, was not taking her seriously. At times she had the eerie feeling that she had gotten rid of Len only to have him come back in miniature.

"Do you understand me?" she repeated and stopped to emphasize her point with a look that he understood—one that meant a good smack on the behind was near.

"Uh-huh," he said, nodding.

As they continued up Seventh Avenue she could feel the cold water creeping down inside her new high heels. She would be glad to change into her tennis shoes when she got to the center. She kept them and a pair of jeans and a paint-smeared old sweat shirt at the center for her work with the children. At noon, when Len would come in to take over the second half of their assigned day each week at the center, her shoes and stockings should be dry, she thought. Then she would head for her part-time job as a fabric designer in Manhattan.

She and Len had helped to found the center in a storefront on Seventh Avenue shortly before the breakup, and despite all that had happened between them—even during those venomous first months of separation—he had maintained the split-day arrangement to keep Teddy in the center. It enabled her to work part time and him to keep his support payments down to fifty dollars a week.

He was good with children. Some of the other mothers who worked in the center had called him a pure delight. A parent of each of the fifteen children in the center was required to put in one day a week of supervision, but Len and one other father were the only men who participated. About half of the women were divorcees, and Susan had an idea that they were not just thinking of his work with the children when they called him a "pure delight."

It made her feel strange viewing him through the eyes of other women. Yes, he was a good-looking man. A hunk, as Chrissy Ludlow, one of her best friends, had called him. And certainly better-looking than Bob Gillet. Oh, that . . . that *wimp!* she thought. Why, why, why, why did I sleep with him? Her mother had brought him around the day after the Christmas party. The most eligible bachelor in New London, she had said. And hadn't she gone to high school with him? She remembered him only after her mother had brought out her old high school yearbook. Not him! she had told her mother, calling him the spookiest little guy in their class. All glasses and pimples in those days. Well, he's not spooky now, her mother had said, describing how he was driving around in a new Jaguar, living in his own seven-bedroom house and prospering mightily as a dermatologist. It figured he'd turn out to be a pimple doctor, Susan had laughed. He arrived the next day, still shorter than she, but the pimples were gone and he'd added a little dash to his style. She found him appealing and they had spent the day zooming around the Berkshires in his sports car—and the night in a fashionable little roadhouse outside of Hartford. He had made love like a tourist and had sped out of her life in a cloud of promises.

It wouldn't have worked out anyway, she thought, remembering the sour face he had made when she told him she had a child. She gave Teddy's hand a loving squeeze. He was walking along looking at everything with that curious brooding look of his and, thank god, ignoring the puddles. Across the street she watched some parents hurrying their children into the new tan brick public school building. All the other children seemed to be wearing hooded yellow rain slickers like Teddy's. Poor Teddy, that's where you'll be going next year, she thought. God, all those plans we had for sending you to private schools. Dreams cost money, she thought, and that one got shot down in the divorce.

Len had told her he wanted Teddy to grow up to be a great scholar, something he had prized since his boyhood in Texas. Even before Teddy was born he had talked of how wonderful it would be to have a son, whose mind he could shape into a thing of brilliance. They would send him to Eastern prep schools, Harvard, then perhaps Oxford or Cambridge—all the things his mother had dreamed for him but made impossible by their transient existence as army dependents. He'd told her of growing up torn between his father's desire to see him tough and manly with perhaps a career in the army, and his mother, who kept plying him with books and idealistic visions of becoming a great educator.

Susan remembered when she had met him at the university and how captivated she had been by this tall rugged-looking Texan who spoke so softly and sensitively about the world of ideas. And how proud she had been of him in the first two years of their marriage, when she would drive up to the Brooklyn campus each afternoon to pick him up after his classes. He'd grown a mustache then and looked so professorial in his tweeds and sweaters.

But there had always been the division deep within him over satisfying his mother's and father's dreams. And in the last year of their marriage it seemed his father's influence was finally beginning to emerge. His father had retired from the army the previous summer and that seemed to mellow Len's attitude toward him. And for the first time he'd started talking about how he'd admired his father's military exploits when he was a child. And there was less talk about Teddy's growing up to be a scholar.

Well, she was not about to give up the dream, she thought, looking down at the boy. You're still going to private schools, she thought. Maybe not this year, but soon. Your old mommy's gonna pull it off. A few good breaks with my job this year, and then watch out. Mommy's got talents you've never heard about.

She felt a twinge of sadness as she thought of him entering his first school year. Taking her baby away. The world already reaching for him. And it doesn't give a damn about you either. It doesn't want to know you, Teddy. C'mere, kid, get in line! Shut up and do what you're told! You'll have to be strong. But I'll make you strong.

Her thoughts were interrupted by the suggestive sucking noise made by one of the young men unloading beef carcasses from a truck in front of Oscar's Meat Market. She had to stop as the young man paused directly in front of her balancing a split quarter-carcass on his powerful shoulders. He looked down at her with deep brown Italian eyes and puckered his red lips and made the sucking sound again. His ruggedly hand-some face was glistening in the soft freezing rain and the great carcass on his shoulders put her in mind of butchery . . . his.

Out of my way, you bastard, she thought as she blazed a look of contempt at him and walked around him.

"Mommy, look!" Teddy shouted, pulling her back so that he could see the racks of beef hanging in the truck. "Are them deaded cows?"

"Hi, there, preddy mamma," another young loader said from inside the back of the meat truck. He was short and squat and wore blood-smeared white overalls. "Have I gotta soup bone for you!"

"Come on," she said, pulling Teddy away and fighting down an urge to throw a finger at the leering ape in the truck.

Then, as she started up Seventh Avenue again, she heard the first young loader make the sucking noise again. This time something exploded inside her and she whirled around and threw both of them the finger.

"Oh-ho! Hey, Mamma, not in fronna da liddle boy! Dat's a naughty-naughty!" the loader in the truck called out and laughed.

"Scum!" she yelled back and turned and stormed away, nearly dragging Teddy off his feet. At the same time she was furious with herself for engaging with such idiots. Their laughter continued to bark along at her heels as she hurried through the rain.

"Are you mad at them mens cause they killed all them cows?" Teddy asked.

In her fury she did not register his question. She hated such men. They were the jackals of the male species. Cowards, too. If Len had been with her those two apes would never have even dared to look sideways at her. Oh, god, Len would have knocked the face off that sucking bastard back there.

"Mommy, are you mad at them mens?" Teddy persisted.

"What?" she asked vaguely, still engulfed in anger.

"Were them bad mens, Mommy?" he asked, looking up at her with wide searching eyes.

"They're pigs!" she snarled.

She knew he didn't understand and after a few more steps she got control of herself and stopped, reached down, pretending to adjust the hood on his slicker.

"I'm sorry, honey," she said, softening her voice. "It's

nothing to worry about. Okay? Those men back there . . . I, they had very bad manners and that's what made Mommy mad. Remember how I told you about having good manners?"

"Yeah," he said, nodding and searching her eyes for what she was really saying.

"Well, it's because I don't want you to grow up like those men back there. Okay?"

"Okay."

"I love you," she said, hugging him to her thigh.

"But Mommy?"

"What, dear?"

"How did them mens kill all them cows?"

"Oh, they— I don't know, Teddy. Come on, we'd better hurry now. Hey, I bet Alexis is coming today," she said, referring to one of his little playmates at the center. "Don't you want to see Alexis?" She wanted to get his mind off the dead cows.

"Mommy, Alexis doesn't have good manners," he said of the little girl who was always following him around the center and hitting him with blocks at times when he wouldn't play with her. "She's gonna grow up and kill cows, I bet."

Susan had to laugh. She gave him one last hug to her thigh and took his hand and laughed again. What a joy he was, she thought.

Chrissy Ludlow and her three-year-old son, Robert, were already in the center when they got there. Susan peered into the front window briefly and saw the willowy young divorcee with long red hair taking quart cans of apple juice from a bag she was holding and putting them into the refrigerator. Must've just gone in, Susan thought, seeing Chrissy was still wearing her green down jacket and big blue earmuffs. Robert was just below her with half his body leaning into the refrigerator.

"Hi!" Susan warbled as she stepped down into the center's main room.

"Suzy?" Chrissy called from the open kitchen area at the back. "Hi," she said, looking over her shoulder and smiling. With the last can in, she pulled Robert out of the refrigerator and closed the door.

"Whew! Smells like a bar in here," Susan said, glancing into the big trash barrel and finding it full of empty beer cans and cigar butts. "Goddam it, Rafferty's been having more of his Saturday night poker sessions again."

"I think he only sends his kid here so he can use his key on weekends," Chrissy said, watching Susan go into the bathroom, which had a long piece of flower-print cloth draped down for a door. "Hey, speaking of bars, Suzy . . ."

"Yeah?" Susan asked from behind the curtain.

"Well, remember what we talked about? I mean, going out on my birthday?"

"Oh, god, that's right! Hey, happy birthday, kiddo. What a time to start our career in barhopping—Monday night. Great timing, Chris! Even bartenders probably don't show up on Monday nights. Did you pick out a bar?"

"Well, everyone I talked to said to go to Larsky's," Chrissy said. She tucked Robert's coat under hers and hung them both on one of the hooks near the door.

"Yeah, Helen Margolis says that's where the action is in Park Slope," Susan said, slipping her old gray sweat shirt down over her bare breasts. "Sure doesn't look like much from the outside, though. Kind of tough-looking. Maybe we should go to the Marlebone? Very elegant, Chrissy—gaslight and mirror-top tables. I've eaten there."

"Well, my deah, I have heard that it's gone quite gay," Chrissy said, leaning in through the curtain and doing a la-di-da with her hand.

"Well, then, my deah," Susan said, flouncing out and stroking Chrissy under the chin, "maybe they won't notice that we came in without dates."

"Oh, you wicked, wicked thing," Chrissy said, flouncing out behind her.

"Besides, I'm just about ready for that after this weekend," Susan said, getting serious again.

"What happened? How was your New London doctor?"

"He wasn't! I got stood up."

"Oh . . . Hey, I'm sorry. What happened, he get called to the hospital or something?"

"Who would know?" Susan exclaimed, clapping a cloud of chalk dust out of two erasers and then wiping off the stick figures the children had drawn on the blackboard the previous week. "The bastard never even bothered to call."

"Damn," Chrissy commiserated. "Look, forget it. Okay? We'll go to Larsky's and have a lot of fun tonight. Trisha's coming along with us, and you know what a riot she can be.

And maybe, just maybe, there'll be old Prince what's-his-name sitting at the bar."

"You know who's liable to be sitting at the bar, don't you?" Susan asked, turning and giving her a meaningful look.

"Nope. Burt Reynolds is going to be in Hollywood all week," Chrissy said. "I follow his movements on a map in my bedroom."

"My ex," Susan said, continuing to clean off the blackboard.

"Len?"

"No, my other ex," she said impatiently.

"Huh?"

"Of course, Len. He practically lives at Larsky's these days, I understand."

"Shit," Chrissy said, biting her lip.

"I'll make a deal with you," Susan said, walking over closer to Chrissy as Marge Deter came in the front door with Alexis. "I'll go to Larsky's if you agree we get up and leave immediately if Len shows up." She dropped her voice to a whisper as Marge drew close. "Or turn around and walk right out if he's already there. Agreed?"

"Agreed," Chrissy whispered back. "But I don't see what difference it makes. After all, you're divorced— Oh, hi, Marge!"

Ian Rafferty, as usual, had forgotten his key and was banging on the window. When Susan got to the door, Rafferty's little daughter, Cathy, was standing there alone and Ian was hightailing it to his car at the curb.

"Ian!" Susan exclaimed. "Wait a minute! Ian!" she shouted and started out after him.

"Susan, my love! You'll catch your death in this rain!" he shouted and then ducked into his car and lurched it away before she could get to the curb.

"Damn you, Rafferty!" she screamed at his departing car, then stood blinking against the misting rain.

The hell with it, she thought as she turned and walked back to the center hugging her arms. Four more months of this crap and they can turn ChildSpace into PigSpace for all I care. Damned Irish. Damned men! Damned rain!

"Oh, goddam it!" she exploded as she reached for the door and found it locked. Cathy must have closed it after she had gone out. Ducking her face from the rain, she walked back around to the front window and rapped . . . and rapped and rapped. Finally after about three minutes, Chrissy walked back into the main room from the kitchen area and noticed. Marge had been sitting talking to Alexis the whole time and had been oblivious of the noise on the window.

"How'd you get out there?" Chrissy asked as Susan brushed past her, boiling.

"Me?" Susan asked, wiping the rain slowly from her face and looking around and giving Cathy a fierce smile. "I was just having a lovely little conversation with Mr. Rafferty."

"Oh, yeah?" Chrissy asked, still looking puzzled.

"Mustn't pick our little nose, Cathy," Susan said, still smiling and then nearly gagged as the tiny three-year-old extracted her index finger from her nose and offered Susan the prize nugget stuck to the end of it.

"Is that for me?" Susan asked sweetly and looked over at Chrissy with a sickly smile. "Here, let me get a napkin so we can save it, darling."

And so it went for the next half-hour with the other children being dropped off by their parents, and Susan, Chrissy and Marge hanging up coats, wiping noses, consoling and generally trying to cheer up the usual Monday morning crabbiness of the children.

"God, you'd think they all had hangovers," said Marge, a tall woman in her late thirties with graying hair and deep-cleft lines in her face.

By eleven o'clock the children had made the transition from tranquil weekend home life to the competitive peer world inside the center, and pandemonium was in full swing. Nearly all of the boys and a few of the girls were engaged in a fierce intergalactical war between the Death Star invaders and Superman, Batman, Spiderman and Wonderwoman. And Wonderwoman's daughter. At the same time, Alexis, Frannie and Marissa were operating a combination restaurant and hospital in the indoor sandbox to take care of casualties.

The rain had finally stopped and Susan was standing near the back window sipping a cup of coffee while she took a five-minute break from the space war and tea party going on behind her. Outside, the little paved-over back play yard was full of puddles and the four-tier wooden complex of monkey bars was glistening with drops of rain.

Len would be showing up in about an hour and she was

wondering if she should tell him about her plan to invade his stomping ground that night. She knew he wouldn't like it. She could see his face when she asked him. Asked him? What the hell was going on here? she wondered. Why should she have to ask him if she could go to Larsky's? I want to go to Larsky's, I go to Larsky's. If he feels uncomfortable with that . . . well, there's a hell of a lot of other bars in New York.

Just then Marissa let out a blood-curdling scream as Alexis threw a tin plate of sand in her eyes. She threw it because Marissa had just married herself to Teddy after he had crawled into the sandbox with forty dozen Krypton bullets stuck in his chest and had his Superman towel cape stolen by the Death Star invaders. When Alexis had tried to fix him up with a piece of her sandmade chocolate cherry fudge cake, Marissa had haughtily stepped in front of her and declared him off-limits. So Alexis gave the chocolate cherry fudge cake to Marissa—in the face.

While Susan and Chrissy were busy in the bathroom washing the sand out of Marissa's eyes, Marge was giving Alexis a good scolding.

"It was a terrible, terrible thing to do," Marge was saying to the uncontrite girl. "You could blind somebody by throwing things in their eyes. How many times have I told you that? You're growing up to be a girl with no manners."

Teddy, who was standing nearby, nodded knowingly.

Susan waited until she saw Len's car pull up outside at noon before she started changing clothes. Usually she was ready to go when he got there, but this time she wanted to be busy and hurry out without having to stop and talk to him for long. Of course, they would have to talk when she picked up Teddy at his rooming house after six o'clock, but she'd have all afternoon to decide what she was or was not going to tell him about Larsky's.

From behind the bathroom curtain, as she was slipping on her now dry panty hose, Susan heard Len announce his arrival with a loud Tarzan yell. The children, who had just been seated at the long table for their lunch, responded with gleeful shouts.

"Daddy!" Teddy called out proprietarily.

"Tarzan hungry!" Len said gruffly as he neared the table. "Tarzan eat up food of boys and girls. Um-yum, Tarzan take!"

Susan smiled as she heard the children squeal with protest as he moved around the table pretending to steal the sandwiches and fruit from their lunch boxes.

"Peanut butter—yum," he said. "Chicken—yum. Ba-na-na! Yum!"

"Here, Tarzan, you can eat my samich!" Jennifer shouted from the end of the table.

"Here, Tarzan!" another child shouted.

"Eat mine!" Alexis squealed.

Then she heard Marge and Chrissy begin to take charge again, trying to stem the uproar before it upset the whole lunch period.

"All right, children, everyone settle down and maybe we can have Tarzan sit down and eat with us," Marge said. "Okay, Tarzan?" There was an edge of anger in her voice.

"Or else Tarzan is going to be sent back up his tree," Chrissy added.

When the shouting and squealing continued, Len brought it to an abrupt halt by shouting, "Shaddup!"

Then two of the little girls down at the end of the table started tittering again and he raced over to them and threw his arms around their shoulders with a fierce growl. Each start of a new titter from them was shut off with a new growl. Then he stood up and glared at everybody with an apelike scowl.

"Okay, everybody eat and then we'll go out back and play. Okay?" he asked.

This appeased them and they went back to eating and laughing among themselves.

"Susan already leave?" he asked Chrissy.

"In the bathroom getting ready," Chrissy said through a mouthful of baloney sandwich.

"Hi!" he exclaimed brightly as he poked his head in around the curtain just as she was lowering her dress down over her head.

"Hi, yourself," she said, knowing he was gazing at her nudity through her transparent panty hose. She took her time adjusting the dress down.

"Nice dress," he said while she still had it rumpled around her waist.

"Nothing you haven't seen before," she said, looking at him calmly as she smoothed the dress down at her thighs.

"Been a while," he said, sniffing. "One forgets."

"I'm late," she said, moving toward the curtain and forcing him to back out.

"Ah . . . the, ah, usual time?" he asked as she headed over to get her coat from the wall hook.

"I might be a little late," she said. "I have to pick up some sketches from Granger's on the way home." She walked over to Teddy as she slipped into her coat. "Be a good boy," she said, leaning over and kissing him on the cheek. Teddy nodded and went back to talking with George, the boy on his right, who was still wearing his rag cape.

"So?" Len asked.

"About six-thirty," she said as she walked past him toward the door.

"No rush," he said. "I'll be home all evening doing papers."

Susan stopped and gave Chrissy a look as she weighed the possibility of bringing up the Larsky's issue. She could call him outside and talk it out with him right then. No, she thought, not sure she wanted to mention it at all. If he was going to be home all night, they could go to Larsky's and he'd never know.

"See you before seven, anyway," she said and turned and went out the door.

"Right," he said to the closing door.

# CHAPTER
# NINE

By eight o'clock that night Susan had still not shown up at Talbot's for Teddy, and he was wondering if he should start getting the boy ready for bed at his place. He was also beginning to feel annoyed that she had not even called. At the moment he and the boy were sitting quietly opposite each other at his heavy round oak table in the window bay.

He watched Teddy leafing through some pictures in one of his books on the Frontier West and then took his reading glasses off and tossed them on the pile of American history essays he'd started grading.

"Good book?" he asked, rubbing his eyes and stretching.

"Pretty good," the boy said without looking up.

Talbot got up and walked in his white wool socks to the window just behind the boy. Peering outside, he could see the rain slanting down out of the darkness past the glow of the streetlamp over near the edge of the park. A few cars slished by on the wet street. But looking down the sidewalk, he could see no one coming. Goddam it, he thought, same old kiss-my-ass Susan. At eight-thirty I'm putting him to bed, he thought, looking again at his watch. He imagined her snotty reaction when she would show up: "I told you I was going to be late. Why'd ya have to put him to bed?" She can kiss my ass, he thought as he watched the rain pelting off the stone railing along the brownstone steps.

The room smelled of hamburgers he had cooked up for their supper and he smiled as he remembered Teddy's ultimate compliment: "Almost as good as Burger King, Daddy."

"That's General Custer," he said, looking over the boy's shoulder at the book.

"Who's General Custard?" Teddy asked, nuzzling his head back against his father's white T-shirt as Talbot leaned over him and placed his hands on either side of the open book.

"He was a soldier back in the days when they fought the Indians," Talbot said, scratching his chin on the top of Teddy's head. "Only he didn't do so well. Looks like a shoe salesman, doesn't he?"

Teddy studied the picture again and tried to think whether looking like a shoe salesman was good or bad. He wanted to ask his father what a shoe salesman was, but instead he just nodded his head and pretended he knew, too. He liked the closeness of his father's strong body hovering over him, and he looked with awe at the big veins on the back of his father's powerful hands.

"Did General Custard kill the Indians, Daddy?"

"For a while—until the Indians got him."

"Was he bad?"

"No, mostly he was a pretty good soldier. Then he did something stupid—and that was that."

"Grampa was a soldier," Teddy said proudly.

"Yep, he sure was," Talbot said, smiling as he remembered his father carrying Teddy around on his shoulders when they had visited him shortly before he retired.

"Did Grampa fight the Indians?"

"No, he isn't *that* old," Talbot said, straightening up and tousling the boy's hair. "But, your great, great Grandpa George did," he said, walking over to the mantelpiece and picking up the sword. "This was his sword."

"Oh, let me play with it, Daddy!" Teddy exclaimed and jumped up from his seat and ran toward his father.

"Whoops! No dice," Talbot said, suddenly remembering the last scene he'd had with Susan over the sword. "Every time I let you play with it you tell Mommy, and then Mommy jumps down my throat. Maybe when you're a little older."

Susan hated anything military, particularly his father, and

went into a rage whenever he talked about the army to the boy. Professional killers, she called them and swore that her son would grow up with a reverence for life.

"Please, Daddy? I wouldn't tell Mommy."

"Huh-uh," he said, putting the sword back and resenting his giving in to her irrational bias.

"If I grow up to be a soldier could I have a sword, too?" Teddy asked as his father escorted him over to the bed and sat him on his knee.

"Sure can," he said. "I might even give you this one. Course, you'd only be able to wear it at parades. They don't fight with swords anymore."

"How come you wasn't a soldier, Daddy?" the boy asked.

"Because I had asthma," he said, bouncing Teddy on his knee and then falling back and holding the boy up over his head and chest. Then he got his feet under the boy's chest and raised him higher. Both father and son were wearing white T-shirts and jeans. Teddy started laughing and begged to come down when he tickled him with his toes.

"What's asthma?" Teddy asked after Talbot lowered him onto his chest.

"Remember how last summer I got sick and couldn't breathe too good? That's asthma."

"Did you want to be a soldier?" the boy asked, leaning on his father's chest.

"Yeah, when I was your age," Talbot said and then felt an old ache as he remembered his father's disappointment in him. The look on his father's face each time the boy had to be put to bed, the same look he'd had when they had gone out that morning to destroy the colt that had been born deformed. The old soldier had always dreamed of having a son at West Point.

"Look, Teddy," he said, sitting up and placing the boy on his lap again. "Being a soldier is not bad. No matter what your mother says. If it were not for soldiers, we would probably not even be here today. They are the ones who go out and protect us when the enemy wants to come and hurt us and take away our country. And it isn't easy to be a soldier. They have to go away from their families and sleep on the ground and sometimes they have to give up their lives."

"You know what I really want to be when I grow up, Daddy?" the boy asked after a moment of thought.

"What's that?"

"A vetinarium. 'Cause they help animals."

"That's good," Talbot said, smiling. "Hey, how'd you like to play Titans?" Titans was their pillow-fighting game, in which they played Olympian heroes hurling great stones at each other. Teddy nodded eagerly.

"Okaaaaay!" Talbot roared as he jumped up and began bouncing high on the bed with a pillow over his head.

Teddy squealed with delight and scrambled under him to grab his own pillow.

"Nobody can kill the great— Oh, wait a minute," he said, suddenly remembering the complaints crotchety old Mr. Richter raised across the foyer every time they got into one of these yowling pillow fights. Stopping his bouncing momentarily and putting his finger to his lips, he said, "Let's have a quiet one this time. We don't want Mr. Richter coming over again."

"I'm the great Herkalees!" Teddy yelled anyway and began bouncing up and down holding a pillow high over his head.

"And I'm the great Zeus!" Talbot yelled and began jumping again.

Then Zeus let out a loud "Yaaaaaaaagh!" and crumpled off the bed onto the floor as Hercules hit him in the stomach with a giant boulder-pillow.

"Yeeeaaa! Herkalees is the greatest!" Teddy yelled triumphantly.

"Zeus comes alive again!" Talbot yelled, jumping up from the floor with his pillow over his head and a ferocious look on his face.

Just then the front doorbell buzzed.

"That's Mommy," Talbot said, going over to ring her in.

Opening the door, he saw Susan stamping her way across the hallway to get the rain off her shoes and frowning as she tried to close the snap on her dripping umbrella. Her cheeks were rosy and moist from the weather, but he could tell as she came up to him that she had had exactly two cocktails just before coming over to pick up Teddy. It had always been that way with her eyes, a slight lidding by which he could calibrate the amount and almost what type of liquor she had been drinking.

"Orange blossoms!" he said, snapping his fingers.

"Martinis," she fired back. "How many?"

"Two—maybe two and a half."

"Two," she said with a shrug and brushed past him into the room.

"Martinis?" he asked, taking one last look out into the foyer. "When'd you start drinking martinis?" he added, closing the door and then jerking it open again—in time to catch Mr. Richter's door opening another inch and then closing across the foyer.

"So, how's my big boy?" Susan asked as she walked over to Teddy, who was now kneeling on his chair with the book open.

"Mommy, look here," he said excitedly. "That's General Custard. He was stupid, so the Indians killed him and that was that."

"Well," she said, going around the table and giving him a hug. "Uh-hum, sure doesn't look too bright in this picture does he?"

"But my great, great Grampa killed the Indians with Daddy's sword. Right, Daddy?"

Talbot was making motions with his hands and face for Teddy to be quiet about the subject around his mother and then stopped and smiled guiltily as Susan looked up.

"God, I wish you'd leave off that soldier and killing business with him," she said, coming back around the table.

"He just wanted to know about Custer," Talbot said defensively, beginning to feel a little irritated about having his man-to-man relationship edited by her—or any woman. These were things that had to do with the man's world.

"Whew! Smells like a giant hamburger in here," she said, crinkling her nose.

"Hey!" he said, raising his hand to shut her off. "Before we get too far into your comments here . . . What the hell kept you?"

"Business," she said, picking up Teddy's boots. "Come on, cowboy, let's start getting ready," she said to Teddy.

"Well, it's nearly eight-thirty and I—" Talbot began.

"Look, I couldn't get away. They've got a new art director over at Granger's and I had to orient him on our lines."

"Over martinis," he added sulkily and went over and sat down at his desk. Teddy, meanwhile, was sitting on the floor pulling on his boots while Susan pulled his jacket out of his raincoat sleeves.

"Len," she said, shaking her head and looking up at the ceiling, "this is beginning to sound like one of our old conversations. I'm sorry I was late, but let's just drop it. Okay?"

"Excuse *me*," he said, picking up one of the essays on the table.

"Come on, Teddy, we've got to hurry. Mommy has a baby sitter coming over in a little while."

"Baby sitter?" Len exclaimed and then shut himself off and waved his hands for her to disregard the question. She was right, drop it.

"It's Chrissy's birthday and me and Trisha are taking her out. That okay with you?" she said as she held the coat for Teddy to slip into.

"None of *my* business," he said, waving away the subject with his back to her.

"Say goodbye to Daddy," she said to the boy after she had zipped up his slicker.

"Hey, c'mere, bucko!" Len said, swinging around and pulling the boy into his lap as Teddy rushed over. "Tell you what. On Saturday we'll go see a movie. Okay?"

"Which one?" Teddy asked, smiling.

"How about *Star Trek?*" Talbot said, giving him a hug and a kiss and putting him down again.

"Oh, sweat!" Teddy exclaimed gleefully.

"Sweat?" Talbot asked, scratching his head and looking at Susan.

"It means swell, I think," she said with a shrug as she held the door open for Teddy to leave. "What time Saturday? Noon, one o'clock . . . What?"

Talbot nodded and went back to the table again.

"What?" she asked again.

"Yeah, noon," he said, slumping down in his chair without looking back at her. "No, one," he added. He heard the door slam. From his chair he could see part of the front stoop through the window. In a moment Susan and Teddy appeared and descended with Teddy's rain hood barely visible above the stone railing.

The book that the boy had been reading still lay open and Talbot reached over and turned it around. There was a picture of an old 1870s desert fort with a grouping of bearded cavalry soldiers posing stiffly in front of an adobe headquarters building. Yeah, Teddy, he thought, I wanted to be a soldier. For a moment he could hear again the distant thumping of cannons and the blowing of reveille bugles that had awakened him nearly every morning of his youth living on the edge of so many army camps in the Southwest.

The asthma had come back in the summer of his thirteenth year, after an absence of nearly four years. Rather, he had returned to it when his family was transferred back to the fort near San Antonio, with its humid climate. He still had a vivid memory of the day it had found him.

In the late morning, he and his mother had been sitting on the edge of the bed watching his father dress for the Saturday ceremonial horse drills at the fort polo field.

"Cap!" his thirty-four-year-old father, then only a captain, commanded while jutting his lean jaw and narrowing his eyes sternly at the mirror. The boy jumped off the bed and held out the marvelous cap with its officer's gold eagle over its burnished leather brim. The well-tanned captain took it like a crown and gently placed it down over his head, adjusting it for some seconds before it was at the precise angle.

"Crop!" he barked.

The boy's mother winked at him and then snatched the riding crop from behind her on the bed and handed it to the captain with a bow. She was so beautiful in her light yellow summer dress and floppy straw hat, the boy thought.

When she continued to stand close, the captain gave her a mock imperious look and snapped the crop against his riding boot. At which point his mother jumped back onto the bed and tucked her legs beneath her.

Then the captain clicked his heels and stood before the mirror again with the riding crop tucked under his arm, tall and splendid in his medals, braid and Peale boots.

"Car!" he commanded and executed a rigid about face and marched out of the room, leaving them to follow, suppressing their laughter and marching in arm-swinging Prussian style.

The ride out to the polo field in his father's dusty old Packard had been lighthearted, with his father singing "My Blue Heaven" and his arm hanging over his mother's shoulder. He remembered that his mother was holding her straw hat in her lap and his father's cap was pushed back on the back of his head. Both of their faces were happy and there was a sheen of perspiration on his mother's cheeks.

"There's a deer, Len!" his father shouted.

"Where?" the boy exclaimed and leaned away to look out at the side of the road. But he could not see the animal and when he turned back his father's hand was slipping away from his mother's breast. Blushing, she quickly put her hat on. He turned away and looked again for the imaginary deer.

For the rest of the way out to the field, his mind kept replaying the image of his father's hand at his mother's breast. She had large soft breasts and he had found himself wondering what it would feel like to touch them. He was also agitated and sweating over the fact that he was having an erection, something that had been occurring frequently and at the most awkward times in the past few months. In the spring he had masturbated for the first time and the feeling that had exploded through him had caused him to nearly fall over in the shower. It had given him a sense of newfound power and dread at the same time. Then there had been at least three times when he had awakened soaked and sticky in his own nocturnal emission. It had made him ashamed and reminded him of the anger his bed-wetting had provoked in his father. God, what if it just spurted out while they were driving out to the polo field, he worried. By darn, he *would* spot a deer, he had thought, trying to get his mind off what he'd seen.

When they pulled into the stable area at the polo field, they were greeted by several ofter booted officers in the Saturday ceremonial riding brigade. He quickly jumped out of the car and ran into the hazy darkness of the big stable to bring out Midnight, his father's mount. He was the captain's boy and treated in comradely fashion by the enlisted men who worked with the army horses. They all liked his mother, too, though they were never as freely cheerful with her as they were with him on those Saturday afternoons. But he had seen them give her shy admiring glances.

It was a few minutes later, after his father had led the troop of mounted officers out onto the field, when he and his mother had been sitting on the sun-warmed grass at the edge of the field, that the asthma had finally found him. He had turned to her and there was something he had wanted to say.

Her face had been so beautiful as she sat there in her yellow dress, leaning on one arm, watching the snaking line of cavalry, her exquisite tanned face calm and partly shaded by her hat, and her full breasts rising and falling slowly under her thin summer dress. The air was heavy and humid and his own breathing had become labored.

And he had had to turn away again and had watched his

father moving the column, and suddenly there had been such a clarity—the horses thundering across the green plain, the rich throating of commands, the grass and dark sod flying and Midnight's wet ebony hide glittering under the high Texas sun. And there was an overwhelming excitement to speak of, but when he turned again to his mother there was no breath in him for words. And afterwards there was not enough breath for a career in soldiering either.

At ten-thirty Talbot finished the last of the essays and slumped back in his chair. He took his glasses off and put them into their leather case.

Time for a good swaller of bourbon, old man, he thought. Man's got to have a little solace before turning in for the night. He got up and stretched and walked in his wool socks over to the bed and sat down and put on his boots.

Going down Prospect Park West with his umbrella angled against the slanting rain, he spotted Tiernan under a streetlamp in front of his apartment. He was standing at the curb with an enormous white and gray shaggy dog and holding a newspaper on his head to keep off the rain.

"Where the hell did you get that?" Talbot said, coming up to him.

"Hey, Len!" Tiernan exclaimed in surprise. "Where'd I get what?" he asked, pretending to ignore the great beast of a dog that was now sniffing Talbot's boots.

"That," Talbot said, pointing down. "What is it, a yak?"

"Oh, that!" Tiernan said. "That's Max. Max, meet Len."

"Hi, ya, Max," Talbot said, grabbing the great dog's paws as it leaped up and nearly bowled him over.

"He's Lynn's," Tiernan said. "Except I have the pleasure of boarding him. Get down, Max," he commanded as the dog leaned with its paws on Talbot's shoulders and panted into his face.

"Jesus, what kind is he?" Talbot said, pushing the dog down.

"The A.S.P.C.A. said he's part Old English sheep dog and part Irish wolfhound. They didn't have any white fluffy puppies, so Lynn chose him instead."

"Goddam, what a dog," Talbot said admiringly. "But he must eat a ton."

"That's only half of it," Tiernan said with a frown and

pulled the dog out into the gutter. "Come on, Max, do your thing!"

"Don't forget the poop law." Talbot laughed.

"What do you think I've got this paper on my head for?" Tiernan said, squinting up at the rain. "Actually, poor old Max is a victim of the poop law. The old lady who owned him told the people at the A.S.P.C.A. that she'd be damned if she'd clean up after him in the street."

"Oh, yeah, I remember that piece in the paper, where that woman said she wasn't going to clean up after her Great Dane. Said it would take a forklift. How are you managing?"

"Well, then there now, ya see, Len, it's all a matter of technique," he said in the tone of a country philosopher.

"Of course, of course," Talbot said, nodding seriously.

"It takes a while to get the hang of it, but I'll explain it to you. First off, you notice where I've got the paper. The cleaning instrument, as it were. On my head, right?"

"Right."

"Well, that's important, see? Cause you always wanta remember that you put the paper on top of your head *before* you pick up the dog shit—not afterward. Cause if you . . ."

"Oh, right! Now I get it," Talbot said, still nodding and then bursting into laughter.

"Then there's the matter of which paper to use—tabloid or fold," Tiernan continued.

"Okay, so how about parking Max and joining me for a short one at Larsky's?" Talbot said.

Tiernan groaned and made a nauseous face. "Think I'm going to lay off it for a while," he said, rubbing his stomach. "Besides, Max doesn't like me keeping late hours."

"Still feeling that toot you went on Friday, huh?" Talbot asked, remembering that Tiernan had been too sick for their run that morning.

"God, you should have seen me at the A.S.P.C.A. on Saturday. Most of the dogs in there looked better than me."

"Okay, get some sleep, old man," Talbot said, patting him on the shoulder. "So long, Max," he said to the dog.

As he started back down Prospect Park West to Fourth on his way to Larsky's, he heard Tiernan yell, "All right, goddam it!" at the dog. He looked back with a smile and saw the dog sitting on the curb and looking up lovingly at Tiernan. Tiernan, on the other hand, had an imaginary Luger finger-aimed between the dog's eyes. "Shit!" Tiernan commanded.

When Talbot got down to Larsky's he was stunned to find the place filled with young brownstoners, most of them wearing three-piece suits or dinner dresses. He recognized Baron Finnerty, a fat little neighborhood Pickwick with a melon face and thatchy red hair, holding forth at the center of the bar. Finnerty had approached him several times along Seventh Avenue with his little membership clipboard, trying to enlist him in his Conservatives for Lynch club. Talbot looked at all the young executive types in the bar and figured he must have gotten a following.

"Lynch that man!" Finnerty yelled, pointing a pudgy little finger at Talbot. At which point a young blond woman standing next to him took a "Lynch for President" button out of a box of them on the bar and headed toward Talbot.

"Len!" Frieda called from the end of the bar, where she was sitting under one of the Tiffany lamps. Her blond hair was glowing like soft gold in that light and she looked exquisite, he thought. She waved for him to come over and made a "save-me" face at the slightly wobbled middle-aged man, one of Finnerty's troops by the look of his three-piece-suit, who was murmuring something into her ear.

"Oh, Len, over here!" This time it was Chrissy's voice coming from the opposite end of the room. He turned and saw the willowy redhead standing and waving to him from a table over near the jukebox. Sitting at the table were Susan and a large very masculine-looking woman he had never seen before. Chrissy's birthday, he thought. He'd have to go over and congratulate her.

Chrissy waved again and he waved back, telling her with his lips he'd be over in a little while. Susan, who was slumped down a little drunkenly, just crinkled her nose disdainfully and turned to speak to the other woman. It gave him a strange panicky feeling seeing her ensconced in his preserve. The feeling was aggravated by the looks some of the men standing at the bar were giving her. Fuck her, he thought. She'd just better not pull anything cute while he was there. God, she looks just like any fucking pickup in the joint, he thought. Worse! He felt embarrassed.

Then as he was turning to go over to where Frieda was sitting, the woman Finnerty had sent to button him stopped him

and reached up to pin a "Lynch for President" button on his
red ski jacket. She was such a tiny woman, he thought, and
behind her enormous false lashes her eyes were almost solidly
bloodshot from drinking. He looked over at Frieda and
shrugged while the woman reached way up and fidgeted with
the pin.

"There, now you know who to vote for," she said, patting
the button on his jacket.

"Thanks a lot—a *horrible* lot," he said with madly earnest
eyes as he backed away holding out his hands.

When he finally made his way over to Frieda, he wedged his
shoulder between her and the murmuring Finnerty man and
then pulled the pin off his jacket and plopped it into Frieda's
glass of beer.

"Hi, I'm Mike," the saggy-eyed Finnerty man said with his
nose bent against Talbot's back.

"God, you ever see anything like this bunch?" Talbot asked
her, ignoring Mike.

"Lynch for President, *Liebling*," she said, raising her glass
and then smiling and leaning over and kissing his cheek.

"God, don't tell me they've got *you?*" he asked.

"Certainly," she said, nodding facetiously. "Mike has just
convinced me. *Ja*, it's true, Mike?" she asked, looking around
Talbot's shoulder. "Helloooo, Mike?"

"Hi, I'm . . . [hiccough] . . ." Mike mumbled as he
took his face out of Talbot's back and glumly nodded along the
bar looking for his drink.

Talbot finally caught Danny's attention and measured a shot-
glass with two fingers of one hand and made a mug grasping
motion with his other hand.

". . . Mike," the befuddled Finnerty worker said, slurping
down his drink and then looking off with a sad smile on his
face.

"Mike has been working very hard for the cause," Frieda
said.

"Hey, Danny, what're you running, a goddam clubhouse or
something?" Talbot teased as the bartender wearily trudged
toward him with his mug of beer and double shot of bourbon.

"A bunch of joiks, if you ast me," Danny said, setting them
down and leaning in exhaustion toward them. "Listen," he
said under his breath and waving with his thick fingers for them
to come closer. "The guy down dere tells me dey got bounced

outa da Pilgrim Club for not paying for de meetin' room. So dey come floatin' in here like some kinda convention. Yeah! Tommy calls me up at home an tells me ta come because the joint is crawlin'. Hey, I been goin' since dis morning, right? I'm beat down to my socks. But I come back, right? It's business, right?" With that, he grabbed Talbot's money and lumbered back to the register.

Talbot's view of Susan's table was cut off by the crowd along the bar, so he turned and gave Frieda a long caressing look. She looked back and did not take her eyes from his even while she brought her glass of beer to her mouth. She swallowed and then slowly licked the trace of foam from her upper lip. She seemed to be taking better care of herself since they'd begun seeing each other quietly, doing her hair more elegantly and dressing in finer clothes when she came in. Tonight she was wearing the white silk blouse she had worn at the Stalingrad party.

"You look good," he said just before slinging down the bourbon.

"And you look tired," she said, handing him his mug of beer to wash down the whiskey.

"Yeah"—he sighed after a long swallow—"been grading papers all night. This is just to help me sleep," he said, raising the mug again.

"There is even a better way," she said, turning away slightly.

"Yes?" he drawled, leaning into her shoulder and caressing her thigh. "And what might that be, mein liddle frauline doctor?"

"Oh, a little back rubbing perhaps," she said, turning and looking into his eyes again, the tinge of a blush beginning to glow on her face.

"Yes?" he drawled again.

"And a little . . . How shall I say? A little special something, perhaps? Frieda is the specialist, *ja?*"

He smiled and half closed his eyes in agreement. *Ja,* he thought, Frieda is the specialist. Within the hour, my lovely Frieda . . . very special indeed. Gazing dreamily at her face, he mentally removed the clip from the back of her hair and let it fall over her shoulders, unlocked her warm lips with the tip of his tongue, and then moved slowly down her body unlocking all her treasures. And then she his. God, did any woman ever know more ways of giving pleasure? Each time a revelation of new pleasure. The last time she had poured oil over her breasts and massaged his back without touching him with her hands.

*"Herr Doktor,"* he said, saluting her with his mug of beer.

"You shouldn't look at me so," she said, feeling very aroused. "I could do something shocking to you just now," she said, glancing slowly down toward his belt.

"Hello!" Finnerty called from behind him, his voice coming like a splash of ice water.

Talbot exhaled his agitation and turned toward the pudgy little party leader, who was posed in open-armed greeting.

"Mind if I join you and your charming friend? Hi," he said, turning briefly to Frieda.

"Oh, well, sure," Talbot said, giving Frieda a hopeless shrug. "Come right in," he said, moving back and accidentally rolling Mike off his bar stool.

"Say, thanks, Mike," Finnerty said, taking the empty bar stool, while poor Mike lurched across the room trying to keep himself from hitting the floor.

"Finnerty is my name, Baron Finnerty," the little man said, holding out his hand. "I know we've met somewhere, but I can't seem to remember your name."

"Duke," Talbot said, shaking the clammy little hand. "And this is Queenie. Queenie, this is Baron."

"Queenie," Finnerty said, holding out his hand again.

Frieda took his hand and smiled as aristocratically as she could.

"Duke!" Finnerty then exclaimed as he leaned back beaming a proud smile.

"Baron?" Talbot replied beaming back.

"It's gonna happen, Duke!"

"What's that, Baron?"

"We are going to put the great man into the White House," Finnerty said and then lost the edge of his smile as he noticed the great man's button lying face up in the bottom of Frieda's glass of beer.

"Lynch, you mean," Talbot said, nodding.

"Yes, but Brooklyn has to come through," Finnerty said, suddenly switching to a baby-face scowl. "This time the East has to make a statement. This time, *we* are the pivot!"

"They're asking us to pivot?" Talbot asked, looking around conspiratorially.

"Brooklyn could do it," Finnerty said, leaning closer and putting his hand on Talbot's arm. "Jesus, think of it!"

"Yeah, Jesus," Talbot said, opening his eyes in wonder.

"So, whatta ya say?"

"Whatta I say what?"

"You in?"

"In?"

"Yeah. Will you help us?"

"Me?"

"You bet," Finnerty said, squeezing Talbot's hand.

"They want me," Talbot said to Frieda, his voice breaking with emotion.

"That's good," Frieda said. "You could use the money."

"Huh?" Finnerty said, taking his hand away.

"I want five hundred—a week," Talbot said, nodding resolutely.

"No, see, we're only a volunteer group," Finnerty said.

"The great man ain't paying?" Talbot said, giving Finnerty a menacing look.

"This is a cause!" Finnerty protested.

"He thinks he's gonna get Brooklyn to pivot for free?" Talbot asked.

"Hey, Duke," Finnerty said soothingly.

"I ain't gonna pivot. You, Queenie?"

"Not for nothing!" she declared. "The nerve!"

"Queenie," Finnerty whined.

"Scram!" Talbot said. "Go get Staten Island to pivot!"

"If that's the way you feel, give me back the button."

"What?" Talbot said angrily and got up.

"Okay, keep the button. . . . See ya," Finnerty said, looking pale and backing away.

After Finnerty had gone Talbot laughed and ordered Frieda another drink. Then he told her he had to go over and wish Chrissy a happy birthday. He'd be right back, he said.

Susan was not at the table when he got there, but two of Finnerty's men were now seated and talking to Chrissy and the big Irish-looking woman, who at the moment had her arm positioned for an arm-wrestle and was nodding to one of the Finnerty men to take her up. He recognized the other man as Joe Moreno, a married lawyer he knew on Garfield. There were still two empty chairs and one of them had Susan's patchwork rabbit-fur coat draped over it. Probably in the john, he thought as he quietly stole up behind Chrissy. He paused for a minute with a half-smile on his face as he watched Moreno trying to charm Chrissy. Neither of them noticed as he quietly stepped in and put his hands on the back of Chrissy's chair. The other two didn't notice either, because by now they were grimacing into each other's eyes as they locked grips in a fierce arm-wrestling contest.

Just as Moreno glanced up, Talbot swung Chrissy's chair around toward him and plopped himself in her lap and gave her a long passionate kiss on the mouth.

In a moment, he let her come up for air and said, "Happy birthday, darling."

"Len, goddam it!" she exclaimed and pushed him off her lap.

"Hey, Talbot, what'sa big idea?" Moreno complained.

"Hi, Joe, how'sa wife?" Talbot said, taking the seat next to Susan's.

"Wife?" Chrissy asked, turning to Moreno and touching the moisture of Talbot's kiss off her lips with her fingertips.

"He's kidding," Moreno said, shaking his head confidently.

She then looked back at Talbot, who nodded his head just as confidently.

"So, we're separated . . . kinda," Moreno conceded.

"I hear you guys got bounced out of the Pilgrim meeting hall," Talbot said, keeping the pressure on the frowning lawyer.

"Where'd you hear that?" Moreno asked, smoothing his dark hair back and touching his mustache briefly. "Hey, Chrissy, I'll talk to you later," he said and got up before Talbot could answer. "When the air is a little fresher around here," he said, giving Talbot a scathing look.

"Hey, Joe, sorry you and your wife are separated!" Talbot called out to Moreno's back. Moreno threw him an underhand finger without turning around.

"Separated?" one of Moreno's friends inquired as the lawyer reached the bar.

Talbot chuckled and then turned back to the table as the other Finnerty man, a blond collegiate type, let out a sighing groan as his hand was forced back and nearly crushed into the table by the big red-faced Irish woman, who was now blowing through her mouth like a weight lifter.

"Trisha, this is Len Talbot," Chrissy said, scooting her chair back around to the table.

"Hi, ya, Len. Wanta try your luck?" Trisha asked, flexing her fingers and giving him a big toothy grin.

"Not me," Talbot said, holding up his hands and scooting down into his seat.

The young man who had just been her opponent looked at Talbot sheepishly and rubbed his reddened hand. Then he started to rise in order to join Moreno at the bar.

"Hey, have a seat, love!" Trisha exclaimed, shoving him back down into his seat. "I always buy a round of beers when I win."

"Sure, why not?" the young man conceded, squirming his neck around in his collar. "The name's Shelton, Bob Shelton," he said, extending the still-throbbing hand weakly to Talbot.

"Len Talbot," Talbot said, giving him a commiserating look and trying not to squeeze the unfortunate hand too much.

"Beer, Lenny?" Trisha asked, rising to her solidly packed six-foot-two height.

"Yeah, thanks," he said and then shook his head in wonder as she swaggered over to the bar and pushed two Finnerty men out of the way and yelled at Danny for the beers.

"God, she could play for the Steelers," Shelton said, trying to flex his fingers.

"Oh, Trisha is very nice," Chrissy said. "A very gentle soul when you get to know her."

"I hate delicate women," Talbot said and then sat up a notch as he saw Susan come out of the ladies' room, weaving slightly as she tried to skirt around the group dancing near the jukebox. Four blossoms, at least, he thought, looking at the condition of her eyes.

Before she could get around the jukebox group, however, a tall Finnerty man with his tie hanging loose and his shirt unbuttoned down to his hairy chest grabbed her by the waist and began waltzing her around to the music of John Denver's "Country Road." A wave of hostility surged through Talbot's brain and he had to check himself from jumping up from his chair. Bitch, he thought, as he watched Susan smile ecstatically at the dark curly-headed young man and lean back against his arm as he swung her around. Talbot knotted his fist under his other hand and imagined bloodying the young man's nose for him.

"Oh, Len, I love this song. Let's dance," Chrissy said.

He just slumped lower in his chair and looked at her with his nostrils flared and his brows knitting. She shrugged and gulped her beer.

"Okay, four beers!" Trisha exclaimed, placing the brimming mugs down in the middle of the table. Then she walked around and sat almost prissily next to Shelton.

"To you," she said, blushing and hoisting one of the mugs to Shelton, who still looked a little ashen.

"Who's your mature lady friend over there?" Chrissy asked Talbot, referring to Frieda.

"What?" Talbot said, coming up out of his black thoughts.

"The blond lady."

"Didn't know you could see us from here," he said, still watching Susan, who was now being escorted over to the bar by her dance partner.

"I walked over. Ah, you seemed a little preoccupied."

Talbot didn't answer but sipped his beer and continued glowering toward Susan.

"A little old for you, isn't she?" Chrissy continued.

"No," he said almost in a whisper. Then he turned and looked into Chrissy's eyes. "Why were you looking for me?"

"Why?" she asked. "I don't know," she said shrugging. "Thought maybe . . . Well, actually, we were getting a little bored."

"I wasn't bored," Trisha said, beaming a look of affection at Shelton, whose lip was curling toward a frightened smile.

"Anyway," Chrissy said, looking up into Talbot's eyes and then down at the table again as she felt a blush rising.

"Just someone I know," Talbot said and looked back at Susan again.

She had that coy little-girl tilt to her head and she was saying something and nervously pushing her blond hair back from her face. Talbot noticed that she had lost a little weight and looked sensuous in her expensive tight-fitting jeans and black sweater. In a moment the young man's face lit up with an eager smile and he took a small black book and a pen from inside his jacket. Goddam it! Talbot thought. He was exhaling pure anger as he watched the young man lean over onto the bar and take down the number Susan was apparently giving him. Fucking goddam slut! he thought, using every bit of will he possessed to keep from leaping out of his chair and going after the smug-faced sonofabitch who was putting the notebook back into his coat and patting it confidently. Not in this bar, you fucking bitch, he thought as she gave the young man a little finger wiggle of a wave and started back toward the table.

"Hello, everybody!" Susan chirped as she got to her chair.

"Well, if it isn't Miss Ginger Rogers herself," Chrissy said.

"Hello, Leonard," she said sarcastically as she looked down at the brooding Talbot and then sat down.

"Too late, Suzy, you just missed the free beer," Trisha said.

"Beer?" Susan said, making a face. "Beer, my dear, is for the peasantry. I would like a little blossie-pooh. Len, be sweet and get me an orange blossom."

"You've had too many blossie-poohs," he mumbled without looking up from his brooding.

"God, what a dreary man," Susan said, looking at him disdainfully. "Bob?"

"Right!" Shelton said and got up eagerly.

"This is really an *enchanting* place," she said, giving Chrissy a wink. "Aren't you just having a simply marvelous time, Chris?"

"Don't get too enchanted," Talbot said with his head still down and his fingers touching together at his lips. "You're not coming back."

"Excuse me?" Susan asked, looking over at him, the whimsy gone from her face.

"Susan, maybe we'd better go," Chrissy said, sensing a storm about to break.

"Were you talking to me?" Susan asked Talbot, her eyes blazing.

"Yes I was, my little enchanted bar-hustling two-bit goddam slut!" he hissed through his bridged fingers.

"Huh-oh," Trisha said, cracking her knuckles nervously and looking over at Chrissy.

"Yep, time to go," Chrissy said, standing up and taking her coat off the back of the chair. Trisha started to rise and then sat down again.

"Just sit down, Chris," Susan said, narrowing her eyes. *"He's* the one who's going!"

"You got three minutes," Talbot said in a barely audible

voice. He and Susan were facing each other now with their knees nearly touching.

"You own this place now, do you, Len?" she asked. "You own me, do you?" Her rising voice brought a quiet across the bar. "You own nothing, you, you . . . dumb bastard! Any man in this bar has more claim to me than you do! You know all you are—"

"Two and a half minutes," he said, turning his wrist slightly to look at his watch.

"Len, please," Chrissy pleaded.

"You're just one of the unpleasant sights around here," Susan continued. "Like . . . like the scummy toilet in there. Well, shit on you, Len. And you can count till you're purple!"

"Please," Chrissy said, sitting down and shaking her head at Susan.

"Shut up, Chris, for once in our little rabbit lives we're not going to go skittering away when some asshole man goes boo!"

A cheer went up along the bar and Susan turned and raised her fist to them.

"God, I could just puke when I think of how we snivel around these bastards," Susan said, turning back to the group at the table. "There we were, for nearly fifteen goddam minutes we waited outside trying to decide if we should come in here tonight. 'Oh, what if Len's in there?' I said. So, who the hell is Len Talbot? Well, thank god for you, Trisha," she said, reaching over and patting the big woman on the arm. "You were the only one with any guts."

"Two," Talbot said.

"Look at him counting!" Susan said, laughing. "A total jerk. Ladies, I give you a completely preserved Neanderthal. It eats, shits and can read a Timex!"

Just then Shelton showed up with Susan's drink.

"One orange blossom for the lady," he said cheerfully and started to put it down in front of her.

But Talbot quickly put his hand in the way and pressed it back on him. "Take it back. The 'lady' isn't going to have time to drink it," Talbot said without taking his eyes off Susan.

"Bob, that's my goddam drink and you'd better put it right down there!" Susan ordered, her eyes glaring.

"I . . . I'll just leave it on the bar for you," Shelton said, backing away after Talbot gave him a menacing look.

"Okay, jerk-face, now you've done it," Susan said, turning on Talbot. "You want war, you've got it. Fellow women, I've decided I like this place. From now on this is going to be *our* little stomping ground. And I've also decided I don't want jerk-face hanging around in our little bar. And jerk-face here knows how I can keep him out, too. Don't you, jerk-face? Jerk-face doesn't want to see it when Mommy goes into her little act, does he?" she taunted.

"One minute," Talbot said, glancing down at his watch and then back into her eyes.

"Oh, god, how pathetic!" She sighed in disgust.

Trisha managed a smile and nodded toward Susan.

"You know what he's thinking right now, Trisha?" Susan asked. "He's thinking he wants to beat my ass right into the ground. But he knows that this time I'll throw his chicken-shit woman-beating ass into jail."

"Susan, please, it's getting late," Chrissy said.

"That's his specialty, did you know that, Chrissy?" Susan asked, knowing that her friend was a little fond of Talbot. "He likes beating up women. Tell her about the two black eyes you gave me, jerk-face, and the cracked ribs. Tell her what a big brave—"

"No, you tell her!" Talbot finally exploded. "And don't take too long, because you've only got about ten seconds. Tell her how you were fucking Garnand while I was away at work. Tell her how I came in and found you with Garnand's cock halfway down your throat!"

"You goddam—" she said.

"The Linda Lovelace of Garfield Street, folks!" he yelled. "And while you're at it, tell her how you locked Teddy up in his nursery so you could fuck your brains out with the next-door neighbor!"

The slap that Susan gave him could be heard all over the hushed bar.

"Tell her, goddam it!" he bellowed as he tried to blink back the tearing that the sting of her slap had started.

Her next slap hit him so hard that several tears splashed into Chrissy's face. And then she wound up and continued slapping until his own hand came up over her head and hung there like a sword.

He stopped its descent when he saw her cringe, but there was an almost irresistible force impelling him to bring it down across her mouth. His anger was sighing out of him in great heaving drafts as he fought against his rage. He saw again her twisting naked body tumbling down the stairs the afternoon he had caught her with Garnand. He saw himself again, a Frankenstein monster moving down after her with his fingers aching to clench her around her throat, to squeeze and break and snap the life out of her.

"God!" he cried out and then brought his elbow down on the table and held the murder-hungry hand up to Trisha.

"Take it," he said with a strangling sound.

"Me?" Trisha asked somewhat shaken.

"Take it," he gasped, trying to hold back the sobs of fury coming from his chest.

Trisha looked over at Susan and then hesitantly reached over and took Talbot's hand. For a moment she held it gently and looked sympathetically into his tearing eyes. Then her expression turned to fear and determination as she felt the power of his hand lock around hers. She instinctively set her muscles against him as their arms moved together for the beginning of the combat.

He waited a moment until he felt she was set and then he unleashed all the fury that was in him and slammed her arm down with so much force that it flipped her out of her seat and sent her crashing into the empty chairs at the next table.

"Don't . . . don't come back in here," he said in a low voice to Susan as he got up. Then he turned and walked out of the bar past the startled patrons.

After a few minutes, Frieda, who had remained in her seat with her head bowed during the entire altercation, quietly got up and put on her coat and slipped out after him.

# CHAPTER
# TEN

From Linda's bedroom window Gemetz looked across the harbor at one of the broad orange ferries as it swung slowly out into the current off the tip of Manhattan and began churning toward Staten Island. There was still a smudgy glow of sunset over the Jersey shore, and higher in the gathering darkness he saw the first star—the constant light of Venus that his mother had shown him from their rooftop on Dean Street one summer night so many years ago.

Standing with his arms folded at the window, he could hear Linda saying goodbye to the last of Mark's birthday guests at the front of the apartment. Then he heard the door slam and for a while there was silence except for his father's reedy breathing where he lay sleeping on Linda's bed. In the dimmed room Gemetz looked over at the old man's upturned face, its open mouth and cadaverous eyes bringing a moan of despair from the son's throat.

He and his father had come from the store together to the party for Mark. Juliet had dropped in at the store at noontime to leave a present for the boy and said she regretted not being able to attend the party. The night before, she and Gemetz had agreed that it would have created a strain for both her and Linda if she went.

But all during the party the old man had had trouble keeping the names "Juliet" and "Linda" straight and had interchanged them without even noticing it. Linda had noticed it, however, and Gemetz had seen the hurt in her eyes each time it happened. He was grateful that she had not made an issue of it with his well-meaning father. The old man had even used Juliet's name once when he had tried to persuade her to sing the "Vissi d'arte" aria from *Tosca* again. It was his favorite and she had smiled and promised him that she would sing it for him after supper when all the guests had gone.

At about five o'clock, after cavorting around in rare playfulness with the children, the old man had slumped against a wall and complained of suddenly feeling very weak. Gemetz and Linda had helped him to her bed and then had gone back outside to try to wind up the party. The old man had declined their suggestion to call his doctor, saying that all he needed was to lie down and recoup his strength. It always happened when he overdid it, he had said.

Mamma, let him stay with us a little longer, Gemetz thought as he looked out at the star again. He was having so much fun with the children, Mamma. They need him, Mamma, and I need him. He was so funny, walking like Uncle Alex for them. I was laughing, too, Mamma. Remember how he was before the operations, Mamma? The boys don't remember him like that. Linda is going to sing for him tonight. I'm sorry about Linda, Mamma. People change. . . . There was no love anymore, Mamma. I want to be happy again.

The Venus light, a pinpoint of warmth in the engulfing night, had always been a consolation to him—from the nights of his boyhood in Brooklyn to the strange sultry nights on the campus of the University of Virginia and the nights of planning from his barracks window in West Germany and even from this same window so many times when he and Linda were still married, times when he had come into the bedroom to be alone. Always out there shining for him, constant and yet remote and solitary and touching that which had always been remote and solitary in his heart.

"Richie, another blanket, could you?" his father called from the bed.

"Sure, Papa," Gemetz said, unfolding his arms and moving toward the closet where the extra blankets were kept on a shelf. "How you feeling now?"

"Good," the old man sighed. "Just a little cold is all."

"You were sleeping," Gemetz said, coming over and distributing the soft brown blanket over the gray one Linda had put on the old man earlier.

"Yeah, sleep is good," the old man said as his bony fingers hooked the blanket up under his chin.

"Want another one?"

"No, this is just fine. Thank you, Richie."

Gemetz smiled down at his father and the father managed a weak almost apologetic smile back. Then Gemetz reached behind him and pulled Linda's vanity chair close to the bed and sat down next to his father.

"Linda's saying goodbye to everybody," he said, nodding toward the closed door.

"I saw Linda in my dream," the old man said, opening his eyes a little wider and turning to his son. "But I couldn't see Sarah's face, Richie. I could see you and I could see Linda . . . and I could see me. But Sarah kept turning her face away. It was her body, but in each picture she turned her face away."

"Dreams are strange, Papa," Gemetz said. "Who can explain?"

"It was the wedding pictures," the old man continued. "I was dreaming of looking through your wedding pictures. But in each picture, even the one with the cake, Sarah had her face turned around."

"Maybe it would be too sad to look at Mamma's face," the son said, feeling his eyes begin to tear.

"No, no, Richie," the old man protested. "I keep Sarah's picture right beside my bed. Each day I have looked at her lovely face. Such a lovely smile your mother had. Even when I tell her I am so angry that she died and left me, she smiles, Richie. So why did she have to die? Tell me. A smile like that and she could die, Richie?"

"Papa . . ." Gemetz said, choking.

"But in the wedding pictures she turned away," the old man said, shaking his head.

"Tell you what," Gemetz said, clearing his throat and wiping his eyes, "you try to get a little more sleep and when you wake up I'll get Linda to take down the old wedding pictures and you can see Mamma hasn't turn—turned away. She liked the wedding pictures, remember?"

"Yes," the old man sighed and laid his head back. "But Linda wouldn't mind?" he asked, raising himself and reaching his hand out.

"I think she'd like to see them, too," Gemetz said, taking his father's thin hand and gently placing it back under the cover. "And don't forget she promised to sing us the *Tosca* aria after supper."

"Such a fine girl, Juliet," the old man said, resting back on the pillow.

"Linda," Gemetz corrected before he thought.

"Yes, Linda. . . . Richie, I get so confused."

"It's all right, Papa," Gemetz said, feeling wretched.

"Linda has been very nice to me, Richie. I am happy we can still be so close. I would miss not hearing her sing. Is it too much? The *Tosca* I would miss, Richie. Such a joy."

"I know," Gemetz said. "But how about getting a few more winks?"

"Yes, a few more winks," his father sighed and closed his eyes.

"I better go help Linda straighten up," Gemetz said rising. "You just . . . " He stopped when he heard his father's breath drift into a sleeping rhythm. "Sleep well, Papa," he whispered and walked to the door.

After leaving the room and closing the door gently behind him, he walked down the hall and caught Jonathan up in his arms as the boy ran yowling from the living room with Mark on his heels.

"Hold it!" Gemetz whispered. "Grandpa is asleep, so cool it, okay?"

"Okay," Jonathan said as his father put him down. Mark turned and walked back toward the front foyer.

"Where's Mamma?" Gemetz asked as he and Jonathan walked hand and hand through the party litter on the living-room floor.

"Doin' the dishes," the boy shouted and ran to the foyer, where Mark was starting to wheel his new bicycle around.

Linda was dumping a pile of ice cream-smeared paper plates into a garbage bag near the sink when he looked in. Her long chestnut hair was tied back in a ponytail and she was wearing jeans and one of his old blue shirts with the tails hanging out and her sleeves rolled up. There were little circles under her eyes, and he could tell that she was going through one of her

insomnia cycles again. He wondered what she was feeling
guilty about this time.

"Want some help?" he asked, leaning against the doorjamb.

"I've just about got it," she said, wiping a little speck of
cake frosting off the tip of her nose with the side of her arm.
"How is Papa?"

"Sleeping," he said and went over to the sink and started
sorting some of the dishes on the drainboard.

"I'll finish them later," she said, pushing him away gently.
"Want some coffee?"

"Yeah," he said and went over and sat down at the table and
then put his face in his hands. "I'm a little worried about
him," he said.

"We shouldn't have let the children tax him so much," she
said. "But I haven't seen him so lively since Sarah's death. He
really can be very funny."

"Yeah," he said, leaning back and looking at her again. She
had always loved his father. That was nice. It had been her
immediate acceptance of his family that had helped get the first
years of their marriage off to a good start. "Do you mind
singing that *Tosca* aria for him tonight?" he asked. "He
mentioned it again."

"Sure," she said, taking down two cups from the cabinet.
"If you can keep Mark and Jonathan from booing. I'm glad
there's at least one music lover in this family."

"Hey, I never booed," he said defensively.

"Yeah, well, come around more often and I'll sing for you."

"Well, old girl, I sort of gave my seat to old what's-his-
name—Steve?"

"Scratch old what's-his-name," she said, giving him an
embarrassed look.

"What happened?"

"I didn't live up to his ultimatums," she said with a shrug.

"How so?"

"He wanted a commitment," she said, spooning the instant
coffee into the cups. "Still take sugar?"

"Just one," he said. "And?"

"I don't know," she said. "I really thought the world of him
until he forced me to look at him as a permanent thing in my
life. Then I started seeing a lot of things I hadn't seen before.
You know, little things that all of a sudden become big things if
you have to live with them forever."

"Yeah, I know the feeling," he sighed and stretched his arms behind his head.

"It's the truth," she said, bringing over the steaming cups of coffee. "It's a problem. I'm beginning to see that now. Not that I want Steve back. But until I solve that problem I don't think I'm ever going to be able to have a long-term relationship with a man. My shrink is hopeful though."

"You'll make it," he said. "Accepting the problem is half the solution."

"How about you?" she asked without looking over at him.

"Starting to feel a little leveled off," he said, putting his leg up on the edge of the table unconsciously, something he had never been able to get away with when they lived together but enjoyed now in his own apartment.

"Still seeing your little . . . I'm sorry, Richie. What is her name? She the 'Juliet' Papa was calling me all day?"

"Yeah," he said, looking at her over the cup of coffee he was sipping. "I'm really sorry about that. She came over at lunchtime, and she and Papa were talking a lot. He was a little confused when he got here."

"I don't mind," she said, taking a sip.

He noticed that he'd put his leg up and then was about to take it down. Instead he thought he would wait and see how long her new casualness about it would last.

"She's—" he began.

"Want an apple?" she asked, getting up and going over to the refrigerator.

"No, thanks," he said, taking his leg down. "She's had a good effect on me. I think I'm starting to trust women again."

"You shouldn't judge all women by me," she said, holding up two red apples. "McIntoshes?" she offered.

"No, thanks," he said, declining the apple again.

"Do . . . do you love her?" she asked, coming back to the table.

"I don't know," he said, lying to spare her feelings. "Oh, listen, Papa wants to know if he can look through our old wedding pictures. You still got them?"

"Of course," she said. "I had them down just a week ago."

"Oh?" he asked, giving her a puzzled look.

"Jonathan," she said. "He wanted to see what we looked like when we got married."

He laughed. "What'd he say?" he asked.

"Well, he thought Mommy looked like the princess and Daddy looked like—"

"—the frog," he interrupted.

"No, he said Daddy looked like Grizzly Adams," she said.

"Ah, yes, my bushy period," he said.

"You do look better since you've trimmed things back a little," she said. "At least you've got more of a face."

"You always did like the conservative type."

"No, you just look cleaner, younger—and sexier, that's for sure," she said.

"Sexier, huh?" he said, rubbing his hand over his tightly trimmed beard. "Think so?"

"I always told you that," she said.

The conversation was beginning to trouble him a bit, because he was beginning to respond to her friendliness. When she didn't have her knives out, Linda had a way of seducing a man by just the magnetic warmth of her femininity. He thought again of his father's gaunt sleeping face and frowned and turned toward the bedroom.

"What's the matter?" she asked.

"Him," he said, shaking his head. "God, Lin, he looks so wasted."

"I know," she said. "I can't get over how fast it hit him."

"Damn," he said. "Now, I bet it's his heart."

"Don't get upset, Richie, he's never had trouble there before. Maybe he did just wear himself out."

"I don't know," he said.

"He was sleeping?" she asked.

"Yeah," he said.

She nodded and then pensively brought the apple to her lips and pressed her tongue against it. He watched her and sighed. Such beautiful fingers, he thought. He had always loved her hands, and they appealed to him very much at this moment as she held the glistening red apple. Then he saw again his father's withered fingers as he pulled the blanket up under his chin.

"God . . . It's just I remember him before all those goddam operations," he said, shaking his head.

She took a slow bite of the apple and then licked the frothy juice from the corner of her mouth.

"Why did he want to see the wedding pictures?" she asked to try to get his mind off it.

"He had some kind of nightmare about Sarah in the pictures," he said. "He . . . he couldn't see her face. Yeah, gimme a bite," he said, reaching out for the apple and trying to stifle the sadness that was rising in him.

"I better call Talbot and tell him I'm not coming," he said after a while.

"To what?" she asked.

"Oh, god, he's cooking up some kind of Mexican meal."

"He's the big dark-haired guy, right?" she asked.

"Yeah, one of your fellow Texicans."

"Still separated from his wife?"

"Divorced. Why, you interested?"

"Not my type," she said. "He scares me a little."

"He's not a bad guy," Gemetz said.

"So, why don't you go?" she asked.

"I'm worried about Papa," he said.

"I can take care of him," she said. "If he wakes up before you get back, we'll keep him entertained with *Tosca* and wedding pictures. Go on. No sense sitting around worrying yourself to death."

"I don't know," he said.

"Richie, don't make yourself crazy. He might even sleep right through till morning. I don't mind; I don't have a show and I can bunk on the couch."

"Ah, yes, the old couch," he said, smiling ruefully as he remembered the times she had walked out of their bedroom with her pillow under her arm when she was down on sex.

Suddenly he was thinking of Juliet again and how willing and loving she was in bed. He felt a great urge to call her and hear her youthful voice. He could call her from Talbot's, he thought.

"I really don't mind, Richie," Linda said again. "Is *she* going to be there?"

"Strictly male," he said.

"So, get out for a while," she said.

"Maybe you're right," he said, stretching his arms again and getting up. "Look, I'll leave Talbot's number on top of the refrigerator," he said, walking to the pad and pencil she kept up there.

"Don't worry," she said, getting up. "Go have a good time with your cooking club. Mexican food, huh? How's your ulcer these days? I've still got some of your tablets if you want to take them."

"If it bothers me, I'll take 'em when I get back," he said. "Should take about two hours—nine at the latest. Jesus, with Talbot cooking I'll need a stomach pump! Sure it's okay?"

"I'm sure," she said, pushing him toward the door.

"You know what we call it—the cooking club?"

"No, what?"

"Ptomaine Tuesdays. My turn is next week. How does 'Le Haut Dog a la Gemetz' sound to you?"

"Wonderful. Who else is in this club?"

"Joe Tiernan. I don't think you've met him. Him you'd like. He's a glutton for punishment."

"That's not my type either," she said, frowning at him.

"I'm sorry," he said and started again for the front door.

Linda followed him to the foyer and took his peacoat from the guest closet while he talked to Mark about the bike's speed gears.

"Daddy, Mark said I could have his old bike," Jonathan said.

"Not till I put some training wheels on it," Gemetz said, slipping into the coat Linda was holding for him.

"Easy on the chili, Pedro," she said as he was going out the door.

"Hey, Lin, I don't know," he said, stepping back inside again. "What if he needs some—"

"Richie," she said, dusting some lint off the shoulder of his peacoat and pushing him out the door, "he'll be all right. He's just a little tired. Now go eat!"

"Sure?" he asked, his face full of doubt.

"Sure," she said, and leaned over and kissed him lightly on the lips.

He looked at her in surprise for an instant and then reached out and touched the softness of her shoulder.

"Okay," he said, smiling.

"Bye," she said. "And don't worry."

As Gemetz walked up Montague toward the subway stop for the short ride over to Park Slope the butterfly lightness of Linda's kiss was still on his lips. A wifely peck that stirred a little glow in the dead coals. Ah, forget it, he told himself. Don't get sucked in. Just in one of her downswings. The Steve thing. Yes, he had been through her swings before, moods that had left him tumbled in uncertainty as she went from vulnerability and need for him to almost belligerent independence.

As he neared the subway entrance he saw two men standing at a sidewalk phone stand. There were three phones on the stand and he thought he'd give Juliet a call before getting to Talbot's. He felt a great longing and tenderness for her as he remembered her anxious smile as she was leaving the store after lunch, worrying about his being submerged in that whole family scene with Linda. He had touched her under the chin and smiled. Not to worry, his smile had said.

Both of the men at the phone stand were talking loudly, their voices almost alternating.

"I *would* like to be friends, Cele," one of them, a young lawyerish-looking man in a tan trench coat was saying. "I'd like very much to be friends. Do you want to try it like that?"

". . . an' it's gotta be by da foist," the other, a short thickset man wearing a trucker's cap and a plaid jacket was almost yelling. "If it ain't da foist, ferget it! Can he get it by da foist? No, March . . . da foist a March! What?"

Gemetz turned his back on their noise and dialed Juliet's number. She answered it on the second ring.

"Hi," he said warmly. He could hear loud rock music.

"Richie," she said happily. "Just a minute. Annie, could you turn it down a minute!" she yelled at her roommate. "Richie?"

"Hi," he said again, putting his finger in his other ear to block out the other two men. "The party was great! Mark loved your gift."

"Well, he's fulla shit if he tinks dat!" the man with the truck driver's cap yelled. "What? Not a chance, Vinnie. No fuggin' chance. I'm tellin' ya!"

"Richie, where are you?" Juliet asked.

"At least let's try being friends, Cele," the lawyer urged. "I want to be a friend."

"I'm at a phone booth," Gemetz yelled. "Look, I'm heading over to Talbot's for his Mexican—"

"Wait a minute," she said. "Annie, damn it, I'm on the phone."

"No, da foist!" the truck driver yelled again. "Whatta ya tink I been sayin'!"

"Okay, Richie, what were you saying?"

". . . special friends. We would be *special* friends," the lawyer continued.

"Juliet, I'll call you from Talbot's. It's too damned confusing. Okay?"

"Richie?"

"Yeah, and we could go out," the lawyer was saying. "I mean if you—"

"I'll call you in half an hour, Juliet," Gemetz yelled, trying to wedge his voice between the two adjacent callers and Annie's rock music. Then he shrugged and hung up the phone.

When Gemetz finally got to Talbot's he immediately called Juliet, but the line was busy. Then he called Linda and she reassured him that his father was still sleeping soundly. She had just looked in.

"How's the Mexican feast?" she asked.

"I don't know. Lennie's still flailing around in the kitchen," he said. "Jesus, you should look at this. He's got flour and other strange shit scattered all over. The place looks like a taco factory that got a direct hit."

"Just watch your stomach, Richie," she warned again.

"He looked okay?" he asked again about his father.

"Fine," she said. "I'm keeping the kids quiet."

"Lin?"

"What?"

"I want to thank you. Really, it's—"

"Hey, he's sort of my Papa, too," she said. "So, just relax and enjoy your meal. I'll see you later."

"Right, about two hours," he said. "Well, goodbye."

"Ta," she said and hung up.

Half an hour later, the three bachelors were seated around Talbot's big oak table. Talbot had darkened the room to obscure the mess he'd made in the kitchen area and now their faces were illuminated by the glow of a candle he had set in an amber bowl in the center of the table. There was only the sound of the scratchy recording of "La Paloma" playing on Talbot's old portable and the clinking of their spoons into their bowls as they each took a breath and simultaneously started into the first course—a cheese and peppers soup that immediately heightened the glow on Tiernan's and Gemetz's cheeks.

"What do you think?" Talbot asked confidently as he continued spooning hungrily.

"Wheeeeeeeeeeee!" Gemetz exclaimed, squinting the tears

from his eyes and trying to blow some of the fire off his tongue.

"Water!" Tiernan gasped.

"Wait a minute," Talbot said, dabbing his lips with a paper napkin and getting up. "I made a pitcher of margaritas."

As he walked back to the kitchen area Gemetz and Tiernan looked at each other in alarm and fanned their scorched tongues with their hands.

"Cooooo coo rrrroo coocooooooo . . . palooma!" Talbot sang along with the record as he returned to the table with the plastic pitcher and glasses on the table and then jumped back as the towel draped over his arm waiter fashion and a lemon tucked up in his armpit.

"Margaritas for the steenking gringos," he said, putting the pitcher and glasses on the table and then jumped back as the lemon accidentally dropped out of his armpit into Tiernan's soup. Talbot nimbly escaped the splash, but Tiernan caught a streak of soup across his right cheek and a good deal more on the front of his red sweater. For a moment he sat there glumly looking at Gemetz with his face dripping green soup.

"Last time we eat in this dump," he said to Gemetz.

"For please to excuse," Talbot said, wiping Tiernan's face with the towel and then rubbing the glop on his sweater briskly until it was driven in against his chest.

"It did sort of clash," Gemetz said.

"Gentlemens, thees ees most unfortunate," Talbot said as he tried to fish the lemon out of Tiernan's soup. "Notheeng neber hoppeen like dees een my place before. Neber!"

"Neber?" Gemetz asked.

"Just get your goddam dirty fingernails out of my soup," Tiernan said, still without moving as Talbot continued chasing the slippery lemon around in his bowl.

"Aha! And now, gentlemens," Talbot announced proudly as he extracted the lemon and wiped it off on Tiernan's portion of the tablecloth, "Leonardo going to make margaritas!"

After he had rimmed the three glasses with salt and poured the drinks, he gave the other two a section of lemon and told them to bite and then drink. The margaritas went down well and they toasted the inauguration of Ptomaine Tuesday and poured another round before they addressed themselves to the soup again. Tiernan watched as Talbot spooned right in and Gemetz took some tentative sips off the end of his spoon. Then he looked down at his bowl and stared at it like a Greek contemplating his hemlock.

"I'm not eating the soup," Tiernan said finally.

"Eat the soup," Talbot said between slurps.

"What's next?" Tiernan asked.

"It's good, eat the soup," Talbot said, already nearing the bottom of his bowl.

"No soup," Tiernan said stubbornly and folded his arms.

"Two hours I spent making this soup," Talbot said, "not counting going over to Manhattan to get the green peppers. Eat the soup."

"No soup."

"No soup?" Talbot said, slamming his fist down and glowering in mock anger.

"No soup," Tiernan said, picking up the sharp knife Talbot had used to slice the lemon.

"Okay," Talbot said with a shrug of indifference and going back after the last drops in his bowl. "How about a chili relleno?"

"Is it hot?" Tiernan asked.

"No, it's good."

"Okay, I'll have a chili whatchacallit. But no soup."

"Me neither," Gemetz said, pushing his bowl away.

"What have we here, gentlemen, a revolt?" Talbot asked, looking at Gemetz, a little hurt.

"The only thing that's revolting," Tiernan said, "is this soup."

"No, no, Lenny, it's probably great soup," Gemetz said. "Just too hot for us greenhorns. Really, man."

"Ah, the hell with it," Talbot said, looking depressed. "You guys don't know what's good."

"Come on, Len, don't take it personal," Tiernan said, reaching over and giving him a shove. "You can take a piss in my Irish stew when it comes my turn."

"Irish stew?" Talbot exclaimed. "That's what you're going to make? Irish stew? That's foreign? That's gourmet?"

"Sure, where do you think Ireland is—Pennsylvania?"

"I ain't even gonna tell you what I was planning," Gemetz said.

"Hey, I've been knocking myself out!" Talbot said, getting up and throwing his napkin on the table in real anger. "What is this? You guys agreed that we'd really try for something. I don't get it. You just fucking around with me or what?"

"Hey, calm down, calm down," Gemetz said. "We were only joking. Right, Joe?"

"You know how much I spent to make this goddam meal?" Talbot asked, shaking his head in disgust. "Twenty-six bucks, and that's not counting the tequila for the margaritas. And you're going to do Irish stew?"

Tiernan looked a little sheepishly at Gemetz. "Well, I was going to put red wine in it," he said lamely.

"Oh, yeah . . . Red wine in Irish stew?" Talbot asked, looking interested. "I never heard of that."

"Hey, I told you," Tiernan said, "it's a special recipe my aunt brought over from Ireland. A very difficult recipe, too. It used to take her two, sometimes three, days to make this kind of Irish stew. I only hope I can pull it off."

"Red wine," Talbot said, nodding.

"That's the easy part. Getting the truffles and wild heath potatoes will be damned hard in this country," Tiernan embellished, lying his head off while he had Talbot on the ropes.

"Truffles . . . wild heath potatoes!" Talbot exclaimed, his face brightening. "Now that's more like it. Wow! What're you going to do, Richie?"

"That is going to be a surprise," Gemetz said, fidgeting with his fork.

"Goddam, okay, gentlemens, now Leonardo is going to bring the chilies rellenos," Talbot said cheerfully as he picked up the bowls and headed back to the kitchen area.

"Wild heath potatoes?" Gemetz whispered over to Tiernan, who simply shrugged hopelessly.

"What's a chili relleno?" Tiernan whispered back.

"You'll love it, trust me," Gemetz whispered. "Linda used to make them. It's like a big green chili, but not hot, and they stuff it with fantastic cheese. Fluffy as a feather, and it goes down like a dream. Trust me."

"No shit?" Tiernan said, nodding as Talbot came back to the table with a platter of chilies rellenos.

Gemetz's smile of anticipation dissolved as Talbot dropped one of the chilies rellenos onto his plate—with a clank.

"Okay, gentlemens, the piece de resistance!" Talbot said, sitting down after he had clanked two on each plate.

"Light as a what?" Tiernan asked as he nearly bent his fork trying to break through the cementlike crust Talbot had cooked onto the rellenos.

"Jesus," Gemetz said as he, too, struggled with his relleno and nearly lost it onto the floor as it popped out from under his fork.

"I think maybe I used too much flour," Talbot said as he tried to get into his.

"I think maybe you could drive a nail with this thing," Gemetz said, picking up the relleno and banging it on the plate.

"Damn it!" Talbot growled as the relleno skittered around on the plate away from his fork. Finally he started stabbing at it angrily and then dropped his fork and grabbed both rellenos and fired them across the room into the kitchen area, where they bounced off the metal cabinets like two sticks of wood.

"Yea!" Tiernan cheered and picked up his rellenos and fired them one after another into the kitchen.

"Remember the Alamo!" Gemetz exclaimed and arced his over the room like two hand grenades.

Then for a moment there was silence as Tiernan and Gemetz watched Talbot, who had his face buried in his hands and was slowly shaking his head.

"What's next?" Gemetz asked.

"It's hopeless," Talbot moaned.

"Aw, come on, Len," Tiernan said soothingly. "All great experiments start off with a few misses. We're going to learn from these Tuesdays. If we were all that good at cooking we wouldn't need a cooking club. Right, Richie?"

"Right," Gemetz said. "We're trying, that's what's important. Come on, Len, what's next?"

"Enchiladas and bean burritos," Talbot sighed in dejection.

"Great," Tiernan said, nodding. "Go get 'em. We'll like 'em, we promise. What's a burrito?"

"Come on, man, bring on the food," Gemetz said, giving him a shove back from the table.

The rest of the meal turned out surprisingly well, especially the bean burritos. And after three more margaritas apiece, the first two courses were a distant memory. By nine o'clock they were all leaning back in their chairs and smoking the big Churchill-style Te-Amo cigars Talbot had purchased for the after-dinner coffee. Except they never got around to the coffee.

"Gentlemen, a toast," Tiernan said, raising his glass. "I give you tonight's chef—brother Talbot. A heroic effort!"

"Hear, hear!" Gemetz added, raising his glass to Tiernan's.

Talbot joined in, smiling modestly. He was satisfied that his enterprise was successfully launched, if not in the execution of the meal then in the forging of their wills to resist.

"Think of it," Talbot said, "our exes are probably home right now picking at some kind of macaroni and tuna fish, or canned string beans and beets or something. Bored out of their minds eating alone and not having a man to cook for."

"Yeah," Tiernan said.

"They would have loved that discussion on the Khyber Pass," Talbot continued, referring to their talk about the chances of the rebels cutting off the Russians in Afghanistan. "They're going to dry up, gentlemen. They're going to sit there night after night picking at macaroni and listening to their minds winding down. Their lives are turning to dry rot even as we sit here, gentlemen," he said, putting his legs up on the table and twirling his cigar.

"Yeah," Gemetz said, leaning back puffing his stogie. "Dry rot."

"That joke you told about the Indian in the snow, Joe?" Talbot asked. "A great joke, a great joke. But they missed it, Joe. Think they can tell jokes like that? They'd cream for a joke like that. Now they can have their macaroni."

"Dry rot, harumph!" Tiernan assented and leaned back.

"Good cigar, good food, excellent conversation . . ." Talbot went on.

"And don't forget the margaritas," Gemetz added, raising his glass and sipping down the last dregs.

"And good drinks." Talbot nodded. "They ever make us drinks like that? Gentlemen, I put it to you that they have acted irresponsibly. And they have lost—profoundly."

"Most profoundly," Gemetz said, sending out a long flume of cigar smoke.

"Dry rot," Tiernan mumbled contentedly.

Just then the phone rang on the mantelpiece and Talbot swung his legs down to get up and get it.

"Hey!" Tiernan exclaimed. "I bet that's Susan wanting to know what you're having for supper."

"Oh, shit," Gemetz said and looked at his watch. "I was supposed to be back at Linda's twenty minutes ago."

"Umm, hello," Talbot said into the phone as he flicked an ash from his cigar into the fireplace. "Who? Oh, hi, Linda. Yeah, just . . . just a minute," he said nodding toward Gemetz, who was already walking toward him.

"Tell her about the chili whatchacallits!" Tiernan yelled and then lost the smile on his face as Talbot came back and shook his head, frowning with concern.

"Hi, Lin," Gemetz said. "Sorry, I— What did you say?"

"Something's wrong," Talbot whispered to Tiernan.

"Oh, god," Gemetz said almost in a whisper and leaned against the mantelpiece for support.

Talbot turned and saw Gemetz standing there like a man who had just awakened in a strange room. For a moment everything in the room seemed suspended. There was no sound or movement except for the wavering shadows of the two men at the table cast by the candlelight against the kitchen wall.

"Richie?" Tiernan asked.

"My father," Gemetz said. "He . . . he's dead."

# CHAPTER
# ELEVEN

"You were dreaming," Juliet said.

Gemetz blinked and then closed his eyes again and breathed through his open mouth. The heat in the little space between the loft-bed and the ceiling was almost suffocating, and he could hear the radiators hissing down below near the window. After another moment he licked the dryness from his lips and turned his head toward her on the pillow.

"God, they've really got it up," he said, pushing the covers down off his chest.

Juliet was lying propped up on one elbow and looking at him with a puzzled expression. She was covered just to the waist by the blue sheet and there were fine strands of her dark hair matted to the moisture on her face.

"What were you dreaming about?" she asked. "You kept saying Linda's name."

"Yeah, it was . . . Oh, goddam it!" He sighed, closing his eyes again.

"What is it?" she asked.

"I just remembered Papa. What time is it?"

"Little after seven."

"Oh, hell, why can't *this* be a dream?" he said, thinking of the funeral services he had to attend in two hours.

"I wish it were." She sighed and stroked her fingers through the beads of perspiration on his forehead. Her touch was light and soothing and he let his dread breathe out of him.

"You don't mind not going?" he asked after a minute.

"I'd like to," she said quietly, "but I understand."

"I wish you could."

"Richie, it's going to be tough enough for you getting through today without getting caught between me and Linda."

"He liked you."

"I liked him, too." She blinked against her tears.

"Strange damn dream," he said, shaking his head. "First time I remember dreaming in color. It was so vivid. Everything in this . . . like peach-colored light. We were on a beach somewhere."

"You and Linda?"

"Yeah, and she was big—pregnant. She was naked and she was walking down this beach. Away from me. I was calling to her and she was turning and waving and smiling at me. But she kept moving farther and farther away from me. And I kept calling to her and telling her not to go too far, because the baby might come. But there was this thing—like a giant sail."

"A sail?" she asked, pushing a damp lock of hair back off his forehead.

"No, not exactly a sail. You could see right through it. It was like a curtain, only transparent, and the wind was coming in off the ocean and it was like blowing into this giant curtain that was hanging down from the sky. And the wind was like bulging it in over the beach. Weird, I mean. And I was trying to get to Linda and there was this big curtain billowing in over the waves and I couldn't get around it. And she kept walking away, getting farther down the beach."

He stopped talking and looked at her again. She pursed her lips in thought and then shrugged.

"Strange," he said.

"Ummm," she agreed. "I read this piece in the *Post*. Some psychiatrist, he said that the important thing about dreams is how they make you feel."

"I don't know," he said, sitting up and pushing the covers all the way down off his perspiring legs. "I have this terrible feeling about going to Papa's funeral, but it doesn't seem related to the dream."

"Okay, Mr. Gemetz, what do you say I fix you a nice cup of

coffee?" She rubbed his back briskly and wished she could get his mind off the subject.

"Rather have an orange juice," he said, leaning forward and grunting under her vigorous rubbing. "I'm melting."

"Any in the fridge?" she asked.

"Yeah, I think so," he said, stretching his neck from side to side.

"Coming up!" She had to climb over him to get to the ladder.

For the next forty-five minutes until Tiernan showed up, Juliet pampered him like a little boy, feeding him breakfast, pushing him toward the shower and laying out his dark suit and a fresh white shirt. She had just finished getting ready to leave for work herself when Tiernan pushed the buzzer.

"Good morning," Tiernan said when she opened the door. He was freshly shaven and his cheeks and nose were ruddy from the cold air outside.

"Hi," she said, stepping aside for him to come in. "There's some coffee on the stove. Have you eaten?"

"Yeah. Whew! It's like an oven in here."

"That you, Joe?" Gemetz called from the bathroom, where he was trimming his beard with the scissors.

"Yeah!" Tiernan shouted.

"Joe?" Juliet whispered as she slipped into her coat. "Stick with him today, will you?"

"Sure, don't worry," he said, smiling fondly at her.

"Len's still not coming?" she asked.

"No, he wanted to, but he's got this exam he's giving this morning. He said he talked to Richie last night."

"I'm glad you could come," she said. "It was good of you. I mean, taking time off from work—"

"I didn't have anything pressing this morning," he said.

She smiled at him and walked toward the bathroom door as she buttoned her coat.

"You'll call me tonight?" she asked Gemetz when she got to the door.

He put down the scissors and smoothed his beard with his hand and walked over to her. Putting his arms around her waist, he looked into her eyes for a moment as though he were weighing something in his mind. He loved her very much and was grateful for the way she had been trying to nurture him through this shock, but he also felt relieved that she was leaving. He didn't understand why he felt this way. All morning it was as though something in him was resisting her efforts to comfort him. It was as though she didn't belong to this . . . this death. He had also been feeling a growing eagerness for Linda to show up with Mark and Jonathan in the car.

"Will you?" she asked again.

"What?"

"Call me tonight?"

"Yes," he said, pulling her to him and rocking her gently in his arms. "Don't worry, okay?"

"Okay," she said and kissed him gently on the lips. "I'll stop in at the church near my office at lunch."

"Thank you," he said and gave her one last hug and then walked with his arm around her to the door.

When she had gone, he gave Tiernan a glance and walked to the mirror over the fireplace and began putting on his tie. He felt his breath coming easier.

"You okay?" Tiernan asked, going into the kitchen and pouring himself a cup of coffee.

"Yeah," he said, pulling the tie under his collar. "Thanks for coming."

"Talbot call you?" Tiernan asked.

"Yeah, he's tied up with classes. You didn't have to—"

"Hey, I'll take a funeral to Alma Reed any day," Tiernan said, walking into the main room with the steaming cup in his hand. "I'm sorry," he said, grimacing. "I didn't mean it that way."

"Relax."

"Well, you're lucky to have Juliet around," Tiernan said, sitting down in Gemetz's frumpy reading chair with his trench coat still on.

"Yeah, but I just . . . Ah, never mind," Gemetz said, slamming his fist into his palm. "Linda should be showing up with the kids any minute."

"How're they taking it?" Tiernan asked, sipping his coffee and watching Gemetz pacing between the fireplace and the window.

"I'm not sure Jonathan understands what's going on," Gemetz said. "We didn't let him go to his grandmother's funeral last year and I thought maybe that was a mistake. She just sort of disappeared from his life—like she moved out of town or something. Now, I'm not so sure. His first funeral . . . the old man dying in Linda's bedroom? It's got him a little frightened, I think."

"How'd Linda get along with the old man?" Tiernan asked.

"Hell, they were real close, even after the breakup. But so far she's been like a rock. Thank god! She made all the arrangements, you know."

"Oh, yeah? Good woman."

"In many ways she's a damn good woman," Gemetz said, nodding as he looked out the window for her car. "She's crazy, but in a crunch she's the one you want to have around."

"My old man died when I was just a kid," Tiernan said. "He was something of a bastard, though."

"You didn't miss him?"

"Not right after he died," Tiernan said, resting back in the chair. "Later I did. Like after I got out of college and went to work and started raising a family. Shit, I don't know. Maybe I just would've liked being able to face him without being terrified."

Gemetz went over to the old canvas butterfly chair and slumped down in it and buried his face in his hands.

"Papa was always so . . . love . . . loving," Gemetz sobbed.

"He had a good life, Richie," Tiernan said sympathetically.

"No!" Gemetz said, shaking his head. "He got screwed by life. He . . . got shortchanged. I wanted him to live, Joe. He never asked anything of me, but I wanted him to live. You know? To take hold of life and make demands on it. Scream and yell and kick the shit out of it for giving him such a small piece of it."

"Wasn't he happy?" Tiernan asked.

"I don't know. He was just there. Hanging in. Always in that store. I woke up this morning and for a second it was just another day and I was going to get dressed and go over to the store and find him in there with that shitty little knit scarf of Mamma's around his neck. I couldn't believe that I was going to get up and go stick him under some dirt in Queens. Is *that* where we're really going this morning, Joe? Tell me, because I don't believe it."

"It's tough," Tiernan said, putting his cup on the floor beside his chair. "You shouldn't feel guilty though."

They sat there in silence for the next five minutes with

Tiernan watching Gemetz rocking back and forth with his face still buried in his hands. Then they heard Linda honk her car horn out front.

"Okay," Gemetz said, getting up and frowning with determination. "Okay."

On the way over to the Kaufman Funeral Chapel in Flatbush, Linda drove and Tiernan sat in the back seat with the two boys. Gemetz sat with his hands jammed into his overcoat pockets and looked at Linda. She had been unusually quiet since they'd gotten into the car and she looked very tired, pinched. God, don't start caving in now, baby, he thought. In the back seat Tiernan was trying to draw the boys into a discussion of the new *Star Trek* movie.

"How're you holding up?" Gemetz asked her.

"Okay, I guess," she sighed and glanced at him quickly, with tears verging in her eyes. "Little trouble with Jonathan this morning."

"Oh," he asked, glancing back at the boy, who was ignoring the discussion going on between Tiernan and Mark.

"Hard to explain to a five-year-old," she said.

The thought of Linda and the boys alone over at the apartment trying to deal with his father's death made him cringe with guilt. He should have been there to give them support. But in the time since the death he had been like a hurt child himself, retreating into himself and allowing everyone else to take care of an impossible situation. Yes, it was a time for allowing, he thought. Once a death was allowed, you— No, no, dammit! he thought. You're copping out, asshole. They needed you and you copped out. Like you copped out of the marriage. Yes, that was the look in his father's eyes that had haunted him. That you could leave them, Richie? No words of recrimination, just that look. She wouldn't sleep with me, Papa! he screamed in his mind. She hated me, Papa!

The lobby of the little funeral home on Flatbush Avenue was filled with thirty or so of his father's relatives and friends when they walked in. Most of them were elderly and well dressed, and they were all noisily engaged in one of those reunions that only take place at funerals. Moving ahead of Linda and the others through the gauntlet of outstretched hands and pats and hastily constructed expressions of condolence, Gemetz made his way to the hallway that led to the service chapel. Here he was met by the funeral director, Mr. Kaufman, a tall gray-haired man who looked like he belonged on Wall Street.

"Rabbi Gold should be here in about fifteen minutes," Mr. Kaufman said. Gemetz remembered him from the previous year at his mother's funeral.

"Fine," Gemetz said as the director escorted them to the chapel door.

"I phoned his wife and she said he was delayed," the director continued. "He was visiting out on Long Island."

"Keep everybody outside for a few minutes, okay?" Gemetz said as Linda and the boys went inside and sat down in a front pew before his father's closed bronze coffin.

"Of course," Mr. Kaufman said, bowing slightly and turning away in time to intercept several of the mourners who were coming down the hall.

"I can wait outside," Tiernan said, starting to go, too.

"No, stay," Gemetz said, pushing him inside. "Sit next to Mark, okay?"

"Sure."

The morning outside had been cold and bright, and inside the chapel a broad shaft of sunlight from a high window slanted down over the rows of polished oak pews and caught a corner of his father's coffin. He sat there quietly for a while next to Linda looking at the motes of dust swirling around in that slant of blazing light and listening to the drone of the reunion continuing in the lobby.

He heard Linda sniff and felt her body shudder slightly against his. She was wearing her fur-collared black coat, and her hair was done up in a tight roll under a black pillbox hat. And turning to her, he saw her pressing her eyes shut to fight back her tears.

"It's okay," he whispered, patting her gloved hands.

"Daddy," Mark whispered as he leaned forward to see around his mother.

"What?" Gemetz whispered back.

"It's just like Grandma's," the boy said, looking toward the coffin.

"Yeah," he whispered back with a nod and tried to give his oldest son a look of encouragement.

"I wish we could get started," Linda said, dabbing her eyes. "Jonathan feels very bad."

Gemetz glanced down and saw the five-year-old pressed

against his mother's side, hiding his face under her arm so that he would not have to look at the coffin.

"Me, too," Gemetz whispered, choking.

The tears were rolling freely down Linda's cheeks now and he felt a sense of panic rising in him. "Good woman," Tiernan had said. Yes, he thought now. The old man had seen that, too. They had become close, Linda and his father. The old man had been his, as much as his flesh and bone were his, but the death had taken from Linda a father he had chosen with her heart. I'm sorry it didn't work out, Papa, he thought.

The chapel room seemed cleft by the long shaft of light that now illuminated half his father's coffin. He wanted to dig his fingers into the coffin's crease and rip open the cover and pull the old man up into the light. But he had to sit there with the panic rising in his throat and feeling more and more that the lid that had sealed his father in darkness was closing down on him as well.

"I need a little air," he said to Linda and squeezed her hand and got up. As he left the chapel, Tiernan rose and followed him out.

As they moved through the crowd in the lobby, Gemetz's Aunt Mimi, a tiny middle-aged woman who looked like a fur ball in her mink coat, reached out a black gloved hand to stop him.

"Richie, I'm so sorry," she said, grasping his arm. "First Sarah, and now it's—"

"Thank you," he said, pulling away. "I just, uh, I have to go out for a minute. Excuse me. Please, Aunt Mimi, try to get everybody to go in and sit down."

"Is Rabbi Gold here?" she called after him.

"Any minute!" he called back and shouldered the front door open and stepped out into the crisp cold air. Tiernan followed a moment later.

For a minute Gemetz turned and leaned back against the imitation brick facade of the funeral home and gulped the air, letting his panic sigh out of him. I can't bury . . . he thought as he mentally tried to strip off all the moldered blankets of sorrow that had been descending on him.

"You okay?" Tiernan asked, eyeing him apprehensively.

"Yeah," Gemetz sighed and opened his eyes.

Across the street two black youths emerged laughing and sparring from Carlo's Pizzeria and continued their casual odyssey up Flatbush Avenue toward Erasmus High School. The pizzeria had replaced a furniture store that had been burned and looted during the blackout in the sweltering summer of '77, the year before his mother died. The store's charred and boarded-up windows were still in Gemetz's memory from the morning of his mother's services.

He thought again of that morning and of her bronze coffin being lowered into the ground in the cemetery in Queens. A coffin identical to the one that now held his father's poor wasted body. Again the panic began to rise. He closed his eyes and tried to quell it with his breathing. Just then one of the big blue city buses hissed to a stop in front of the funeral parlor, stalled by the line of traffic from the corner.

In its windows drowsy-eyed passengers looked out on the scene, giving little notice to him as they surveyed the row of small stores and shops along the avenue. A mother held a sleeping child against her shoulder, an elderly man read his paper, others looked out, looked toward their destinations— homes, jobs, stores, bars but not cemeteries. The bus started moving again and suddenly Gemetz found himself walking toward it as though he were being pulled by a magnet. Tiernan stood back watching for a moment and then started after Gemetz as he saw him yank the little black silk yarmulke from the crown of his head and begin running alongside of the bus. When Gemetz got to the front doors he started pounding to be let on. The black driver looked over at him with a bored expression and kept driving.

"Richie!" Tiernan shouted. "No, Richie!"

"Stop! I have to get on!" Gemetz shouted as he ran and continued pounding and tried to keep up. Finally the bus came to a halt at the corner and flapped its doors open. He leaped on gasping. Tiernan was still some distance behind, calling to him.

"Exact change," the driver said, closing his eyes and slowly shaking his head when Gemetz drew a dollar out of his pocket and handed it to him.

"Oh, right, right," Gemetz said, still trying to get his breath and digging through his pockets for some change. Nothing in his overcoat pockets, a dime and three pennies in a jacket pocket, nothing in his pants. His head seemed to be bursting. He wanted to sit down and hide. Sit down and feel the bus taking him away.

"Let's go, Mac. We got a schedule," the bus driver said.

"Look, I'm sorry, I don't have the change," Gemetz said, holding the dollar toward the driver again. "You can change a buck, huh?"

"Exact change," the driver said, frowning.

"Here, take the buck. Keep it," Gemetz said, fidgeting and looking at an empty seat toward the rear of the bus. A hole he could dive into.

The driver shook his head and turned away. "Go get some change and catch the next bus," he said.

"Come on, asshole!" Gemetz exploded.

"Here, sir!" an elderly black woman sitting a few seats down called out as she held out four quarters on her palm. "I'll change yo' dollar."

"Thank you, I . . ." Gemetz said, rushing back to her and taking two of the quarters and giving her the bill. "Keep it."

"Richie!" Tiernan called as he jumped into the bus. "For god's sake, Richie, what the hell—"

"Outa my way!" he shouted, shoving Tiernan aside and lunging toward the driver.

"Exact change!" Gemetz yelled angrily and slammed the quarters in his palm toward the coin-box opening.

But only one of them went through the opening and the other spanged off its lip and went sailing past his shoulder out the door. He made a sweep at it with his hand and then leaped out of the bus after it. Tiernan leaped off behind him, trying to grab his arm. Gemetz pulled away and frantically chased the coin, stamping on it as it nearly rolled into a sewer grate. But just as he was leaning over to retrieve it he heard the bus door hiss shut.

"No, goddam it, wait!" he shouted as the bus pulled away.

"Richie, wait a minute!" Tiernan pleaded and threw his arms around him to hold him back.

"You sonofabitch!" he screamed at the bus as it crossed into the intersection, and then he swung free of Tiernan and began pounding his fists on the hood of a car that was parked along the curb.

"No, no, no, god . . . I can't do it," he cried, cringing his face against the top of his fists on the hood. The yarmulke was still clenched in his hand. In a moment he slowly opened his hands and buried his face in the yarmulke and began to weep, letting go for the first time since his father had died and feeling the ache that had been hanging in his chest begin to dislodge at last.

"Let it all out, Richie," Tiernan said, putting his arm around Gemetz's shoulders.

"Papa, Papa, Papa, I don't want to do it," Gemetz wailed. And the black silk skullcap in his hands was like a dark well into which he sent his cries.

Tiernan held him tightly and let him cry it out, turning occasionally to tell curious passersby to keep moving.

After a few minutes, Gemetz stopped crying and stood up, wiping his tear-stained face with the yarmulke. "I'm sorry," he said, looking at Tiernan and shaking his head.

"Come on, babe," Tiernan said, brushing Gemetz's coat off and leading him gently to the sidewalk. "What say we go someplace and grab a quick drink?"

"No, I'm okay . . . crazy . . . I'm sorry."

"It's gonna be okay, babe," Tiernan said, putting his arm over Gemetz's shoulder. "You can do it."

"Yeah, I can do it."

As they neared the front of the funeral chapel, Gemetz took off his coat and dusted it briskly and folded it over his arm. Then he looked at Tiernan, took a deep breath and walked in. Yeah, I can do it, he thought.

"In here, Mr. Gemetz," the funeral director said, motioning to them from his office. "They're in here with Rabbi Gold."

Inside the office they saw the elderly white-haired rabbi talking with Linda and the two boys. Linda was holding Jonathan by the hand and they were all now wearing the traditional little torn black ribbons pinned to their lapels to signify a rending of garments. The funeral director took one from his pocket, made the tear in it with a little silver knife and handed it to Gemetz. He needed no symbol of his grieving heart, but he nodded his thanks to the director and pinned it on.

"Where were you two?" Linda asked as they joined the little gathering around the rabbi.

"Richie just needed to get it together," Tiernan said.

Gemetz smiled at her and took Jonathan up in his arms. "How's my man?" he asked the boy.

"You are feeling better, Richard?" the rabbi asked, touching his arm.

"Yes, thanks," he said. "I'm sorry I haven't had a chance to call you." The rabbi had been close to his family for as long as he could remember and he was grateful to have him perform the service, as he had for his mother's funeral.

"I understand," the rabbi said soothingly. "Linda has been most helpful."

"If we could," the funeral director urged, looking at his watch and beginning to worry about having the chapel cleared for the next service. They started to follow him to the door.

"Richard, a minute," the rabbi said, putting his hand on his arm again as Tiernan, Linda and the others went ahead.

The old man, whose soft white hair formed a wreath around his bald pate, looked into his eyes for a moment and searched deep into his sorrow.

"Do you know what I remember most about Martin . . . your father, Richard?"

Gemetz shook his head and sniffed back the sob that was rising in his throat.

"We were young men together—friends, here in Flatbush," the rabbi went on. "And we both fell in love with the same lovely young woman who lived on our block. Richard, that was Sarah. Richard, we were such rivals for Sarah, I cannot tell you! And when she chose Martin, I—"

"It's okay," Gemetz said, smiling and wanting to save the old rabbi from this confession.

But the rabbi shook his head. "No, let me finish," he said. "Oh, I was . . . I think I even wanted not to live, Richard. But I managed to survive, and over the years as I saw how much love there was between them I even became glad that he had won her. Such a love between them, Richard. Do you understand?"

"Yes," Gemetz said, turning his head to hide the tears that were starting.

"And in a little while, they will be together again," the old man said, his own eyes beginning to redden. "Will you try to think of that, Richard?"

"Thank you," Gemetz said, and walked into the chapel with the rabbi. After Richie had taken his seat with Linda, Tiernan and his sons, the rabbi went to the front and began the service.

"We have gathered here this morning to express our love and to pay our respects to Martin Gemetz," the rabbi said from the little pulpit to the left and behind the coffin.

Linda reached over and took Gemetz's hand and squeezed it. He put his other hand over hers and pressed it warmly.

"In our Jewish tradition we turn for strength, comfort and consolation to the words of our tradition and especially to the Book of Psalms. I would like to share with you several appropriate psalms in the Hebrew and English. The first from the Twenty-third Psalm: *"Mismor l'David, Adonai roe lo echsar . . ."*

Oh, Papa, Papa, go to her new, he thought, remembering the rabbi's words about the young lovers. Be young and strong and gay again, Papa. Smile for him, Mammá.

"He leadeth me beside the still waters . . ." The rabbi's voice moved slowly outside his thoughts.

And as the fifteen-minute eulogy continued he looked at the coffin and imagined his father far away walking in the sun, a young man wearing a gleaming white shirt and chuckling in his way as he spoke to the young Sarah holding his arm. The compression and panic he had felt before in the chapel were gone and there was only the voice of the rabbi.

*"Ayl maleh rachamen . . ."*

Driving Linda's car out to the cemetery, Gemetz felt at peace with himself. He watched the hearse bumping along ahead of him over the potholed Brooklyn-Queens Expressway and thought of his father going to join his beloved Sarah. Just a little longer, Papa, he thought. Linda sat next to him with the still-silent Jonathan on her lap. She was nuzzling his face with hers and telling him they would soon be coming to the little high-arched Kosciusko Bridge, the boy's favorite of all the spans in the city. In the back seat, Tiernan and Mark were talking about the Pittsburgh quarterback Terry Bradshaw.

I'm going to be all right, Papa, Gemetz thought. I have some good friends who love me. And, Papa, I feel very close to Linda today. I will keep an eye on her for you, Papa. I want her to be happy, too.

"How's Jonathan doing?" Gemetz asked her.

"Just fine—a big boy," Linda said, kissing Jonathan on the cheek and smiling sadly at Gemetz.

A little later at the graveside Gemetz faced the last thing he would do for his father. The Kaddish had been recited and now with the others waiting quietly behind him he stood on the edge of his father's grave holding the first shovelful of the orange earth that would be thrown in. At the bottom of the new grave next to his mother's resting place his father's coffin lay half in shadow and half in the morning light. A cold wind coming up the cemetery slope caused him to squint his eyes and it dusted some of the dirt from the shovel onto his coat.

He shook his head and looked out across the thick gray clusters of tombstones on the descending slope. About fifteen yards down the slope two overall-clad cemetery workers leaned on tombstones and chatted and smoked. A third sat huddled against the cold on the seat of the tractorlike grave-digging machine.

"Richard?" the rabbi's voice urged behind him.

"It's all right, Rabbi Gold," he heard Linda say.

Yes, it is all right, he thought, taking courage from the soft warmth of Linda's voice. "Goodbye, my wonderful, wonderful papa," he murmured as he let the soil slip off the shovel down into the grave.

As he turned back to the gathering, Linda came forward and put her arm around his waist and led him toward the cars at the top of the slope. Gemetz stopped for a moment and picked up Jonathan. Tiernan followed, holding Mark's hand. But before they could proceed very much farther the cluster of mourners trapped them in one last huddle of condolences, touching him, stroking him, holding him. God, he thought, let me just leave this place quietly. He smiled and nodded and tried to press through the gathering. Then over their heads he saw the great jaws of the digging machine lurch up with a hundredweight of orange earth and let it drop with a sickening whump onto his father's coffin. The bastards, he thought as he caught a glimpse of the cemetery workers quickly trying to fill in the grave so they could get back out of the cold. He looked at Linda and cringed as he tried to escape. And all the way up the slope the clacking, grinding sound of that machine, the grasping hands of his relatives and the incessant crashing of earth onto that drum over his father's face nearly drove him into a frenzy.

In the car again he sat behind the wheel panting and shaking his head to expunge the image from his brain. When everybody was in the car he threw it in gear and sped away down the cemetery road.

"That fucking machine," he snarled through his teeth as he pulled out through the cemetery gates.

"Those ghouls!" Linda exclaimed, her own anger surprising him. "They could have waited a few goddam minutes!"

"What happened, Mamma?" Mark asked from the back seat.

"It's okay," Tiernan said soothingly.

They drove along for the next ten minutes in silence, Gemetz feeling a little better because of Linda's partnership in his anger.

"They're not going to get away with it, Richie," she said suddenly. "Turn around!"

"What?"

"I want to go back," she said, looking at him with fiery determination.

"Oh, Linda," he said, "I can't take that again."

"No," she said. "I'm not going to have our last memory of Papa's funeral be that grotesque crap they pulled back there. Please, Richie, turn around."

"If we go back, I'm liable to kill that guy on the machine," Gemetz said.

"They should be finished when we get there," she said. "Besides, there's something I promised Papa."

Gemetz looked at her for a minute and then back at Tiernan. Then he nodded his head with determination. She was right, he thought. They weren't going to ruin his father's funeral. He took the next cutoff and headed back to the cemetery.

When they got back to the cemetery slope, Gemetz could see the digging machine moving away with the three workers on it, leaving his father's grave neatly piled and tamped. He stopped the car and they all got out. But as they started down the slope, Jonathan balked and started crying. Mark, too, seemed hesitant about returning to the grave.

"You two go on ahead, I'll keep the boys here with me," Tiernan said, holding the boys against his thighs.

"Thanks, Joe," Gemetz said, taking Linda's hand and continuing down the slope.

Tiernan watched them walking down between the gravestones and patted the two boys on the shoulder. The wind was still blowing up the slope, and he saw Linda reach up to keep her hat on as Gemetz steadied her other arm. For a moment he could glimpse the bond that had once existed between them.

He watched them stop at the edge of the grave and stand silently hand in hand, their heads bowed. They were about twenty yards from where he and the children were standing. Linda had been right, Tiernan thought. Just the two of them saying goodbye in a way the old man probably would have liked.

Then he saw Linda step away from Gemetz and sit down beside the fresh rise of orange earth over the grave. And in a moment he saw her lean forward and place her hand on the grave. Then he heard the rich sounds of her voice rising hauntingly over the silence in the cemetery in what he recognized as an aria from *Tosca*.

*"Vissi d'arte, vissi d'amore, non feci mai male ad anima viva . . ."* There was a melancholy power in her voice that sent a shiver down Tiernan's neck and brought tears to the brim of his eyes.

And when she finished he let his tears fall as he watched Gemetz step over to her and help her up and then take her in his arms and kiss her. A good woman, Richie, he thought, sniffing. A good woman, indeed.

That night Gemetz and Linda stood at the window of her bedroom looking out at the Venus light over the harbor. They had spent the day together consoling the children and quietly talking about the things they remembered of his father. And now the children were in bed and soon it would be time for him to go.

"You can stay if you want," she said quietly.

# CHAPTER
# TWELVE

There were still wet footprints on the bedroom carpet where Juliet had walked in from her bath. The thick blue towel she had haphazardly dried off with lay crumbled near a corner of the bed, and on the night table there was an empty bottle of Cabernet Sauvignon and beside the bottle a glass half filled with the deep red wine. Juliet lay nude on her brown corduroy bedspread, her pale lithe body stretched out in catlike languor. Looking along the length of her arm with half-closed eyes, she sighed drunkenly and toyed with the white Princess phone perched on the edge of one of the pillows.

She poked at the phone with her fingers and told herself that when it tumbled from the pillow she would dial Linda's number. Of course, Richie was there, she told herself. It was now Sunday night and she had not heard from him since Thursday morning just before he was to go to his father's funeral. She had called his apartment and the store at least a dozen times and had even gone over to his place. On Saturday morning, thinking that he might have done himself in in a fit of depression over his father's death, she had made the superintendent of his building let her in to look around. The apartment had looked exactly as it had been when she left it Thursday morning, except Richie wasn't there.

For four days he had left her fretting in limbo, she now thought. "Twisting in the wind, Richie," she mumbled in self-pity. "You left me twisting in the wind, Richie."

Just then the phone toppled from the pillow onto the bed, its receiver falling free next to her outstretched hand. "Okay." She sighed and grasped it and rolled on her back.

"Okay, Richie, this is it," she said, sniffing and looking over at the night table for the little piece of paper she had written Linda's number on after looking it up in the phone book earlier in the evening. The slip of paper was sticking out from under the wine glass.

"You don't have t'say anything, Richie," she slurred as she stared at the little piece of paper. "Just hello. Just a word. Just so I know you're alive. Just so I know you went to her. That's all, Richie. Just a little word, Richie. Then it's goodbye, Richie. All over. Yeah." She sighed with a wistful smile. "All over."

Just then the phone receiver in her hand began making little clicking noises and then she could hear a man's squeaky voice, a telephone company recording, saying, "Please hang up . . . there appears to be a receiver off the hook. Please check your . . ."

"Oh, fud!" she said and slapped the receiver back onto the phone. "'Please hang up! . . . Please hang up!'" she minced, imitating the recording that came on whenever a phone was left off the hook for more than thirty seconds.

But as she started to reach for the piece of paper with Linda's number on it, it suddenly struck her that Linda might answer the phone. It would be humiliating to ask her if Richie was there. How can you do this to me, Richie? she thought.

"You're a rotten creep, Richie!" she shouted and slapped the bed with the palm of her hand.

Then she thought of how miserable he looked on the morning of his father's funeral and began to cry.

"You didn't have to go to her," she whined as the hot tears washed down over her cheeks. "I . . . I cared, Richie. Didn't you know I cared?"

"Well, he's a big boy," she sniffed and flung her arm out to pick up the piece of paper again. But instead of sliding it out from under the glass she picked up the glass and brought it over to her lips. Sniffing again and rubbing the tears from her cheeks with the back of her other hand, she took a sip of wine. There was only the light from the lamp on the night table, and the room was cool and silent except for the light ticking of her fingernail against the glass she was holding to her chin. Annie had gone out on a date and would not be back until well after midnight, if she came back at all that night. The luminous dials on the Big Ben clock on the bureau at the other side of the room told her it was only a little after ten o'clock.

"Pretty . . . pretty pur— pretty purple wine," she sighed, holding the glass up to the light. She had slowly worked her way through the bottle, sipping little glassfuls of it during a supper of cheese and plums, keeping the bottle and slender little wine glass beside the tub when she took her long soaking bubble bath, carrying them in one hand with her as she walked into the bedroom drying off.

"Shit," she sighed and took another sip.

Lying on her back in the stillness, she felt a little dizzy and imagined the room floating down a wide river. I want my Richie, she thought and pouted her lips. Then she dipped a finger into the wine glass and touched the cool liquid to her lips and began to feel a warm tingling spreading through her body. After dipping her finger into the wine again, she slowly inserted it into her mouth and began sucking it and licking it lasciviously. And after a moment she took another drink from the glass and pouted again.

"Is she better than me, Richie?" she asked. "Is that it?"

Then she dipped her finger again and touched little drops of wine around the pink aureoles of her nipples, and dipped again and traced a long pink line down the center of her abdomen. "Oh, Richie," she sighed and sought escape from her unhappiness, imagining his fine strong hand caressing her body, murmuring to her to open to him, licking and biting the edge of her ribs, moving down in moans as he always did until his mouth was feeding hungrily on her sex, lapping and sucking great hot waves of feeling from her, and she arching her body toward his ravenous ghost as her own fingers strummed the deep rhythms into orgasm.

And afterward, as she lay there spent and sighing deep breaths, she glanced down at the wine glass she had been clenching in her hand. She brought it to her mouth and finished what was left in one gulp and then tossed the glass over the edge of the bed with a little flip of the hand.

"Oh . . . oh, god," she sighed, feeling a mild nausea

starting down in the pit of her stomach. "Gotta call Richie," she said, starting to rise and then falling back on the pillow out of dizziness.

For a while she just lay there until the nausea subsided. And then she opened her eyes again and looked over at the little slip of paper. She reached out and took it between her fingers. "Two-three-seven . . . two-three-three-seven," she murmured several times and then turned over on her side to the phone again.

She picked up the receiver and dialed several times before she could do it without hitting wrong numbers.

"Hello?" Linda answered.

Juliet shook her head and breathed several times through her nose while she tried to decide whether to talk.

"Hello?" Linda asked again.

"I wanna . . . I'd like to talk to Richie," Juliet finally said, trying to control the slur in her voice.

"Who is this please?" Linda asked.

"Talk to Richie," she said, nodding and trying to keep her eyes open.

Then there was a pause and she heard Linda's voice farther away from the phone: "Rich, I think it's your little friend."

Juliet let out a whimper of rage.

"Hello?" Richie asked.

Juliet shook her head and hung up the phone.

After a moment her phone rang. She lay there with her head on her arm looking at it. Inside of her there was a war going on between her anger and her nausea. Linda's words kept striking like a knife through her mind: "I think it's your little friend . . . your little friend . . . your little friend."

She slapped the receiver off the phone and jumped up on her knees and began pounding the pillow with her fists.

"Fuck you, Richie Gemetz!" she screamed into the receiver as she picked it up. "And you can tell your little wife she . . . she can . . . you can tell her she deserves you!" she shrieked and threw the phone against the wall over the bed. It bounced back onto the bed and rolled down against the depression made by her knees. "Ooooooh!" she howled in rage as her hands shook over it as though she could strangle it.

Then she got up and staggered around the bed looking for something she could smash the phone with. She spotted the empty wine bottle on the night table on the other side of the bed and threw herself across the bed to get it.

"I hate you! I hate you! I hate you!" she screamed as she kneeled over the phone and pounded it with the bottle.

However, the smashing had little effect on the tough plastic phone and she missed it half the time as it bounced around on the bed.

Finally she released the bottle and knelt there crying with her face in her hands. Her sobs of anger and loss came racking up out of her for a long time and then she felt her nausea taking command. As she knelt there fighting it back she could hear Richie's squeaky voice coming from the phone receiver: "Juliet . . . Juliet . . . Juliet." She reached down and picked it up finally.

"I can't talk to you, Richie, I have to throw up," she said, still crying.

"Juliet, I'm sorry . . . I . . ." he said in a pleading voice.

"I know, forget it," she said, coughing. "I've go to go because I'm . . ." And then she hurled the phone to one side and leaned over the edge of the bed and retched up the purple wine.

When she was finished she wiped her mouth against the bedspread and fell back on her pillow exhausted. And after a minute she blinked the tears out of her eyes and picked up the phone. Gemetz was still on the line. She could hear him talking to Linda.

". . . I don't know. It sounds like she's being sick," she heard him say.

"Maybe you should talk to her later," Linda said.

"Look, will you just . . . Hello, Juliet?" he said.

"Richie, you don't have to say anything," Juliet said, feeling very calm and sleepy. "Just promise you won't call me anymore. Okay?"

"Juliet, I feel very ashamed," he said after a pause.

"You don't have to feel ashamed, Richie. Guys go back to their wives, right?" she said, wiping her nose.

"I should have called you," he said.

"Yeah, I know it," she said, closing her eyes.

"I don't know how to explain it," he said. "I'm just as surprised as you are. It just—"

"I can understand," she said. "The kids and . . . Look,

Richie, I don't want to talk about it. I drank too much wine and I shouldn't have called you. But I . . . I . . . just didn't . . . know, Richie," she said, fighting back a new wave of tears.

"Can you forgive me?" he asked.

"Yeah," she said. "But promise you won't ever call me. Okay, Richie?"

"Juliet, I just want you to know—" he began.

"Goodbye, Richie," she said and hung up.

# CHAPTER
# THIRTEEN

"Woman, open this bloody door or we'll be breakin' it down!" Tiernan roared outside Mary's apartment door.

Lynn was sitting on his shoulders laughing and banging on the door with the beribboned toy shillelagh he'd bought for her at the St. Patrick's Day parade in Manhattan. The little girl was wearing a shiny plastic green top hat, and both their faces were bright and ruddy from being hours out in the cold watching the parade.

"Are ye in there, woman?" he called out again.

"Okay, I'm coming, I'm coming!" he heard Mary say as she hurried to let them in.

"Break the door, Daddy!" Lynn squealed.

"Sure'n' we'll crash it!" Tiernan exclaimed and swooped around and ran back about ten paces. Then he narrowed his eyes and scratched his shoes against the floor as he prepared for the grand charge. "Hold on, love, we're goin' in!" he called to Lynn and adjusted her on his shoulders as Mary unlatched the door. His timing was perfect and he sailed into the apartment going "Wheeeeeee!" just as Mary swung the door open and jumped out of the way.

"Up the Irish!" he crowed from the living room, lifting Lynn high over his head.

"Daddy, Daddy, Daddy!" she squealed.

Mary followed them into the dusk-shadowed room, smiling and shaking her head. The Chopin nocturne she had been quietly listening to seemed to have been chased into the woodwork by Tiernan's booming voice and high spirits. All the wind and color and Irish brashness from the parade seemed to have wafted into the apartment after him.

"Ah, ye should ha' been there, Mary, me love!" he said, putting Lynn down and striding over and snatching Mary into his arms. "A glorious, *glorious* day it was for all the wee green people!" he exclaimed as he waltzed her around the coffee table and nearly knocked one of her potted plants off the parson's table near the window.

"My zebra!" she cried out, looking back over her shoulder at the plant lying on its side on the corner of the table.

"Ah, ta hell with yer zebra. Oy'll buy ye a camel!" he cried out, and started on another whirling circuit around the coffee table.

"Help!" Mary squeaked, trying to catch her breath and keep her legs from being flung out from under her.

"And you, look at ye," he said to her as they came to an unsteady stop near the couch. "Ye look like ye haven't kissed an Oirishman all day," he said, brushing a long blond lock of hair from her flushed face.

"Here, you loony!" she said, taking his face in her hands and giving him a loud smacky kiss on the lips.

"Faith, ye've dizzied me wits!" he said, slapping his head and falling onto the couch in a swoon.

"It's nearly six o'clock," Mary said, walking over to straighten up her zebra plant and move it in closer to all the other plants that covered the top of the long green table. "Are you two leprechauns in the mood for a little dinner?"

"Mommy, I'm hungry," Lynn said, unzipping her coat.

"Joe, would you like to stay?" Mary asked as she helped Lynn off with her coat. "I've got a meatloaf in the oven."

"Darlin' of ye," he said, squinting his eyes like Barry Fitzgerald. "But Oy've got this terrible droivin' thirst, don't ye see," he rasped and stroked his throat.

"Right, one beer coming up," she said, folding Lynn's coat over her arm and hurrying toward the kitchen. Lynn trotted along side her.

"Bliss ye for a foin woman!" he rasped after her.

After they were gone Tiernan got up and took off his trench coat, draped it over the arm of the couch and walked over to the window. Regular goddam nursery she's got in here now, he thought, looking around at all the new plants covering the table and growing out of big pots in the corners and hanging from long knotted macrame slings in the windows.

He looked out the window pensively for a while and listened to the peaceful strains of Chopin filling the room again. In the brownstone across the street the shutters were closed in the window where a busty young woman used to stand naked for his eyes at times in the evening. He turned around and went back to the couch and sat down, a curious loneliness beginning to gather in him. The room was so different now, he thought, looking around. He could no longer find himself or what he had been in it.

It struck him that Mary seemed to be re-creating the quiet cloistered world of plants and music that she had known growing up with her divorced mother on Long Island. The world he had taken her from—but not completely. The red parson's table that he had once used for his desk, always overflowing with his papers and always messy with his pipe ashes, was now painted pale green and overgrown with plants; there was a new slipcover on the couch, its subdued gold pattern more elegant than the threadbare brown they had shared; a new curved glass vase was on the coffee table, once the cluttered repository of his *New Yorker* and *Fortune* magazines. Even the walls were freshly painted white. And over near the French doors to the dining room the chip in the wall he'd once made by angrily throwing a tumbler of Scotch—the fury of those last months—smoothed over, painted, gone.

So peaceful now, he thought, leaning his head back against the couch. The quiet heart of the woman he had married had crept out of hiding now that he was no longer around to bluster at it. They were so different, he thought, and he had married her hoping that some of the stillness and quiet that were at her center would somehow enter his troubled soul. All his life there had been the explosions of anger that ruined everything, their seeds embedded in him since childhood, waiting to break through the tranquillity and order he had desperately sought all his adult life.

"Hey, what's the long face?" Mary asked, coming into the

darkening room with his beer. "Where's our rollicking son of Ireland?"

He smiled wistfully at her and took the beer. Still wearing those old jeans and sweat shirt, he thought, remembering those fresh spring days when they walked along the North Shore beach near her mother's Long Island home. The memory brought an ache to his throat, and he eased it with long swallows of the cold beer.

"Ah, now that's heaven," he sighed, licking his lips. But the playfulness had gone out of him and he felt a great desire to try to enter her world again, to sit quietly with her again and talk of things—little inconsequential things. Things that he had belittled to her when she had brought them up during their marriage.

"Want to finish it in the dining room?" she asked. "I'm going to start putting dinner on the table."

"Great, I'm famished," he said, rising and taking another swallow of beer. "Um, what's that? I like it," he lied, nodding toward the music coming from the record player.

"When did *you* start liking Chopin?" she asked, nudging him gently as they walked together into the dining room.

"Hey, Chopin?" he asked, putting his arm around her waist. "Chopin is my life."

"Oh, great," she said, kidding him back. "After supper I'll put on the 'Polonaise Fantaisie' and maybe even *Les Sylphides*. You always *loved Les Sylphides*," remembering how he hated it.

"Oh, yeah, I remember we went to the ballet—all those wood nymphs flitting about."

"You fell asleep," she said with a laugh.

"Hey, it was my first ballet."

Lynn was still in the kitchen playing when Mary got there. The little girl was busy constructing words like DADDY and CAT and MAX on the refrigerator door with her little plastic magnetic letters.

"Go wash your hands now, dear," Mary said.

As she took the meatloaf and carrots and potatoes from the baking pan and arranged them on a large serving dish, Mary smiled to herself. That big idiot, she thought, remembering the look of appreciation he had tried to screw onto his face when he told her he liked the Chopin nocturne. He had forgotten that she could read him like an old book. He wanted something from her. . . . What? Well if she knew Joe, he would tell her before he left. Probably make an oblique allusion to it during supper and then just before he was to go out the door he would go into one of his "Oh, by the ways."

Money? No, he was doing pretty well now with the raise Alma had given him. He seemed so relieved to be able to give her support money. The job had helped a lot; he seemed more settled down and sure of himself these days.

"Dinner is served!" she said, carrying the big dish into the dining room.

About halfway through the meal, Mary nearly burst out laughing at the way Joe was exulting over her meatloaf. There was still the blush of the outdoors on his and Lynn's cheeks and they were both eating with great appetite. But Joe was embarrassing her with his unabashed praise.

"God, Mary, I've never seen anyone do a meatloaf like you," he said, nodding and munching ecstatically. "Is there such a thing as a gourmet meatloaf?"

"Is there such a thing as gourmet blarney?" she asked back, shaking her fork knowingly at him.

"Ummmmm, I mean it," he said through a mouthful of food. "Delicious . . .[chomp, chomp] . . . delicious!"

"You and the guys still running every morning?" she asked.

"Me and Len are," he said, leaning back in his chair again. "We've lost Richie to the 'Great Reconciliation,' as Talbot calls it."

"Oh, how are they doing?" she asked.

"Great, I guess," he said, reaching over and picking a little crusted piece of meatloaf from the serving dish and chewing on it with his front teeth. " 'Cept Talbot thinks he made a big mistake—going back. Let's see, how did he put it?" Tiernan said, tilting his chair back. "A typical Talbot way of putting it. . . . Oh, yeah, 'Character is destiny,' he said. 'Once a bitch, always a bitch.' "

"He sounds a little bitter," she said, shaking her head and getting up to clear the table.

"Wait, I'll help you," Tiernan said, drawing a look of surprise from her, which he ignored. "As a matter of fact, I'm having dinner with Richie and Linda on Thursday. At this restaurant I'm promoting. Should be a riot."

Tiernan sneaked a last chip of meatloaf off the serving dish and then picked up the dish and his own plate and headed down the narrow hall to the kitchen. Mary stacked the dirty plates and silverware and followed.

"Why a riot?" she asked behind him.

Tiernan explained his Gemetzschernsteiner scheme as Mary took the dishes from him and moved about the kitchen cleaning up. She had to laugh at his description of Alma and General Van Dong, but she was happy to see Joe back to his old Irish spirits again.

"Except, there is no Gemetzschernsteiner," she said after he finished.

"A mere detail," he said with a shrug and started back toward the dining room for more dishes.

"Joe," she called after him, "I can't believe you make a living this way."

"Illusion, my dear," he said, turning and wiggling his fingers in her face. "I am a master of illusion."

"And Richie is going along with this?" she asked.

"Are you kidding? Richie is one of the great all-time hams. He jumped at it when I told him. He's been practicing his German accent for a week. Besides, he gets a free meal out of it."

"Linda is going, too?" she asked. "God, you're all crazy."

"Look, it's probably going to be a lot of fun," he said, picking up the glasses and Mary's coffee cup from the table. "The only problem we'll have is keeping straight faces."

"Oh, I'd love to see it," she said, laughing.

"Why don't you?" he asked.

"What?" she asked.

"Come along," he said, trying to keep his voice casual. "It's an interesting place and the food is pretty good—kind of spicy Oriental with French overtones."

"Oh, I couldn't," she said.

"No, really, Mary," he persisted. "The fact is, we could use your German." The memory of her having taken some German language courses in college flitted across his mind as he was talking and he grabbed it and pressed it into service. "You know, somebody to throw in a few German-sounding words."

"So that's it," she murmured, feeling that she had finally discovered what he was after all evening. He wants me to help him pull off this little public relations scheme, she thought.

"That's what?" he asked.

"Oh, uh, nothing," she said, reaching up for the dish towel

over the sink and drying her hands. "Joe, don't be ridiculous," she said, turning around and pushing him away as she went to put away the food. "I only remember little scraps of my German. Stupid things like 'Is this the table?' or, let's see, 'The snow is on the roof.'"

"Oh, yeah, what does that sound like?" he asked, following behind her.

"Oh, god," she said, getting a little flustered. "Okay, here goes: *'Ist das der Tisch?'*" she said, pointing to the table. "And, uh, oh, yeah: *'Der Schnee ist auf dem Dach.'* The snow is on the roof."

*"Der Schnee ist auf dem Dach?"* he asked, laughing and grabbing her by the hands.

*"Ja, der Schnee ist auf dem Dach!"* she repeated and started laughing herself.

"Mary, that's terrific!" he said, swinging her around a bit. *"Der Schnee ist auf dem Dach!* All you've got to do is keep saying that. Anybody asks you a question, you just say, *'Der Schnee ist auf dem Dach!'*"

"Joe, you're out of your flaming skull," she said, pulling her hands away from him and going back to putting things away.

"Listen, nobody's going to know what you're saying. Just so long as it sounds German. We'll sound like we just blew in from the Third Reich. *'Der Schnee ist auf dem Dach!'*" he said gruffly and then clicked his heels together and made a Hitler mustache with his index finger.

"We can pretend you're Gemetzschernsteiner's mistress or something," he continued enthusiastically. "What do you say?"

"Oh, I don't think so, Joe. I'd be too embarrassed," she said, moving away.

"Okay, so think about it, okay?" he asked. "It's no big deal."

"How'd you like some coffee?" she asked, trying to change the subject.

"Naw, I guess I'd better get going," he said and walked down the hall to find Lynn to say goodbye. By the tone of her voice he knew that she wasn't completely against the idea. He would take the pressure off for the moment and bring it up again. He had four days until Thursday.

"Lynn!" he called when he found she was not in the dining

room. When he got no answer he went into her room and found her on the floor watching an *I Love Lucy* rerun on her little television set.

"I'm going now," he said, leaning in through her door.

"Okay, Daddy," she said without looking up.

"Did you have a good time today?" he asked.

"Yep," she said, still engrossed in the show.

"Well, do I get a kiss, for crying out loud?" he asked.

"Oh, okay," she said, getting up slowly and walking to him while still watching the screen and reaching up and kissing him quickly while only taking her eyes from the screen for a fleeting second.

He walked back into the living room shaking his head and smiling. Mary was standing over near the window behind the parson's table. She had turned on one of the lamps.

"Hey, the place really looks nice," he said, nodding toward all the plants. "Reminds me of your mother's."

"Oh, god, I think I went a little overboard," she said, looking around at her plants with embarrassed pride.

"No, really, they give the place a nice peaceful feel," he said, picking up his trench coat from the arm of the couch.

"I shouldn't have done it. They really cost too much. But I love them . . . all the plants I . . . You must think I'm silly," she said, looking down.

"I don't, really!" he protested. "Mary, this is you. You have a right to express yourself. And, hey, it's beautiful. What the hell are they, anyway?"

"Oh, just a little of everything," she said, walking around and touching the leaves lightly with her fingertips. "I got dieffenbachia, schefflera, philodendrons, a ficus over there in the corner, asparagus ferns, Boston, you name it."

"Well, Mrs. Tiernan, Oy've had a foin time, and yer cookin' was grand, but, now Oy'll be takin' me leave," he said, slipping back into brogue as he put on his coat and waited for her to escort him to the door.

"It was nice of you to take Lynn to the parade," she said, walking with her arm around his waist to the door. He put his arm around her shoulder and gave her a light hug.

"We had a great time," he said. "Sure you won't change your mind?" he asked as he opened the door.

"Oh, hell, I'd like to help, Joe," she said. "Well, when is it?"

"Thursday, eight o'clock," he said, shrugging.

She looked up at him for a minute and twisted her mouth pensively. She knew that he wanted it very much despite his efforts to appear casual. Maybe his job was depending on it. She could practice her German a little in the next few days. God, he'd been so nice all day, taking Lynn, turning himself inside out praising her crummy meatloaf, even pretending to like Chopin. She hated to send him away in defeat.

"Okay," she finally said. "But only if I can get Juliana to baby-sit."

"Fantastic!" he exclaimed and kissed her on the lips and hopped out the door.

She waited, smiling at him, while he stood in front of the elevator door. After the door closed behind him she could hear him singing "Blackball the Derrio!" all the way down.

# CHAPTER
# FOURTEEN

Mel, the maitre d' at the French East, was leaning against a wall yawning into his hand when he noticed General Van Dong frowning at him across the sea of palm plants in the dining room. Snapping his fingers over his yawn, the sleepy Frenchman gathered himself off the wall and tried to look more alert. After a moment he had the luck to spot a waiter coming out of the kitchen with a full tray on his shoulder and hurried over to detain him.

"Ah, *oui*, just so . . . just so," he said, nodding his approval as he lifted each covered dish. Then after a few imperious sniffs over the tray he snapped his long fingers again and waved the struggling little Vietnamese waiter on his way.

Returning to his post near the entrance, he gave his jacket lapels a little tuck and surveyed the sparsely occupied dining room with as much hauteur as he could muster for a man who always looked three nights behind in his sleep. Then by slow degrees he allowed his glance to creep back to the general's table.

Henri Van Dong just shook his head slowly in dismay and beckoned him with a little motion of his finger to come over. But then, as Mel was halfway to him, scissoring his long legs hastily between the tables and palm plants, the general seemed to have a change of mind and waved him away. Then, with Mel hanging precariously in midstride, Henri changed his mind and motioned him to come forward.

"Monsieur?" Mel asked when he got to Henri's table.

"How is it going—over there?" Henri asked, tilting his head toward the Gemetzschernsteiner table near one of the front windows.

"I think, ah . . . so far, so good?" Mel replied with a shrug.

"They don't look pleased," the general said, taking a glance at the table where the Tiernans and the Gemetzes seemed to be bickering under their breath.

"Well, ah, *certainement,* it could not be the food," Mel said a little defensively. "Monsieur Gem— Gemetzenschttt—the German, he praised the zucchini to me personally."

"Ah, the zucchini," Henri said, nodding and feeling a little encouraged. "He said what? 'Good,' 'nice' . . . what?"

"He said, *'Wunderbar!'* " Mel replied.

"He said that?"

*"Oui."*

"So, he likes my zucchini," Henri said, leaning back and smiling his little Vietnamese smile. Then he clapped his hands once and barked an order: "Go and see how Wang is doing with the bass *en papillote!"*

*"Certainement,"* Mel said with a little military bow and turned sharply toward the kitchen.

"No, wait!" the general said, leaning forward. "I will go. I want to taste the garlic sauce. Wang is an idiot with the garlic. You go and see how it is at their table," he said, getting up. "Wait!" he snapped as Mel executed an about-face and started toward the Gemetzschernsteiner table. "Slowly . . . don't be obvious!"

Whereupon Mel began a slow, ambling, table-tidying odyssey around the edge of the dining room. Along the way he kept taking sly bearings on the German's table. They were all involved in some kind of disagreement, but it seemed to be mainly between the Gemetzschernsteiners, who were leaning toward each other over the table.

Herr Gemetzschernsteiner was wearing a little pair of round wire-rimmed glasses down on the end of his nose and had his hair parted down the center. He had on a dark three-piece pin-striped suit with an antique watch chain across his vest. Frau

Gemetzschernsteiner's hair was done up in a crown of braids and she was smoking a cigarette from a long ivory holder. Between them they looked like two refugees from the Weimar Republic.

The wire-rimmed glasses and other little quaint touches had come from Linda's box of theatrical props, kept in the closet since her college acting days.

Definitely the look of a gourmand, Mel thought as he drew closer to their table. Ah, thank god, he liked the zucchini fritters, he thought. And, please, Mary and Joseph, let him like the bass, too. For Wang's sake. If it is a flop, Henri will cook him in the big wok.

Mel cringed as the German slapped the table with his hand and said something in anger to Frau Gemetzschernsteiner. He hoped this little contretemps would not spoil the dinner. Henri had been preparing his staff for nearly a week for the diplomat's arrival, warning them that his reaction could make or break French East. The general himself had seated the party and at one point Mel had seen the entire kitchen staff peeking out to get a look at this formidable guest.

Tiernan glanced up and saw Mel approaching and gave a stilted cough to warn the others. But Gemetz and Linda missed his signal and continued arguing.

"No, that's not the point, that is not the point," Linda was saying.

"Hell, yes, it's the point!" Gemetz replied.

"The only point is on your little head," she said and stuck her tongue out at him.

Tiernan coughed again and gestured with his head toward the approaching maitre d'.

"*Ein sprechnen mit zer Krauten,*" Tiernan said through his teeth and smiled warmly at Mel as he stepped up to the table with a little bow.

"Everything, it is satisfactory, *oui?*" the maitre d' asked.

"*Ja, ja . . . ist gut, gut. . . . Schnell, schnell,*" Gemetz said with a flourish of his hand.

Linda gave Tiernan a mischievous wink and turned her head around and looked up at Mel with a pouting sultry expression. Then she took a long draw of her cigarette holder and blew a cloud of smoke up into his face.

"*Guten Tag,* French!" she said in a low suggestive voice.

"Ah, everything is fine, Mel," Tiernan said hurriedly, hoping to cut off any more hamming it up by Linda.

"Ouch!" Mary yelped as Tiernan tried to prompt her into the act with his foot under the table. She looked at him angrily for a moment and reached down and rubbed her foot, where Tiernan had clipped her. His eyes pleaded with her for help.

"Oh, ah, er, *ist das der Tisch?*" she asked.

"Ho, ho, ho!" Tiernan laughed with forced heartiness and nodded his agreement. "Oh, *ja, der Schnee ist auf dem Dach!*"

"*Auf dem Dach?*" Mary replied, trying to sound impressed.

"*Ja,*" he said, nodding confidently. Then he turned to Linda. "*Ist dot not zo,* Linda—*der Schnee ist auf dem Dach?*"

"*Das Dach ist Schmach!*" she said with bored disdain and smiled again at Mel.

"*Ist dot not zo, Herr Doktor?*" Tiernan asked, turning to Gemetzschernsteiner. "*Der Schnee ist auf dem Dach?*"

"*Ummmmmm,*" Gemetzschernsteiner mused in consideration as he hooked his thumbs in his vest pockets and leaned back in his chair. "*Der Schnee ist . . . umm, schnell . . . undt das Dach ist . . . ummmmm,* how do you say? . . . *ummm,* mouth water?"

"Mouth-watering, *ja!*" Tiernan agreed, smiling and nodding.

"*Ummmmmm, ja,*" Gemetzschernsteiner continued and then, looking over the top of his glasses professorially at Linda, he said, "*Undt zer Linda trip to California ist outenzieleftenfieldenschtingk!*"

"*Dropenziedeadenstink!*" Linda replied and wrinkled her nose at him.

"Ho, ho, ho!" Tiernan laughed again. "Well, Mel, you can see our guests are having a marvelous time."

"*Ah, très bien,*" the maitre d' replied with a polite nod and backed away slightly bewildered by all the German mishmash.

Then he turned and hurried toward the kitchen, while Tiernan let out a groan of relief and slumped down in his chair. He looked at Gemetz and Linda and didn't know whether to laugh at their weird Gemetzschernsteiner performance or punch Richie in the nose for screwing up his other scheme for the evening—letting Mary see their blissful reunion. Ha! he thought. They're making reconciliation look like the second Ali-Frazier fight.

"How'd we do?" Gemetz asked, feeling uncomfortable under Tiernan's stare.

"Fine, only it ain't the Gemetzschernsteiners," Tiernan said, shaking his head. "It's more like the Katzenjammer Kids. And can't you guys act a little less married?"

"He's the one who wants to argue," Linda protested.

"I'm not the one who wants to abandon her family for two fucking months!" Gemetz shot back and then grimaced and bent forward.

"What's the matter?" Linda asked, sitting forward as she saw the pain on his face. "Ulcer?"

"Yeah," he grunted. Then he picked up his Scotch and started to drink it.

"Damn it, Richie," Linda said, holding his hand with the glass in it. "That's going to make it worse!"

"You okay?" Tiernan asked, ducking his head to see Richie's bent-over face.

"It's been kicking up the last two weeks," Linda said. "How bad is it?" she asked Richie. "You want to smoke one?" she asked referring to the marijuana that he sometimes took when he got one of the bad cramping pains.

"No, uh," he grunted. "I think it's easing. Shit!"

"Jesus, Richie," Tiernan said, becoming worried about the pain on Gemetz's face. "Maybe we ought to leave. What do you think?" he asked, turning to Linda.

"I've got some pot in the car," she said. "It helps when he gets one of the bad ones. Richie? You wanna go?"

"Whew!" he sighed and straightened up. "There, I think it's passed. God, comes on like a kick in the gut," he said, drawing deep breaths and pushing the glasses farther back on his nose.

"Sure you don't want to go, Richie?" Mary asked.

"No, no, it's okay, now. Sorry," he said, looking around at each of them and looking more at ease.

"You seen a doctor?" Tiernan asked.

"He won't go!" Linda complained. "Afraid he'll wind up getting it cut out like . . . like . . ." She decided not to mention his father.

"Look, I'm okay!" Gemetz said, waving away any more talk on the subject. "See?" he said and picked up his Scotch and took a long drink.

"Richie, that's not going to help your—" Linda protested.

"The only thing that is bothering my ulcer tonight is your goddam plan about taking off for San Francisco!" he said, slamming his drink on the table.

"Did I say I was going? Huh?" she asked. "I wish I'd never told you about it," she said, and turned away from him.

"You're going," he said.

For the past three days they had been arguing about a phone call she had gotten from a former assistant conductor at the Met who had recently been fired and had gone out to the Coast for a better job with the San Francisco Opera. He had offered her two major singing roles in the spring season and said that it would be her big chance to break out of the chorus. Gemetz had been against it because she would have to quit her job at the Met and because he felt they should be putting in full time trying to make their reconciliation work. It was only a trial reconciliation, he had kept reminding her.

"If I do, it will be my decision," Linda said.

"Well, don't mind me," he said.

"Let's . . . Hey, you guys," Tiernan said, trying to head off a continuation of the argument, "let's declare a time out. How about finishing this when you get home. Okay? My job is at stake here."

"I'm sorry, Joe," Linda said. "You're right. Okay, Richie?" she asked, holding her hand out to him.

Tiernan reached over and took up Gemetz's hand and put it in Linda's. "Please?" he asked Richie.

"Yeah, sure," Gemetz said, grasping Linda's hand and nodding. "Sorry. This is bullshit anyway. Ve must put aside personal considerations for the greater glory of Germany. *Sieg Heil!*"

"You okay?" Linda asked him sympathetically as she held on to his hand.

"Yeah, I'm sorry," he said and smiled at her.

"That's the stuff," Tiernan said, smiling.

"Joe, I think you broke my poor little toe," Mary complained and rubbed her foot.

"God, I'm sorry," Tiernan said contritely. "Look, maybe we ought to just get the hell out of here and go get drunk someplace."

"Relax, relax," Gemetz said. "I'm feeling fine now. The show must go on, right, Linda?"

"Right, *mein Führer!*" she said, giving him a little Nazi salute.

Tiernan let out a sigh and looked across the deserted center of the dining room. The ceiling fans were sending a breeze through the little palm grove and except for the few diners along the far wall they almost had the place to themselves. Henri was probably in the kitchen rallying his troops, he thought. God, the whole thing was ludicrous.

"When do we eat?" Mary asked.

"Soon," Tiernan said. "It should be good—to impress the great Gemetzschernsteiner," he said, turning to Gemetz. "You know what to do, right?"

"Right," Gemetz said with a confident nod. "If I like the meal, I stand up and make a little bow toward the kitchen."

"What do you mean, *if* you like the meal?" Tiernan exclaimed.

"Oh, Joe, this is mad," Mary said and started to laugh.

"It's what I told Henri," he said, looking down in embarrassment at the corniness of his scheme. "You know, like it's Gemetzschernsteiner's trademark—a little bow after the meal to compliment the chef."

"So, I'll bow," Gemetz said with a shrug. "No problem, Joe: little click of the heels, little bow, little Nazi salute—"

"No goddam Nazi salute!" Tiernan exclaimed, rubbing his fingers through his scalp in exasperation.

"Okay, so how about if we *really* like the food we get Linda up on the table and have her belt out Brünnhilde's battle cry from *Die Walküre?*" Gemetz asked, keeping the needle in Tiernan.

"Ho-yo-to-ho!" Linda sang out operatically.

"Aw, gimme a break, you guys," Tiernan pleaded. "I need this account. You promised, goddam it! Richie? Just a little bow—please?" he asked, measuring a little bow with two fingers.

"Hey, the San Francisco is doing Wagner in the spring schedule," Linda said enthusiastically. "They've offered me Brangäne in *Tristan und Isolde,*" she said and then ducked her head guiltily as she remembered the moratorium on the subject.

Gemetz clenched his teeth and took another long swallow of Scotch. As he put the glass down he could feel the spasm of pain beginning to gather in his stomach again.

"Ah, the main course!" Tiernan exclaimed as he saw the waiter bringing a large tray of food from the kitchen.

From the kitchen window, Henri and Mel watched the waiter placing the dishes of bass *en papillote* and garlic sauce on the Gemetzschernsteiner table. Mel had his fingers crossed behind him. And Wang, the cook, stood off to one side watching their faces like a defendant awaiting a verdict in a capital-punishment case.

After the waiter finished serving the table and returned to the kitchen, Henri and Mel again pressed their faces to the little window in the swinging door and resumed their vigil. Gemetzschernsteiner had his back to them but they could see the others beginning to eat.

"I don't wish to look," Henri said, turning his back to the door. "Tell me everything they do," he said to Mel as he folded his arms and looked menacingly at Wang.

"Ah, Monsieur Tiernan is smiling and nodding his head," Mel reported.

"He has tasted the bass?" Henri asked.

"Ah, *oui!*" Mel replied enthusiastically. "I see him chewing. . . . He is very happy!"

"Good," Henri said with a nod toward Wang. "And the German?"

"I cannot tell . . . Yes, there, he has lifted his fork!"

"And?" Henri asked almost in a whisper.

"He is eating!" Mel said.

"Yes?"

"Wait! Now he is putting his fork down and looking at Monsieur Tiernan."

Henri bit his knuckles and looked over at Wang.

"Now he is beginning to stand up!" Mel exclaimed.

"What, already?" Henri asked, thinking Gemetzschernsteiner was going to deliver his famous bow to the chef after only one bite. What stupendous luck, he thought, giving Wang a victory sign.

"Now he is bending over," Mel said.

"Ah, the bow to the kitchen!" Henri exclaimed. "I must see this!"

"No, he is bowing to the coatroom," Mel said. "He . . . he seems to be in a great deal of pain."

"What!" Henri gasped and turned to the window.

Through the window Henri could see Tiernan hurrying

around the table to assist the stricken Gemetzschernsteiner. The two women were also coming to his aid. The German was doubled over and his face was contorted in pain.

"I am ruined," Henri sobbed as he turned around and buried his face in his hands. It was Tet all over again. Then he looked up and saw Wang standing against the nearby wall, his arms down at his side, his face set in stoic resignation to his fate.

"Monsieur Tiernan is helping him toward the front door," Mel continued reporting from the window. "They are going out! Now the ladies, they are collecting the coats!"

"Hurry!" Henri shouted, and pushed Mel through the swinging door and followed him. *"Assassin!"* he yelled back over his shoulder at Wang, who flinched and then resumed his sad communion with his ancestors.

# CHAPTER
# FIFTEEN

An hour after their emergency bail-out from the French East restaurant, the Gemetzes and the Tiernans were sitting in Linda's car across the street from Roosevelt Hospital. It had taken them only a few minutes to get to the hospital, but the rest of the time they had spent sitting in the car because Richie refused to go in. At the moment he was slumped down in the front seat—sound asleep for the last twenty minutes after having smoked an entire joint of marijuana to kill the pain in his stomach.

Across the street an ambulance pulled into the hospital's emergency bay, its oscillating red light reflecting like an angry pulse on Tiernan's face as he looked broodingly from the back seat of the car.

"Well," he sighed, rolling down his window to air out some of the marijuana smell. "What do you think, Linda?"

"Yeah, we might as well go," she said, sitting up from where she was reclining against her door. "I can watch him sleep at home." Their lowered voices seemed not to disturb Gemetz, still sleeping with his chin on his chest and the antique glasses still riding the end of his nose.

"The pot must have worked," Mary whispered.

"I still think he's nuts to rely on it," Linda said as she put the car in gear and turned on the ignition.

"How's that?" Tiernan asked, keeping his voice down.

"I don't know," she said, pulling away from the curb. "It seems to kill the pain, but maybe the pain is there for a reason—like trying to tell him he's bleeding inside or something."

"Hmmm," Tiernan said, nodding. "He won't see a doctor, huh?"

"He just won't, dammit!" she said. "He's afraid they'll cut him up like his father. I don't know how many operations the old man had."

"Boy, that was scary tonight," Mary said.

"It's been worse since the funeral," Linda said, looking down at Gemetz and shaking her head.

"I'll give you a hand getting him upstairs," Tiernan said.

"He'll probably be okay, Joe," Linda said. "Sorry about tonight."

"Ah, it was a dumb idea," he said, rolling the window up.

Fifteen minutes later they were on the East River Drive, heading south toward the Brooklyn Bridge. They had not spoken again and Richie continued to sleep peacefully. Tiernan was looking glumly out the window at the lights on the other side of the river and thinking of what a disaster the evening had been. All of his plans had been blasted out of the water: his great gourmet being carried out of the restaurant, the wonderful Gemetz reconciliation he wanted Mary to see turning into a cat fight, and now Richie bombed out of his mind and maybe bleeding internally. What else you got in mind for tonight, God? he wondered. Maybe You can get Linda to drive off the Brooklyn Bridge. That I might welcome.

Never saw Henri looking so scared, he thought, remembering the panic on the little general's face when he had rushed into the street with Mel. Tiernan had turned back to reassure them, while Linda and Mary had continued to the parking lot with the grunting, bent-over Gemetzschernsteiner. Richie had been pleading with Linda to get him the pot she kept under the front seat of the car.

"Poor Henri, he's probably chewing his palm plants." Tiernan sighed, looking out the window at the Manhattan and Brooklyn bridges spanning the dark river farther ahead.

"What did you tell him?" Mary asked in a whisper.

"Appendicitis," Tiernan replied glumly.

"You didn't," she said. "Why?"

"So he wouldn't think it was the food," he said. "I'm sure it made him happy."

For the next few minutes they were silent again. Then Gemetz sneezed, opened his eyes, looked around for a moment and then seemed to go right back to sleep.

"Brooklyn Bridge coming up," Linda said.

"Chicken Bridge," Gemetz murmured without opening his eyes.

"Well, look who's back among the living," Linda said, looking down at him.

"Richie, how are you feeling?" Mary asked. "You really had us worried tonight."

"Old Chicken Bridge," Gemetz murmured again.

"How come 'Chicken Bridge'?" Linda asked, glancing down again and wondering if he was really awake.

"Brrrrock, bluck-bluck-bluck," Gemetz clucked with his eyes half opened and his chin still down on his chest. Then he smiled sadly and closed his eyes again, and in his marijuana dream he again saw Juliet's shivering face looking up at him that cold night on the bridge—the night of his cowardly retreat from a commitment to her.

"Hey, how're you feelin', old man?" Tiernan asked.

But Gemetz appeared to have drifted off to sleep again, and after a moment Tiernan shrugged and went back to looking out the window. As Linda drove onto the bridge the steel brads on the roadway sent a vibrating hum up through the car, a veil of noise that Tiernan always imagined hanging down between the different worlds of Manhattan and Brooklyn. Manhattan only asked for your wit, he thought, but Brooklyn tested your soul. Off to his left he saw a snake of subway-train lights crossing the Manhattan Bridge. In a few minutes he would be standing with Mary in front of her brownstone, he thought. And she would once again send him on his way. Perhaps a little sympathetic kiss this time—but not enough to change the frog into a prince.

"You hungry?" Mary asked him in a lowered voice.

"Uh, yeah," he replied, sitting up at this unexpected invitation. "We sure didn't eat much at Henri's."

"I fried up a batch of chicken wings—if you want some when Linda drops us off," she said.

"Great," he said, smiling. Well, well, he thought, sensing the fates wiggling their fingers at him again. So the night is not over yet, Tiernan, me boyo, he thought. Coming in on a chicken wing and a prayer. She gave him a frown and a push on the knee to protest the leer that had slid onto his face.

"Hunger," Gemetz mumbled from the front seat.

"What, honey?" Linda asked.

"Hunger," he growled.

"Aw, Richie's tummy all better now?" she asked him in a cutesy little mommy's voice.

"Hunger!" he growled again and fell onto her lap. "Yaaaaarrrr!" he roared and bit her on the thigh.

"Yiii!" she screamed and nearly veered the car into the curving exit ramp.

"Jesus." Tiernan sighed and closed his eyes.

"Hey, would you guys like to come up for some chicken?" Mary called to the front seat. "There's plenty—and I think about a quart of chocolate ice cream."

"Well, it's for sure we can't take this maniac into a restaurant," Linda said, prying Richie off her thigh. "Sounds terrific, Mary. I *am* famished!"

"Good," Mary said, settling back in her seat. "Sure it won't hurt Richie's ulcer?" she asked on second thought.

"Hunger," Richie growled again from down in his seat.

"Down, boy," Linda warned. "Yeah, any kind of food is probably a good thing now," she said, turning to Mary.

Juliana, the dark-haired twelve-year-old baby sitter, was lying on the sofa watching television when the four of them quietly entered Mary's apartment, tiptoeing down the hallway into the living room.

"Oh!" the girl exclaimed and nearly jumped off the sofa when she glanced up and saw them nearly already in the room.

"We're back early, hon," Mary said. "How'd it go?"

"Fine," the girl said, straightening her blouse and looking a little apprehensively at Richie's stoned face. "Ah, Lynn went to sleep about an hour ago," she said to Mary, who was taking off her coat and going into the adjoining dining room. "I let her watch the Peanuts special."

"Well, well," Tiernan said, mustering a fatherly smile. "Juliana is growing up. Very pretty, too."

"Hi," Gemetz said, wrinkling his nose in a little smile and waggling his fingers at her.

Juliana blushed and then hurried into the dining room after Mary. "You got two calls," she said almost in a whisper. "I, uh . . . pinned the message on the kitchen board."

"Thanks," Mary said, taking some bills from her purse and handing them to the girl. Then she accompanied her to the front door. Juliana lived at the other end of the hall with her parents.

"I'll give you a hand, Mary," Linda called out and went to the kitchen.

"Feeling okay, now?" Tiernan asked Richie, who had flopped down on the sofa.

"Yeah, great," Gemetz sighed.

"Be back in a minute," Tiernan said, taking the coats into Mary's bedroom.

After placing the coats on Mary's bed, Tiernan sat down on the edge of it for a moment and looked around. This room she had not changed very much, he thought. The walls still needed painting, and there was that old crack in the ceiling he used to stare at lying in bed. Same collection of perfumes and hair curlers on the dresser. He was tempted to go over and look through its little top drawers, where she kept personal things like her diary and letters and snapshots. Cool it, he told himself and got up.

On the way out he tiptoed into Lynn's room and stood next to her bed for a moment. That angelic sleeping face had haunted him so many nights when he was away. He could hear her pleading with him on those nights he used to tuck her in. She loved him to swing her in his arms. "Swing me, one for the money, Daddy."

He touched his fingers to his lips and kissed them and then touched them to her forehead. Sleep well, my Lynn, he thought and felt his eyes begin to burn.

Walking over to the window, he looked down at the street below. Old Mrs. Whitman was passing under the yellow streetlight with her two little dogs. Still the same awful orange wig and wide watery blue eyes—forever oblivious to muggers as she walked the neighborhood for hours every day. Two calls, he thought, remembering Juliana's attempt to keep her voice low. Probably the Italian upstairs, he thought. Tough shit, creep, he thought. The old lion is back with some new moves, so watch your skinny little ass.

"Womenfolk is in the kitchen," Gemetz said as Tiernan

came back into the living room and found him reclining on the sofa with his bare feet stretched out onto the coffee table.

"Well, see you've made yourself to home," Tiernan said.

"A'yeah," Gemetz drawled, looking over the tops of his glasses at Tiernan.

"Feelin' a mite better now, Abner?" Tiernan drawled back at him and walked over to the record player to put on some music.

"A'yeah," Gemetz replied and wiggled his toes.

"Had us a mite worried back there, Abner," Tiernan said as he picked up the record that was on the turntable.

"Oh, little colicky is all," Gemetz twanged.

But Tiernan barely heard him as he stared down at the record in his hand. It was Fauré's *Requiem*, the only classical piece that he ever liked, despite Mary's long efforts to get him interested in long-hair music. My record, he thought. Maybe she's been thinking about me lately. Playing my record. Maybe . . . Take it slow, boy, he warned himself. He heard Mary and Linda coming in from the kitchen and quickly put the record down and went over and sat in the easy chair near the coffee table.

"I hope there's enough here," Mary said, coming in with a big platter of fried chicken wings. Linda followed with a stack of plates, spoons and the quart of ice cream.

"That's enough for me," Gemetz said, taking his feet down and reaching for a wing as Mary put the plate on the table.

"Richie, where's your shoes?" Linda asked.

"Abner here is just feeling homey," Tiernan said, getting up and pulling another easy chair close to the coffee table for Mary to sit on.

"Oh, god," Linda said, sitting down next to Gemetz on the other side of the coffee table. "Richie, if you go into one of your little routines this time, I'm gonna . . ."

Gemetz looked at her in wide-eyed innocence with a chicken bone sticking out of his mouth.

For the next ten minutes the four of them hungrily bent over the table and devoured all of the chicken wings, groaning with delight as they picked each bone clean and tossed it onto the spare plate. Then as they were about to serve up the ice cream, Gemetz held up his hand for them to stop.

"Wait, we can't eat it yet!" he declared. "Lin, remember our Bicentennial Pot Party?"

"Yeah," she said, smiling. "Pete and Marty brought those joints wrapped in red, white and blue rolling paper."

"No, the chocolate ice cream," he said, nudging her.

"Oh, yeah!" she exclaimed. "The pot really turned it on. Oh, god, Mary, I have never tasted anything like chocolate ice cream after being stoned. Too bad we didn't bring any up from the car."

"Ladies and gentlemen," Gemetz said, smirking as he drew a joint from his vest pocket.

"Oh, goodie!" Linda exclaimed. "Mary, you've got to try it. Hurry, light it up, Richie!"

"Gee, I don't know," Mary said, turning to Tiernan.

"Oh, come on, just a little to turn on your taste buds," Linda urged.

"I . . . I'm game," Tiernan said, looking at Mary. "Anything to take the bummer off this evening."

"No arguments," Gemetz ordered and lighted the joint.

"You guys are crazy," Mary said. "I probably can't even get high. I haven't smoked in years."

"So, who's talking about getting high?" Gemetz asked and then took a long drag on the joint and handed it over to Tiernan. In a moment he exhaled wheezing. "This . . . [cough] . . . this is just gonna turn on your tongue. Mary, you're gonna think chocolate ice cream is the second coming!"

Tiernan had taken his drag and was now handing the joint to Mary with a nod of encouragement.

"Go on," Linda urged.

"Oh, god," Mary sighed and then put the joint to her lips and drew in. Gemetz made an air-sucking noise with his mouth to encourage her.

"Gimme," Linda said, holding out her hand eagerly for the joint when Mary had finished. "This is really first-rate pot."

For the next five minutes or so they passed the shrinking joint around and then sat back and waited for its effects. It didn't take long, and in a minute Mary was shaking her head as a fuzziness began to creep over her brain. "Whew!" she said, "I already feel it."

"Ummmmm," Tiernan sighed, rolling his head a bit and smiling stupidly at her.

"And now the ice cream!" Linda declared and began heaping it onto their plates with the big serving spoon.

Soon there were more groans of ecstasy as they spooned into the nearly melted ice cream.

"Oh, god," Tiernan gurgled with ice cream thick on his lips. "My mouf is having an orgasm."

"Ummmmmm," Mary moaned and closed her eyes as she let the rich cream melt in her mouth.

"Didn't I tell you?" Linda said between mouthfuls.

"Oh, man," Gemetz said, looking up to the ceiling. "I'm thinking of fresh strawberries. Chocolate ice cream with fresh, ripe, juicy, succulent, red, ripe strawberries," he said, slowly and sensually mouthing each word.

"Oooooooh," Linda groaned and slowly licked her lips.

"This is getting indecent," Mary said and giggled.

"Haaaaah, this pot is unbelievable," Tiernan said and fell back into his easy chair. "Where'd you get it?"

"Linda knows somebody at the Met," Gemetz said.

"Ummmm, very sensual," Mary said, feeling warm waves rippling through her.

"I know," Linda said. "It's great for fucking."

"You're telling me," Gemetz said and leaned over and began sucking on her neck.

"Hey, you guys, bedroom is in there," Tiernan said.

"Joe!" Mary protested and then had to giggle again.

"One time Richie and I went to this party over in the Village," Linda said and then started laughing and covered her mouth with her hand as she looked at Richie, who was sprawled back against the couch again. "And we got so turned on . . . Remember, Richie?"

"We did it in their bathroom," Gemetz said, smiling with his eyes closed.

"Um, that had to be the best ice cream I've ever tasted," Mary said, resting back in her chair and trying to move the conversation away from an area that was warming her up uncomfortably. Then Gemetz started giggling to himself. Fearing something obscene, Mary was about to get up and take the dishes into the kitchen. Richie was liable to propose anything, she thought.

"Tweenie, tweenie toes," Gemetz murmured as he looked fondly at his feet and began wiggling his toes.

"Oh, no, not your feet again, Richie," Linda complained.

"Say, what is this foot fetish—or toe fetish—of yours, Richie?" Mary asked, feeling relieved at the playful turn.

"Every time he gets stoned, he thinks his feet look like little boys' feet," Linda said. "I mean, he thinks he sees his feet as he remembers them when he was a boy. What happens, actually, is his brain runs backwards. Right, Richie? Pretty soon Mommy going to have to change your widdle diaper?"

"Tweenie, weenie feeties," Gemetz continued with a stupid smile on his face while he wiggled his toes.

"I gotta try that," Tiernan said. "Hold your noses everybody," he said, taking off his shoes and socks.

Then, with Mary and Linda laughing, he put his bare feet up on the table and began wiggling his toes at Gemetz's wiggling toes.

"How old are they?" Gemetz asked after a moment.

"I can only get them down to nineteen," Tiernan said with a frown. "My corns throw me off."

"Keep wiggling," Gemetz said authoritatively.

"You guys are nuts," Mary said.

"Uh, uh, uh, uh . . ." Tiernan grunted with effort as he wiggled his toes as rapidly as he could.

"How old?" Gemetz asked again.

"Down to twelve," Tiernan grunted.

"Wiggle!" Gemetz commanded.

"Wheeeee!" Tiernan exclaimed. "Just passed six . . . uh, uh, uh, heading for five!"

"Oh, yeah? Five? What's that like?" Gemetz asked, looking with great awe at Tiernan.

"Ooooh, dat feels vewy nice," Tiernan said in baby talk and turned to Mary with a moronic smile on his face.

"The new champ!" Gemetz exclaimed and leaned forward and raised Tiernan's hand, whereupon Tiernan crossed his eyes and made gurgling sounds. "Okay, girls, now you try it!" Gemetz said, turning to Mary and Linda.

"Ha! We can outwiggle you guys any day of the week!" Linda declared and began wiggling her toes inside her nylons.

Mary laughed and began wiggling hers, too.

"Nope!" Gemetz exclaimed and waved his hands for them to stop. "No panty hose. Can't tell how old your toes are all covered up like that."

"Who says?" Linda asked pugnaciously.

"The champ does. Right, champ?" he asked Tiernan.

"Glurg!" Tiernan affirmed.

"Right!" Gemetz went on. "This has to be a bare-toedied fight or nothin'!"

"I concede," Mary said. "Joe's the winner." The pot was sending strange sensations through her and she was afraid she was slipping beyond her depth.

"Well, I don't!" Linda said and got up and walked over behind the plant-covered parson's table near the window. There she pulled up her dress and hooked her thumbs into the elastic tops of her panty hose and, cocking an eyebrow at them, she slowly undulated them down. As she was bending over to step out of them, Gemetz hooted and told her she was giving a royal moon to the apartments across the street.

"Oh, god!" Mary exclaimed and rushed over behind the table and pulled the curtains shut. When she turned around, Linda was waving her panty hose at the two men.

"Woo-woo!" Tiernan called.

"Okay, Mary!" Gemetz shouted.

"This is silly," Mary said, blushing as Linda patted her on the behind and walked back to the couch with her panty hose.

"Come on, Mary, they can't see you," Linda said and plopped down beside Richie again.

Tiernan nodded to her and smiled; and then, after another moment of hesitation, she shrugged and hiked up the back of her deep-green velvet skirt. Gemetz and Tiernan immediately started whistling and clapping and then joined in humming the tune to "The Stripper." She quickly struggled her panty hose down over her legs and stepped out of them. Then she smoothed down her skirt and white cashmere sweater and hurried back to her chair, leaving the nylon undergarment piled on the floor under the planter. The nakedness she felt under her slip and the fuzzy erotic warmth the marijuana was fanning through her caused her to blush brightly.

"Mary, you should see your face," Linda said teasingly and put her feet up on the table.

"Ho, ho, ho!" Gemetz said, pointing a knowing finger at her.

"Okay, on with the wiggle!" Tiernan declared, wanting to get Mary off the hook.

"We're *all* nuts," Mary said, putting her feet up on the table.

For the next five minutes the four of them wiggled their toes furiously on the coffee table until they finally had to stop from exhaustion and laughing. Linda was declared the winner, having regressed to the prime toe-wiggling age of nine months.

"Whooo, I never would have thought toe-wiggling could be so strenuous," Mary said, feeling more at ease.

"Hey, don't I get a prize or something?" Linda complained.

"Yeah, I've got it right here," Gemetz said, reaching into his vest pocket and slowly drawing out another joint of marijuana. "Everybody ready for another round?" he asked.

"Oh, not for me," Mary said. "And, Linda, you have to drive home. How about a little music?" she said, getting up and trying to shake the dizziness from her head.

"Booo!" Gemetz said with a frown and put the joint back into his pocket as Linda shook her head at him.

"I, uh, see you were playing Fauré's *Requiem*," Tiernan said as Mary walked over to the record player.

"Oh, Joe, I meant to tell you," Mary said with enthusiasm. "They're doing it at Carnegie Hall tomorrow night for Good Friday! Your favorite piece. And guess what? I got a free ticket to it for you. How about that? One of the women I work with couldn't go and asked me if I wanted her ticket."

"Yeah, thanks," he said. "I should be able to make it."

"Wait a minute, I'll get it out of my purse," she said and hurried into the dining room.

"So, how come you were playing it?" he called after her.

"Well, if you didn't want it, I thought I'd go anyway. And you know me, I always like to listen to the music before I go to a concert."

"Oh," he said, feeling disappointed that she had not been playing it to remind her of him.

"Here," she said, coming in with the ticket. "Joe loves this music," she said to Linda and Richie, who were sitting back and letting the pot wear off a bit.

While Tiernan tucked the ticket into his wallet, Mary went back to the record player and turned it on. In a moment the soft haunting opening of the requiem crept into the room, instantly displacing the playful mood Richie's games had stirred up. Mary came over and sat down quietly and Tiernan leaned back with his hands behind his neck and looked at her sadly for a moment. Then he closed his eyes and let the music carry him away from her, back into the time when his world was in its early morning, and one of its boundaries was made of gray cathedral stone and stained glass, and his were the child's footsteps echoing in the flagstone courtyard of St. Joseph's and the gray wet air moved around his face like a sea of ghosts. And behind him an old priest coughing and carrying the precious Eucharists in a gold chalice, priest and altar boy crossing a court toward the church. The music rising now and carrying him inside the great towering house of God, the once-splendid mystery.

"I haven't heard Fauré's in such a long time," Linda said after a while.

Tiernan opened his eyes and smiled at her, his eyes still sad and calm.

"Lin, didn't you sing in this one . . . remember, before you got the Met job?" Gemetz asked.

"That was Mozart's *Requiem*" she said. "At St. John's, I think."

"Yeah, remember those days?" he asked, smiling fondly at her.

"I liked church work," she said with a shrug.

"She . . . Linda used to get, oh, I think it was fifty dollars for singing in those big churches on weekends," Gemetz said, turning to Mary and Tiernan. "When we were first married. God, I never could keep up with her. One week she'd be singing for the Presbyterians, the next week for the Episcopalians, then in a synagogue."

"A synagogue?" Mary asked.

"A name like Gemetz?" Linda replied in a Jewish accent. "For me it was easy—and they paid wonderfully. Are you interested in music, Mary?"

"I try to get to the concerts," she replied. "Especially if they're doing Chopin. And I've been to the Met. I'll look for you next time I go."

"Don't bother, I'm just one of the mob," Linda said, looking down.

"Not much longer," Gemetz said, turning to her and taking up her hand. While they were talking, the memory of all those struggling years had come into his mind again. All the hours, days, months and years she had worked to develop her voice. The nights he had listened to her cry because she had been turned down again for solo parts. Watching her in recent years as her hope slowly sank in the quicksand of the Met chorus.

"What do you mean?" Linda asked, looking up at him.

"I mean I'm sorry . . . for being such an ass about your

trip to San Francisco," he said, raising her hand and kissing it gently. "I want you to go. It's your chance. And . . . and, goddam, you earned it," he said choking up a little.

"You do?" she asked, beginning to smile, not sure he was putting her on.

"Hey, great!" Tiernan exclaimed and nodded his approval to Gemetz.

"Bet your ass," Gemetz said proudly. "This little lady's gonna knock San Francisco on its butt! Then, she's gonna come back and the Met'll *have* to take her back. And no more goddam chorus! Right?" he asked her. "Ladies and gentlemen, I give you the next *prima donna assoluta!*" he said, applauding her.

"Bravo, Linda!" Tiernan shouted and clapped, too.

"Oh, Linda, it's so exciting!" Mary said, beaming at her.

"I don't know, Richie," Linda said, looking down again.

"You'll do it!" Gemetz exclaimed, and squeezed her hand.

"Pretty good roles?" Tiernan asked.

"Fantastic!" Gemetz replied. "Listen, it had to happen. You got talent and it has to happen. I'm just sorry I was such a pig about it. I just thought . . . Well, anyway, our thing can wait. Right? But a break like this—how often does it come?"

"How did it happen?" Mary asked.

"This guy . . ." Gemetz said, turning to Mary and Tiernan. "What was he, Lin, some kind of assistant conductor or something?"

Linda nodded and looked over at Tiernan. He started to smile at her and then looked at her quizzically as he thought he saw some kind of fear creeping into her eyes.

"So, this assistant conductor," Gemetz went on, "gets himself fired from the Met about three months ago. Some disagreement, I don't know. And right away he goes out to San Francisco and they hire him for a top position. Then a few days ago he calls Linda. He *remembered* her, goddam it! Offers her two really juicy roles in the spring season. I think he was your coach or something, wasn't he, Lin?" he asked, turning to her.

"He worked with me last fall when I had that understudy part in *Rosenkavalier,*" Linda said, looking away nervously. "Richie, let's not talk about it, okay?" she asked. "I really haven't decided to go yet."

"*Now* she gets cold feet!" Gemetz laughed and sat back smiling proudly at her.

"I think I read about him in the *Times*," Mary said. "Last January . . . something about his objecting to the lead in *Billy Budd?* Yes, yes . . . and he went out to San Francisco! He's the one, Linda?"

Linda nodded, but there was a look of deep misery on her face.

"Whoever he is, he's a goddam genius in my book," Gemetz said, giving Linda's hand another squeeze. "Because he was able to see what the goddam Met couldn't—a great, great talent."

"Hey, I heard her sing out at the cemetery, remember?" Tiernan said, getting up. "It sent chills through me—beautiful. You'll make it, Linda. You guys sit still. I'm just going to clear off some of this mess," he said, gathering up the plates and silver from the coffee table.

"You sure you want me to go, Richie?" Linda asked.

Gemetz raised her hand and kissed it again in affirmation.

"Rhodes! That was his name!" Mary exclaimed. "Or was it DeRodes?"

Linda closed her eyes and bit her lip, wishing Mary would drop it.

"Yes, DeRodes!" Mary continued enthusiastically. "Steve DeRodes! They even had his picture—very handsome!"

Tiernan was halfway out of the room with the stack of plates when he heard the name "Steve" and nearly stopped in his tracks. He looked back over his shoulder and saw that it had registered on Gemetz, too.

"Steve?" Gemetz asked, looking at Linda, the color going out of his face.

"Richie, I . . ." she stammered and looked down as a blush of shame spread over her face.

She had never mentioned the name of the assistant conductor who was offering her this big chance out in San Francisco, but Gemetz was now certain that he was the "Steve" she had been having an affair with until shortly before his father died. The look on her face confirmed it.

Gemetz let out a long breath and slumped back on the couch. He closed his eyes and let his head fall back and slowly he released his hand from hers and put it in his lap.

"Mary," Tiernan called quietly from the dining room.

"I'll be right back," she told the Gemetzes after Tiernan had motioned her to follow him. "You guys want anything from the kitchen? A beer? Some coffee?"

"Huh-uh," Linda said, shaking her head without looking up.

"Richie? You okay, Richie?" Mary asked Gemetz, who was very pale and breathing short little rapid breaths through his nose. "Your ulcer acting up?"

He shook his head but did not open his eyes.

"It's okay," Linda said and motioned her to go ahead.

"Be right back," Mary said and hurried over to Tiernan, who turned and continued on toward the kitchen.

"Hey, I think Richie's having another attack," Mary said to Tiernan's back as he lowered the dishes into the sink.

"Yeah, I know, this whole trip thing," Tiernan said, trying to keep her from the enormity of the disaster that had just occurred in the living room. Unbelievable, he thought. How could I have been so wrong about Linda. She gets him away from Juliet, and then this shit out in San Francisco. Poor bastard, he thought, remembering the stunned look on Richie's face.

"Well, it sounds like he's all for it, doesn't it?" she asked.

Tiernan turned around and smiled at her. Good, honest Mary, he thought, pushing a strand of blond hair off her forehead. Sometimes brutally honest, but you'd never be capable of that kind of monstrous deceit.

"Why so sad?" she asked, looking up into his eyes.

"I . . ." He shook his head and closed his eyes for a moment. "Could I have a little kiss, maybe?" he asked, opening his eyes and smiling sadly.

"Little kiss for sad little boy," she said and pulled his head down and kissed him gently on the mouth and then on the forehead.

In the living room Richie was still sitting with his head back against the couch and almost appeared to be sleeping, except for a little smile that now and then teased at the edges of his mouth.

"Richie?" Linda asked in a tiny voice. "Richie, would you please open your eyes?"

After another moment he turned slowly toward her and opened his eyes. She smiled and reached over and took his hand from his lap and kissed it.

". . . I didn't want you to know . . . for a reason," she said, her eyes pleading for understanding.

He let out a little laugh and looked at her with an amused expression, waiting for what else she would say.

"Richie, try to understand this. . . . I mean it from my heart," she said, squeezing his hand. "Richie, in the long run it would be for us. My going out there will give us a better chance."

"Ummmmm," he said, nodding and looking over his glasses with great interest.

"Everything you said tonight is true," she went on. "It *is* my big chance, Richie. But it's also *our* big chance, don't you see? I can come back to you fulfilled. A whole woman—the woman I've always wanted to be. That will *really* be the new beginning for us, Richie."

"Ummmmmm," he said, nodding agreeably.

"Oh, Richie," she said, kissing his hand again. "In a way I'm glad it came out. I want us to be open and honest with each other. I . . . I love you, Richie. Do you understand that?"

He seemed to be considering that for a moment and then he looked at her seriously and nodded again.

"Let's go home and talk about it," she said, smiling and giving his hand another squeeze.

He smiled at her and got up and reached out his hand to assist her up. Then he started to say something, shook his head and smiled at her again.

God, he's still stoned out of his mind, she thought as he put on his socks and shoes. Then she followed him into the bedroom to get the coats. Still without saying anything or changing the eerie benign expression on his face, he helped her on with her coat and then put his on. She noticed that he was no longer wearing the glasses.

"I like Joe and Mary," she said, buttoning her coat. "When I get back, I think we should—"

But her voice was cut off as his slap caught her in the face and sent her sprawling onto the bed.

"There isn't any *we* anymore, cunt!" he snarled and walked out.

Tiernan and Mary were still in the kitchen talking when they heard the front door open and slam shut. They looked at each other for a moment and walked into the hall in time to see Linda running toward the door. She was holding her face and her eyes were brimming.

"Linda?" Mary asked and started to intercept her.

"Later," Linda growled, and brushed past her and hurried out the door.

"Hey, Linda!" Tiernan shouted after her as he leaned out the door and watched her pause for a moment in front of the elevator door, look back at him and then head for the exit stairs farther on. Then she was gone.

"Richie?" he called, stepping back into the apartment. "Mary, see if he's in there," he said, nodding toward the living room, and then trotted past her to see for himself. "Hey, Richie?" he called again as he found the living room empty and then continued on at a trot into the bedroom. Both of their coats were gone and the only thing on the smooth bedspread was Richie's comical glasses.

"Joe!" Mary called from the living room.

When he rushed out he saw her standing by the living-room window holding back a curtain and looking down at the street. Joining her there, Tiernan could see Gemetz down below running and waving to a cab that was disembarking its passengers about a half a block up. Then he saw Linda come out of the building and run to her car, which was parked just below the window.

"Poor bastard," Tiernan murmured and shook his head.

"God," Mary sighed. "Those two have to be the craziest couple I've ever seen."

Tiernan watched Richie get into the cab and walked away from the window shaking his head. The *Requiem* had played through but the record was still turning. He walked over and turned off the machine.

"There goes Linda," Mary reported from the window. Tiernan could hear her tires screeching as she sped off.

"Show people," he said, going over and flopping down on the couch. "They're all temperamental," he sighed, still trying to keep the full truth from Mary.

"What do you think set them off?" Mary asked, dropping the curtain and walking over toward the record player. "I thought everything was finally going great. About the San Francisco trip. Richie really came around—really backed her up."

"Who knows?" he moaned and buried his face in his hands.

"You think it was the pot?" she asked. "God, that was very strong stuff," she said, shaking her head to try to clear the wooziness that was still there.

"Probably," he mumbled, his head still down.

"You okay?" she asked as she took the record off the turntable and put it into its album cover.

"This hasn't been the greatest night of my life," he said and straightened up and looked at her sadly. "That whole German thing at Henri's had to be the all-time stupidest idea of my life."

"Aw, Joe, it was funny," she said, smiling at him. "I mean, except for Richie getting sick, I never laughed so hard."

"Well, I'm glad you liked it," he said, smiling back. "Henri is probably ordering mass executions at this minute."

"He won't hold it against you," she said, unable to restrain herself from chuckling. "It was an emergency . . . uh, an appendix attack, right?"

"The number-one dummo," he said, and buried his face in his hands again. "How'd you ever put up with me all those years?"

"Come on," she said. "Hey, how about some John Denver to cheer you up?" she asked and knelt down in front of the record collection.

"Naw," he moaned.

"Little Chopin?" she teased.

"Know what I'd like to hear right now?" he asked, straightening up and rubbing his face. "Don't laugh."

"What?"

"Johnny Mathis," he said, remembering how they used to dance to it when they were first going together. "I don't know why, but I feel like that would really sound terrific right now. Must be the pot, huh?"

She looked at him for a moment, wondering what he was thinking. She, too, was thrown into a reminiscent mood when he mentioned it but one that signaled a little warning from somewhere. She was feeling very tender toward him and had a great urge to lift him out of his despondency, but she did not want him to shift into a romantic mood. The almost erotic warmth the pot had stirred up in her and the attraction she had been feeling for him most of the evening made her worry about her vulnerability. She did not want to hurt him again, and any door she would open for him tonight she would only have to shut on him later. Still, he looked so woebegone, she thought.

"Okay," she said, smiling. "Then it's on your way. I gotta get my beauty rest."

"Yeah, poor old Max is waiting," he said.

"Aw, how's dear old Max?" she asked, pulling out the Mathis album.

"A noble dog," he said with a flourish of his hand. "A true and noble companion. Except when he takes an ignoble shit on the carpet. God, when Max makes a drop, it's . . . it's . . . profound," he sighed, measuring a mound rising to two feet over the floor.

"Then, we mustn't keep him waiting too long," she said, putting on the record and walking over and sitting down in the easy chair opposite him.

"Don't worry, don't worry. . . . I'll go," he said, resting back and giving her a knowing look. Then he put his hands behind his neck and put his bare feet up on the coffee table.

"I'm sorry," she said, blushing a little and then smiled and put her feet up, too. "Richie was so funny with his toes, huh?"

"A total maniac," he said.

"In a way, I thought they were very suited for each other," she said. "Both of them are—"

"Crazy," he said.

"Yeah, but I mean they're both very funny, you know?"

"Yeah," he lied, thinking Linda was about as funny as a kick in the balls. God, no wonder they broke up in the first place, he thought. Poor goddam bastard, he thought. Gotta give him a call in the morning.

"Do they always blow up like that?" she asked.

"Yeah, I think so," he said, wishing she'd get off the subject.

They sat quietly for a moment as the singer began their old favorite, "Misty," in his rich alternatingly deep and lilting voice. She smiled at him as the nostalgia evoked by the song moved through her. He smiled back and closed his eyes.

"It's still nice," she conceded.

"Come on," he said, getting to his feet and reaching across the coffee table to her, "let's see if we can still dance."

"Joe . . ." she began to protest but instinctively took his hand and let him pull her up. "Joe, let . . . let's keep it light," she said, looking into his eyes with concern. "We're both a little stoned."

"One dance," he said with a guilty little smile. "Then I'm on my way . . . really." Before she could protest further he stepped closer and took her into his arms. "Besides, Max would never forgive me," he said.

The shag rug was soft under their bare feet and he held her lightly, moving around slowly to the familiar music. In a moment he closed his eyes with happiness as she finally acquiesced and let herelf rest against him. He loved the feel of her flesh under her cashmere sweater.

". . . as restless as a kitten up a tree," he crooned along with the singer and traced his fingers down the crease of her back and then slid his hand around her slender waist and drew her into him. The soft fullness of her breasts against his chest made him open his mouth in breathless excitement. He could feel her breath, too, against his neck.

"We always did this pretty good," he said.

"Uh-huh," she said, choking on a little dryness in her throat. She knew that he was going to try to take her and she knew, too, that she could stop him at any point. Surely she would have to—gently—after the song. But not right now, she thought, feeling a radiating warmth wherever their bodies touched. Yes, there would be time after the dance, she thought, and then breathed in deeply the manly cologne-tinged smell of him. His neck was so near and her lips were becoming so hot, she thought, and then remembered Linda's comments about the erotic qualities of the marijuana. His hand was moving farther down on her hip and she felt a shudder of excitement course through her. Oh, dear god, I'm not going to make it, she thought.

"Ummmmmm," she moaned in protest as he shifted his hips a bit and pressed the immense rigidity of his penis between her thighs. But she was now unable to act against the hungry pressing of her body against him.

"Joe . . . ," she sighed and made a feeble effort to pull away and then pressed against his penis again as another shudder went through her.

"So good," he breathed, and moved his hand down slowly, caressingly over her buttocks, loving the feel of her velvet skirt and the slide of her slip over her bare ass—her fantastic ass, now loose and wanton without the constraints of her panty hose.

"Please," she moaned and opened her famished mouth against his neck as his hand reached farther down and drew up the back of her dress, exposing the nakedness of her legs and then her ass. Now she was overtaken by the wave and bore into his neck with ravenous sucking. She felt she could devour him and thrust her pelvis against his penis in a frenzy as his hand began searching up her inner thigh and into the wet heat of her vagina. Her mouth was on fire now and her tongue licked out like a flame over his neck and then up until his mouth came down and met hers with equal hunger. In a moment she was tearing at his belt and falling, falling, sliding down over his chest, her mouth gasping.

Later—after he had carried her into the bedroom and had made her stand while he slowly and lovingly stripped her and had made love to her again and then again—they lay beside each other under the sheet, completely spent and breathing out the last remnants of their desire.

"Ohooooo," he crooned in ecstasy and exhaustion, his right arm flung over his forehead. "The best ever," he sighed.

"Mmmmmmm," she agreed and rolled on her side and lay with her head on his chest. "That pot . . . I went a little crazy, I think."

"You were fantastic!" he said, raising his arm in tribute. He closed his eyes and remembered the wild and almost painful ecstasy on her face as she rode on top of him during their last orgasm, her head swinging and her long blond hair swishing down across his face.

"I'm so weak, I'm trembling," she whispered against his chest.

"Sleep . . . sleep," he said and stroked her hair soothingly.

"So tired, so tired," she murmured. "So—"

"I love you, Mary," he said.

In a moment he could feel her breathing evenly in sleep and gently pressed his arm around her shoulder. So childlike, he thought, remembering all the nights she had snuggled up to sleep in the protection of his arms. Oh, Mary, Mary, let me come home, he thought, and felt himself sliding into sleep. For the first time in so many months the world was in order again.

He had been sleeping for several hours when something, a noise, a movement, awakened him from a dream. Strange images of Linda taking off her panties in a cemetery. Richie nearby digging like a dog into his father's fresh grave. Blinking his eyes in the darkness of the bedroom, he thought at first he was in his apartment and that perhaps Max had barked or growled. Then he saw Mary's back as she sat on the edge of the bed. Mary, Mary, he thought with a smile and slowly drifted off to sleep again.

In about five minutes he awoke again, this time opening his eyes wide. She was no longer in the bed. He blinked and tried to make out the forms in the darkness. Probably gone to the bathroom, he thought. Then he heard a man's barely audible voice at the farther end of the apartment. Then Mary's whispering reply. He flung the sheet off and swung his legs out of bed, feeling dizzy and weak as he tried to stand up.

Quietly he tiptoed naked to the entrance of the living room and listened again in the darkness. The low voices were coming either from the kitchen or from the front door. He padded quietly across the living room to the entryway of the hall and peeked around it.

"Look, that's up to you, Michael," he heard Mary say. "Good night, Michael."

Tiernan had looked around the entryway just in time to see her closing the door on the slight, delicately featured Italian, who seemed to be wearing a dark silk bathrobe. As Mary turned to go back to the bedroom, Tiernan sucked in his breath and tiptoed rapidly back across the living room, hurried into the bedroom and leaped almost from midroom into the bed and slid under the sheet. With his heart pounding in his chest he closed his eyes and tried to control his rapid breathing. Thank god, he thought as he heard her go into the bathroom. Time to get my breath. Don't want her to know I saw them.

After a few minutes he heard the toilet flush and the bathroom door opening. Just cool it, Tiernan, he told himself. It's not her fault the little jerk came down from his apartment. Jesus, in his bathrobe—how cozy. Little guy, almost shorter than her. Probably all wang. He kept his eyes closed and feigned sleep as she came back into the room and slipped into bed beside him. He debated whether to feign a little snoring.

In a moment she let out a sigh and turned to him and tapped him on the shoulder.

"I heard you," she said.

"Oh," he said, opening his eyes.

"You tiptoe like a buffalo," she said.

"What'd he want?" he asked, turning to her and rising up on one elbow.

"You wouldn't believe it," she said with a weary sigh.

"I've got an idea," he said, frowning.

"Popcorn," she said.

"What?"

"Yep," she said and sighed again and rolled over on her back and draped her arm over her eyes. "He was watching the late late show and got an irresistible urge for popcorn."

"You're kidding?" he laughed.

"Well, it's his popcorn," she said. "He brought some down the other evening for us to pop and forgot to take it back with him."

"Likes popcorn, huh?"

"Popcorn and television," she said.

"Give him his popcorn?"

"Yeah," she sighed. "God, there was only a tiny bit left."

"He seemed a little unhappy," he said.

"I wouldn't let him come in."

"That was thoughtful," he said.

"Men!" she exclaimed.

"What did you ever see in him anyway?" he asked.

"Joe?"

"Yeah?"

"Go to sleep."

"I *am* tired," he sighed. "That was really powerful tonight, you know, Mary?"

"Shhhhhh," she said, feeling an anger growing in her over the proprietary tone in his voice. Please, Joe, she thought, tonight was a big mistake. Don't push me. Go to sleep and tomorrow we'll talk.

"Good in bed, or what?" he asked, referring to Michael again.

"Don't, Joe," she said, gritting her teeth.

"Well, what are you going to tell him?" he asked.

"About what?"

"About us," he said.

"What is there to tell him, Joe?" she asked, feeling the anger surfacing now.

"Tonight meant nothing to you, then?" he asked, rising up on his elbow again.

She rolled over and put her back to him. It's not going to wait until morning, she told herself.

"Mary?" he asked.

"I enjoyed it," she said. "The pot turned me on and I enjoyed it."

"That's all?" he asked.

"Joe, there's . . . there's something we have to talk about. I was going to wait until after Easter, but we might as well get it over with now."

"Don't tell me you're in love with that little . . . that . . ." he said, his hostility flaring.

"Goddam it!" she said, and sat up. "You never will understand, will you? You think that I only exist in relation to you or some other man. You never will understand that I very well goddam like being just me—alone!"

"No, I *do* accept that you're an individual," he said, defensively. "I've always seen you as—"

"Joe, I hired a lawyer yesterday," she said.

"What do you mean, you hired a lawyer?" he asked and lay back with his hand over his eyes, not wanting to accept what was happening.

"Joe, we've been separated for nearly a year. It's time!"

"It is *not* time!" he bellowed. "I know you, Mary, you . . . you're going through something right now. But I can wait, goddam it. Even if it takes years, I can wait. No, we don't need a lawyer!"

"That's why we do need one, Joe," she said. "Because you *are* waiting. You're holding up your life, waiting for me to come back to my senses or something. I feel guilty, Joe. I don't want you to wait for me. I am where I want to be. Free! I have my life, and it's the way I want it."

"And Lynn?" he asked.

"Lynn is Lynn, and Mary is Mary, and Joe is Joe," she said. "Why can't you understand that?"

"I understand one thing!" he shouted and whipped the sheet off him and got up. "I understand that you don't give a shit about *anything* but Mary!" he roared at her.

"Don't shout at me," she said and closed her eyes.

"No divorce!" he said, searching around in the dark for his underwear.

"I don't need your consent," she said.

"Then you do it, Mary!" he said, hurrying into his pants. "Yeah, you do it . . . you get your goddam divorce. And later on, later . . . when you wonder what ever happened to the man who loved you, *you* can tell yourself that *you* threw him in the shitcan! You can just go fuck yourself!"

"Get out!" she shrieked.

# PART
# THREE

# CHAPTER
# SIXTEEN

Two weeks after Easter, Talbot was leaving his tiny office in Whitehead Hall at Brooklyn College feeling shaken by the news that he'd just been turned down for an associate professorship. There had been a delay until July in the publication of his "Lorenzo" paper, so the board had made its decision against him on the basis of something else. What that was he didn't know for sure, but he suspected it was the general lack of interest he'd shown toward teaching during the past year.

"Len, wait!" Chuck Freedman called to him from behind as he started down the nearly deserted corridor outside his office. It was twelve-thirty on Saturday and nearly everyone had gone home.

"Chuck," he said without enthusiasm as the lanky bald-headed young professor came alongside and hooked his arm in his. Freedman, who also taught history, had just received his promotion from assistant to associate professor, and Talbot wasn't in any mood for the words of commiseration he was sure his colleague was about to bestow on him.

"How about coming over for supper with Phyllis and me tonight?" Freedman asked. "We'd love to have you."

"Nah, tonight I wanna get blind," Talbot said. "Thanks

anyway. And, listen, you ought to be celebrating. You don't want a gloomy Gus around."

"I don't understand it," Freedman said, shaking his head. "I was sure you'd get it. You deserve it. Len, you're twice the teacher of anybody in the department."

"Not this year," Talbot said as they walked down the steps toward the front door. "Been a crazy year, you know?"

"Yeah, you looked like you were going through some kind of personal hell. The marriage breakup, huh?"

"Yeah. Too bad, too. I think I've screwed myself pretty well here. Might start looking for another school. Fresh start, you know?"

"Damn, Phyllis was saying the same thing! Said a change of scene might snap you out of it."

"I like Phyllis. How is she?"

"Oh, god, I'll be glad when she gets through her goddam psychoanalytic studies. We barely see each other. Then, when we do, she's so whipped from those long hours she just wants to be left alone."

"Never should have given them the vote." Talbot laughed.

"I don't know. Couple a years and she'll be dragging down forty grand as an analyst," Freedman said with a shrug. "That won't be so bad. Might even get to lay her now and then."

"What more could you ask for?" Talbot said, smiling.

"Listen, if you are serious about looking someplace else, I have a friend who's a dean at the University of South Dakota. He's been after me for the past year to come out there. They need some talent in the history department and he promised a full professorship within two years."

"Thanks, I'll keep it in mind," Talbot said, slapping him on the back as they stepped outside into the sunlight. "Buddy of mine's waiting across the street in my car. Gotta run. Tell Phyllis I'll take a rain check!" he yelled over his shoulder as he trotted toward the car.

Tiernan was leaning out the window with a frown on his face, having been parked there for half an hour waiting. Talbot had told him to have the car back at noon sharp, when he'd loaned it to him that morning to go over to Queens to pick up some used furniture for his apartment.

"Sorry I'm late," Talbot said as Tiernan moved over and let him slip into the driver's seat.

'No sense of time, you academic types," Tiernan chided.

"All locked up in your little ivory worlds, preying on all them pretty little coeds who wander in there. Boy, you've got it knocked. I saw some real beauties, sitting here. Maybe I'll come over more often."

Talbot pulled the car away without responding to Tiernan's kidding. For a while he just drove along the tree-lined street toward Flatbush, his brows knit in thought. "I didn't get it," he said finally.

"What?"

"The associate professorship. Ah, well, fuck it," he sighed.

"Aw, man, I'm really sorry. I know it meant a lot."

"I didn't really deserve it. Been going to hell this year. I think I'm losing interest in teaching, anyway."

"Nah, nah. I know how you feel. It's a big—"

"You get your furniture?" Talbot asked, trying to cut off further discussion on his lost appointment.

"Yeah! Great kitchen table and a big leather reading chair. Thanks for the car. Oh . . . uh, I put a few new scratches on your roof."

"So, who'd notice?" Talbot laughed. "This thing's been through the wars."

"Yeah, like all of us," Tiernan replied. "Oh, and the woman also had this old antique dollhouse I picked up for Lynn. Only five bucks and it plays nursery-type music on a little box when you open the doors. Lynn'll love it . . . when I see her again," he said, and then shook his head and looked out the window.

"Come on, Joe," Talbot said, glancing at his friend, who seemed to be sinking into his depression again. "Why don't you go over there? No sense punishing Lynn because you're mad at Mary."

"I want to. I want to more than I can tell you," Tiernan said, slamming his fist into his palm. "It's tearing me to pieces. But, it's the only way I know to fight the divorce. I can't give in to it without a fight."

"Joe—"

"No, I know Mary. She doesn't know what she's talking about. She gets these stupid stubborn ideas into her head and they have nothing to do with reality. She thinks she wants me out of their lives. . . . Well, I'll give them a taste of it. She'll feel it. . . . She'll feel it just like I've felt it."

"It's totally crazy," Talbot sighed hopelessly.

Talbot didn't say any more after that but continued driving back toward Prospect Park West. He had his own sorrows. God, Richie was right, he thought—the three basketeers. Now all three of them could get drunk and cry in their beers at Larsky's. For the past three weeks, since the night of the massacre—the crazy Gemetzschernsteiner fiasco, Richie's second breakup with Linda and Tiernan's latest painful rejection by Mary—Talbot had been listening to their laments until he wanted to slug them. But, Christ, what could he do? he thought. Richie was back living in his old unlighted apartment, while Linda had moved out to San Francisco with the kids for the spring opera season, and Tiernan had nearly gone berserk after receiving his divorce papers in the mail. What a night that was! He and Richie had had to sit on Tiernan to keep him from going over to Alan Curtis's and beating the lawyer to a pulp for taking the case. In the end, Tiernan just tore the document to shreds and mailed it back to Curtis.

No, he couldn't sink into the swamp with them, he thought. Jesus, after all their big New Year's resolves they were in total retreat again. So I didn't get my associate. So, to hell with it! There are other goddam colleges. And I don't have to go to South Dakota, either. New York University was still a possibility. He'd applied there, but they'd only hire him as an instructor. But it would get him out of Brooklyn, this damned swamp, he thought.

"That's it!" he exclaimed, jolting Tiernan out of his reverie.

"Wha—?" Tiernan said.

"We're going to Manhattan—you and me and Richie!"

"Manhattan?"

"Bet your ass! I just figured it out. We gotta move. We gotta get out of the swamp. It's killing us. We're gonna cross the river, man. Ride for high ground!"

"What're you talking about?" Tiernan asked, looking at him as though he'd just gone crazy.

"Brooklyn, man—the whole brownstone fucking swamp of Brooklyn. What the hell are we doing in Brooklyn anyway? That's where you go after you get married—where you set up house, have babies, and tear each other to pieces! We got no more business in Brooklyn, we've done all that."

Tiernan let out a whistle and frowned at him.

"We're single, goddam it! We're single and we're drowning

in postmarital shit! It's destroying our lives. And man we are going to ride. Get on our horses and ride."

"Manhattan . . . hmm. I never thought of that," Tiernan said, considering the idea and getting caught up a little in Talbot's enthusiasm.

"First, I'm going to line up a teaching job over there—maybe N.Y.U. Right?"

"Right," Tiernan said.

"Then we're all going to start hunting for apartments over there, preferably in the Village."

"I like the East Side," Tiernan said, his enthusiasm growing.

"Okay, okay. You take the East Side, I'll take the Village and Richie can have the West Side. We'll have the place covered."

"Right on!" Tiernan said, smiling, but still only half believing what Talbot was saying. At least it was lifting his spirits for the moment.

"Then, we're gonna ride hell-bent through the Manhattan singles world. Man, we're gonna be up to our asses in women—new women, single women, sharp, ever-lovin' Manhattan women!"

"All right!" Tiernan exclaimed.

"Only we're not gonna do that last. We're gonna do that tonight. Tonight we ain't gonna go to Larsky's, man! New ground, man!"

"Shit, let's go find Richie," Tiernan said and punched Talbot on the shoulder causing him nearly to swerve the car over into the other lane.

# CHAPTER
# SEVENTEEN

That night the ride was on.

Tiernan and Gemetz were ready to follow Talbot into the new hunting ground across the river. For nearly the whole afternoon he'd been pounding at them, trying to raise them from defeat with the idea of taking on the singles scene on Manhattan's East Side. Brooklyn was a brownstone swamp that would swallow them up if they did not break out, he'd said. Let all the Marys and Lindas and Susans and Juliets rot in it, he'd said; but the high ground, the future for them as males with their balls still intact, lay in Manhattan.

Crossing the Brooklyn Bridge in Talbot's old VW, they were in high spirits—passing Talbot's flask of bourbon around and bantering up their courage.

"Gentlemen, twenty bucks here says I'll be the first to score!" Talbot said, flashing a crisp new bill in front of their faces.

"You're on, turkey!" Tiernan said, snatching the bill and tucking it into his jacket breast pocket.

"Hey, gimme!" Talbot said, fishing it out and trying to keep his eye on the road as he drove.

"Don't bet him, Joe," Gemetz said, taking a swig from the flask. "For twenty bucks this guy'd make it with a bag lady."

"Ha! Lemme at 'em!" Talbot exclaimed and turned off on the exit ramp on the East River Drive.

Feeling the glow of the bourbon in his chest, Gemetz looked at his two friends and smiled. For the first time since his second breakup with Linda he was feeling his old spirit again. Talbot was right, he thought: Forget 'em all! Juliet, too. She wants to cling to her anger, that's okay with me, he thought, remembering her cold refusal to talk to him on the half-dozen times he'd called her. He wanted her but, by god, he wouldn't die for her. For a while, until Talbot had goaded him back to life, he was ready to drink himself into oblivion over her.

Now more than ever he valued his friend's energy and will to fight back. He needed to draw on that energy. Everything had blown apart—his father's death, Linda's departure, Juliet's rejection—almost too much to deal with. Yes, thank god for Talbot, he thought. Maybe he's a little overboard with his military bullshit, he thought, but maybe even that's right on the mark. Maybe man's natural fate is to ride and conquer and let the woman pick up the pieces. Everything else seemed to be quicksand. You rode or you sank. Yes, literally, he thought, remembering his father's burial. The pain from his ulcer had been growing since the breakup.

"Man, this shirt is fantastic," Tiernan said, referring to the white silk shirt Talbot had made him put on after he'd shown up for the ride wearing his usual red sweater.

"Looks great, looks great," Talbot said, nodding in agreement. "You'll knock 'em dead in that shirt."

"I feel like it," Tiernan said, pulling the sporty collar out over his jacket lapels and rising up to get a look at himself in the rearview mirror. "I gotta get one—maybe two or three."

Tiernan, too, was feeling better for the first time in weeks. Talbot had managed to tap into the anger that was eating him up and get it directed outward. He envied this quality in Talbot—this ability to harness his anger into decisive action. His own anger lacked the dedication and constancy of Talbot's—always seeming to subside and allowing him to drift back toward Mary. Now he must keep it hot, keep it directed outward.

"Here," Talbot said, taking three tiny black books from inside his jacket. "A present to mark the occasion."

"What's this?" Tiernan asked, taking one and giving another to Gemetz.

"Ze leetle black book, eh?" Gemetz said, flipping through its tiny pages.

"Ze leetle passport, you mean," Talbot said. "We're gonna fill 'em up with new names. Fill up our lives now with new women."

"Right on, brother!" Tiernan said, smiling and putting his in his pocket.

"So even if you guys don't score tonight, I want you to come back with no less than four new names. Right?" Talbot asked and took a long drink of bourbon from the flask.

"Think we're gonna turn up that many women tonight, huh?" Gemetz asked.

"Hit and run—hit and run, that's our tactic," Talbot said.

"Yeah," Tiernan agreed.

"Just be cool," Talbot went on, still looking ahead with grim determination. "Don't get soapy and serious with 'em. These chicks are sharp. They've heard every dumb-dodo line there is. We come in cool—cool and sharp."

"Yeah," Gemetz chimed in, winking at Tiernan.

"Sharp, sharp, sharp!" Talbot emphasized, hitting his fist against his palm three times.

"Hit and run—hit and run," Tiernan said, and slammed his fist against his palm, too. Then he turned to Gemetz and asked, "What the hell does that mean?"

"It means we're cavalry, man!" Talbot said, looking at them with a little smile. "It means we come at them from the flank, we dazzle them, we confuse them, we overwhelm them with our pure masculine charm. Then . . . the *coup de grace!* We act like they're wasting our time. They're suckers for a pullout."

"Yeah," Tiernan agreed, sneering.

After leaving the East River Drive, Talbot continued north on Third Avenue past all the singles bars and finally pulled into a parking garage at 72nd Street. Then they got out and headed down Third, walking at an eager clip, three abreast and ready to do battle. It was just after nine o'clock and they had decided they would work their way down the ten-block strip, bar by bar. Of course, they wouldn't get to more than two or three bars on any of these Saturday night forays, Talbot had assured them, because by then they'd be up to their necks in fantastic women. It might take them until midsummer to complete the strip, he had said, but they would take their time and master the terrain. Then it would be theirs—new territory, new women, new lives.

By ten-thirty they'd hit about eight bars and were more than halfway down the strip. There had been many fine-looking women, but most of them seemed to have dates and the others acted like they were waiting for their dates to show up. Gemetz and Tiernan had never seen Talbot get frosted so many times in one evening. The last bar they'd trooped into was for gays, and they had just wheeled and trooped out.

"Shit, we've had better luck at Larsky's," Gemetz said as they crossed Third Avenue and headed for a bar on the corner called Peaches.

"Better-looking women, too," Tiernan added.

"Hey, take a look!" Talbot called to them from where he was peering in through the front window of Peaches. Most of the bar's long window was covered with stained-glass designs of ripe peaches intermingled with what looked like peach-shaped women's buttocks.

Looking in through a clear portion of the window, they could see a long bar jammed two and three deep with chicly dressed young singles—most of them women. The bartenders were passing drinks over the heads of the first rank and there seemed to be a loud party atmosphere inside.

"Diz muz be de plaze," Gemetz said, rubbing his hands.

"Wow! I told you we'd find 'em!" Talbot exclaimed. "Come on!"

"No, wait!" Tiernan said. "Before we go in, I, uh, I think maybe we need a little new strategy."

"Huh?" Talbot asked, starting for the door and then coming back.

"I, uh . . ." Tiernan stammered and looked down uncomfortably. "Well, I think we're blowing it with this super-stud approach," he continued and looked up at Gemetz for support.

Gemetz nodded and looked over at Talbot, hoping he would take it right. Talbot's idea for coming to Manhattan had been a stroke of genius, he thought, but he had been coming on like a goddam idiot in the other bars. Pure Hollywood, Gemetz thought, not like Talbot at all.

"Yeah, he's right," Gemetz finally said with a shrug of apology to Talbot.

"Oh?" Talbot asked, eyeing them both.

"It's too macho, Len," Tiernan said. "Phony . . . and,

well, look, it just ain't my style. And it isn't yours either. Hey, just hang easy like you do at Larsky's, Len. The women eat you up at Larsky's."

"Yeah, a little *too* cool maybe," Gemetz offered.

Talbot knitted his brows, looked around and started for the door again. Then he walked back. "The hell it is," he said. "Come on, let's get in there!"

"Okay, you guys go on in," Tiernan said. "I'll come in in a few minutes and hit another part of the bar."

"Wait a minute, wait a minute," Talbot said, trying to keep his anger down. "What's wrong with my approach? At least it's an approach. Your idea of picking up women is to sit there verrrry quietly until one of them jumps in your lap."

"'Hey, Mamma, let's get down,'" Tiernan said, snapping his fingers and mimicking one of Talbot's unsuccessful lines of the evening. "Where'n hell did you get all this Johnny Cool bullshit? It's embarrassing, Len."

Talbot looked at him angrily for a minute and then by degrees his face broke into a grin and then he started laughing.

"Hey, man, this is Manhattan. Gotta be cool, man," Talbot said, jiving around and snapping his fingers in self-mimicry.

"All I say is we quit trying so damned hard," Tiernan said after pushing Talbot away in good spirits. "Like in Brooklyn, man—mellow down easy. Women're the same anywhere."

"Mel-low," Talbot said slowly and smiled. "Okay, I got it. You're right. Mellow, right? Now let's get in there!"

"God, look at the talent in here," Tiernan said as they pushed in through the front door of the bar.

"Check the end of the bar," Talbot said and let out a little whimper of joy.

"Oh, god, the mother lode," Gemetz sighed.

Gathered at the end of the bar and talking to each other were six of the most stunningly beautiful women they had ever seen. And nobody had moved in on them yet.

"Let's get 'em," Talbot said under his breath and gave Tiernan a push.

"Mellow," Tiernan reminded him.

"It's your play," Talbot said, pushing him on ahead of them.

When they got down to the end of the bar, they wedged in beside the women and Talbot and Gemetz were facing him, making little urgent expressions with their faces for him to turn around and get busy. Instead, Tiernan sipped the foam off the top of his beer, and looking wistfully off in the distance, he began talking about the chances of the Yankees taking another pennant this year, as though they had been discussing it all night. "It's all up to Guidry," he said. "If his arm holds up, they could go—"

"Enough already," Talbot said, glaring at him. "Get your ass in gear. Jesus, one of 'em's looking at you," he murmured under his breath.

"Gossage should be back in shape, though," Tiernan went on. "What's the first game, Richie?"

"The Dolphins," Gemetz replied with irritation. "Who gives a shit! Joey, we're losing it," he hissed and nodded toward two other young men who had come up and were now talking to the beauties.

"I can't believe this," Talbot whimpered as three more young men joined the group of women.

"What a great place," Tiernan said, saluting the bar with his mug of beer but still keeping his back to the women.

"Shit!" Talbot grumbled, and pushed in next to the bar, where he lowered his head and ran his fingers through his hair in exasperation.

"Great goin', Joey," Gemetz griped and slid in beside Talbot at the small opening at the bar.

For the next five minutes Talbot and Gemetz ignored Tiernan, who was still standing out from the bar and looking benignly over the crowd. Inside he was a mass of nerves as he tried to think of something to say—if he could work up enough courage to turn around and take on the six beauties. He was taking a deep breath in preparation to do this, when a long lovely arm came snaking past his neck over his shoulder.

"What does it smell like?" a sultry feminine voice whispered in his ear.

"Huh?" he asked, starting to turn.

"No, don't," she said, holding him in place and stroking her hand over his face. "Name the scent."

He sniffed the fresh perfume on her arm and smiled. Meanwhile, Talbot and Gemetz were gaping in wonder at what was taking place. One of the best of the beauties, an almond-eyed Sophia Loren type, was stroking their friend's face.

"Let's see," he said, taking her hand gently in his and turning around. "It's either Old Spice or Mennen Skin Bracer."

"Ha!" she laughed and took her hand back and patted him

on the face as he turned around and immediately fell in love with her Italian brown eyes. "Hey, Maggie, man here says it smells like aftershave!" she called over her shoulder to the tall brunette standing just behind her.

"Well!" Maggie exclaimed and tilted her nose in the air in disdain.

"That's twelve out of twelve, Mag," another of the women, a lithe redhead, said.

"She models this stuff on TV and she believes half the men in America are buying it for their girlfriends—or wives," said the one with the lovely brown eyes. "You married?"

"Uh, no," Tiernan said biting his tongue as he was about to add "separated." "Ah, my name's Joe."

"Debbie," she said and then, striking a sultry pose, added, "But you can call me Deborah."

"Here, let me try," Gemetz said, pushing in beside Tiernan and taking Debbie's hand. "Ah, lemme guess," he said after sniffing her wrist. "It is definitely familiar. . . . Yes, Juliet's perfume. She . . . she called it . . . Wait . . . wait . . . wait . . . something like . . . something with a 'song' in it." He sniffed again.

"Yes, Skin Song!" Maggie exclaimed and came over and threw her arms around Gemetz. "I won, I won!"

"Well, I'm not paying," Debbie said with a pout. "He only got half of it."

"You were just about to say Skin Song, weren't you, sweetie?" Maggie asked Gemetz, pressing her cheek to his and giving him a squeeze around the waist.

"Yeah," Gemetz sighed, rubbing his cheek back against hers. "Just what I was going to say—Skin Song."

"Bet's off," Debbie protested. "Game called on account of coaching."

"Are all of you models?" Talbot asked, moving closer.

"Of course, dahling," Debbie said. "Ummm, and who are you?"

"I'm Len and this is Richie—and that's Joe," he said. "What kind? I mean, what do you model?"

"Hands," Maggie said, serpenting a hand toward him.

"Hair," Debbie said, flogging her long brown hair across his face.

"Jeans," said the redhead. "I'm Sharon."

"She means buns," Debbie corrected.

"Oh, yeah, let's see," Tiernan said, moving closer to Sharon and peeking around behind her.

"Watch it, Buster," she said and pushed him back playfully.

For the next half-hour the three Brooklyn interlopers were indeed up to their necks in fantastic Manhattan women. At one point, just as Tiernan was about to say they'd come over from Brooklyn, Talbot jabbed him in the ribs with his elbow and said they were all advertising executives living on the East Side. Gemetz denied this, saying he was a belly-button model with a loft in the Village.

"Yeah, he's into lint," Tiernan said.

"Of course, of course, and we're handling the account," Talbot added. "Lint's the big growth industry now. Gathering and gathering every day."

"Buy lint, make a bundle!" Tiernan declared.

"It's all in the belly button, all in the belly button," Gemetz said, spreading his shirt open between two pearl buttons and exposing his own.

"Ooooooo, there is some lint in there," Sharon said, peering into the opening.

"Of course there is," Gemetz said confidently. "Even as we speak, I'm collecting material, as it were, for my next TV appearance."

"Best little button in the business," Talbot said with a confident nod.

"How's this?" Gemetz said, taking a stance protruding his hairy stomach forward. "Ladies and gentlemen, this is where it's at!" he declared and then plunged two fingers into his navel and drew out an imaginary gob of lint.

"So, what do they do with it?" Maggie asked, laughing.

"Ear plugs!" Gemetz said proudly and stuck the gob into his right ear.

As they talked and joked, a pairing of sorts began to evolve: Maggie with Gemetz, Sharon with Tiernan and Debbie with Talbot. And for the next hour they kept the beer flowing, with the men buying, the women drinking thirstily and Talbot and Gemetz giving Tiernan approving nods for the success of his low-key approach. The Peaches was becoming jammed to the walls with new arrivals, however, and they found themselves being edged farther and farther away from the bar.

"You have to clear this aisle," a huge Indian bouncer with

massive shoulders and a purple turban grumbled at them as he pushed his way through.

"God, where'd he come from?" Gemetz asked after the bouncer had shoved him into Talbot's chest. "Looks like that guy in Orphan Annie—Punjab."

"That's Vijay," Sharon said, sipping her drink. "A lovely man."

"Don't fool around with him," Debbie warned almost in a whisper. "Totally crazy."

"Aw, Maggie thinks he's cute. Right, Mag?" Sharon said, wrinkling her nose at the hand model.

Maggie stuck her tongue out at the busty redhead.

"First time I ever heard of an Indian bouncer," Tiernan said. "I thought they were supposed to be little guys."

"Jesus, his arms are as big as my legs," Gemetz said.

"Maggie's his big love," Sharon sniped again.

"You know him, Maggie?" Gemetz asked.

"I let him buy me dinner once—and for dessert he asked me to marry him," Maggie said. "Very weird. I think he's out on loan from some loony bin."

In the next half hour Vijay cleared the aisle with his towering bulk four more times, each time seeming to go out of his way to bump Gemetz.

"Hey, whatta ya say we get out of this dump?" Sharon exclaimed after Vijay's last clearing operation.

"I want to dance!" Debbie said. "The Hot Fizz is just down the street."

"Not again," Maggie griped. "My feet can't take another night."

"The Hot Fizz?" Talbot asked.

"Disco," Sharon said. "You guys disco?"

"Not—" Tiernan started to say.

"Sure!" Talbot exclaimed, cutting him off. "The Hot Fizz it is."

"You guys go ahead," Maggie said. "I'm gonna have another drink and go home." Then she looked meaningfully at Gemetz and slipped her arm through his.

"Uh, well, yeah," Gemetz said. "I'm kinda pooped, too. Guess I'll just see Maggie, uh, gets home okay."

"Mmmmmm," Maggie said and squeezed his arm tighter.

"Oh, ho, ho!" Sharon exclaimed and gave them a knowing look.

"Come on!" Debbie said, pulling Talbot.

"Okay!" Talbot said enthusiastically and then reached into his inside jacket pocket and took out the twenty-dollar bill. "Richie, before we go, uh, here's that twenty I owe you," he said, giving Gemetz a wink and poking the bill down into his shirt pocket.

"Huh? Oh, yeah, thanks," Gemetz said, looking a little embarrassed.

"Yeah, watch out for muggers," Tiernan said, giving Gemetz a congratulatory pat on the back.

"And Vijay," Sharon said.

After Tiernan and Talbot left with Debbie and Sharon, Maggie asked Gemetz to buy her a Scotch and water. He ordered two of them and then had to jump back as Vijay came lumbering through again.

"I told you to keep this aisle clear," Vijay warned him. "Next time you have to leave."

"So, where're we supposed to stand, on the bar?" Maggie shouted at his broad back as he walked away. "Creep!"

"Don't rile him," Gemetz said and gave a shudder.

For the next fifteen minutes they were free of Vijay's clearing operations and had a chance to talk quietly. They were jammed up against each other by the crowd, talking mostly about her TV appearances as a hand model, keeping another conversation going with their eyes, slowly sipping their drinks, trying not to get them jostled by those squeezing past them in the aisle.

"You do have lovely hands," he murmured.

"They're insured," she said, looking at her long tapering fingers. "I have to wear gloves when I go outdoors. It's really a drag."

"So soft," he murmured, taking one of her hands in his.

"No cracks about hand jobs," she warned, giving him a wary look.

"Ha! I hadn't thought of that," he said, smiling.

"Let's have one more of these and then go," she said. "God, that tastes good after all that beer."

Her next Scotch led to a third Scotch and then a fourth, and pretty soon she was leaning against him for support. Vijay was practically hovering over them by now, coughing and making pained little animal sounds each time she snuggled against Gemetz.

"I am not going to tell you again—clear this aisle!" Vijay finally thundered and shouldered Gemetz roughly aside.

"You leave him alone, you . . . you big mongoloid!" Maggie shrieked at the bouncer, her face suddenly blazing with anger.

"Jesus, don't they ever feed this ape," Gemetz said, loud enough for Vijay to hear him.

"Okay, now you go!" Vijay said, stepping between Gemetz and Maggie.

"We'll both go," Maggie said, reaching in and jerking her coat off the back of a bar stool. "Come on, Richie!" She pressed through the crowded aisle with her coat thrown over her shoulder and her glass of Scotch still in her other hand.

"Maggie, wait!" Gemetz yelled as he put his drink on the bar and hurried after her.

"Maggie!" Vijay called out forlornly.

Gemetz and Maggie got blocked temporarily by the crowd about midway to the door, while Vijay pushed and shoved his way down the side of the bar and made it to the entrance ahead of them. As they were about to go out the door, Vijay was there waiting, looming over them with a wild look under his bushy eyebrows.

"Give me the glass, Maggie," Vijay ordered. "I will not allow you to steal our glasses."

"You got it!" she yelled at him and threw half a glass of Scotch onto his chest, splashing his chin and soaking his gray three-piece suit.

Vijay immediately reached out and captured her hand with the glass in it in his big paw.

"Aaaah! My hand," she screamed. "Let it go, you goddam freak!"

"Maggie, Maggie," the giant groaned, looking like he was about to cry as he continued to hold her hand in his fist.

For Gemetz it was the moment of truth—a final truth, he feared. The minute he made a move, he knew, the monster holding on to Maggie would turn and crush him. Okay, Richie, in two seconds you're going to be unconscious. But you've got to do it. He felt his ulcer contract and send a knife of pain up through him.

"Turn her loose, Godzilla!" he roared up at the giant and placed his hands on the huge forearm that was holding Maggie.

"Maggie, Maggie," Vijay moaned again, peeling the glass from her hand and now holding her by the wrist.

"Help!" Maggie yelled over her shoulder toward the bar.

"I said turn her loose," Gemetz said, trying to pry the iron fingers from around her wrist. At the same time he knew that once the hand released Maggie it would destroy him. His stomach was knotting in excruciating pain.

"I can't stand it!" the giant finally roared.

"Huh?" Gemetz asked and looked up in surprise.

"I will kill myself, Maggie!" Vijay sobbed and held the glass to his throat, while still holding on to her with his other hand.

"Vijay, please," Maggie said in a soothing tone. "Just let me loose and we'll talk about it. Tomorrow, Vijay. Goddam it, turn me loose," she said, slipping free as he loosened his grip.

"I want to die!" Vijay howled, pushing the rim of the glass into his throat and looking to the sky.

"Come on!" Maggie yelled at Gemetz and started running.

"Jesus," Gemetz said, looking in awe at the towering bouncer's agony. Then he took off after Maggie.

In a moment the manager of the bar came out with two other young men and tried to calm the big Indian down. Gemetz sighed with relief as he looked back over his shoulder and saw them leading him gently inside.

When they got around the corner, Maggie stopped and leaned against the side of a building panting. Gemetz was nearly doubled over with the pain in his stomach.

"Ugh!" he grunted and tried to straighten up.

"Oh, god, did he hit you, Richie?" she asked.

"No, just, ugh, my gut. Be okay in a minute."

"Oh, Richie, you were so brave back there," she said, putting her arm around his shoulder. "My brave little Richie."

Fighting back his pain, he straightened up and hailed a passing cab. As they rode uptown to her apartment on 86th Street in the Yorkville section he began to feel a little better.

"Whew!" he sighed. "I thought I was gonna be dead by now. A total nut job."

"Indians, who can figure them out?" she said.

"I don't know, maybe that's the way they bounce people in India," he said. "They really get mad at you, they'll set themselves on fire or something. Like those Buddhist monks during the Vietnamese war."

"No, Vijay doesn't have any trouble being mean," she said. "I've seen him crack heads lots of times over there. Vijay's problem is love. It's my fault, I guess. I keep going back there knowing it's driving him up the wall."

"He hurt your hand?" Gemetz asked.

"I don't think so," she said, rubbing it. "Just a little red."

He took it and kissed it.

"This is it, driver!" she called out as they came to a row of old buildings on 86th near the river. "Come up for a drink?" she asked.

"Why not?" he said, sliding out after her. "After that I need a couple."

"Shit, I just remembered. All I got is tequila."

"Great!" he said, putting his arm around her, and then turned and paid the driver.

When they got inside Maggie's tiny apartment, the phone was ringing and she pulled away from his attempt to embrace her and ran to answer it.

"Bobby!" she said after picking up the phone. "Where are you tonight? Charlottesville? Where's that? Oh!"

As she talked she carried the phone trailing a long extension cord over to a bookshelf where she tucked the receiver under her chin and picked up a half-empty bottle of tequila and a slightly dirty glass and handed them to Gemetz with a nod.

"No, I've been in all night," she said. "You did? Oh, yeah, I went out for cigarettes. Of course, I miss you, chubby-wubby!"

Gemetz shook his head and poured himself a drink and was about to sit down on a soft lounge chair when Maggie shook her head and pointed her finger at the sofa. Then she made a pulling motion at him, and after a minute he figured out what she was gesturing about. He put his drink down and pulled out the sofa bed.

"Aw, Bobby can't sleep again?" she said, flopping down on the bed and making a face at Gemetz.

He shook his head at her and then walked into the tiny kitchen off the studio room and found a glass on the sink. Bringing it back, he poured a tall drink and handed it to her. She took it and made a pained face at the phone.

Gemetz went back to his chair and sat down and began sipping his tequila. The harsh liquid went down hot and

seemed to set his ulcer on fire. Jesus, I hope she's got some
pot, he thought. Think I'm going to need it tonight.

"Daddy needs a little quickie-wickie?" she said.

Jesus, Gemetz thought. What the hell is going on?

"Are you lying down?" she asked the man on the other end
of the line. "Ummmmmm," she moaned. "Oh, Daddy, it's
sooooo big!" she sighed and then made an inch sign with two
fingers to Gemetz and shook her head. "Mmmmmmmmm
mmmmmmm," she moaned, "I can't get it all in my mouth."

Gemetz made a grimace and looked at her inquiringly. She
shrugged apologetically and made a male masturbatory motion
with her hand.

As she went on with more lascivious talk, Gemetz felt a
nausea rising in him and tried to quell it with the tequila. In a
moment he felt a tightening pain gathering in his stomach and
an uncontrollable urge to vomit. He put the drink on the arm of
the chair and looked around frantically for a door that would
lead to a bathroom. He spotted it at the other end of the room
and rushed toward it. Meanwhile, Maggie was going on with
her verbal quickie for Bobby Wobby.

He had barely made it to the commode when the black gush
came exploding from his mouth. What the hell had he eaten
that was black? he wondered. At the same time he felt his body
trembling and a cold sweat breaking out all over him. Jesus, he
thought, must've been something wrong with that tequila.

Afterward, he went over to the sink and splashed cold water
on his face to wash off the perspiration. The sweat was pouring
from him. Drying off his face and hands, he looked in the
mirror and was shocked by the pallor of his face. The sweat
was beginning to soak through his jacket, so he took it off and
pulled at his shirt to keep it from clinging to his body. What the
hell is happening to me? he wondered, feeling a panic starting.
Never this bad. Gotta get some pot quick.

Leaving the bathroom, he felt a growing heaviness in his
legs and a great desire to sit down and rest. Maggie was just
hanging up the phone as he crossed the room.

"God, that man can never sleep without his little orgasm—
and I mean *little*," she said, shaking her head. "You know how
I can tell? He makes a little squeak and then I hear him snoring.
Can you believe it—three hundred twenty pounds and he
makes a little squeak!"

Gemetz flung his damp coat over the back of the chair and

fell into it with a sigh of exhaustion. So tired, he thought. The trip across the room seemed like a mile.

"Say, you look awful!" Maggie said, sitting up a bit in the bed and squinting at him.

"Tequila hit me wrong," he sighed.

"My god, you're soaking wet!" she said.

"You got any pot, Maggie? It's my gut. Pot usually fixes it."

"Sure," she said and hopped up and went into the kitchen and opened the refrigerator. "I've got brownies or joints!" she called back.

"Joint!" he called back and tried to shake the growing drowsiness from his head. His breath was becoming shorter and his hands were trembling.

"This is good stuff," she said, coming in taking a drag on the lighted joint and handing it to him. "Oh, Richie, you look like you just took a shower."

"This'll do it," he said, reaching for the joint and taking a deep drag on it. "Who . . . who . . . [cough] . . . is Bobby?" he asked after he exhaled.

"My boyfriend," she said, kneeling down at his feet and taking the joint from him after he'd taken a second drag. "He's on the road a lot—sells pharmaceuticals."

"Hoh!" Gemetz gasped. "You say he's three hundred twenty pounds? Huh! Man, you like 'em big," he said, gasping for breath.

"I love fat men," she said, exhaling the drag she'd just taken on the joint. "Always have. My papa weighed nearly four hundred pounds—before his stroke." She handed him the joint and then she wrapped her arms around his knees. "But every now and then I really dig someone who's small and cuddly."

"Hoh, boy!" he gasped, finding it hard to keep his eyes open as another wave of drowsiness spread over him. He was becoming numb and found it too difficult to raise the joint to his mouth. "Take it," he said to her as it nearly fell from his limp fingers.

"Richie, you gonna be okay?" she asked, looking a little worried now.

"Yeah," he sighed. "Pot's working. . . . Don't feel the pain anymore. Damn ulcer . . . had it forever. Feel so sleepy now."

"You seeing a doctor?" she asked, getting to her knees.

"Nah. Gotta find a good one, I guess."

"My friend Nan, downstairs, has a terrific ulcer doctor," she said. "Cured her in just a few months. Brandt, I think she said his name was. Yeah, Brandt."

"Brandt," he said, feeling himself sinking down into the chair. Feeling so damned sleepy, he thought, and stretched his legs out. No more pain. So damned sleepy.

"Brandt, right," she said. "In the new Fuller Building, right around the corner on Eighty-fifth. Big glass building, you can't miss—Richie? You okay, Richie?"

"Sleepy," he sighed again. "Pot made me sleepy. Okay . . . okay," he murmured.

"Richie, come over and lie on the bed," she said, getting up and taking his limp hand.

"Sleepy," he murmured. "Just let me sleep a minute here."

Maggie watched him for a few seconds more and then let his hand down gently on the arm of the chair. He now seemed to be sleeping deeply and comfortably. She put out the joint in a nearby ashtray and knelt down and took off his shoes. Then she pulled an ottoman over and propped his legs on it, drawing a sleepy murmur from him. After that she took a blanket from her bed and brought it over to him. As she was covering him she could see the folded twenty-dollar bill Talbot had given him showing through the wet transparency of his shirt.

Let him sleep for a while, she thought, and went into the bathroom to get ready for bed. After she came out she sat on the edge of the bed and stared at him. Such a finely built man, she thought. So brave of him to stand up to Vijay for me. Poor man, I hope he's not seriously ill. Seems to be breathing easily.

"Well," she sighed in resignation and crawled over the bed and slipped under the cover. "Good night, Richie," she said softly and reached over and turned out the light.

At the Hot Fizz, Talbot and Tiernan were leaning over its long horseshoe bar and looking glumly at their dates being whirled and discoed around by two swarthy Latin young men dressed in tight-fitting light slacks and open-chested silk shirts.

"How can you compete with that?" Tiernan asked as the young man dancing with Sharon whipped her through a series of spaghetti twirls.

"I think I could learn," Talbot said, "but that greaseball out there has her hypnotized."

"Oh, well, at least Richie scored tonight," Tiernan said and took a long drink of beer.

The barnlike dance palace was pulsing with the Bee Gees recording of "More Than a Woman," with the red lighting around the edge of the rectangular dance floor giving a Danteesque aura to the writhing bodies in its glow. After they had paid their way in and stopped at the bar briefly for a drink, they had been literally dragged out onto the dance floor by Debbie and Sharon. While the girls had immediately gone into their exotic disco routines, Talbot and Tiernan had clumped around awkwardly like two farm laborers stepping through cow patties. The girls had almost fled from them after that and took up with the Latin whirling machines.

"Fuck it, I didn't come here to watch a teenybopper puberty rite," Talbot said and finished his beer.

"Wanna split?" Tiernan asked, pushing himself back from the bar.

"Yeah, let's hit a few more bars," Talbot said. "Quiet bars."

"What time is it?" Tiernan asked.

"Nearly one-thirty," Talbot said, looking at his watch.

"Hell, let's go home," Tiernan said, yawning.

"One more bar, then," Talbot said. "No telling what we might pick up."

"That's what I'm afraid of," Tiernan said, walking toward the exit.

"Look, we can't go down without a fight," Talbot said, catching up to him. "We set out tonight to score, right?"

"Come on," Tiernan complained. "Now you're sounding like one of them teenyboppers. We made a start, man. Next Saturday maybe we'll get lucky like Richie. It's still a good idea."

"One bar," Talbot insisted.

"All right, all right. . . . Maybe we'll run into a whole pack of nymphomaniacal insomniacs," Tiernan said, giving him a shove.

An hour and four bars later, they were driving back over the Brooklyn Bridge, with Tiernan looking sadly out over the harbor and Talbot frowning so hard his eyebrows were almost meeting.

"Fuck!" Talbot growled.

"Aw, forget it," Tiernan said, snapping out of his reverie about Mary.

"So, we'll learn to dance, right?" Talbot said, turning to him.

"Not me, brother," Tiernan said. "If I can't get them without turning myself into one of them disco dipshits I don't want 'em."

"Yeah, you're right," Talbot said, nodding resolutely. "We just picked a couple of losers. Plenty of women over there who don't dance. Look at Richie. His chick wanted no part of it."

"Jesus, she wasn't bad either, you know? Bet she makes him forget Juliet. That would be nice—Richie hitting it off with someone like that. Great chest on her."

"Dumb dropping Juliet like that," Talbot said.

"You gonna make a play for her again?" Tiernan asked.

"She turns me on, I'll admit," Talbot said, looking over but then shook his head. "But it would be a stab in Richie's back. We hang together, right?"

"Right," Tiernan said, admiring Talbot's sense of loyalty.

After leaving the bridge on the Brooklyn side, Talbot drove up Flatbush Avenue toward Park Slope. The rows of shabby stores and dimly lighted bars along the strip near the Slope were depressing after the East Side glitter. The night was mildly warm for late April and there were a number of derelicts hanging about the bars in this black section. On several street corners there were packs of black prostitutes standing out waving at cars.

"Ah, it must be spring," Talbot said. "The hookers are out in force."

As they stopped for a light a few blocks from the Plaza one of the hookers came over and leaned on the hood of the car wiggling her finger at Talbot. She had a tough broad-nosed face, but she had a huge bosom which was almost canted up toward her chin by her brassiere. When Talbot gave her a smirking grin, she pulled down the neck of her white knit sweater and exposed one of her breasts. Then she licked her finger and touched it to the nipple that was protruding through the hole in the middle of the black bra.

"I think she loves you, Len," Tiernan said and laughed.

Talbot smiled and shook his head at her and made a naughty-naughty gesture by rubbing his two index fingers. She responded by throwing him a finger and sliding off the car hood. As Talbot pulled the car ahead again after the light changed, he suddenly swung his head around and slowed down as he spotted two fairly innocent-looking young black women standing near a doorway on the corner. They appeared to be in their mid-twenties and were attractive in an almost housewifely way. Still, they might be hookers, he thought, judging by the slacks and sweaters they were wearing. Nice ass on that young one, he thought as he cruised slowly past them.

"What do you think?" he asked Tiernan as he kept the car moving almost at a crawl.

"You're kidding," Tiernan said, looking at him. "Come on, let's get out of here."

"They weren't bad," Talbot said, looking back at them through the rear-view mirror.

"Len, for Christ sake," Tiernan protested. "They're just probably going home from a party. Those were definitely not hookers."

"They're not going, they're standing," Talbot replied and stopped the car. "That makes 'em hookers."

"Who cares? We're not fucking any hookers."

Talbot pulled the car ahead and Tiernan let out a sigh of relief. But instead of driving straight ahead to the Plaza he turned right on the next street intending to circle the block.

"I wanna look at 'em again," Talbot said as Tiernan groaned.

"Len, you're out of your goddam tree!" Tiernan finally exclaimed as Talbot made another right.

"I just want to see if they're hookers," Talbot said. "I'm intrigued. I mean, what if they're amateurs—you know, married and out picking up a little extra money. That turn you on?"

"No, goddam it!" Tiernan sighed and slumped down in his seat. "Hey, you can't be that horny."

"Look, we set out tonight to do what?"

"Try the East Side," Tiernan replied.

"We also set out to change the way we look at life. We were going to get off our asses, quit being pissed on, right?"

"So?"

"So, dammit, Joe, it's important that we start taking what we want. We wanted to find some new ass tonight, right? Here we are going home with our tails between our legs. I don't like that. I say when we go after something we damn sure take it."

"So you wanna pick up a couple of black hookers?" Tiernan said and shook his head. "Man, that's not taking it—that's buying it!"

"Right now we're just going to see if they're hookers. Okay? We'll decide what to take later."

"Christ, I don't believe this," Tiernan said but feeling an excitement beginning in his guts. He'd never picked up a hooker before. He'd seen the black ladies of the night numerous times along Flatbush and had often wondered what kind of world they lived in. Right now the dark side street they were driving down scared the hell out of him. Dim shapes moved into doorways and ducked out of the light like cockroaches. When Talbot made his next right, the two women were still standing near the corner, talking to each other and giving wary glances toward their car.

"They are definitely not hookers," Tiernan protested.

"Just take it easy," Talbot said, easing the car up to the women. When he got abreast of them he stopped and smiled at them.

One of the women turned her back to him and said something to the other. She looked up and stared at him for a moment and then nodded hesitantly as he waved for her to come over. The other remained where she was with her back turned.

"Roll your window down," Talbot said as she came over.

"Len, for Christ—" Tiernan said, but then began rolling the window down.

"Hi," Talbot said cheerily as she came over to the car and folded her arms barely looking at him.

Tiernan looked at her and thought he recognized her from the neighborhood. A light-brown smooth-skinned woman with soft features.

"You cops?" she asked.

"Not us," Talbot laughed. "We're just looking for a little company. How . . . uh, how much?"

"Twenty," she said, looking in apprehensively.

"Joe?" Talbot asked, looking at Tiernan.

Tiernan frowned and glanced into the black woman's eyes. They were full of mistrust and impatience, yet there was something else there, some flickering excitement that matched his own. She's new to this, he thought. That makes two of us,

honey, he thought, letting his eyes stray down over her body.
She was nicely built, he thought.

"Where do you live?" Talbot asked.

"Round the corner," she said without taking her eyes off
Tiernan.

"Joe?" Talbot asked.

"I get her?" Tiernan asked, feeling his heart pounding.

"Right on!" Talbot exclaimed and slapped him on the
shoulder. "Let's get out. Okay, honey, go tell your friend," he
told the black woman.

Leaving the car parked at the curb, they followed the two
women around the corner to a rundown tenement and then up
four flights of rickety stairs to an apartment at the end of a
dank-smelling hall.

"You both live in the same apartment?" Talbot asked his
hooker, a younger woman than Tiernan's with the bony
youthfulness of a teenager. She had a delicately pretty face
though and was wearing heavy red lipstick.

Instead of answering him she just snorted a laugh and poked
the other woman, who was opening the door with her key.

"We splittin' it," the woman with Tiernan answered his
question.

"No men in here, are there?" Tiernan asked nervously.

"Huh-uh, no way," the younger one answered.

"We splittin' this place just *cuz* they ain't no men," the older
one said ruefully.

"I told you," Talbot whispered to Tiernan.

"Twenty apiece," Tiernan's woman said after they'd
stepped inside the apartment. "Just fuh one come."

"That's plenty," Talbot said, taking out his wallet.

They were standing in a long narrow hallway just inside the
door and after taking the money the women led them down it to
two adjoining bedrooms. As Talbot was about to step into one
behind his hooker, he turned and gave Tiernan a thumbs-up
sign. Tiernan shook his head in doubt and followed behind the
other woman.

"Nice room," Tiernan said to be polite and stood with his
hands in his pockets as she closed the door behind him. There
was a sickly sweet aroma of an incense stick burning in a glass
on the bureau. The room was bathed in purple light from a
lamp on the floor near a shade-drawn window. In the center of

the room there was a slightly sagging bed covered with a drab green bedspread.

"Be a minute," she said, pulling her sweater off over her head and tiptoeing into an adjoining room.

Through the wall on the opposite side of the room he could hear Talbot's laughter and the young hooker's squeal. In a moment the woman came out of the other room and motioned him to come over to the bed. She was wearing a pink see-through brassiere and had lovely perfect breasts.

"So," he said nervously, "what's your name?"

"Brenda," she said, coming over and putting her arms inside his jacket and wrapping them around him. He liked the feel of her soft breasts against him and the sure strong feel of her fingers massaging his back.

"Tha's a fancy shirt," she said, stroking across the silk garment Talbot had persuaded him to wear.

Then she stepped back from him about a foot and pulled down her slacks. He took off his coat and walked over to put it on the back of the kitchen chair in front of the dressing table, but on the way he stepped on something small that made a crunching sound. Reaching down, he picked up a child's black baby doll, its face crushed by his shoe.

"Oh, god," he said, holding it out to her. "I'm sorry. . . . I'll pay for it."

"It's okay, come on," she said, climbing naked onto the bed, her lithe shapely body glowing in the purple light.

"No, really, I'll—" he started to say but stopped when he heard the bronchial cough of a small child in the next room.

"Come on, damn it!" the woman almost snapped at him.

He came over and sat on the bed looking at her, the broken doll in his lap. God, you must hate me, he thought, looking at the anger in her eyes. Probably forced into this kind of crap to feed your kid.

"Well, you sho' cain't do nuthin' with all a them clothes on, boy!" she said, leaning toward him and starting to unbutton his shirt.

The child coughed again sending a shudder through Tiernan. He closed his eyes and shook his head slowly. Lynn had sounded just like that two years ago when she had bronchitis, he remembered. It was the sickest she'd ever been and they'd stayed up three nights watching her. Oh, Lynn, what am I doing?

"I . . . I'm sorry," he said, pulling her hand away from his shirt. "I can't, lady. It's too . . . it's—"

"You a fag, honey?" she asked sympathetically. "Hey, that's okay, honey," she said, reaching out to pet him.

"God . . . damn!" he howled at this final outrage and flung her arm back. Then he jumped up, rushed over and grabbed his coat off the chair and bolted from the room.

As he ran down the hallway, Talbot stepped out of his room stark naked to see what had happened.

"Hey, Joe!" he called out as Tiernan was going out the front door. "Hey, for Christ sake, wait!" he yelled and darted back into the room to get his clothes.

Outside, Tiernan shook his head and cried with fury and self-hate. He wanted to smash something and started running down the garbage-littered sidewalk punching his fists at the air.

"I won't live like this!" he howled and swung his fist at the sky. "I won't live in this sewer, God!" he yelled at the darkness over him. "I want my home . . . I want my home . . . I want my home!"

# CHAPTER
# EIGHTEEN

On Sunday morning Gemetz emerged from Maggie's bedroom pale and shaken after having thrown up and defecated enormous amounts of acid-blackened blood. He started unsteadily toward the chair he'd slept in during the night and then had to stop as another wave of dizziness caught him. He stood there weaving slightly and breathing through his nose. Can't panic, he thought, looking over at Maggie sleeping peacefully on her side of the sofa bed. Sunlight was beaming against the ceiling from over the tops of the heavy red drapes, but otherwise the room was dimmed and still. In a moment he continued to the chair and collapsed into it exhausted.

His body felt leaden and it took a great exertion of his will just to raise his legs onto the ottoman in front of him. Panting through his open mouth, he gazed tiredly at Maggie's sleeping face and shook his head. Maggie, wake up, he thought. One of your Saturday night bozos is bleeding to death.

On the night table near her outstretched hand a digital clock was flashing away the seconds in green illuminated numbers. Nearly eight-thirty, he thought. God, I've probably been bleeding all night. Feel so tired . . . feel like I've been filled with sand. Gotta get up . . . get a cab. Come on, Richie, get up. You wanna just sit here and die looking at Maggie's clock?

He watched the numbers changing steadily on the clock and felt himself sinking deeper into lethargy. Gotta go when your number's up, man, he told himself and watched the clock. Pick a number, Richie. What's your number? Flip, flip, flip . . . lotsa numbers. One of 'em's mine. Richie's number.

Poor Maggie, he thought, looking at the young woman sleeping across from him on the bed. Dirty trick to play on you, waking up with a stiff in your apartment. What'll old chubby-wubby say? Flip, flip, flip . . . pick a number.

Wonder if Juliet will come to my funeral? he thought. He closed his eyes and imagined her looking down at him in his open coffin. Yes, there he was, serene and handsome. Great-looking corpse, Richie, he congratulated himself, and so heartbreakingly young. Tears breaking over Juliet's cheeks now, her hand reaching out to touch him back to life. Too late, Juliet, he thought, smiling sadly. I'm gone, Juliet. I love you with all my heart. I didn't want to die, I—

What the hell are you doing, he thought, opening his eyes wide. Get your ass up or you *are* going to die! He pushed himself up from the chair and stood for a moment to get his balance. The nausea was starting again. That meant more blood pouring into his stomach. Body throws it out . . . won't tolerate it in the digestive system, he remembered from his father's bouts with bleeding ulcers. Both ends, he thought, feeling the same urgency in his bowels again. Gotta get to a hospital. Keep me on my feet, Papa, he prayed, stepping into his shoes. Then grabbing his still-damp jacket from where it was plastered against the back of the chair, he headed for the front door.

Leaving Maggie's building, he had to squint against the bright morning sunlight. The tree-lined street was deserted and quiet—that eerie ghost-town quiet of Manhattan on Sunday mornings. I'm dying, he thought, pushing his heavy legs toward York Avenue at the corner, going to be tough finding a cab. Should have called for one. Should have called for an ambulance. Come on, come on, he urged himself and tried to still the panic that was driving up his nausea.

Can't throw up more blood, he told himself. Can't have much left in me. The amount he'd evacuated in Maggie's bathroom had frightened him. At least a quart, he thought. How many quarts in the body? Come on, come on. He panted and staggered on toward the corner.

When he got to York, there was only a few cars going by and not a cab in sight. He turned toward 85th and felt the resistance against his legs increasing. His vision was blurring in the bright glare of the morning, and midway down the block he had to stop and lean against a building to keep from falling down. God, please help me, he prayed. Give me a cab . . . gonna die. He drew in deep breaths through his mouth to stem the nausea and could smell the East River over beyond the line of buildings across the street.

Cab, he said to himself as he spotted something yellow and tiny at the end of his blurred vision. But his nausea was insisting now, coming up. He lurched out to the curb and vomited a rush of the black tarry blood. Oh, god, I'm pouring inside, he thought and kept raising his head to keep track of the cab. It drew near just as he let go with another gush and veered away and kept going.

"Wait . . . wait!" he moaned after it and waved, "Oh, fuck, I'm dying, man. Gimme a break!"

He wiped his mouth on his sleeve and continued down the street. In a moment, he was standing on the corner of 85th and looking diagonally across at a new glass office tower with wide marble sidewalks. Over the canopied entrance there was a sign in gold lettering: FULLER MEDICAL ARTS BUILDING.

"Fuck it," he murmured, realizing that on Sunday there wouldn't be any doctors within fifty miles of it.

Feeling himself about to topple off the curb, he grabbed onto a bus-stop stanchion and held on. Still no cabs in sight, he thought. Gotta get help . . . gotta stop somebody's car, he thought. He waited a moment and drew in as much breath as he could and resolved he would step out into the middle of York Avenue and keep waving until somebody stopped. Can't just drop dead on the sidewalk, he thought.

Then glancing back toward the Fuller Building, he saw two young men in doctor's whites walking into the building. He couldn't believe his eyes. Interns, he thought, probably coming from some hospital. "Hey, wait! Hey, I need . . . ," he called and then started moving his legs in the direction of the Fuller Building entrance.

Even if I miss them, there's gotta be a security guard at the door. He can get me an ambulance. Come on, come on, he thought, walking faster and trying not to fall.

Entering the building, he found the security guard's desk

next to a bank of TV monitors beaming pictures of empty
corridors inside the building. But the guard was gone and there
was no sign of the doctors. Looking toward the elevators, he
saw the numbers changing over one of them and hurried
toward it. He would watch where it stopped and take another
elevator up to that level. But when he got to it the numbers
were descending again—18,17,16 . . . Has to be somewhere
around the twentieth floor, he guessed and stepped into the
nearest open elevator and pushed the button for the twentieth
floor.

Thank god, he thought, leaning tiredly into a corner of the
now ascending elevator. A miracle seeing those two doctors. A
miracle! He grimaced as the pressure to move his bowels began
to surge. Blood filling up my guts, he thought. They'll have
some kind of shot that can slow it down. Wonder what the hell
they're doing in here on a Sunday morning. A miracle!

When the elevator stopped, he pushed himself from the
corner and stumbled out into an orange-carpeted hallway.
There were about ten closed doors along the hall with various
doctors' names on them. Which one, which one? he wondered
as he forced himself along the hall. Try 'em all, he told himself
and started ringing the little doorbells on each one.

Oh, Christ, I've gotta shit, he thought, holding his breath
and praying someone would hurry out. God, there must be a
restroom somewhere along here. He was beginning to panic
now, fearing he would mess himself before help came.
Moaning with the effort he was making to resist his body's
effort to drive the blood out, he began pounding on the doors.

"Please," he cried and moved down the line of doors
slamming them with his fist.

At that moment, the young security guard had returned to his
desk near the closed-circuit TV monitors and was about to sit
down when he saw Gemetz on one of them. "Goddam!" he
gasped and put down his container of coffee. "Another
druggie," he said, watching the figure on the TV screen
staggering along and trying the doors. He quickly dialed the
Nineteenth Police Precinct house and asked for help.

By now Gemetz had tried all the doors and was crying with
desperation as he could no longer hold back the pressure in his
bowels. At the same time, his nausea was building up toward
his throat and bringing him to the edge of collapsing onto the

floor and just letting go. He couldn't allow them to find him like that, lying in his own shit.

A few feet away he saw the exit sign to the stairwell and decided he would try to get down it to the next floor, where he would hopefully find the doctors. Pulling open the painted steel door, he lurched into the stairwell and nearly toppled over its railing down into the twenty-story air shaft.

"Oh, dear god, please . . . please," he cried and grunted with his efforts to constrict his bowels. "Give me strength," he panted and started down the cement stairs to the next floor.

But when he got to the nineteenth-floor exit door he found it locked. Christ, I'm trapped, he thought, realizing that for security reasons the doors would be locked from the inside. He started back up the stairs to the twentieth-floor door again, hoping that by opening it from the inside he'd disengaged the security lock. His panic was full-blown now and sent him staggering and crawling up the stairs. The door was locked.

"Can't hold it," he gasped and began tearing at his belt to let down his pants and relieve himself of the agonizing pressure. But he'd barely started pushing them down when his bowels gave way in an explosion of black diarrheal fluid, saturating his pants, legs and hands. He collapsed to his knees sobbing in despair as the blood continued to spasm out of him. The stench sickened him and he began vomiting as he crawled toward the stairs through his own muck.

"Help me," he cried, raising a besmeared hand out before him. His vision was blurring out and he felt some paralyzing force closing around him. In the next instant he was tumbling into space and then pitching headlong like a lifeless dummy down the stairs.

He came to rest at the turn of the stairs, his stained legs twisted in his pants and his face jammed into the corner of the stairwell. He could no longer feel his body and lay there with his eyes open, staring at his blood-grimed fingers. The numbing force had closed over him now, and as his mind slipped into darkness his own small voice was echoing somewhere deep within him, "I died . . . I died . . . I died." The force was stronger than the voice and he closed his eyes slowly and let it carry him away, down through the stairs, down, down, through the air shaft and into a black endless abyss.

Descending now into peace . . . a lovely floating peace

that he yearned for . . . taking him away from all his torments . . . so soft and good, he thought, loving the enveloping darkness. A strange and wonderful journey taking him deeper and deeper into a void that had no meaning other than direction.

Then from somewhere above him voices, distant and alien, searching down through his lovely darkness to find him.

*"Got a pulse?"*

Swimming away in darkness from the sounds. Hands touching his body, rolling it, lifting it. Darting deeper, escaping into the rising black clouds. Never find me, never find me, he thought joyfully.

*"Mount Sinai's closest . . . better take him in the squad car."*

Never find me again, never find me . . .

*"Get the door!"*

Light coming from somewhere. . . . Where?

*"No, you drive."*

He swam toward the light that was flowing toward him over horizons of darkness. Oh, there . . . there . . . how beautiful, he thought as he came out of the night onto a placid lake shimmering in soft dawn light. Juliet bathing at its edge, smiling serenely at him. Come in, come in, her smile said, reaching for him, laughing and kissing him, washing away his stains.

*"Easy buddy."*

*"What'd he say?"*

Juliet's soft hands cupping water over his face, bathing and stroking him tenderly.

# CHAPTER
# NINETEEN

"All right, ladies and gentlemen, she's going to go for it!" the announcer shouted and triggered a riot of applause and cheers from the studio audience. "This is it, Mrs. Brunson, this is for the eighteen thousand dollars, the new Thunderbird, the trip to Honolulu for you and Mr. Brunson. This is your 'Fling at Fortune'!"

More screams from the audience along with a cacophony of honks, buzzers and blats from the quiz-show band.

The noise from the television set above the patient in the next bed awakened Gemetz into a world of intense pain—clutching pain, as though some grotesque thing were sitting on him with its claws embedded deep into his abdomen. He groaned and tried to brush the thing away but his hand only bumped against a numb mound of bandages. Something was stuck in the back of his throat, moving and making him gag as he tried to swallow.

Opening his eyes in panic, he found himself in a sunlit room with tubes running down from plasma bottles on either side of him, red into his left arm, clear into his right, and a tube running from his nose down over his chest and over the side of the bed, this one passing some kind of green slime in little jerky movements from inside of him. He panted to control his fear and reached up and touched where the green tube was taped to his nose, realizing by its slight movement that it was the thing hurting the back of his throat.

"You have thirty seconds, Mrs. Brunson."

"Help me," Gemetz rasped in a weak voice and twisted his head from side to side in pain.

To his left he saw a deeply tanned middle-aged man with a bald head sitting up in bed and eagerly watching Mrs. Brunson struggling in thought on the television screen. To his right he saw Tiernan rising out of an easy chair and coming toward him.

"Richie?"

"Pa—Pain," Gemetz said, touching the lump of bandages under the sheet.

"Hold on, Richie, I'll get the nurse!" Tiernan exclaimed and hurried from the room.

Oh, god, it's happened, Gemetz thought, closing his eyes and trying to hide in darkness from the pain. I've been cut open. Just like Papa. Oh, god . . . oh, god . . . He tried to remember how it had happened, but his mind was a tumble of images—Maggie's digital clock . . . numbers lighting up over an elevator door . . . a long orange-carpeted hallway . . . a musty stairwell . . . bright lights burning his eyes . . . doctors leaning over him in white surgical masks . . . Juliet's face.

"Richard?" a woman's voice asked over him.

He opened his eyes and found a heavyset nurse leaning into his face. Her blue eyes were magnified down over her fat cheeks by thick glasses.

"Richard? Do you know where you are?"

"Hel— Help me," he whispered. "Pain."

"You've had surgery, Richard. You're at Mount Sinai Hospital, and you're going to be all right."

"No . . . pain," he protested as the pain sliced through him, making him feel he was coming apart in sections.

"Well, well, Mr. Gemetz," a young doctor said, coming up alongside of the nurse. "Good to see you awake finally. Do you remember me, I'm Dr. Schwartz?"

Gemetz could only shake his head.

"When was his last shot?" the doctor asked.

"Three hours about," the nurse replied.

"No, you idiot!" the man in the next bed howled and shook

his fist at poor Mrs. Brunson, who had just flubbed the big question.

"Okay, give him another hundred milligrams of Demerol," the doctor said. "You'll be okay in just a minute, Mr. Gemetz."

"I . . . I . . . thought I was dead," Gemetz said, remembering fading out after his fall in the stairwell.

"You were a lucky man, Mr. Gemetz," the doctor said. "Five more minutes and you would have bled to death. Those officers saved your life."

"What . . . officers?"

"You were found on some stairs in the Fuller Building yesterday morning and—"

"Yesterday?"

"Yes, you've been mostly asleep since surgery. But Dr. Slattery did a terrific job on you and you're going to be fine."

"Ulcer . . . per— perforated?"

"Well, it ate into a complex of arteries in your duodenum, and you sprang one hell of a leak. I'd say you were running on empty when they brought you in."

"That was some snooze you took, old man," Tiernan said from the other side of the bed.

"Hi . . . hi, Joe," he said and smiled weakly at Tiernan. "How'd you know I was here?"

"Juliet," Tiernan said. "You must have been conscious enough to give them her number. She called me and Len."

"Juliet!" Gemetz exclaimed and tried to sit up and look around. "Owwwww!" he yelled as the pain sliced through him.

"That's the young woman who was in?" the doctor asked Tiernan.

"Yeah, Richie, she's been in twice to see you but you were too unsociable to wake up and say hello."

The nurse came over then with a hypodermic needle and after turning him slightly gave him an injection of the pain killer in the hip. In a few minutes it began to take effect and he felt himself sinking into a pink warm drowsiness.

"Tell Juliet . . . tell . . ." he said and fought against the perspiring sleep that was overtaking him.

"Don't worry, Rich," Tiernan said, stroking his shoulder. "I'm bringing her and Len over tomorrow night. You just get some sleep. Glad you're back with us, man."

"Tell . . . Jul . . . et . . ." In a moment he was drifting away on the pink Demerol cloud, his mind full of Juliet coming to see him.

The rest of the afternoon and evening was a blur of more television quiz shows, pain, Demerol injections and sweaty sleep. Somewhere in all of it, Dr. Slattery had come in and explained his operation—small piece of the stomach removed, vagus nerve cut, very little chance of another ulcer occurring— and told him he would probably be in the hospital for two weeks. A lot would depend on how soon his intestines started working again. Surgery always paralyzed them briefly and stopped the peristaltic motion that would eliminate his food. Until then the tube running down through his nose and throat into his stomach would have to remain and he would be fed intravenously. Two or three days, the doctor said, and then they would begin feeding him very bland food for a few more days and then have him eating almost regularly within ten days.

"What can I eat after I get out?" Gemetz had asked.

"With the vagus nerve cut, you'll probably never have another ulcer," the doctor had said. "You can eat tin cans if you want to."

The next morning, Drs. Slattery and Schwartz dropped in again and changed his bandages and assured him that he was doing fine. Dr. Schwartz listened to his intestines with his stethoscope and said that they had not started moving yet.

"Be good to get up and try to walk as soon as you can," Dr. Schwartz said, "that helps to get them started."

"Oh, god, I'll do it," Gemetz said. "I can't stand this thing in my throat."

Gemetz got through the rest of the day marking time in Mr. Kadin's TV quiz shows and the Demerol shots the nurse came in to give him every four hours. Every minute and hour that passed brought him closer to the moment he would see Juliet that night during visiting hours. He had not seen her since the morning of his father's funeral, but now it seemed like another lifetime. And it was, he thought, because he'd come back from the dead to a new life . . . his life . . . and Juliet would be a major part of it.

As far as he knew, Linda and the kids did not know of his situation and he intended to keep it that way. By the time she came back from her opera engagement in June, he'd be out of the hospital and back to work. No need to worry the kids now by telling them. It was fantastic, he thought, that the cutting of the vagus nerve would keep him from getting another ulcer, keep him from being slowly whittled away with a succession of new operations as had happened to his father. Now if Juliet only would hurry up and get here, he thought.

That evening, just before visiting time, the pain had become too intense again and he'd been given another shot of Demerol. As he started to drowse off he begged the nurse to tell him when Juliet arrived.

He was awakened by the smell of lavender. Opening his eyes, he turned to see the little table beside his bed and found a lush sprig of it resting in a glass of water. It was her favorite flower. She'd been here and gone, he thought and let out a moan.

"About time," Tiernan said, standing on the other side of the bed.

"Juliet . . . she's gone?" Gemetz sighed and tried to look around.

"I'm here, Richie," she said, coming from behind Tiernan and followed by Talbot, who gave him a thumbs-up sign over her head.

"Juliet!" He gasped and tried to raise himself but was pressed back by the pain.

"How ya doin', Richie?" she asked and came closer to him so he'd lie back down. "You sure had us worried."

"Juliet, I . . ." he stammered and then looked over at Tiernan and Talbot.

"Uh, Len, what say we go take another look at that nurse down the hall," Tiernan said and winked at Gemetz.

Gemetz nodded his appreciation and closed his eyes as he tried to get his breath. When they were alone, he looked up at her and took her hand. She had cut her hair a little shorter and her face looked thinner but lovelier. Oh, god, I love you, he thought. She was wearing a light blue flowered spring dress and he felt himself almost dizzy with the sight of her.

"I'm glad you're okay," she said, smiling calmly at him.

"Marry me," he said, looking intently into her dark blue eyes.

"Richie," she said in surprise and started to draw her hand from his.

"Marry me, Juliet. . . . I'm so sorry. . . . I love you so much."

"Richie, please don't," she said, biting her lip and turning her head away. "I—"

"Marry me!" he almost shouted.

Mr. Kadin who had been watching them, lifted his eyes to the ceiling and turned on his television set to remove himself.

"Can't . . . can't I just be concerned about you?" she asked him as her tears began to form. "I just wanted to say I was sorry what happened to you. Please don't talk like this, Richie."

"Will you think about it, then?"

"No, Richie," she pleaded and pulled her hand away. "I don't want to get into that again. It's too painful. I've got my life together now and I'm doing fine, Richie. I just want you to get well . . . and be happy."

"June first," he said, reaching for her hand.

"What?" she asked and took her hand away again.

"On the bridge," he said, still looking intently into her eyes. "I'm going to be there waiting for you, Juliet. At noon on June first. At the place where we left off . . . I'm alive now, Juliet. I can't tell you what's happened to me. I am alive and I want to live . . . and it's because of you. I had this dream about you . . . when I thought I was dying. Maybe I was dying—"

"I don't want to hear it, Richie," she said and started crying.

"Just remember June first, Juliet. Just remember that I am going to be on that bridge."

"I gotta go now, Richie," she said, turning from him. "You don't know what you're saying."

"At noon, don't forget," he said.

"No, Richie. Just . . . just . . . no," she said and ran from the room.

"I love . . . you," he shouted after her and then closed his eyes and began to cry, each sob wrenching up pain from his abdomen.

For a moment there was only the sound of Mr. Kadin's television set and then Tiernan came into the room shaking his head. Mr. Kadin looked at Tiernan and then at Gemetz and sighed. "Oy veh!"

"Richie, what the hell happened?" Tiernan said. "Juliet just ran down the hall crying."

"She, ah, wouldn't marry him," Mr. Kadin said after

Gemetz continued to lie there silently with his eyes closed, gritting his teeth against the pain.

"Aw, Richie, buddy," Tiernan said and put his hand on Gemetz's shoulder. "Don't push it now. Just get well. She'll be there when you're ready for her. I know it. Come on, Rich—"

"I love her," Gemetz moaned.

"I know, I know," Tiernan said soothingly.

Talbot walked in and gave Tiernan a shrug. He had followed Juliet down in the elevator and tried to talk to her, find out what had happened. All she would tell him was that he had to make Richie understand that she was just a friend, that she cared about what happened to him, but that the rest was over. He couldn't persuade her to wait and let them drive her back to Brooklyn.

"How's Juliet?" Tiernan asked.

"She went home," Talbot said. "What happened?"

Tiernan shook his head for Talbot to shut off the subject.

"Oh, oh . . . get the nurse," Gemetz grunted as the pain became too intense for him to bear. "I need . . . a shot."

Talbot wheeled around and ran out to get the nurse. Tiernan stayed by and patted Gemetz on the shoulder and tried to get him calmed down.

"You never did tell us about Maggie," he said, trying to get Richie's mind off Juliet. "I won't even tell you what me and Len wound up with. You might bust all your stitches."

"I'm going to be there, Joe!" Gemetz grunted.

"Where's that, Rich?"

"Just tell Juliet . . . tell her every time you see her . . . tell her I said I'm going to be there!"


Toward the end of the week, Gemetz felt able enough to get up and try walking a few steps around the room with the help of a nurse or one of his friends. In between quiz shows, Mr. Kadin encouraged him. But the paralysis in his intestines showed no signs of letting up and he had to remain hooked up to his glucose bottle, pushing it on ahead of him on a wheeled pole. The Levine tube also remained in place, sticking out of his nose and pinned to his shirt after it was disconnected from its suction machine.

On Sunday morning, a week after his hospitalization, Tiernan found him walking slowly down the corridor, dressed in an old red bathrobe, his hair and beard shaggy, and he was

pushing his plasma bottle on its pole. He appeared gaunt and
weary and did not look up as he trudged past Tiernan in his
slippers.

"Hey, you're beginning to look like John the Baptist!"
Tiernan called after him.

"Oh, hi, Joe," he said, looking halfway around and then
resuming his circuit of the corridor.

"Still no luck, huh?" Tiernan said, coming alongside of him
and walking slowly with his hands in his pockets.

"No," Gemetz sighed. "Just call me the gutless wonder."

"Aw, they'll start up," Tiernan said. "It's only been a week.
Some people go a month, according to Dr. what's-his-foot."

"This is to cheer me up?" Gemetz asked.

"Shit, I'm sorry," Tiernan said, frowning.

"Seen Juliet?" Gemetz asked.

"Oh, yeah, I meant to tell you. I saw her in the Korean
market yesterday. Looks great."

"And . . ."

"And what?"

"What'd she say?"

"Nothing. Just hi. I, uh, didn't tell her that business about
'you'll be there.' What the hell does it mean?"

"Just tell her. She'll know. I've gotta get out of here, Joe."

"How do they know when your intestines are working?"

"I fart," Gemetz said with a little smile.

"No?"

"Yeah, half the hospital is waiting for me to fart."

"All you gotta do is fart?"

"Man, I'd give anything just to fart. My kingdom for a fart!
Oh, God, grant that I may sound my horn once more!" Gemetz
said, calling to the heavens.

"Well, how do you know you haven't already farted
. . . in your sleep, I mean?"

"I keep a nurse on watch."

They trudged along like this for another half-hour, Gemetz
pushing his glucose bottle and Tiernan cracking jokes to keep
his friend's spirits up.

By Saturday of the next week, Gemetz's intestines were still
paralyzed despite hours of walking in corridors each day. He
had not shaved and after two weeks of being fed intravenously
his face was looking hollowed out. There were now raw
swollen patches on his wrist where the intravenous needle had

irritated the flesh from being in so long. The greatest toll, however, had been on his spirit.

Tiernan and Talbot had been visiting nearly every day, trying to cheer him up, walking the circuits with him, dredging up every bit of anal humor they could find to encourage his flatulence.

At one point they had spent an entire hour walking around the corridor making different farting noises with their mouths and drawing frowns from the nurses. At night and at various times during the day, they would phone him, making a farting noise and hang up. Once Mr. Kadin had picked up the phone, winced and handed it to Gemetz saying, "It's for you."

Nothing had helped, but on Saturday night Talbot had gotten Gemetz to laugh by persuading two of the nurses to come in and chant a bunch of Apache words, which he insisted were an ancient prayer for wind.

After leaving Gemetz that night, Tiernan and Talbot drove back to Brooklyn and decided to stop in at Larsky's. It was nearly ten o'clock, and as they were entering, Susan was coming out with a tall brawny fellow, who looked like he might have played guard for the Giants. She didn't say anything but just smiled and took the big man's arm and started across the street toward Garfield. Talbot was about to go after her when Tiernan grabbed his arm and pulled him toward the door.

"Keep it mellow," Tiernan said. "She's leaving."

"Jesus, now she's going with a black," Talbot said, stepping back outside to get one last look at her companion, who was only slightly tanned but had very kinky brown hair.

"Come on, I'll buy you a beer," Tiernan said, pulling him back inside.

The bar was fairly crowded, but Talbot immediately spotted Frieda sitting at her usual place down at the end under the Tiffany lamp. Sitting beside her was someone they had not seen in months, Verna. She had fallen madly in love with a drugged-out rock singer and had gone off to Denver with him to try to get him back on his feet in the good clean Rocky Mountain air. Now she looked like she'd been on drugs—hollow around the eyes and down about twenty pounds.

"God, is that Verna?" Tiernan asked.

"Yeah, she looks like she's been under a rock."

Frieda nodded to them as they pushed in beside her. Verna

looked up briefly and reached for her drink with a shaking hand.

"'Lo, boys," Verna said after taking a gulp.

"Hey, babe, how was Denver?" Tiernan asked, giving her a hug.

"Bad," she said and pulled his arm from her waist.

"How is Mr. Gemetz?" Frieda asked and made an expression with her face for them to go slow with Verna.

"Nothing yet," Talbot said, shaking his head.

"I was telling Verna about him," Frieda said.

"Yeah, tough break," Verna said and took another drink.

"I see we just missed Susan," Talbot said and gave Danny a two-fingered sign for two beers.

"Oh, god! I was hoping you would not come," Frieda said.

"Some clown she picked up this time," he said and grabbed up his beer as soon as Danny put the two brimming mugs on the counter. "She let him pick her up?"

"They came in together," Frieda said, stroking his arm. "Len, don't think. Okay?"

"Don't advise me. Okay?" he shot back and pulled his arm away from her.

"Of course," she said and turned away.

"Ah, boy, a great night, a great night." Tiernan sighed.

For a while they just quietly drank their beers and watched the crowd. Talbot noticed Juliet's roommate, Annie, leaning against the jukebox and waiting for someone to ask her to dance. He did not see Juliet around anywhere, but he remembered how she and Gemetz used to dance and play around down at that end of the bar. He couldn't imagine Richie playing like that again. He looked so old and wasted now, walking his legs off trying to get his lifeless gut moving again. Jesus, they had all seemed to age. Everything seemed to have gone to shit since Susan had invaded Larsky's . . . poisoned it somehow.

At eleven o'clock the phone behind the bar rang and Tommy Larsky answered it.

"Hello? Who? Yeah, deah both heah. Who's dis, Richie? How ya doin', Richie? I hoid about your operation."

Talbot looked at Tiernan, who looked back and shrugged. Jesus, what now? Tiernan wondered.

"Okay, hold on a minute, Richie," Tommy said and handed the phone over toward Tiernan. "It's Richie."

"Hey, Rich, what's up?" Tiernan asked.

There was a quiet now at their end of the bar as those standing around waited to hear what was going on. Tiernan looked over at Talbot and raised his hand in anticipation.

"You're kidding," Tiernan said in awe.

"What?" Talbot asked.

"What happened?" Tommy asked.

"You're sure?" Tiernan asked.

"For Christ sake!" Talbot exploded with impatience.

"How big?" Tiernan asked.

Tommy turned to a noisy patron near him and shushed him to be quiet.

"Two?" Tiernan asked in surprise.

"Goddam it!" Talbot cursed.

"One little and one big?" Tiernan went on.

"Gimme the fucking phone!" Talbot said and made a grab for it.

"Hallelujah!" Tiernan yelled.

"You mean he . . . ?" Talbot asked.

"He farted!" Tiernan roared. "Richie farted. . . . Richie farted!"

"Oh, how wonderful!" Frieda exclaimed and clapped her hands.

"Yeeeeeeeeehaaaaaaagh!" Talbot yelled and grabbed Frieda off her chair and started dancing her around the floor.

"Three cheers for Richie!" Tiernan yelled across the bar. "Free beers for everybody!"

A great applause went up across the bar and the Larsky brothers started running for the beer taps, laughing and patting each other on the back.

"Hey, he's coming home on Thursday!" Tiernan announced.

# CHAPTER
# TWENTY

On the following Thursday, Gemetz was released from the hospital and given a ride back to his apartment by Talbot. Tiernan and Frieda and Verna were on hand when they got there and for most of the day, until Gemetz got tired and slowly made his way up into his loft-bed, they stayed around and tried to create a party atmosphere.

"Two weeks, Richie boy, then it's back on the jogging trail!" Talbot had yelled to him as they were leaving.

"I have to get a note from my doctor," Gemetz replied from the loft-bed. "I'm sure he'll want me to take it easy for at least six months."

"Two weeks!" Talbot repeated. "That goes for you, too, Joe," he said to Tiernan, who was sneaking around behind him. "You haven't gotten your ass out of bed to run in more'n a month."

"Get me one of those notes, too, Richie!" Tiernan called out.

"Two weeks!" Talbot exclaimed. "After that, all malingerers will be shot!"

"Go suck a tennis shoe!" Gemetz shouted back and flopped back on his pillow.

"Yeah!" Tiernan agreed. "See ya, Richie!"

On Saturday morning, Talbot was standing in front of his
dressing mirror making facetious muscle-man poses in the
classy blue jogging pants Frieda had bought for him the day
before. She was sitting on the bed with just his white silk shirt
on taking pins out of the sailor-styled top to the new jogging
outfit, and looking up occasionally to raspberry one of his
hairy-chested poses.

Turning sideways to admire the double line of silver piping
running down the side of each pant leg, he suddenly snapped
into his best Mr. America pose—gut sucked in, shoulders
bunched forward, fists pressed together at his groin. Then in
magnificent disdain he slowly turned his head toward Frieda—
a picture of indestructible manhood, except for his cheeks
being blown out from holding his breath and his eyes being
crossed.

"There, you idiot!" She laughed and threw the shirt in his
face.

"Igor like," he grunted and pulled the shirt on, mussing his
hair down over his eyes in the process.

Facing the long stained mirror again, he squatted his knees
out and assumed a shaggy-haired gorilla pose.

"No, Len, stand up straight, it looks beautiful on you," she
said, lying down on the bed and looking at him admiringly.

"Ah, yes, splendid—absolutely splendid," he said, pushing
his hair back and turning this way and that in a foppish manner.

But he did like the outfit and he loved Frieda for the sacrifice
she must have made to buy it. The piping down the arms and
legs gave him a military feel, and for an instant the image of
his father dressing before his mirror on those parade-drill
mornings came to mind. He straightened himself into military
attention and narrowed his eyes the way he had seen his father
do when he was a boy.

"Cap!" he ordered and snapped his fingers toward Frieda.

"What?" she asked, smiling.

"Crop!" he barked and snapped his fingers again.

"A crop? What is this—a crop?" she asked, looking
amused.

Brushing down the few wrinkles in the jogging shirt, he
squared his shoulders, stood erect and the saluted himself. And
then he made a military right-face toward Frieda, regarded her
with a superior air and leaped from where he was standing on
top of her, pressing himself in between her legs.

"I have your crop," he murmured and nuzzled into her neck.

"Good," she murmured back and dug her fingernails into his buttocks. "I think it's so silly to tire yourself running."

"Nope!" he asserted and raised himself on his hands and knees over her. "The jogging trail calls me. Duty doth beckon me with distant trumpet. Alas, my lass, I am called away!"

"Oh, shut up!" she said and pulled him down on top of her again.

"Nope!" he said, springing up on all fours again. "A man's duty is his . . ." But he stopped as she began licking her lips lasciviously and reaching between his legs for his *crop*.

"That is, I . . ." he moaned and started to give way under the slow stroking.

"Yes, *mein General?*" she asked seductively.

"Funny thing about duty," he sighed and lowered himself slowly onto her, groaning with pleasure as she locked her legs over his buttocks.

In a moment her mouth was hungrily on his and they were writhing together over the bed. But just as she had pulled the elastic-waisted pants down over his hips there was the metallic rapping of a coin against the window.

"Damn, it's Tiernan!" Talbot gasped, raising his flushed face and looking toward the shuttered windows.

"What does he want?" she asked.

"How the hell do I know?" he said, rolling from the bed.

Tucking his erection between his legs, he pulled his pants back up and hopped over to the window. When he opened the shutters and peeked out, Tiernan was peeking in with a maniacal grin on his face. He was dressed in his jogging clothes and wiggling his fingers. Talbot scooted his feet forward awkwardly to keep his erection tucked and hidden and then reached down and threw open the window.

"Now you pick to run, asshole?"

"So come on, come on!" Tiernan said. "It's great out. De boids is choipin' in de trees, de flowers is . . . Why in the hell are you standing like that?"

"Never mind," Talbot laughed and closed the shutters.

"Buzz me in. I've gotta piss!" Tiernan called from outside.

"Just hold it a minute!" Talbot said, hopping back across the room to where Frieda was hurrying into her jeans. "Now see what you have done?'' he whispered and pointed to the enormous bulge in his jogging pants. "It won't go down!"

"I can't hold it!" Tiernan called from outside.

"Wait!" Talbot called back and looked at Frieda frantically.

"Boooo!" she said to the erection.

"Don't let him in for a minute," he whispered and ran over to the sink and started splashing cold water on his face. Outside, Tiernan was making whimpering noises.

"Hurry," Frieda urged.

"It won't go down, goddam it! Down!" Down!" he scolded it. "Okay, prick, you asked for it," he warned and prepared the ultimate squelch. "Miss McCormack!" he shouted at it, invoking the name and memory of the skinny old teacher he'd had in the seventh grade, a hawk-faced harridan who could freeze boiling water with a glance. The effect was immediate and he nodded to Frieda, who pushed the front door buzzer.

"I am convinced you are a madman," she said as she heard Tiernan bounding through the foyer outside toward the community bathroom upstairs. "Both of you."

In a few minutes, Tiernan was knocking on the door. Talbot went back over to the mirror and posed a few more times and then started jogging in place.

"Okay, open the door!" he said to Frieda as he circled away from the mirror and prepared to jog out the door the minute she swung it open.

"Hi, Frie— Oof!" Tiernan said as he was barged into by Talbot jogging out the door just as she opened it.

"Hi, Joe," she said waving.

"Ummm, you look delicious this morning, Frieda," Tiernan said after recovering himself.

"Come on!" Talbot called from the front door.

"Oh, Joe," she called as Tiernan turned and started toward the door, "why don't you come back with Len and have breakfast with us?"

"Thanks, I will," he said, waving to her as he trotted past Talbot, who was holding the door open. "Jesus, where'd you get the fancy schmancy outfit?" he asked Talbot.

"Oh, just a little something Frieda picked up for me," Talbot said casually, but feeling very proud of her.

"Buying you presents. Aha, things are getting serious," Tiernan said, slapping him on the back as they trotted across the street into the park.

"Hey, I'm worth it!" Talbot said, kidding defensively.

The fresh new feel of the jogging clothes inspired Talbot and he set a grueling pace across the meadow toward the riding trail. He had been feeling better all around since Gemetz had gotten out of the hospital and looked like he was going to be actually in better shape—minus the ulcer—than before. He was still a little worried about Tiernan and his determination not to call Mary again or see his daughter until Mary stopped her divorce proceedings.

"I'm gonna pick up Teddy at noon today," Talbot said as they ran sliding down the side of the gorge toward the cinder trail. "Why don't you pick up Lynn and come to the playground with us?"

"No, I'm not going over there," Tiernan said and was irritated that Talbot would bring up the subject again. He felt miserable about not seeing his daughter in nearly a month but he felt it was the only way he was going to drive home to Mary the seriousness of what she was doing.

"Come on, you're not mad at Lynn, are you?"

"Hey, just fucking can it, will you?" Tiernan spat out.

"Suit yourself. . . . Come on," Talbot replied and began pushing the pace a little faster.

Tiernan responded by pushing it even faster, pulling ahead of Talbot. Then Talbot overtook him and turned it into a race as they went under the bridge. After they had gone along full steam like this for another half-mile, Tiernan began to feel a knifing in his side and slowed up.

"Big deal!" he said as Talbot slowed and ran alongside of him shaking his head.

"Getting soft, Joey," he taunted. "Been lying around feeling sorry for yourself."

"Think so, huh?"

"Sure," Talbot said and then laughed as Tiernan took off at a sprint ahead of him.

When they finally got back to the rooming house, Tiernan was soaking wet and wheezing from the three-mile footrace that only ended when Talbot had tripped him on their way back across the great meadow. He had sprawled and then tumbled across the grass and had gotten up and started swinging at Talbot, who had ducked and darted around him laughing and egging him on until they were both laughing at the absurdity of it all. After that Talbot had apologized for pushing him on the

subject of Lynn and they had raced one last time back to the
rooming house. In a way he was glad that Talbot had put him
through the ordeal, because it seemed to mitigate some of the
guilt he had been feeling about Lynn.

Frieda greeted them at the door with two glasses of orange
juice and told them to sit down while she finished cooking up
the eggs and sausages. They spent an hour eating and talking
about Gemetz and about Talbot's latest scheme—a camping
and fishing trip upstate when Gemetz was well enough. Finally,
at about eleven o'clock, Tiernan said he had some work to do
at home and got up to leave.

"How is Lynn?" Frieda asked as he was going out.

"What, you, too?" Tiernan asked and shook his head and
closed the door behind him.

"What did I say?" she asked Talbot.

"I don't understand you, Frieda," Talbot said, walking over
to her with a mischievous glint in his eye. "How could you
have said something like that?"

"What?" she asked in bewilderment.

"Digging into his private life," he said, backing her up
toward the bed.

"All I asked was—"

"Insinuating like that," he said, continuing to push her with
his chest.

"What did I insin— Oh, ho, you . . . !" she exclaimed as
she felt the bed at the back of her legs. "Len!" she cried out as
he threw his arms around her and toppled onto the bed with her.

"Now, where were we before we were so rudely interrupted," he said, reaching down and unbuttoning her jeans.

An hour later, as he was wearily getting back into his jogging
suit to go and pick up Teddy, she asked him why he was putting
the sweaty thing back on.

"I, uh, want Teddy to see it," he said, feeling a little
embarrassed about liking it so much.

"I don't know who is the oldest, you or Teddy," she laughed
and got up and put his silk shirt back on.

"Teddy, for sure," he said. "Why don't you stick around
and come over to the park with us?"

"Maybe you would rather have some time alone with him?"
she asked.

"We're just going over to the playground. You can keep me
company while Teddy plays in the sand."

"You are sure?" she asked, walking with her arm around him toward the door.

"Yeah. Anyway, he's staying over tonight, so I'll have plenty of time with him."

"Good. That means you won't be at Larsky's getting angry if Susan comes in again."

"That reminds me," he said, suddenly frowning. "This will be a good time to talk to her about that."

"Len, please, don't fight with her, especially in front of Teddy."

"No, don't worry. I have a new idea. We're going to have a truce talk—try to iron things out a little. I've decided to tell her I'm sorry, ask her if we can at least try to be civilized with each other. After all, we do have Teddy in common and we can try to build some kind of relationship around that."

"Ah, that sounds marvelous, Len," she said, giving him an approving hug.

"All she has to do is agree to some kind of territorial arrangement," he said. "I'll agree to stay away from her social areas and she only has to agree to stay out of Larsky's. There are at least a dozen other bars she can go to. She can have them all. I'll stay out of them. But, goddam it, Larsky's is my stomping ground. I was there first!"

"Lenny, Lenny," she said, trying to soothe him. "Just be sweet to her. You can charm any woman when you're sweet. Don't give her orders. . . . Especially with Susan it won't work."

"I know, I know," he said, kissing her on the forehead. "I'm going to be the charmingest asshole in creation. She'll agree, I know it. I only wish I'd thought of it sooner."

Walking over to Garfield Street, Talbot felt tired from his morning of racing with Tiernan and sex with Frieda. But he also felt a calming relief that at last he was going to be able to end the war with Susan. It would be nice to see her, and he envisioned her softening under his apology. He had provoked the whole thing with his warning to her the night he had arm-wrestled her friend Trisha. He had put her down publicly and of course she had answered his challenge with defiance. That was Susan. Nobody had ever told her what to do. He loved that pride in her. It was the one thing he hoped Teddy would inherit from her.

Susan met him at the door with an expression on her face

that reminded him of a concrete bunker. No matter, he thought, she still thinks the war is on. She looked very sexy in cut-off jeans and a white T-shirt that showed the shape of her nipples.

"Hi," he said warmly as he stepped into the apartment.

"He'll be ready in a minute," she said glumly. "If you want to wait outside, I'll send him out. He's just on the john."

He smiled warmly at her again and walked around the living room. The place looked a little messy and he figured she was feeling agitated at his seeing it like this before she had time to clean it up.

"Hey, the place looks great!" he lied, walking over to the bookshelves near the window. "God, all my old books." He sighed, looking over the worn history and philosophy volumes. "Ever read them?" he asked, turning back toward her. She was still standing near the door with her arms folded, still frowning hostility.

"No, you can pick them up any time you want."

"Oh, no hurry," he said, smiling again, trying to soften her expression. "Hey, what do you think?" he asked, pointing his hands inward toward his new jogging suit. "Pretty sharp, huh?"

"Okay, what is it?" she asked. "You don't want to keep Teddy overnight. Is that what you're building up to?"

"Hey, Susan, for Christ sake," he said, shaking his head at the unfairness of her remark. "Of course I want to keep him tonight. Come on and sit down a minute," he said, going over to the couch and sitting down. "I want to talk for a minute. I've been a total asshole and I would like us to get back on some kind of friendlier basis. Okay?" he asked, patting the couch.

"Len, there—" she started to say but was interrupted by Teddy's running into the room and jumping into Talbot's arms.

"Where'd ya get the blue suit, Daddy?" the boy asked, pulling on the material at his chest.

"At the *jogging* store!" Talbot exclaimed and raised the boy over his head playfully.

"Len—" Susan started to say again, looking a little nervous.

But she stopped as the bedroom door opened and the large kinky-haired man Talbot had seen her with at Larsky's the previous Saturday stepped out. He was bare-chested and holding a dark polo sports shirt in his massive hands.

"Hey, sugar, could yuh sew a button for me?" he asked without noticing Talbot sitting over on the couch with Teddy.

"Jesus," Talbot said, and gritted his teeth.

"Ray, why don't you go back in and put your shirt on," Susan said.

"Huh?" he asked and then looked over at Talbot. "Oh, who's he?" he asked.

"Ray, ah, this is Len, ah . . . my, ah, Teddy's father," she said and went to the piano and snatched the package of cigarettes off of it and nervously put one in her mouth.

"How yuh doin'?" Ray asked while he measured Talbot and gripped the shirt a little tighter so the muscles in his arms would bulge intimidatingly.

Talbot caught the barely perceptible warning and felt his anger begin to boil. He ignored the brute and stood up with Teddy in his arms. Putting the boy down, he looked at Susan with an expression she understood: Get rid of him or there's going to be an explosion.

"Ray, please," Susan said, indicating the bedroom with her eyes. Then she took a drag from the cigarette she'd just lighted and blew it in his direction.

"Everything okay?" Ray asked her and then gave Talbot a look of disdain.

"Yes, we just have to talk for a second," she said. "They're just leaving. Please, Ray."

"Sure, baby," he said, rolling his shoulders and flexing more openly as he turned and went into the bedroom. "Cute outfit," he said over his shoulder with a sneer at Talbot as he went in and closed the door.

"Where'd you find him, at the zoo?" Talbot asked.

From inside the bedroom they could hear the sharp smacking of flesh.

"That's Ray, Daddy!" Teddy said. "He can climb up telephone poles."

"And banana trees, I imagine," Talbot said loudly toward the closed bedroom door.

The sound of smacking flesh grew louder.

"He sleeped in Mommy's room, Daddy," Teddy said.

"Go get your baseball jacket, Teddy," Susan said.

As Teddy ran down the hall to his bedroom, Talbot walked over to the piano and stood next to Susan, his face contorted with the effort to control his anger, the bottoms of his fists pushing down on the piano. She started to move away from him and he snatched her by the wrist.

"Now you're bringing this bar scum in to live around my son?" he growled at her.

"Stop it," she said through her teeth and pulled her wrist free of him. "Don't start anything, Len, or that bar scum you're talking about is liable to come in and put a dent in your stupid head. Just take Teddy and get out. And don't you ever tell me who I can have in here or not!"

"You fucking slut!" he yelled at her and grabbed her by the wrist again. "You want to take your life down the sewer, that's your business. But you're not going to do it in front of Teddy! And you're going to stay out of Larsky's, do you hear?"

"Len, you're hurting me!" she whined and tried to pull away from him.

Ray burst out of the bedroom, flexed out his chest a moment and then headed for Talbot. "Okay, that's it, blue boy!" he yelled.

Talbot flung Susan aside onto the couch and lunged toward Ray. But just as he threw his first punch, Ray grabbed his fist in one hand and whipped it around Talbot's back in a judo move. Then, with Talbot grimacing in pain, Ray forced him across the room to a wall near the door and slammed him against it, one hand pinning his arm behind him and the other mashing his face into the wall.

"You leave my daddy alone," Teddy wailed as he came into the living room and started punching Ray in the thighs.

"Ray, stop it!" Susan called and rushed over and took Teddy against her legs.

"You gonna leave peaceably, pal?" Ray asked.

"I'm gonna kill you!" Talbot grunted and then groaned in agony as Ray responded by forcing his arm behind him, almost to the breaking point.

"Len, please," Susan pleaded. "He's a black belt in judo. Please, Len, for Teddy's sake. Just take him and go home, Len, please."

"Stop hurting my daddy!" Teddy wailed.

Talbot felt himself nearly on the point of passing out from the pain. Worse was the pain of humiliation he felt at having Teddy see him being beaten. He wanted to cry with shame.

"Please, Len," Susan pleaded again.

"Daddy, Daddy, Daddy!"

Teddy's anguish was cutting through him like a knife. He had to quit—take the boy out and try to calm him down. He'd settle with this ape some other time.

"Your decision, pal," Ray said, pushing the arm up another notch and drawing another groan from Talbot.

"Okay," Talbot grunted.

He nearly collapsed to the floor when Ray suddenly let go and stepped back in a fighting stance. His arm felt paralyzed and he let it swing loosely and tried to rub some feeling back into it. At the same time he found it impossible to look either at Teddy or Susan. He stared into Ray's eyes with an expression that told the other man he was going to kill him.

"Anytime," Ray said, opening and closing his outstretched hands.

"Go with your father, Teddy," Susan said, releasing the boy, who ran and threw his arms around Talbot's legs. "Please, Len," she said, going over to the door and opening it for him to leave. "Just take Teddy. . . . He's very upset by all of this. Teddy, Mommy will see you tomorrow, honey."

Without taking his cold gaze from Ray's eyes, Talbot reached down and picked up the trembling child. I'm coming back and I'm going to destroy you, asshole, he thought, looking at the smirking face of his bare-chested opponent.

"Stick around," he said.

"I ain't worried about you, baby blue," Ray replied.

"Stop it, dammit!" Susan exploded.

When he got to the door, Talbot stopped in front of her and looked into her pale face. Her nostrils were flared with fright and anger.

"You've brought this down, Susan," Talbot said to her in a choking voice. "Now there's going to be hell like you've never dreamed of."

"Please . . . just leave," she said, turning away.

As he walked out she slammed the door behind him with a loud bang. He could hear Ray murmur something and Susan snapping at him: "Shut up!"

"Daddy, make him go away," Teddy said, clinging tightly to his neck as he carried him down the stairs to the front entrance.

"Don't worry," Talbot said through his choking rage.

Outside, the afternoon was bright and quiet on the tree-lined brownstone street. Talbot hoisted Teddy up on his shoulders and headed for the park. All the way to the meadow he was barely aware of the child's light weight on his shoulders and the touch of his little hands on his temples. Ray's sneering face filled his mind, and with each breath he spoke a silent curse.

As he crossed the meadow toward the playground, Talbot was deep into his wounded manhood. Images of his father's face flashed before his eyes—that warrior's face he'd remembered from his childhood. Cold gray eyes staring out of a leathered face, measuring him, looking through his child's skin to the savage lying deep within. And now he felt the savage rising to his father's call. He remembered the sword lying on the mantel back at the rooming house.

He felt the sun on his face and hurried now across the meadow to leave Teddy with Frieda at the playground. His hand ached to grasp the sword. He saw himself raising it against Ray's out-stretched hands. His breath was coming in panting rhythms now, his feet moving across the grass with predatory eagerness. The savage was awake, acutely aware of every tree and contour in the park, every sound, every step of the way it would take to the playground, then to the rooming house for the sword and then back to Susan's. God, let him still be there, he thought.

He wanted to cry out his blood lust as the exultation of hatred poured through his body in heated waves. The smell of his father's sweat and leather filled his nose and he could hear the thudding of cavalry horses rolling distantly on those Texas fields. Sun glinting off raised swords. The cry of men wheeling the cavalry line into position for a charge.

In a few minutes he had reached the gates to the playground and saw Frieda sitting on a bench in the sun with her eyes closed. He put Teddy down gently and smiled at him. I'm going to make him go away, Teddy. Yes, go and play in your little world, he thought as the boy scampered toward the sandbox and then stopped short when he saw Frieda.

"Frieda!" Teddy called and ran to her.

"Oh!" she said, opening her eyes in surprise as Teddy clambered onto her lap. "Teddy, darling! How are you? Where is your papa?"

"Frieda, Ray hurted my daddy!" the boy exclaimed.

"What? Where is your daddy?" she asked, hugging him to her and looking around for Talbot. She saw him standing at the gate looking at them with a strange expression on his face. Something about his look she had seen before . . . long ago.

"Ray made my daddy leave Mommy's house by hurting his arm behind his back," the boy said and began to cry.

*"Ach, meiner Liebling,"* she said, holding the boy to her and looking inquiringly at Talbot as he walked slowly toward them. "Len, what is going on?" she asked. "You had a fight?"

"No, it was just a little scuffle," he lied and sat down heavily beside them.

"Oh, poor Teddy," she cooed into the boy's ear and stroked down his hair. "Did you become scared?"

"He's all right," Talbot said, taking the boy from her arms and standing him up on his lap. "Right, Teddy? Remember what I said? He won't be there anymore. Now, you gonna let Daddy see his big boy crying?"

Teddy wiped his nose and shook his head. Then Talbot hugged him powerfully to his chest and whispered something into his ear and set him down. "Now, let me see what kind of a castle you can build this time. And don't forget the moat."

"It's gonna be this big," Teddy said, measuring his hand up about two feet from the pavement.

"Okay, get busy!" Talbot said, patting the boy on the behind and sending him toward the sandbox, where several dozen other children were already at play.

"So, what happened?" Frieda asked.

"God, what a mess," he sighed and put his hands behind his neck and stretched his legs out. He had to put Frieda off guard about his intention to go back to Susan's, and that would take sitting around for a few minutes, he thought.

"You fought with this friend of Susan's?"

"She's got some kind of mongoloid living with her now," he said, gritting his teeth. "Goddam, I can't believe she would stoop to such scum!"

"Len, you are no longer responsible for her life. It is hers."

"Not when she's bringing scum like that around my son, turning his home into a sewer."

"Teddy was very frightened. It is not good to fight around him, Len."

"I know it. . . . I know it," he said, shaking his head. "God my head is killing me. Migraine, I think."

"I have some aspirin in my purse," she said, reaching down for her bag under the bench.

"Nah, what I need is a shot of bourbon. Something to quiet me down. Do you mind watching Teddy for a bit while I trot home and knock down a few shots. I won't be gone long at all," he lied.

She looked into his eyes searchingly for a moment and then leaned back and looked out over the playground. "You are lying to me, aren't you?" she asked.

"No, honest, Frieda. . . . I just need a drink, goddam it."

"You want to go there and finish your fight, don't you?"

"Are you kidding? She can have that ape if she wants him. Really, Frieda, my head is killing me. I'll just be a minute," he said and started to get up.

"No!" she nearly shouted at him and narrowed her eyes.

"What?" he asked, surprised by the intensity of her look.

"I will not stay with Teddy," she said and started gathering her things.

"Wait. . . . Where are you going?"

"Home," she said.

"Frieda, sit down, dammit," he said, pushing her back down. "What the hell has gotten into you?"

"You will not leave Teddy alone and that is the only thing that is going to keep you here. I am going," she said and started up again. And again he pushed her down and sat down beside her, holding her in place.

"You're acting crazy," he said. "All I want to do is get a goddam drink."

"No, you are going to kill," she said, looking him in the eye.

"Ah, what are you talking about?" he asked, sitting back with his arms folded and looking away. At the same time he felt that she was looking right into him.

"It is there. . . . I see it . . . I see it," she cried almost frantically.

"You see nothing!" he said, turning and glaring at her.

"Yes!" she hissed back. "It makes me sick to see it."

"I'm going," he said and got up and started toward the entrance.

She immediately grabbed her bag and hurried ahead of him, leaving the playground before him. Outside the gate, he grabbed her arm and swung her around. She was crying hysterically and twisting to get free of him. Finally she slapped him in the face and broke free and started running again.

"Dammit, wait!" he said, running after her and catching her by the arm again.

"Admit it!" she yelled at him. "You want to go back there and kill him. And maybe her too."

"I'm not going back," he said, pinning her arms down to her side and holding her in an embrace. "Just don't leave me right now . . . or I *will* go over there." He pressed her into him and tried to soothe her crying. "Please, Frieda."

"I can't lose you . . . like him . . . not again," she said, sniffing and burying her face in his chest.

"Who?" he asked, pulling her down on the grass with him.

"It seems like it was just last week," she cried, and shook her lowered head.

"Your soldier?" he asked, reaching out and touching her hair.

*"Ja* . . . Werner, my soldier," she said almost in a whisper.

They were sitting under the thick orange-hued limb of an Osage tree about twenty yards from the playground. Talbot looked over at the high chain-link fence around the playground and listened to the sounds of the children playing. Teddy might be wondering where they were, he thought.

"Come on," he said, lifting her chin. "I'm sorry. . . . I won't . . . You were right, I was angry. I promise I won't go back. Let's go sit in the playground so Teddy'll know where we are."

"Oh, Teddy!" she exclaimed, remembering the fear in the boy's eyes when he had climbed into her lap. *"Ja,* we must hurry."

Talbot got up and helped her to her feet. Walking back, he put his arm around her.

"Tell me about Werner," he said.

"He was killed. . . . But that look. Oh, Len, I remember that look. He had it on his face when they sent him off to kill, and also when . . . when—"

"I know, I know," he said, holding her closer.

They went back into the playground and sat down on one of the benches near the sandpile. Teddy was busy making a castle with two other little boys and a girl.

"Look at him," Talbot said, smiling. "Didn't even know we were gone."

"This is not good for you, Lenny," she said after a while. "Living so close to Susan."

"I'm not running anymore, Frieda. I was not raised to run

away. God, if my father could have seen what happened today!
Do you know what he would have said? I feel disgraced,
I . . . Oh, god, you can never understand. Women have no
idea of men," he said, resting his head back and closing his
eyes.

"No?"

"No."

She looked at him sadly for a moment and then closed her
eyes. "Shall I tell you how Werner died?" she asked, turning
and looking at Teddy building his sand castle.

"I thought he was killed in the war," he said, turning to her.

"No," she sighed.

"You don't have to tell me," he said, not wishing to increase
her pain.

"It was in the last months of the war," she began without
looking at him. "There were many deserters hiding in the city.
Berlin was—"

"He deserted?"

"The Russian armies were nearing the city," she continued.
"And the SS was hanging deserters . . . in the streets, from
the light poles. There was no food and we were being bombed
and we could not hide. The SS would flood the subways to
keep us from hiding in them. And everywhere the young men
hanging over our heads from the streetlamps. I prayed the
Russians would come.

"And one night I came home and found Werner in my room.
He was wearing his uniform . . . but so thin you could have
fitted two of him in it. He had been eating out of garbage cans
at night and hiding. His friends had just been captured and
were to be hanged. So frightened . . . I can still remember
his eyes."

"Frieda," Talbot said, resting his hand on hers in her lap.
"Don't go into it."

"No," she said and shook her head, determined to go ahead.
"I will prove to you that I understand. Do you know what I
saw in his eyes?"

"Fear?"

"Yes, fear, but something else, too. There was an animal
looking out at me from that corner he was sitting in. Werner
could have killed me easily if I had acted in any way to threaten
him. He was like a wolf waiting to see which way I would
turn."

"He loved you?"

"Yes, even then he loved me very much. For weeks he had not come to me for fear that it would endanger me."

"And they found him?"

"We . . . One morning we were riding on the subway. We were coming back from his sister's with some packages of food she was able to obtain. For a month Werner had disguised himself as a woman. His sister was much larger than me and he was wearing one of her dresses and a shawl. Each morning I would help him put on some of my makeup. He had delicate features and I was able to make him look quite feminine.

"When the subway was about ten minutes from the stop near my house, a young SS officer came into the car and sat down opposite us. He kept looking at Werner, and at first I thought it was because I had made him beautiful. But . . . I . . . I turned to look at him a moment out of the corner of my eye and it suddenly was apparent to me what he was looking at. Werner's dark beard was very evident that morning. He must not have shaved closely. My heart was beating like a hammer and I decided we should get off immediately."

"Christ," Talbot said.

"And Werner was becoming very nervous under the staring of the young officer. I nudged him as the train was coming to a stop and we were just getting up to leave. But the officer stood up and pushed Werner back down in his seat and drew his pistol. He called him a swine and pulled the shawl from his head."

All the while Frieda was talking her eyes were staring at the sand castle Teddy was building and her tone was distant and weary.

"I cannot forget the way he looked up at me," she continued after a moment. "Dead. There was no more fear in his eyes. I remember that most. Just dead."

"Did they arrest you, too?"

"They brought us to the courthouse. They took him into a room and told me to wait in a hallway filled with people who had been called on various complaints. I . . . I just walked out. I went home. And they didn't come."

"And Werner?"

"They hanged him . . . that evening."

"I'm sorry," he said, putting his arm around her and pulling her to him.

"I saw him. At first I thought they had hanged a woman. They hanged him in the dress. And everyone thought they had hanged a woman. He had delicate features—Werner. He was a man . . . and for a while he wanted to be a soldier."

"Goddam." Talbot sighed.

"He once told me that when he was a boy his father teased him for being too pretty and made the barber shave his head. I think he wanted to be a soldier to prove to his father that he was a man."

"Poor bastard," Talbot said. "To be hanged like that."

"Do you see how Teddy is playing?" she asked.

"Yes."

"He is beautiful, *ja?*"

"Yes."

"There is a man, too, Len. Not to be created—just to be loved."

"I don't understand."

"Perhaps he will help you," she said, leaning forward and burying her face in her hands.

He reached out and gently touched her hair. Her telling him of Werner had moved him deeply, with horror at first over the degrading manner in which he had died but also in another way which he did not quite understand. She seemed to be implying some kind of comparison between himself and Teddy and Werner and Werner's father. And that was wrong. He loved Teddy and would always accept the man that was arising in him. He wanted Teddy to love him, and perhaps someday look back and admire him. The way he admired his father. And as he turned and looked at Teddy playing in the sand he thought of the many expressions of love Teddy had shown for him, and he could not remember ever being that way with his father. The thought troubled him and he tried to push it away.

"Hey, what say we go back and have a drink?" he asked, rubbing her back. "I'm sorry you had to remember. . . . It was a terrible thing, Frieda."

"*Ja*, a drink would be nice," she said, sitting up.

"Teddy!" Talbot called to the boy.

"Yeah?"

"Come on!"

"Aw!" Teddy said, making a face. "Can't I just—"

"We're going," Talbot said, getting up.

After returning to the rooming house, Talbot set Teddy to

playing with some of his Star War toys and then got down the bottle of bourbon and two glasses for Frieda and himself. She was sitting at the table looking very tired.

"This'll fix you up," he said, pouring her a tall drink.

Then he poured one for himself and went over and sat at the table with her, reaching out and taking her hand. You're some woman, Frieda, he thought. You've journeyed through hell and back and here you sit, tired with all your wisdom yet still ready to reach out.

The bourbon seemed to have a softening effect on both of their moods, and for the rest of the afternoon they sipped and talked and played with Teddy. He insisted that she stay for supper and continued refilling her glass. By five o'clock he was yawning and stretching and giggling at just about anything she or Teddy said. The light outside the window was diminishing. Finally, with a long weary sigh, he fell back on the bed and closed his eyes. Frieda looked up from where she was sitting on the floor and playing with Teddy and shook her head.

"I think your papa is going to take a little nap," she said, chucking Teddy under the chin.

"I hate naps!" Teddy exclaimed and traveled his little space car up her hand and arm and rested it on her shoulder.

"I bet you are getting a little hungry, *ja?*"

"What means *ja?*" he asked.

"That means yes."

"Yes. Can we have hamburgers, Frieda?"

*"Ja, meiner Liebling,"* she said.

"Oh, boy!" he exclaimed.

"Shhhhh," she said, putting her finger to her lips. "How would you like to go with me to Burger King and pick up some hamburgers?"

*"Ja!"* he said, getting up.

"We will bring them back and by that time your papa will be ready to eat with us."

"Okay. Can I get a double cheeseburger?"

"You bet," she said, getting up.

As they were going out, Frieda looked down at Talbot's sleeping face and blew him a kiss. Then she turned out the light and closed the door.

There was just a shaft of light coming in through one of the shutters in the dimmed room. Teddy's toys were scattered over the floor and on the table stood the half-empty bottle of

bourbon and Frieda's glass. Talbot was still holding his empty
glass in his hand as he lay sprawled across the bed.

In a moment he opened his eyes and sat up. He could still
hear Teddy and Frieda talking as they walked down the steps
outside. Swinging his legs out of the bed, he got up and walked
over to the mantel, where he put down his glass and picked up
the sword. The metallic swish of the blade coming out of the
scabbard cut the silence of the room. Picking up the whetstone,
he walked back to the bed, tossed aside the scabbard and sat
down.

"Soon, soon," he murmured lovingly to the sword as he
stroked the stone down along its edge. And the singing blade
answered him.

# CHAPTER
# TWENTY-ONE

It was a little after six o'clock when Frieda and Teddy reached the top of Ninth Street at the park on their way back with the hamburgers. Behind them the broad street sloped down from the park into a dusky haze of brownstones, storefronts and aerial-spiked rooftops. And farther off, beyond the descending congeries of warehouses and decaying tenements, the great blood-tinged orb of the sun was settling toward the harbor.

"Oooooo, look, Frieda!" Teddy exclaimed as he pulled her back and looked squinting into the sunset.

"Oh, *ja,* it's beautiful, Teddy," she said, turning her eyes from its red glow and finding much lovelier its reflection on the boy's face. "It looks like a big red ball, *ja?*"

"No, it looks like a napple."

"Oh, *ja,* that's right, Teddy," she said, smiling at him as they turned down Prospect Park West to the rooming house. "A big, delicious apple."

"Have you ever seen my mommy's apple?"

"No."

"It's this big!" he exclaimed, holding his arms out wide.

"Oh, Teddy." She laughed.

"It's true, but it's only a picture. She has a picture of a giant apple in her bedroom."

"That must be very nice," she said and began to feel a strange ominous sensation rising in her.

The brownstones on their left were casting deep shadows across the street and into the park, but the tops of the trees were tinged with red. She thought again of the burning red eye of the sun and then the image of Talbot lying asleep on his bed came into her mind. His body seemed to be glowing in the same red of that incarnadined sun and then she saw him getting up. Oh, my god, she thought and began to hurry her step. I should not have left him alone.

When they got to the rooming house she hastily opened the door with the extra key Talbot had given her and rushed to his room.

"Len!" she cried out and then sucked in her breath as she saw the room empty and the sword's scabbard lying on the bed.

"Where's Daddy?" Teddy asked, looking around.

"Go and look in the bathroom upstairs, Teddy," she said, trying to control the panic in her voice.

When the boy was gone she reached into her purse for her address book and turned through its pages quickly as she ran to the telephone. Finding Tiernan's number, she snatched up the phone and dialed quickly. "Oh, please!" she begged, hoping he would be at home. She was also worried that Teddy would come back before she could tell Tiernan that Talbot was heading over to Susan's to kill someone.

"Hello?" Tiernan answered.

"Joe? Oh, Joe . . . something terrible!"

"Frieda?"

"Please, Joe . . . Oh, hurry. Len has taken his sword and he is going over to Susan's to . . . Her boyfriend beat him up and threw him out today. Joe, I'm afraid—"

"Jesus!" Tiernan gasped. "When did he leave?"

"I'm not sure. . . . Maybe just a few minutes. Please, Joe!"

"I'm on my way!" he said and hung up.

Tiernan's apartment was not far from Garfield Street, and as he raced from his building down Prospect Park West he tried to think of what he might say to stop his friend. God, he must have cracked, he thought. That goddam sword. . . . I may have to tackle him. Can I handle Talbot?

As he turned down Garfield Street he could see Talbot in his blue jogging suit at the end of the next block, waiting a moment for traffic to pass before crossing the street. Tiernan started sprinting. "Thank god, thank god," he kept saying as the line of passing cars held Talbot in place. Then there was an opening and Talbot started across the street to Susan's block.

"Len!" Tiernan hollered at the top of his lungs.

But he was still too far away and Talbot continued on with the gleaming sword resting point-up on his shoulder. Crossing the street without slowing down, Tiernan was almost hit by a cab that had to swerve around him on screeching tires.

"Len!" he called out again and this time Talbot heard him and stopped.

Talbot looked at him for a moment with a strange dead expression and then turned and resumed his walk toward Susan's in the middle of the block.

"Wait, Len, please!" Tiernan gasped as he caught up with him and grabbed his arm.

"Go on back, Joe," Talbot said and pulled his hand off his arm.

"Len," Tiernan gasped, trying to get his breath. "Wai— Wait. I . . . I'm out of . . . Len, you can't," he said, getting in front of Talbot and putting his hands on his shoulders.

"Frieda called you?"

"Yeah. What . . . what the hell, Len?" Tiernan asked, still panting as he looked into Talbot's eyes and then at the sword. "Len, I don't believe this."

"Nothing to worry about," Talbot said, looking back at him without blinking. "Just going to clean some scum out of my son's home."

"Okay, okay, okay. . . . Just a minute, okay? I just, just . . . uh, I just . . . I just want you to tell me about it first. Come over here. . . . We'll just sit down and talk for a minute. . . . Just a minute, okay?" Tiernan said and gently moved Talbot toward the steps of the brownstone adjoining Susan's.

Talbot looked at his friend sadly and shook his head. Tiernan would never understand . . . the man in him buried under too much civilization. His concern was touching though . . . a good friend.

"Just go home, Joe," he said after a moment. "This is something I can take care of."

"*What*, for Christ sake?" Tiernan exclaimed. "What in the

hell are you gonna do with *that?*" he asked, looking at the
sword that was still resting on Talbot's shoulder.

"Don't worry. . . . If he goes quietly, I won't use it. But
no goddam half-breed fucking mongoloid is going to come into
my home and throw me out!" he snarled, his face tightening in
rage.

"Your home?" Tiernan asked.

"Wherever Teddy is—that's my home!" Talbot bellowed at
him and shoved his hand off his arm.

"Okay, wait," Tiernan said, regretting his further agitating
him. "Look, I agree. . . . I, uh, I'll help you."

"What?"

"Yeah, sure, just calm down a minute. Look, all you wanta
do is get that guy out of there, right? So we'll *both* go in and
throw him out. But no swords, okay? Okay?"

"It's my fight, Joe," Talbot said, smiling at his friend. "But
thanks, I appreciate your loyalty."

"No, it's my fight, too. I'm going in with you," Tiernan
said, feeling this would be one way of controlling what
happened inside. If he could just keep Talbot from cutting
somebody up, anything would be justifiable.

"It's not your concern," Talbot said, turning away.

"Hey, I've been listening to you for months now spouting
this cavalry shit, and the first chance we get to act together you
want to hog the whole show. Come on, Len? You go in there
and cut him up and she wins! Don't you see that? We throw
him out and there's no cops later—no getting your ass thrown
in jail so she can laugh at you. We take him like cavalry—bam,
bam, from all sides. Right?"

"You're right, she would love to see my ass behind bars,"
Talbot said, lowering the sword and looking toward Susan's
second-floor window.

"Bet your ass she would," Tiernan said, sighing in relief.

"I don't know," Talbot said. "Guy is big . . . knows a lot
of judo."

"Are you kidding? You've never seen me in action, man.
You telling me this guy can take both of us?"

"Ha!" Talbot laughed and slapped Tiernan on the shoulder.
Maybe you aren't so civilized, he thought. "I like your spirit,
man. Let's go get this turkey!"

"Oh, he's going, man," Tiernan said, putting his arm
around Talbot's shoulder as they walked toward Susan's front

steps. "Only let me do the talking—and, and no fucking swords."

"I'll do the talking."

"Okay, okay, but no sword."

When they got to the front door, Talbot rang old Mr. Cowl's buzzer on the top floor. He remembered that the old man always rang people in without asking who was there on the intercom. He wanted to be at Susan's apartment door before letting her know he was in the building. The release buzzer sounded and he and Tiernan entered and started up the stairs.

At Susan's door, Talbot and Tiernan stopped for a moment to gather their courage, each looking into the other's eyes for any last-minute wavering. Then Tiernan reached over and lifted the blade off Talbot's shoulder and lowered it to his side. Talbot nodded and then turned and rapped on the door.

"Yeah, just a minute!" they heard Ray call from inside.

Tiernan drew in a breath through his nose and clenched his fists. The deep sound of Ray's voice told him he would be encountering no small man. Talbot stepped a little closer to the door so he'd be the first in.

"Oh, it's baby blue," Ray said, opening the door a crack and not seeing Tiernan. "Sorry, we don't want any," he said with a little laugh and started to close the door.

But Talbot lifted the sword up just in time to jam the door and then Tiernan threw his full weight against it and burst into the room knocking Ray back a few feet with the impact.

"Oh, ya brought some help this time?" Ray said, recovering himself and preparing to do battle. But catching a glimpse of the shining thing in Talbot's hand, he backed up a step. "What the fuck is that?"

"I won't need this for you, shitface," Talbot said, and tossed the sword over onto the couch.

"Ray?" Susan called from the kitchen at the back of the apartment.

Her voice triggered Talbot and he lunged at Ray and threw a wild right that glanced off the taller man's cheekbone. But it had little effect and Ray was able to slip into him and whirl him around with a stranglehold on his neck. But just as Ray did this, Tiernan hit him with a sickening wallop in the side of the head that buckled his knees and sent him and Talbot to the floor.

Talbot then scrambled up and kicked Ray three times in

rapid succession in the ribs as he shook his head from Tiernan's blow and tried to rise. Despite this, Ray managed to rise, but just as he got set again Talbot brought a punch up from the floor and hit him in the mouth, sending him spinning into another roundhouse right from Tiernan. Then Tiernan tore into him with a barrage of punches to the body and face. Talbot was winding up for another roundhouse punch when Ray glanced over at him bleary-eyed and sank to the floor.

Just then Susan came up the hall from the kitchen drying her hands with a dish towel. She was still wearing her white T-shirt and cut-off jeans. Seeing Tiernan and Talbot standing over Ray, who was sitting on the floor dazed with blood pouring out of his nose and mouth, she dropped the towel and screamed.

"Now, get out!" Talbot roared at the sitting man.

Ray looked up at him and slowly wiped some blood from his mouth on the back of his hand. Then he reached down and started to push himself up, but as he did so, Talbot kicked him in the ribs again and sent him sprawling to the floor screaming in pain.

"Crawl out, scumbag—the way you crawled in," Talbot said.

"Stop it!" Susan screamed and ran at Talbot with her fists. He grabbed her arm and threw her into a nearby easy chair.

Ray continued to lie at his feet moaning.

"Out!" Talbot yelled again and kicked him three more times in the ribs, this time causing Ray to start crawling frantically toward the door.

"Joe, open the door for Mr. Scumbag, here," Talbot said, following him.

"Right!" Tiernan said and ran to the door and opened it.

When Ray got to the door, he stopped and looked up at Talbot again and started to curse him, but Talbot turned his utterance into a scream of pain by kicking him in the ribs and sent him clambering out on all fours.

"So glad you could call," Tiernan said after him and closed the door.

For a moment Tiernan and Talbot looked at each other and smiled.

"All right?" Tiernan asked. "That good enough for you?"

"Man, that was just purely fine," Talbot said with a look of calm on his face.

"You bastards!" Susan said, walking toward them with rage

pouring from her eyes. "You *animals!*" she shrieked as she got to Talbot, nearly bent over with the force of her cry.

"Told you I'd be back," he said, smiling smugly at her.

"Where did you leave Teddy, you . . . you . . . Where is my son?"

"Don't worry, he's with Frieda," Talbot said, still smiling.

"Susan, I'm sorry. We . . . that is, I . . ." Tiernan stammered, feeling overwhelmed with guilt for the pain she was going through. He wanted desperately to tell her that he'd come and joined in this to prevent a hell of a lot worse from happening.

"I'll see you both in jail!" she screamed at him and ran to the door. As she opened it she caught sight of Ray limping down the hall toward the stairs.

"Ray!" she called after him and ran out.

"God," Tiernan said, shaking his head and looking miserably at Talbot.

"Don't sweat it, man," Talbot said, coming over and putting his arm around him. "She'll get over it. Hey, didn't we give him a send-off? Did you see him take off? Wow!"

Thinking of the burly Ray, so cocksure when they'd come in, crawling furiously out the door, caused Tiernan to smile and laugh in spite of himself.

When Ray was halfway down the stairs, still moaning and grasping his sides, Susan caught up with him and begged him to wait.

"Oh, Ray, I'm sorry," she said, in tears at the sight of his agony.

"Fuck it," Ray gasped and leaned for a moment against the stair wall. "And fuck you, too!"

"Ray, please," she pleaded. "If you'd only left when I told you. I told you he'd come back."

"You . . . Goddam! You didn't say nothin' about two of 'em," he grunted and looked at her in pain and disgust. "And he comes at me with a sword? He was that kinda nut and you didn't warn me? Oh . . . oh . . . I'm all busted," he said, gingerly fingering his ribs.

She buried her face in her hands and sobbed in frustration. Her mounting hatred of Talbot was overwhelming even the pity she felt for Ray. She wanted to kill him.

"Ray, please don't blame me," she said.

"You told me you wasn't married," he said, shaking his head at her and starting down the stairs again.

"I'm not, Ray. . . . He has no right . . . He—"

"Stay away, bitch!" he said, shoving her back as she tried to stop him.

"Ray, don't!"

"Fucking dingo broads," he moaned as he kept going down the stairs. "It's what I get."

As he disappeared around the turn of the stairs, Susan sat down and began to cry and pound her thighs in frustration. He has no right—no right, she thought. "Len, I'll kill you. I'll kill you!" she wailed.

While Susan was outside the apartment, Talbot had roused Tiernan into a better mood with his joy over what they had done. It was the most exuberant Tiernan had ever seen him. Soon Joe was dancing around with him, too, and celebrating their victory. Talbot had reclaimed his manhood and Tiernan felt relief at having prevented a murder.

"What a punch! What a punch!" Talbot crooned, taking hold of Tiernan's fist and admiring it. "Where'd you learn to hit like that?"

"You rebels, always underestimating us Yankee boys."

"Wham!" Talbot exclaimed and threw a punch in the air. "And down he went like a sack of shit. I thought he was going to crush my windpipe before you hit him."

"I told you we could handle him," Tiernan said, trying to flex his sore fingers.

"The old cavalry rides again!" Talbot howled.

Just then Susan stepped into the apartment and stood quietly by the door watching them.

"Colonel Talbot, suh, we has sighted the enemy and kicked his ass!" Tiernan said, drawing up and giving a salute.

"Yeeeeeeeeeeeeeeegh!" Talbot yelled and swung Tiernan around.

"Too bad Richie couldn't a been here," Tiernan said, not noticing Susan standing there watching them with fire in her eyes.

"Oh-ho, he'd have loved it!" Talbot exclaimed and threw some more punches in the air, stopping and bowing as he noticed Susan.

"I say, uh, Colonel, suh, I wonder if you'd mind if we, uh,

just saddle up our cayooses and ride on down to the canteen for a victory libation . . . uh, suh!" said Tiernan.

"Right you are, Sergeant," Talbot said, pretending to flick some trail dust off his sleeve.

"Sergeant?" Tiernan asked with a frown.

"Make that captain, Sergeant," Talbot amended.

"Thank you, suh. Will there be any more of Susan's asshole boyfriends to kick out, suh?" he asked, still with his back to Susan.

"Not *today,* Captain," Talbot said, looking meaningfully into Susan's eyes.

You arrogant sons of bitches, she was thinking as she looked back at Talbot with total hatred. Her eyes were tearing and her lips were compressed in anger and she looked around the room for anything she could pick up to start smashing them. On the couch she saw the gleaming sword and felt a great urge to run over and get it and plunge it into Talbot's guts. Oh, how poetic, she thought.

"Very impressive, gentlemen," she said coolly and walked over between them letting her hair down over her shoulders.

"Yipe!" Tiernan said, turning in surprise.

"Yes, I thought you'd appreciate it, Susan," Talbot said with a superior smile.

"Ah . . . I . . . Susan," Tiernan stammered and tried to work up a miserable smile. "Len, maybe we'd better get going," he said, blushing with guilt.

"Oh, you don't have to leave right now," she said, turning and tracing her fingernail lightly along Tiernan's jaw line. "You've just had a great military victory, gentlemen—routed the enemy. Right, Colonel?" she said, turning to Talbot.

"Not quite," Talbot said, sensing a counterattack in her tone and manner. Still maneuvering, still defiant, he thought, looking around the room.

There was just the light from the big clay floor lamp near the piano, and the last red reflections of the sunset were on the windows.

"When I came over here to pick up Teddy today there was something I was going to ask you," Talbot continued.

"Uh, Len," Tiernan said, nodding toward the door.

"Oh, let the colonel speak," Susan said, moving closer to Tiernan until she was rubbing her hip against his.

Talbot noticed and put his hands behind his back and started pacing back and forth in front of them, trying to keep down the anger she had already managed to spark in him.

"I was going to *ask* you to please stay out of Larsky's, Susan," he said, glancing over and narrowing his eyes as he watched her moving her hip against Tiernan. "Yes, I was going to suggest a truce between us—something on the order of mutual respect. Your respect for my privacy—my favorite bar—and my respect for wherever the hell else you might want to sell your sluttish ass."

"Such a way with words, don't you think, Joe?" she asked him and put her arm lightly around his waist.

"Now . . . no, now, I'm not going to *ask* you, Susan," Talbot said, controlling his mounting anger. "Now I'm *telling* you."

"Masterful," she said, looking up at Tiernan and tracing her nail sensuously down the middle of his back. "Don't you think he's masterful, Joe, dear?"

"I, uh . . . Time we got going, Len," Tiernan said, moving away a bit as Susan's hand came down and started massaging his ass.

"I know what you're doing, Susan," Talbot said, stopping his pacing and turning on her. "But I hope you're getting my message. I want you out of Larsky's! And I want you out of this neighborhood—out of Brooklyn, in fact. Out! Or by god, I'll drive you out!"

"Oh, and you can make me do it, too!" she shot back. "Yes, all you have to do is round up your half-baked cavalry and come in and terrorize me and beat up my 'asshole' boyfriends, right?"

"You got it!" Talbot said, his eyes blinking with rage.

"Len, goddam it!" Tiernan exclaimed. "Come on!"

"Oh, don't go yet, Joe," she said, running over and standing in front of the door. "You boys have just won the war. You have to celebrate—enjoy the spoils," she said and slowly drew her white T-shirt over her head exposing her round white breasts.

"Oh, mother of Christ," Tiernan moaned and looked apprehensively at Talbot.

"That's what women are, aren't they, Len—spoils of war?" she asked, unbuttoning her cut-off jeans and stepping out of them totally naked.

"Ah, yes, the last refuge of a slut," Talbot said as fear began to mingle with his anger. She was calling for an all-out battle, throwing down the ultimate challenge. The sight of her nakedness set his emotions warring—the love and tenderness he had once associated with her body and the revulsion he felt at her exposing it to Tiernan.

Susan looked at Talbot, knowing what was going on in him, and then walked slowly and provocatively over to where Tiernan was standing.

"No!" Talbot ordered. "Don't turn away, Joe. Take a look— a good look at the slut I once mistook for my wife."

"I'm going," Tiernan said and started for the door.

"No, Joey, that would disappoint your leader," she said, getting in front of him and pressing her breasts against him. Then she reached down and began stroking her fingers up his thigh toward his groin. "He wants *men* in his outfit. Don't you, Len?" she asked, turning her head toward Talbot.

"You're really pathetic," Talbot said in disgust.

"Are you a big man, Joe?" she asked, unzipping his fly and reaching slowly into his pants. "Ummmmmm, he is big, Len," she murmured and rubbed her face against Tiernan's chest. "Bigger than some men I know," she said, looking slyly back at Talbot.

"Ah, Susan, don't," Tiernan said, pulling her hand out and pleading with her to stop with his eyes.

"Take her!" Talbot nearly yelled and then smiled defiantly at Susan.

"What?" Tiernan asked in surprise.

"I said, Take her! You heard her. She's garbage—spoils. Throw her down and fuck her slutty brains out!"

"Len, for Christ sake!" Tiernan said, pulling back farther from Susan, who just followed him and wrapped her arms and thighs around him lovingly. "Susan, stop it. . . . I—"

"Take her, goddam it!" Talbot bellowed at him.

"See, Joe, he wants you to fuck me," Susan said, reaching into his pants again. "He wants to watch while I suck your cock. Don't you, Len?"

"No, goddam it!" Tiernan said, throwing Susan aside and turning his anger on Talbot. "Just take her—is that what you said?" he asked.

Talbot looked at him in surprise for a minute, feeling his condemnation, and then at Susan, who was leaning against the piano smiling in triumph.

"You can stand there and tell me to fuck your wife?" Tiernan continued. "That's what it all adds up to. Oh, god, Len. . . . I can't handle this, man."

Talbot was reeling inside, stunned by Tiernan's mutiny, yet still on the hook of Susan's challenge. She resumed the attack.

"Come on, Joe, don't be bashful," she said, walking over to him again and stroking his shoulder. "You'll like me. . . . Won't he, Len?"

"See, the whore really digs you, man," Talbot said, choking on his anger.

"No, goddam it!" Tiernan exploded and shoved Susan away roughly. "Man, you're twisted—really twisted," he said to Talbot, shaking his head and going out the door, slamming it resoundingly behind him.

The concussive closing of the door shuddered through Talbot's brain like artillery fire. He stood there looking at the door, his hands hanging at his sides, his eyes sad and vacant. Susan let out a laugh of contempt and walked over near the door where she'd dropped her clothes and began putting them on. There was only the small light of the floor lamp and the room was suddenly quiet and full of shadows. He felt as though he were standing alone out on an empty plain . . . deserted . . . reft of command . . . awaiting the enemy. She had destroyed him and consigned him to the fields of the dead. He could hear her laughing as she pulled her T-shirt down over her breasts, but her laughter was irrelevant now, like distant sounds in the ears of the mad.

He turned his head slowly and looked over the room, looked at the world he'd sought to regain, everything nearly as he'd left it—curtains he had hung, books he had gathered over the years, books he'd left on their shelves knowing he'd come back to them, his shelves, lovingly made and finished with his hands, pictures, chairs, lamps, rugs—all hallowed objects in a painting that had been hanging in the shadows of his mind. The picture of his home—a home created and that had to be returned to.

"I think you better go, Len," she said.

He looked at her and wanted to ask why and then glanced toward the floor. Beneath his feet again the old Persian carpet he'd found in the Village—designs he'd memorized. His heel marks etched into it in front of the leather reading chair. How many times Teddy had fallen on this carpet taking his first steps toward him. How many times he had looked across it from his reading chair at her lowered face behind the piano, smiling at her as he listened to her lovely playing. That face now full of contempt and waiting for him to disappear.

And near her the sword glinting on the edge of the couch, beckoning to him, calling something up in him.

"Did you hear me?" she asked impatiently.

The sword was in his hand now and the look of impatience was gone from her face as she walked hurriedly over to the other side of the piano. The defiance still in her eyes, though now betraying an invading fear. Her nostrils widening, her chest rising and falling rapidly as she watched him.

"It's funny," he said, looking at the sword with a strange smile on his face and then looking at her. "You want me to leave, and . . . I want you to leave."

"You don't scare me with your stupid little sword, Len," she said but continued to keep the piano between them.

"You want to see a ghost, Susan?" he asked, looking around the room. "All around us—this place. This home that we created, this . . . this *fantasy!*" he snarled and lopped the neck off the thin glass vase on the piano with a quick swish of the sword.

"Damn you!" she yelled.

"Well, there, you see—it's gone," he said, scraping the pieces of vase off the piano top with the sword. "It was there and now it's gone. It's going, Susan!" he howled and raised the sword again. "It's all going, goddam it!" He brought the sword down on the raised lid of the piano and chopped a piece out of its edge.

"Stop it!" she shouted.

"Watch me, Susan. Watch me slay the ghost!" he said and began chopping more chunks out of the piano in a growing frenzy of hatred.

"You'd better get out of here, Len, or I'm going to call the police," she warned and flinched as a chip of wood sailed past her face.

"Yes, call 'em. Call 'em, by god!" he shouted and continued chopping into the piano. "But first I'm going to destroy this place—destroy it for you, and destroy it in my mind forever!"

"Go on," she said. "Chop your brains out. . . . I'm not

leaving. Chop my piano to bits, if you want. I'll get another one, Len!"

"Your piano, Susan?" he said, panting and looking around the room. "I bought that piano for you! Like everything else in this place. Everything!" he bellowed and ran over to the wall and slashed down two small pictures.

"Go on, go on!" she shrieked at him as he cut a large slash in the leather reading chair. "Let's see what a big man Lenny is with his toy sword!"

"Ha!" he yelled malevolently at her. "Now you're going to see what a lovely toy this is, bitch!"

Feeling the savage heat pouring into his veins, he started across the room, taking sweeping cuts at everything in his path, sending glass shards from vases and figurines whistling over her head. She ducked and followed him, goading him on.

"Here, don't forget this!" she said, pointing to the white plaster bust of Keats on the mantel and then ducked as he swung the sword and pulverized it.

With his breath now coming in grunts, he swung the sword again and cleared the mantel of her little silver-framed photos and brass sculptings, then grabbed the sword in both hands and hacked the mirror over the mantel into shards. Next he went after the long green drapes, rending them with long vertical slashes and tearing down the remaining shreds with his free hand and flinging them in her face. Then the windows, blowing them out explosively with powerful cuts of the sword. Grunting and sighing, he turned back toward the room to continue his orgiastic revenge. Bookshelves pulled down and pages slashed up into the air. Soon everything in the room going before his fury and she hopping over the debris behind him, biting at him with her words, propelling him on and he plunging lest he turn and cleave her, too.

From room to room he went on with the destroying sword, bedroom windows bursting out, drapes coming down, bedclothes slashed, her clothes torn out of the closet on the point of his blade, and on and on through every room—everything in his vision objects for obliteration until at last he was staggering down the hall nearly falling with exhaustion.

"What, you're not going into Teddy's room?" she screamed from behind him as he neared the living room again. She darted into the child's room and then came out holding up a handful of the boy's clothes.

"Here, cut these, too, you bastard!" she cried and ran around in front of him pushing the clothes up into his face.

He looked at her with an agony of hatred and exhaustion and raised the sword away from him and embedded its tip into a door, where it hung for a moment and then dropped to the floor.

"It's over," he gasped and stumbled toward the door.

But as he opened it and started out there were three police officers waiting. He swung his arm at them and plunged ahead trying to break through.

"Hold it, buddy!" one of them yelled and tackled him. The other two jumped on him in an instant and wrestled him down to the floor.

"Get him! Get him!" he heard Susan screaming as the officers piled on and wrestled and pummeled him, trying to subdue him. "He's an animal! An animal!"

Half an hour later, after two more carloads of officers had arrived and Talbot had been beaten into unresistant half-consciousness, he was led out of the brownstone. The building's tenants who had called the police when they heard the windows blowing out were now gathered on either side of him as the police pushed him toward one of the patrol cars. Faces staring at him, faces he'd known during his years with Susan, faces he'd often conversed with—now looking fearfully on the animal being taken away. His hands were shackled behind him and as he came up to the police car he turned his bloodied face back toward Susan's window and saw her standing there behind the jagged remnants of glass smiling bitterly at him.

"In!" an officer ordered and pushed him into the back seat of the car.

Later that evening, after he'd been thrown into the green steel-walled drunk tank because his bellowing had disturbed the other prisoners, he knelt with his bloodied hands on the floor and stared at the door in numbed exhaustion. There was a bright light overhead and behind him two derelicts were sleeping on the cement floor like two sacks of coal. A guard passed by the tiny observation window in the steel door, looked in for a moment and passed on. Just below the rivet-studded square window there was a welter of bloody pockmarks where Talbot had slammed the door repeatedly with his fists and howled to be let out.

And now staring dumbly up at the observation window, he

inhaled the heavy disinfectant smell of his cage and thought of
the gorilla he'd seen that afternoon in December when he and
Tiernan and Gemetz had taken their kids to the Bronx Zoo. He
saw again those brown unblinking simian eyes and understood
that he had been looking into two primordial mirrors.

Late the next afternoon, Tiernan was sitting near the front of
Judge Barragan's courtroom in the Brooklyn Criminal Court
Building, waiting for Talbot's name to be called up. So far, he
had not seen Talbot, who was being held in the detention room
with the other jail prisoners on the docket that afternoon.
Sitting next to Tiernan was Alan Curtis, the only lawyer he
could obtain for his friend on such short notice, though he'd
had to swallow his considerable anger at the little man who was
also handling Mary's divorce action. Curtis had seen Talbot
shortly before noon and said he looked like hell.

Before coming over to the arraignment proceeding, Tiernan
and Curtis had gone over to Susan's to try to talk her into
dropping the charges against Talbot. He had been stunned by
the wreckage Talbot had wrought on the apartment after he'd
left him the previous night. Teddy was being kept over at
Chrissy's, and Susan's two brothers had already arrived from
New London to take them back. They had all—Tiernan, Susan
and her two brothers—sat in the ruined apartment for an hour
while Tiernan had tried to plead Talbot's case.

Now, sitting in the courtroom, Tiernan looked back over his
shoulder and smiled at Susan, who was sitting across the aisle
with her brothers. He had met her at the courtroom entrance
when she came in and told him she had decided to drop the
charges, provided she obtained a restraining order preventing
him from ever coming back to her apartment. She would have
a neighbor bring Teddy over to his father's place on visiting
day. And providing that all of the damage was paid for, Curtis
agreed to all conditions on his client's behalf. Finally she had
declined to sit with them.

"Leonard W. Talbot!" the court clerk called, and Tiernan sat
forward in his seat.

In a moment Talbot was brought forward from a door to the
right of the judge's bench. Tiernan gasped and closed his eyes
when he saw his friend's battered condition. Talbot's bandaged
hands were shackled in front of him and his face was a mess of
cuts and bruises. His blue jogging suit was torn and hanging

open at the chest. But worse was the look of defeat in Talbot's lowered eyes.

"Jesus," Tiernan sighed and shook his head.

"Your honor, I request that the handcuffs be removed from my client!" Curtis called out as he hurried forward to the bench. At the same time, Susan got up and walked toward the gathering in front of the judge as well.

". . . criminal mischief, burglary, menacing, harassment, resisting arrest, obstructing justice," the clerk was saying as he read the charges against Talbot, most of them proffered by Susan.

At the end of the proceeding, Talbot was freed without bail and a date set for June 25 for trial on the charges filed by the police arising out of the fight to subdue him. Susan had stepped forward to drop her charges, and in setting the trial date the judge had suggested that the trial, too, might be dropped if the police reconsidered their complaints. In view of the beating that showed on Talbot's face, that might be agreed to, the assistant district attorney said.

During the time that Susan had been at the bench, she had not looked at Talbot. And he, with his hands shackled in front of him, had merely looked down as she spoke. He knew from her tone that she was not acting out of any compassion, that somehow even in freeing him she was doing it to remove any connection with him. It's all right, Susan, he thought, glancing up at her. We killed it all last night—even the ghosts.

As she turned to leave she looked up at him and started to frown but stopped and walked away down the aisle when he just smiled slightly and shook his head to say, Don't bother. He stood there for a moment watching her leaving the courtroom with her brothers, and then he smiled at Tiernan, who was coming up the aisle toward him, his face full of shame.

"I'm sorry," Tiernan said, "I . . . I guess I let you down"

"No you didn't," Talbot said calmly. "It wasn't your war."

"I'll see you guys later," Curtis said, patting Talbot on the back. "Gotta clear up a few details here. Call me Monday, Len."

"Gemetz sends his best," Tiernan said as they left the courtroom and walked toward the elevators. "And money, too. He came up with the bail. . . . I mean if we needed it."

"Thanks," Talbot said and drew in a deep breath.

When they got outside the sky was heavily laden with dark

clouds and there was the smell of rain in the air. A breeze whipped across the courthouse steps and flapped open Talbot's torn jogging shirt. He pushed it back into place and regretted the ruin of it. Somehow during the night in the cold drunk tank it had been a comfort to him, as though Frieda's warmth was embracing him. She had been right again, as usual, he thought. He had to go away. There was the job offer at the University of South Dakota in July, and now he knew he had to take it. It would be nice if she'd come with him, but he hated the idea of her having to uproot her life again. And for what? He didn't know what he had to offer her, or anyone, other than the moment.

"I thought Frieda might come," he said, stopping and looking out over the square.

"She's waiting at your place. She was afraid she might set Susan off if she came to the hearing."

"I couldn't believe it when Susan showed up," Talbot said, shaking his head. "Figured she'd like to see me buried under the jail."

"She finally calmed down after we promised to pay for everything . . . and that you'd stay away."

"She doesn't have to worry about that anymore. And don't worry about the damage—I'll pay for it. Damn, why is it so deserted?"

"It's Sunday," Tiernan said, ducking his face against the wind.

"Oh, yeah. Seems like I've been locked up for a year."

"Well, it's over. You're gonna be okay now. I think maybe you got a lot of shit blown out of your system last night."

"Nah. . . . I've gotta leave, Joe. She's won. If I stick around it'll all just build up again."

"Ummm," Tiernan said, looking up at him, knowing he was right.

"It's no good here. I don't fit."

"So maybe we'll all go to Manhattan."

"No," Talbot sighed and tried to bend his taped knuckles. "There's a teaching assignment opening at the University of South Dakota. Friend of mine's got a good connection."

"You gotta be kidding—South Dakota?"

"Yeah, lots of open country, Joe. Maybe I'll find room to breathe out there, you know?"

"Ah, come on, that's crazy," Tiernan said as they walked down the courthouse steps.

"I gotta get out of here, Joe," Talbot said, looking sadly into Tiernan's eyes. "I can't be locked up again—not here in that filthy little iron room like an animal, not in this city, not in a world run by women. They're turning everything into jails, Joe. . . . But maybe not out in South Dakota, huh? Maybe there's a few real women left out there."

"What about Teddy?" Tiernan asked. "You telling me you're just gonna pack up and tell him, 'Goodbye, come and see me out in Dakota sometime?'"

A grimy newspaper page blew up against Talbot's leg. He reached down and peeled it off and then held it up and let it blow out of his hand. After watching it swirl up over the roof of a building on the other side of the street, he turned to Tiernan.

"Maybe that's why I'm doing it, Joe. At least he'll know he has a father somewhere—a whole, real man. If I stay here I'll be a madman."

"But . . ." Tiernan stammered still unable to see Talbot moving away from Teddy.

"He has my blood, Joe. That makes him my son. And someday that blood will bring him to me."

# CHAPTER
# TWENTY-TWO

Max's whining and pawing at the venetian blinds awakened Tiernan late the following Sunday morning. At about the same time, the phone started ringing. He yelled at the dog to stop and sat up, swinging his legs out of the bed and holding one hand to the top of his aching head. Before reaching for the phone on the night table he looked at the clock—ten forty-three—and knew who it was.

"Yeah, Richie?" he answered it in a froggy voice.

"You're not up yet?" Gemetz exclaimed.

"I'm up," he groaned and closed his bloodshot eyes. "Stop it, Max!" he yelled at the dog again.

"You know what time it is?"

"Yeah, I'm almost ready," Tiernan lied and shook his head wearily. "Goddam it, Max!" he yelled at the dog, who was now tearing frantically at the blinds and window with his paws. Then the downstairs buzzer sounded in the living room.

"Shit, that's Talbot," Tiernan said, getting to his feet. "Hold on a minute, Richie."

He then threw the phone on the bed and walked unsteadily into the living room and buzzed Talbot in. Then he unlocked the front door, let it hang open a crack so Talbot would come in and made his way sighing back to the bedroom.

"Okay," he said, "we'll . . . we'll be over in a few minutes, Richie."

"Jesus, I'm going to be late," Gemetz lamented.

"You're not going to be late. Besides, you spent the whole night telling Lenny and me *she* wasn't going to show."

"I know, I know. . . . But what if she does, for Christ sake. And I'm not there?"

"Richie . . . Max! Damn dog is digging a hole in the window. Look, Richie, sit quiet a minute, okay? We'll be over in fifteen—no, make it twenty minutes."

"Christ!"

"Bye, Richie," Tiernan said and hung up the phone and went over to pull Max away from the venetian blind slats and peeked out into the bright morning. "Oh, now I see—cute little poodle down there. Cute little owner, too," he said, squinting down at the young brunette standing with the poodle at the curb. "Where'd she come from?" The young woman was wearing a white tennis outfit and seemed to be glowing in the morning sunlight.

"Joe?" Talbot called from the living room.

"Yeah, just a minute," Tiernan replied and let the blind slat down.

"Hey, you better move it, man," Talbot said, poking his head into the bedroom and then walking in shaking his head. "Richie's already called me twice. He said he had a dream last night that my car broke down on the way to the bridge."

"Yeah, I know. I just talked to him. He's shittin' green apples."

"Let's go, let's go," Talbot said.

Tiernan scratched his fingers through his hair and went over and took his jeans from the chair and then went over to his dresser and took out clean underwear and a clean shirt.

"Take me about two minutes," he said, walking past Talbot into the bathroom. "You bring a basket?" he called out.

"Basket?" Talbot asked, turning to Max and shrugging his shoulders.

"For Richie—when we take 'im home after Juliet doesn't show up."

"You know what? I've got this funny feeling—"

"What's that?" Tiernan asked as he brushed his teeth.

"I think she's gonna be there."

"Oh, yeah?" Tiernan replied, spitting into the sink. "Well,

it would surprise me. She hangs up every time he calls, sends back his flowers. *Sure* she's gonna be there!''

Talbot walked over to the window where Max was pushing his snout between the blinds and whining eagerly. The young woman was walking across the street toward the park with the poodle now.

"Hey, some new talent downstairs!" Talbot called out. "I saw her when I was coming up. Very nice, and I don't think she's married."

"I saw her," Tiernan said, coming out of the bathroom with his jeans on and pulling the shirt on over his head. "On my block, man, so she's mine."

"I'm leaving anyway in two weeks," Talbot said, walking away from the window and sitting on the edge of the bed. "I leave all of Park Slope to you, my man."

"Wish you'd change your mind about that, Len," Tiernan said, digging some clean socks out of the dresser. For the past week he and Gemetz had been trying to dissuade Talbot from his South Dakota idea. In fact, part of his hangover was due to their long boozy deliberation the previous night at Gemetz's. Gemetz had just sipped milk.

"Naw, I'm going . . . best thing," Talbot said, lying back with his hands behind his neck. There were still many bruises on his face.

"Too bad. I've decided to move over to Manhattan. Your idea, too. My lease is up in a month. Thought I'd go then."

"Well, that sounds like progress," Talbot said, sitting up. "What about—"

"I called Mary last night," Tiernan said, cutting him off.

"Jesus Christ, that's great, Joe. You're not going to fight the divorce?"

"Nope. Been thinking about it all week, trying to get my head clear about it. I still don't want it—still love her— but . . . Well, maybe moving will help. You know?"

"Yeah. I'm the one who's shipping out to South Dakota, remember? Now, will you go over and see your daughter, for Christ sake."

"I told them I'd come over this afternoon. Bring Lynn's dollhouse over, you know. God help me, I hope I can pull it off—I mean without going to pieces again. Something happens to me over there."

"You'll do fine," Talbot said, getting up and patting him on the back.

"Thanks. You tell Susan you're going?"

"Yeah. . . . Actually she's been very agreeable since I told her. She even said Teddy could come out and live with me during the summers. And I'll come back on holidays."

"Great. You can put up at my place."

"Thanks. . . . And look, you and Richie might want to come out there for a visit. Little fresh air might do you some good."

"You're on," Tiernan said, zipping up his boots and going over to the mirror to brush his hair. "Now, how are we supposed to handle Richie's thing?"

"What do you mean?"

"Richie's great rendezvous on the bridge. Should we just drop him off at the entrance and wait with the car in case he comes down . . . ah, empty-handed. Shit, I still think he's leaving himself wide open."

"I think maybe one of us should walk up with him—at least until we see if she's up there. Then come back and leave them alone. They'll find a way to make it back. But he's still pretty weak."

"Okay, I'll go with him, since you're driving."

On the ride over to the bridge, Gemetz sat up front with Talbot, fidgeting and checking his watch every few minutes. It was already a quarter to twelve and they were still at least ten minutes from the bridge.

"Relax, man," Talbot said.

Gemetz just let out a long nervous sigh and gazed out the window. He was wearing a new tan corduroy sports coat and his beard and hair were freshly trimmed, but there was still a hollowness about his eyes from the ordeal he'd been through and he looked pale and sickly. As they neared Brooklyn Heights on Flatbush Avenue, he began fidgeting even more and nervously clearing his throat.

"Oh, god." He sighed.

"She ever answer your calls?" Tiernan asked.

"No. Maybe the roses worked though," he said. "I sent a half-dozen every day for a week. With one message: 'June first—Bridge. Love, Richie.' "

"Hell, Richie, this is about as romantic as it gets. She's a woman, she'll respond," Talbot said.

"I don't know. . . . I don't know."

"Just try to calm down," Tiernan said. "Life is long."

"Good luck, friend," Talbot said, glancing at him with a smile as he pulled the car over opposite the entrance to the bridge.

"Come on, Richie," Tiernan said, moving forward in his seat. "Ze moment of truth, as they say."

"Look, you guys," Gemetz said, turning to them with a softened expression on his face. "I wanna thank you. . . . I mean, it's for sure she's not gonna show, but I wanna thank you for coming along for moral support."

"Will ya get outa the car?" Tiernan chided. "The lady is probably waiting."

"Fat chance," Gemetz said, opening the door and getting out. "You're coming with me, aren't you, Joe?" he said, turning around once more.

"If you get your ass out, I am," Tiernan said, smiling and pushing on the seat.

"Right. Well, here goes. Right?"

"Right. Open the door and get out," Tiernan said.

"Well, just—"

"Will ya get out for Christ sake!" Tiernan hollered.

"It'll be okay, Rich," Talbot said, and nodded confidently.

When they got outside the car and were about to cross the street, Tiernan leaned toward the window and said, "We'll . . . I mean, I'll be back in a minute, Len."

The walk up the long flight of stone steps to the bridge walkway was slow because Gemetz still had very little energy. Tiernan stepped along slowly beside him, smiling encouragement when they stopped midway to rest.

"Jesus, I'm scared, Joe," Gemetz said, breathing rapidly and looking pale.

"You gonna be all right?"

"I've gotta be there, Joe, no matter what."

The sun was bright and gleaming off the cablework of the bridge as they started along the walkway to the first tower, where Juliet was supposed to meet him. He had dreamed it would be clear and bright like this a hundred times, and that gave him fleeting encouragement. What would he say to her? he wondered. Nothing, he thought. Their presence at the rendezvous would be statement enough for a lifetime.

There were dozens of people moving along the wooden

walkway, some of them pushing bicycles, some of them
jogging and glistening with sweat, others just out for a sunny
promenade over the harbor. How different from that night in
February, Gemetz thought. Oh, god . . . oh, god, he thought
as he remembered the beauty of her face looking up at him that
night.

"You guys can still come back with us," Tiernan said as
they approached the steps to the tower.

"No, we'll— Jesus listen to us. You'd think she was going
to be there," Gemetz said, stopping and panting to get his
breath before going up the steps.

"It's only just twelve, Richie," Tiernan said, looking at his
watch. "You gotta figure she'll be a little late. Just for
appearances. We'll go find a bench out on the span."

"Yeah, right. We'll wait half an hour—maybe an hour. But
you don't have to stay."

"Come on, quit stalling," Tiernan said, taking his arm and
starting up.

As they cleared the top of the stairs, Gemetz's pounding
heart sank as he saw the observation area at the side of the
tower deserted. Too much to hope for, he told himself. But then
as they walked around the great stone tower and more of the
observation area came into view they saw her leaning on the
railing and looking over the harbor. In her arms she was
cradling the roses that Gemetz had sent to her that morning.

"You're a winner, Richie," Tiernan said softly and stopped,
giving Gemetz a little push on the arm to go on.

Gemetz turned to him to say thanks but bit his lip as the tears
of relief rose in his eyes. Tiernan nodded his understanding to
him and Gemetz nodded back and went on.

When Talbot saw Tiernan coming back down the stone steps
alone he let out his wildest rebel yell and raised his fist high out
of the window in victory. Tiernan let out his own whoop and
danced down the steps with both fists raised and ran to the car
laughing with joy.

"He did it! He did it! He did it!" Tiernan yelled.

"Yeeeeeeeeeehaaaaaaagh!" Talbot yelled again and pounded
on the side of the car with the flat of his hand.

"She even brought the roses!" Tiernan said and leaped onto
the hood of the car and down the other side to get in.

"God . . . damn!" Talbot exclaimed and started up the car
as Tiernan jumped in and slammed him on the shoulders. In a

moment Talbot lurched the car away from the curb and whirled it around in a U-turn that almost flipped it over and then drove back toward Flatbush zigzagging and blowing his horn in celebration.

As they neared Park Slope again, having almost exhausted themselves with exclaiming Gemetz's good fortune, Talbot suggested that they go immediately to Larsky's and drink the bar dry.

"Len, I want to go over to Mary's first," Tiernan said, turning and speaking in a suddenly serious tone. "I mean, I can meet you over there in a little bit, but first I want to see my little girl. I feel rotten about staying away."

"Absolutely!" Talbot said, nodding and giving him a smile of encouragement. "Joe, it's going to be fine. I feel it. Hey, this day is turning out okay, right?"

"And I want to try to get on some kind of talking basis with Mary. This is no good."

"Joe, listen to me," Talbot said as he turned the car off on Plaza and headed for Mary's street. "You were acting out of hurt—you know?"

"I know, and it still hurts."

"But we heal, man. I believe we can all heal."

"Yeah," Tiernan said, looking sadly out at the brownstones passing as they neared Mary's.

"Call me when you get home and we'll head over to Larsky's," Talbot said as he stopped the car in front of Mary's brownstone.

"Right," Tiernan said and got out and took the dollhouse from the back seat. Then he looked at Talbot, gulped and turned toward Mary's building.

Talbot watched Tiernan pause in front of the brownstone and then start up the steps. He looked at the ornate stone archway over the door and the tall gleaming windows and thought of Susan looking out at him behind the teeth of glass on the window he had left shattered in his former home. He thought of the brownstone world he had lived in for the past decade, with its elegant nineteenth-century facades and all the torn twentieth-century lives behind those facades. In a moment, Tiernan disappeared behind the high engraved glass door and Talbot felt a shudder go through him and pulled the sputtering car away from the curb.

At Mary's door, Tiernan stopped as he was about to rap and

nearly turned away. God, all the anger that had divided them in recent weeks. She had sounded very sympathetic on the phone—urged him to come for Lynn's sake. He thought of Richie's courage going forward on the bridge and knocked three times.

"Joe, you're early!" she said in surprise as she opened the door. "Oh, that's pretty. Lynn will love it," she said, admiring the dollhouse in his arms.

"Mary, I—"

"Come in," she said and reached out and took his arm. "Oh, Joe, you shouldn't have stayed away. Lynn missed you so much."

"Yeah, I missed her, too," he said, choking and following her down the hall to the living room. He could hear the sound of her record player as they approached. Ah, yes, listening to her music. . . . *Les Sylphides,* too, he thought, smiling. She will always be the same.

"Nina Probst is visiting. You remember Nina, don't you?" Mary said as they came into the living room and saw the young friend of theirs who lived on the first floor.

"Hi, Joe," the tall dark-haired woman said, getting up from the couch. "Long time no see."

"Hi, Nina," he said, nodding to her.

"We were just talking and listening to some music. Oh, god, you would show up when we were playing *Les Sylphides,* Joe," Mary said and started toward the record player to turn it off.

"No, don't, Mary," he said. "It's nice. I only wanted to see Lynn for a minute if I could."

"Damn, she just fell asleep," Mary said, frowning. "I'll go wake her up. She can take her nap later."

"No, please," he said, putting the dollhouse on the coffee table. "I'll go in and take a look at her. Maybe I'll come back later this evening. I mean, if you're going to be free."

"Sure," she said, smiling at him. "Want to have supper?"

"Meatloaf?" he asked.

"Chicken."

"Great," he said with a little smile. "You guys go ahead with what you were doing and I'll be a minute," he said, walking softly into Lynn's room.

"Oh, what a lovely dollhouse," he heard Nina say as he went in.

The bedroom was in deep shadow except for little streaks of light breaking around the drawn curtains, and Lynn was lying without any covers on her bed. She was wearing a blue jumpsuit and her fingers were spotted with pink and purple watercolors as she lay with her hand near her open mouth. He stood beside her listening to her breathing and looking at her sleeping face, and slowly he sank down to his knees. Forgive me, Lynn, he wept silently. I'm never going to stay away again. . . . Never, never, baby, he thought and tried to keep himself from shaking.

Drying his eyes on her sheet, he leaned over and lightly kissed her hand and got up. God, I've been a damn fool, he thought, walking over to the window and parting the curtains a crack to look out. Over the rooftop of the brownstone across the street he watched some seagulls wheeling and thought of the many times he and Lynn had stood at the window and counted it lucky to see them on the rare occasions they would wander so far inland from the harbor.

He could hear Mary and Nina talking quietly in the living room and was glad that she still had the comfort of this old friend. The voices of Mary and her women friends had always played around the outside of his interest when she'd had her visitors—conversations too trivial, he'd always thought, to pay much attention to. And now, without discerning their words, he sensed just the importance of their sound, as though these were somehow nearer the pulse and beat of life than all the concerns of ambition that had occupied his mind.

And mingled almost organically with their sounds was the music of *Les Sylphides* that was filtering into the bedroom. It moved around him delicately, touching at him, moving elusively away from him, insubstantial and beyond his embrace—her music. He thought of the illusive nymphs in the ballet he and Mary had seen. And finally he understood as he now understood her—beautiful and enchanting to the dark heavier creature living within him, yet never to be his . . . and yet still a part of his life. And now he could accept that—accept what was beautiful in her and not need to possess her.

He walked to Lynn's bed and touched his fingers to his lips and laid them gently on her cheek. Then he turned and walked back into the living room. Mary was standing by the window and Nina had resumed her seat on the couch. Sunlight flooded in through the windows around Mary and illuminated the green leaves of her plants on the parson's table. And as he watched her for an instant in the bright light behind the plants, she seemed to appear and disappear in the glare. Finally she turned and saw him and stepped toward him.

"God, I really missed her," he said, looking into Mary's eyes. "Stupid of me—"

"It's okay, Joe," she said with a comforting smile.

He nodded and looked down at his shoes, trying to conceal his emotion from Nina.

"We'll see you this evening?" Mary asked.

"Yeah," he said. "About six?"

"Uh-huh," she said, walking toward him. "But you can come earlier if you'd like. Oh, and you've got to bring Max. That's all she's talked about."

When she drew close to him and took his hand for the walk to the door, he looked into her eyes and wanted to tell her something—the thing he had discovered in the room with Lynn. He wanted to tell her that she was free, that he could finally let her go. And that he did not need to live in her world nor she in his, but that he could still love her as someone beautiful and dear.

"Mary, I . . ." he began, but stopped as he glanced over and saw Nina watching.

"What is it, Joe?" Mary asked looking into his eyes, seeing the urgency there.

"Walk me to the door?" he asked.

"Hey, nice seeing you, Joe," Nina said and waved impishly.

"Yeah, you, too," he said and smiled at her.

Then he walked with Mary down the hall to the door. And there he turned to her and nodded and started out.

"Joe?" she asked, touching his hand. "What is it?"

He leaned forward and kissed her lightly on the lips and winked.

"I just . . . I guess I just wanted to tell you goodbye."